THE RANGER'S PATH

The King's Ranger Book 2

AC COBBLE

Cobble Publishing LLC

FALVAR

EASTWATCH

YARROW

SPINESEND

THE DUCHY OF

·· EERON ··

EASTERN
PROVINCE

IYRE

MORDENHOLD

CARFF

JABAAN

THE KINGDOM OF
· VAELDON ·

KEEP IN TOUCH AND EXTRA CONTENT

You can find larger versions of the maps, series artwork, my newsletter, and other goodies at accobble.com. I hope you enjoy the book, and when you're ready for more, **Remove the Shroud: The King's Ranger Book 3** is penciled for an April 1st, 2021 release!

Happy reading!
AC

I

"You're gripping the hilt like you're trying to strangle it, lass," advised Rew. "Loosen up, or in minutes, your hand will cramp, and you'll be as useless as a cat with a fork and a knife."

Hissing in frustration, Zaine relaxed her grip on the dagger. She frowned at him. "A cat with a fork and a knife?"

He nodded but did not respond.

"A cat with a fork and a knife?" Zaine laughed, glancing to see if Anne and Cinda were listening, but the other two women were engrossed in their own discussion. Zaine turned back to Rew and said, "I don't think I've ever seen a cat using a fork and a knife, Ranger."

"Exactly," he said.

Blinking at him and shaking her head, Zaine raised her daggers again. "I hope using these isn't half as complicated as holding them."

He felt a small grin creep onto his lips before he tightened them and kept a straight face. He circled her, assessing her stance and her grip. She had a point. They'd spent close to an hour training, but so far, she'd done nothing but stand there and learn a few stances. One of his old instructors in Mordenhold, when Rew had been close to the girl's age, had described it as the beginning of the dance before the music had begun to play. It was the kind of thing an old man told a young man, assuming that anything with a whiff of the opposite sex would catch the younger man's interest. The instructor had not been wrong, and years later, Rew still recalled those lessons.

Rew grinned, but he supposed Zaine knew even less of dances than she did of fighting with daggers, so instead, he offered, "A few more minutes and then we'll break for supper. It smells like Anne's stew is nearly finished."

Zaine nodded and raised an eyebrow, as if to ask whether there could possibly be any problems with her stance now, and if she was actually going to learn to fight.

"Attack me but move slowly," instructed Rew. "We're only working on the beginning motions, not on true sparring. Anne's still mad at me about this morning, so I'd rather not end up with one of those blades stuck in my ribs and begging for her healing."

Zaine snorted. "As she should be. No sparring, though? I've seen you fight, Ranger. There's little risk of me putting steel into your ribs."

He shook his head. "There's always a chance. The most talented swordsman in the kingdom could lose to a straw-chewing farmer if the swordsman were to stumble at the wrong time, and if those two unleash something like they did before, stumbling is a real possibility."

Grinning, Zaine glanced at where Anne was instructing Cinda on how to gather and release her magic. It seemed they'd moved back into theoretical exercises only, after a rather loud, frightening burst of sound and light had exploded from Cinda's hands earlier.

Rew nodded to the thief, and Zaine stepped forward, extending her dagger ahead of her. The sharp point of steel was aimed at his chest, and Rew gently brushed her arm to the side and stepped around her guard. "See how easily I moved your arm? It's because you didn't put your weight behind the thrust. Don't give me that look, I know it's difficult at slow speed. This is about understanding the mechanics. Now, step forward with your leg, bend at the hip, and put your weight behind it."

Zaine did, and Rew asked her to keep practicing. Stepping, lunge by lunge, across the campsite, the thief learned to deliver a blow with some force behind it, thrusting her daggers in front of her.

"Good, good," said Rew. "I think that's enough for tonight. Tomorrow, I'll talk to you about what is wrong with attacking like this and the risk of overextending."

"What's wrong with—" spluttered Zaine. "Why would you tell me to do that if it's going to get me killed? Pfah, I'm on the empath's side, you know."

Winking at her, Rew walked to their fire and squatted down, peering into the bubbling kettle of Anne's stew. He declared, "It smells good."

Behind him, the empath snorted. "You won't find yourself out of this wilderness so easily, Ranger. It takes more than complimenting my cooking to break the bars on my jail cell door."

"Oh," said Rew, standing quickly. "I didn't hear you walking up."

"The King's Ranger doesn't hear two women walking across a forest floor?" Cinda laughed before plopping down on the other side of the fire. "Remarkable. And just so you know, I'm on her side."

Rew put his hands on his hips, but the three women turned to pulling dishes out of packs, gathering utensils, discussing the day's travel, and utterly ignoring him. He waited a moment, but none of them glanced his way, so he scooped out a heaping portion of Anne's stew. It had been no lie. It smelled good, and he was famished.

They ate quietly, all consumed with their own thoughts, and it wasn't long before they'd finished eating. Anne moved between the girls, placing her hand on their foreheads and whispering a quiet prayer over them. She was taking their pain, relieving the muscle aches and chafed skin caused by the day's hike. Rew quietly cleaned the dishes as the girls sat a minute. Shortly, both of them crawled off to their bedrolls.

Once the two girls were wrapped up and breathing evenly, Anne raised her hand to Rew. "And you?"

He shook his head. "I'll sleep well enough without your assistance, Anne."

The empath smirked at him. "I offered."

"Did they know you were going to put them to sleep, or did they think you merely offered healing?"

"I don't know what they knew or did not know," claimed Anne, her chin rising slightly.

"Ha," said Rew, drying their bowls and spoons and tucking them away in the packs. "I thought not."

"They need the rest," stated Anne.

"That's why I suggested we stop earlier this evening," said Rew. "Those two aren't strong enough. They're chomping at the bit like a nobleman's war horse, but they don't have the stamina for a long, hurried journey. We have to take it easy, even if they resist it. We can't wear them down in the first few days, and if you put them to sleep every night, it won't be long before you're exhausted as well."

"Is Raif taking it easy?" argued Anne. "We have six days, right, before he makes it to Spinesend? That boy is a fighter, Rew. He's going to walk until he drops every night. We can't catch him by coddling the girls."

"That's why I wanted to head out alone!" complained Rew. "I'll have the lad back in two days if I go after him alone. What's the sense in all of us going together?"

"We're going together, and that's final," declared the empath. "Your job is to push us until we can no longer continue. I want to see them collapsed and unable to rise in the evenings. I'll give them what healing they need, and I'll put them to sleep when they need that. If they find out what I'm doing and complain, I'll deal with it. If I wear down... I won't. We have to stay together, and we have to keep going."

"But why, Anne?" demanded Rew. "Tracking down quarry is what I do, whether it's a beast in the wilderness or a lad off to get in trouble. Listen to my expertise. Let me get this done, and then we can take the children somewhere safe where they can ride out the Investiture."

"We stay together," insisted Anne.

He frowned at her.

Anne shook her head and looked at the two girls who were softly snoring in their bedrolls. "I yelled at you this morning, Rew, because they need to be involved, and everything you do is an attempt to keep them out of it. This journey is not simply about the King's Ranger tracking down an errant noble. It is about a girl trying to find her brother and a thief trying to find redemption. We are not doing this because it is easy, but because it is necessary."

Rew rubbed the top of his head, feeling the tight stubble there. "I don't understand."

"Last night, before I fell asleep, I couldn't stop thinking about what you've said," replied Anne. "All day today, I couldn't stop thinking about it. You said Alsayer told you there was power in the blood, that when the bloodlines are crossed in the right manner, the child was always stronger than the parent? You said he told you to keep the children alive, and that he'd be coming back for them?"

Rew did not respond.

"They have to be ready when that happens," said Anne. She gestured to the two sleeping girls. "It's as plain as sunrise they aren't ready now. We must train them so they're physically capable of meeting the coming threats. We must encourage them so they're mentally prepared. That is why you cannot go alone, because we have to show them how to survive. We have to teach them that they can. Their parents are gone, Rew. The onus is on us."

"On us!" exclaimed Rew. "They're not our children, Anne!"

She smiled at him. "They are now, Senior Ranger."

He spluttered, flabbergasted at the statement.

Anne reached behind her and opened her pack. "I got you something in the market when we were supposed to be packing for the trip to Eastwatch." She pulled out a brown, glass flask and tossed it to him. "It's a spirit from south of Spinesend, where they breed all of the horses. It's distilled from corn and aged in barrels, the vendor told me. The stuff smells like fire, but he was selling it for gold. I figured at that price, it had to be good."

Rew held up the glass flask and watched the firelight flicker through the liquid.

"Have some," encouraged Anne.

"I thought I wasn't going to find an easy way out of the jail cell of your heart—or whatever ridiculous thing it was that you said," muttered Rew.

"Listen to me when it comes to the children, and you will," suggested Anne. "What's happening with them is important, Rew. I can feel it."

He uncorked the top to the flask and sniffed the liquid inside. "You can feel it?"

Anne nodded. "When an empath heals a person, there's a connection. I can sense something of the patient through that connection for a time, even when the healing is finished. With these children, I can feel the maelstrom swirling around them. It's like a giant, spinning tidal wave swooping out from Mordenhold and washing over this kingdom. The Investiture has caught them in its fury. I don't feel that power around myself, and it's not bestirring the natural balance in this part of the world. It's directed, Rew. Someone, the king or the princes, is making sure they sweep up these children in this madness. They're tied inexorably to the Investiture, and through them, I am as well."

Rew grunted and did not respond.

"Damnit, Ranger!" snapped Anne. "That's why you've been refusing my healing, isn't it? That's why you only let me look at your injuries after the fight with the thieves. Not enough time to heal you, you'd said! Pfah! Why did I listen to that?"

Raising the flask to his lips, Rew took a sip and let the spirit burn down his throat.

Anne stood. "I'll heal you now. Your aches after a day of hiking along the highway will be a feather-light burden for me, and I've plenty of time to recover tonight."

"No, Anne, I... ah—"

"You don't want me to feel the Investiture's pull on you," stated Anne, crossing her arms over her chest, glaring down at him. "Why?"

Rew sat silently, sipping the liquor she'd given him, wondering how much he should tell her.

"Tell me, or you really will be in trouble," she threatened.

He twisted his lips and then forced the cork stopper back into the flask. "I can't tell you everything, Anne. I would, but it's not... I cannot. I'm sorry."

"Tell me what you can," she insisted, sitting back down on the other side of the fire.

He sighed and admitted, "I can feel the pull of the current from Mordenhold as well. It's like ropes wrapped around my soul, trying to drag me in. I've fought it, and I'll keep fighting it, but eventually I will break. It's the way it is. Everyone breaks."

"I don't understand," said Anne.

"The pull you feel is the king's magic," said Rew. "Vaisius Morden, Eighth of the Name, is at the center of that whirlpool. He's cast it out across all of Vaeldon, and those with noble blood, the others he means to ensnare in his mad game, will feel the relentless tug. Some may avoid it for a time if they understand what is happening. Others will be too weak or ignorant. Even more people, sadly, won't want to avoid the pull. They've been preparing for years awaiting this call."

"T-The king..." stammered Anne. "The king is the one pulling on these children?"

Rew shook his head. "Not exactly. The king cast the spell, but I worry one of his sons perverted it. I believe it is the princes who are trying to get their talons into the children."

"How is that possible?" wondered Anne.

"It's the way the blood flows," responded Rew. "The child is always stronger than the parent. The king is the one casting the spell, but at least one of the princes has figured out a way to manipulate the current of that magic. What you feel through the children is the king's might. How it found the Fedgleys... that was a prince."

"Prince Valchon, you think?" asked Anne. "He's the one Alsayer is working for."

"Alsayer said he was working for Valchon," replied Rew, "which means he probably isn't. Baron Fedgley thought that's who the two of them were working for, and maybe the baron really was, but Fedgley has never met Prince Valchon and certainly never discussed Alsayer with the prince. Whatever that spellcaster was doing, he did for his own purposes."

"Fedgley hasn't met Valchon?" asked Anne.

"Fedgley hasn't left this duchy in a decade, and none of the princes have entered it," said Rew.

"How can you know that?" questioned Anne.

"I just know," said Rew, meeting her gaze over their fading fire.

"Why would the princes want anything to do with the children?"

"The strength of the blood is always stronger with the child," said Rew. "Alsayer claimed Fedgley was the most powerful necro-mancer outside of the royal line, which means Cinda could have even greater potential. Either one would be a highly valuable ally during the Investiture, but I suspect there is more to it. It's a guess, only, and my suspicion is what I cannot share. I am sorry, Anne, but it is for the best. One thing we can be sure of, the princes will want the girl, and what they want is not what we want."

Grim-faced, Anne glanced at the sleeping girl. "So the pull I feel through our connection is one of the princes using the king's power to reel her in, in case her father fails at whatever task

AC COBBLE

they've planned? Or perhaps it's a rival prince trying to counteract what her father may do?"

Rew nodded. "It could be either one or both, I suppose. The pull of the Investiture is natural magic, ancient magic. It's older. It is before what we call high or low. The net that was cast across Vaeldon by the king is undirected. It's a current that will swallow thousands, but it's rare the king would direct it at an individual. That's not the way natural magic flows. The Investiture draws like a whirlpool into the center. Not a geographical center, mind you, but the center of the conflict. It catches those with an affinity for it. I'm not sure it would have found the children unless the princes corrupted the spell."

"Which prince?" asked Anne.

Rew shrugged. "The only way to find out would be to follow the pull, which I think we both agree is inadvisable."

"And Raif, why him?" asked Anne. "The boy has no high magic."

"Maybe they don't know that," guessed Rew. "Or maybe they want him for leverage over his family. People do strange things to protect their families."

They sat for a moment. There was nothing more that he was willing to say, and she seemed to understand that. She asked him, "You'll take the first watch?"

He nodded, and Anne crawled to her bedroll.

The fire popped and crackled. Rew sat before it, his senses unconsciously extended, monitoring the area around them, his mind churning with confused, frustrated thoughts. He let his attention float, following the current of power that swirled over Vaeldon. He knew its source, but he couldn't find it. He didn't have the skill necessary for such a thing, but regardless, he lost himself in the waves of silent urgency as he mulled over their situation. Come dawn, he was still sitting in the same place. At the first blush of daylight, he stood, his muscles and joints protesting, his body aching like he'd aged ten years throughout the night.

Anne's eyes fluttered open, and she scowled at him. "You stayed up all night?"

"I did," he said. He ignored her look and added, "If you plan to take their exhaustion each evening, then you need your rest."

Anne flipped back her bedroll and staggered to her feet.

"Eat quick. We've a long way to go," advised Rew.

REW TOSSED THE THICK BRANCH UP INTO THE AIR IN FRONT OF THEM, and a sputtering, crackling stream of blue sparks raced after it, flashing a pace to the left of the flying wood in a disorganized, curving flight. The sparks blinked out a dozen paces beyond the branch before it thumped unharmed onto the dirt road in front of them.

"Not bad," said Anne.

"More sparks than lightning," remarked Zaine.

"I missed," groused Cinda.

"You missed," acknowledged Rew, "but you flung high magic. Your aim is something we can work on, but we can't do it until you're able to consistently release your talent. You're doing well, lass. Don't get discouraged."

Anne, walking beside him, glanced at Rew out of the corner of her eye and offered him a knowing smile. Encourage the children, she'd told him. He would do the best he could.

"I'm not sure those sparks would have done anything had you hit the branch anyway," said Zaine.

They kept walking, and Rew stooped as they passed the branch he'd thrown. He picked it up and hefted it. "Your bow, Zaine."

"What?" asked the thief.

"Let's see how you fare."

Frowning, the girl unslung her bow off her shoulder and awkwardly stretched the string between the two ends. The party kept walking, and she had to hurry to catch up to them. "Stop for a minute?"

Rew shook his head. "We didn't stop for Cinda."

"Well, I can't shoot while I'm walking!" cried Zaine.

Rew looked at her and did not respond.

"Fine," barked the thief. She drew a feathered shaft from her quiver and nocked the arrow. "I'm ready."

Rew tossed the branch back into the air, throwing it high and slow so that it flew on an easy arc.

Zaine's bow twanged, and her arrow streaked well in front of the branch and soared down the highway. It landed in the tall grass beside the road several seconds before the branch came back to earth and two dozen paces past where the branch landed. The thief cursed, but no one commented as she strode ahead to search the grass for her arrow.

Rew winked at Cinda, but the noblewoman frowned back at him.

Two days outside of Falvar, and the girls were ignoring each other when they could, tolerating each other when they could not. Despite nearly opposite backgrounds, they'd grown close during the flight from Yarrow to Falvar, but that relationship had been shattered when it had been revealed Zaine had been part of the plot to betray Baron Fedgley. She'd offered profuse apologies, she'd explained she didn't know what was going to happen, and she'd declared she wouldn't rest until she could make it right, but words only went so far. Cinda still recalled the grisly death of her mother and her father's outraged confusion as he was flung through Alsayer's open portal. Cinda's parents had been killed and captured, and it wouldn't have been possible without the role performed by Zaine.

Rew couldn't tell what the noblewoman thought of the thief's apologies, but he appreciated that the two of them had avoided the hair pulling and screeching he'd been worried was going to happen.

When they paused to eat their midday meal, Rew caught Anne

away from the girls and whispered, "At least they're being quiet, not wrestling each other in the dirt, right?"

Anne rolled her eyes and responded, "There will be frost between them until they're forced together again. When we find Raif or when we find trouble, they'll come together."

Rew frowned. "You think? If someone betrayed me like that, I'm not certain I'd handle it as calmly as Cinda has. I certainly wouldn't forget anytime soon."

"Zaine betrayed Cinda, but given the turmoil in the noble-woman's life, Zaine is also her only friend. Not to mention, Zaine is the only hope Cinda has of recovering her father," reminded Anne. "And of course, without Cinda, what chance does Zaine have of a better life? She can't approach any of the thieves' guilds in the duchy now, and how would a girl her age, coinless and alone, travel to anywhere outside of these lands? They've reasons to dislike each other, but they also have reasons to cling to each other tighter than ever."

Rew grunted.

Anne smiled. "Love and hate, it's not the first time a relation-ship between two girls has been defined that way, Rew. Give it time, and you will see."

"I'll take your word for it," muttered the ranger.

"You never had a sister?"

Shifting uncomfortably, Rew responded, "Not really."

"A brother, then?"

"Not… not like you mean."

Anne pursed her lips and raised a hand as if she'd ask more, but she dropped it. She knew some of his story; enough of his story that she must have realized delving into further detail was dangerous. Instead of probing, she offered, "I'm here to talk, if you ever want to. You don't have to tell me all, but maybe if you told me some…"

He nodded his thanks but did not respond. He looked over to where the two girls were sitting on opposite ends of a fallen tree trunk. They were both eating the hard biscuits and salted ham the party had brought from Falvar, and both were staring straight ahead, barely acknowledging each other.

"They'll be fine," assured Anne.

"We should get moving soon," advised Rew.

Anne adjusted the shawl on her shoulders and said, "I'll tell them. They're already complaining of blisters and sore legs, but they know we can't catch Raif unless we move faster than him. If we get moving, at least we'll be a bit warmer." She paused and then asked, "Have you seen signs of his passing?"

Rew shrugged. "I've seen signs on the road, but none I can be certain were the lad's."

"If he didn't come this way…"

"He did. He came this way, and we'll catch him."

$\underset{\sim}{\cancel{\cdots}}$ 2 $\cancel{\cdots}$

Later that afternoon, as they were still hiking along the flat highway, Rew held up a hand to slow them. Beside the road, the tall grass was bent. He leaned over, peering at the bowed and broken blades. He looked up and down the border of the road. Decades of traffic had compacted the soil into a hard surface where no vegetation grew. He couldn't discern anything from the scuffs in the dirt, but it was obvious someone had walked away from the path.

"One person left the road here," he said. Then, carefully, he followed the trail.

It was not difficult. He suspected any of their party could have done it. Someone had stomped through the grass one hundred paces off the road to the edge of a forest. There, just short of the trees, Rew found signs that the person had laid down, tossing and turning, flattening the grass. They'd also collected an armful of wood, arranged it into a pyramid, and failed to light it.

"Raif," surmised Rew.

"How do you know?" questioned Cinda, glancing around as if her brother might be lurking just out of sight, waiting for them.

"What other traveler wouldn't know how to light a proper campfire?" asked Rew. "He stormed out of Falvar in a rage in the middle of the night, and I suspect forgot to bring anything to start a fire with. If he forgot food as well, this chase may be shorter than we expected."

The others watched as the ranger methodically circled the camp, looking for additional signs, but there were few.

"He did bring something to eat, at least. There are crumbs here from a loaf of bread, but I don't think there's anything else we can learn. At the very least, it's confirmation we're on the right track."

Cinda wondered aloud, "How far ahead is he?"

"He camped here last night, so two-thirds of a day," replied Rew. "He could be moving faster than us, but he's not far out of reach. Look there, that's the impression from where he set down his pack. It's small, which makes me think he brought minimal supplies. He'll eventually have to find food, and that will slow him down."

Cinda nodded, looked around the group, and said, "Let's go get him, then."

They began hiking, but an hour later, Rew called for another pause. They were on a straight stretch of road, the river five hundred paces to one side, the edge of a forest five hundred paces on the other. The travel was easy, the scenery bucolic. Because of the recent trouble in Falvar, they'd seen few other travelers. Those that they had seen were merchants guiding long trains of wagons or the individual coaches favored by the wealthy. All of them were headed to Falvar. No one stopped to speak to them, and they didn't bother waving their fellow travelers down. It was possible someone had seen Raif, but they didn't need word of a missing nobleman traveling alone getting out.

The land between the Falvar and Spinesend wasn't any more dangerous than other highways within the kingdom, but any time control passed from one noble's domain to another, there was risk; a risk of soldiers during hostile times, a risk of bandits during peaceful ones. With the Investiture beginning, Rew had no idea what to expect. Was Duke Eeron involved in the capture of Baron Fedgley, and would he have soldiers on the road? Would bandits take advantage of the confusion and hop back and forth between the two territories, raiding inadequately protected travelers?

There'd been no time for bandits to have established themselves following the attack on Falvar, but such men were like roaches. They had an incredible sense of opportunity. The attack might have been days ago, but for months, the protections of the baron would have been drawing back as he dedicated his resources to the barrowlands where he was harvesting wraiths for Prince Valchon. Bandits, with the unnatural senses such men had for weakness, could have already been moving into the gap for weeks.

Rew, looking at the grass along the highway in front of him, shuddered at the thought of Prince Valchon and the rage the man would feel when he realized Alsayer had betrayed him, taken the wraiths, and the baron. Bandits were hardly a concern beside that. Rew frowned and stared curiously at a small spot in the dirt.

"What are we looking at?" wondered Zaine. "Did Raif relieve himself here earlier this morning?"

Anne shushed the girl, and Rew paid her little mind. He turned, studying the grass on the river side of the highway then crouched, looking closely at the thin, emerald green blades.

"I don't see anything," complained Zaine.

Rew drew his bone-handled hunting knife and used the tip of the blade to move grass aside, peering at the soil underneath.

The women, even Zaine, were quiet behind him. The thief had spoken true. She wouldn't see anything. It wasn't like the grass that Raif had disturbed the night before. This was something else. Rew worried what it portended. He kept moving the grass aside, looking at the dirt underneath, until he found what he'd been looking for. Small impressions of a clawed foot that had padded lightly across the earth, barely disturbing it, hardly leaving a visible trace, but everyone and everything left some mark upon the world.

Rew stood and sheathed his hunting knife.

Zaine raised her hands, palms to the sky as if seeking answers from above. "Well?"

"Look there," instructed Rew, pointing down.

"At...?" asked Zaine. The other two women remained silent, but he could see their skeptical expressions.

"Rangers you are not," he said. Then, he walked to the far side of the road and tapped his boot on the dirt. "This discoloration, the dots where it's darker, see that? That's water that fell hours ago. You can tell from the pattern of the droplets the direction of movement. Something came from the river, crossed the road, and headed toward the forest. It moved with incredible stealth, and if it wasn't for those droplets of water, I never would have spotted the tracks."

"An animal?" wondered Cinda.

"An animal, but one that should not be here," said Rew. "These tracks appear to be from a northern river otter, but we're not in the north, are we?"

The women blinked back at him, not comprehending.

"The otters are native to the Northern Province and thrive there," explained Rew. "They're larger and more cunning than the variety you'd find in the eastern province, and for centuries, the northerners have trained them to perform simple tasks."

"You think a trained river otter crossed this road several hours ago but are worried because these creatures are native to the Northern Province?" questioned Cinda, looking between the ranger and their other companions. "And you're gathering all of that based on a few droplets of water on the highway?"

Rew nodded and did not respond.

"How does that help us catch up to my brother?" asked the noblewoman.

Rew sighed and gestured for them to continue. "It doesn't, I hope. The Investiture has started, lass, and we need to keep our eyes open for any and all signs. Anything that is unusual is as like to be trouble as it is not. And trouble is something we cannot afford to deal with if we're going to catch Raif before he reaches Spinesend."

"Fair enough," muttered Cinda.

"If we encounter a river otter, should we hide behind you?" asked Zaine, failing at a valiant attempt to keep the sarcasm from her voice.

"It's not the otter we need worry about, lass. It's the otter's master," said Rew, ignoring the jest in her tone. "And yes, if we encounter a river otter and its master, get behind me."

He opened his mouth to add more but stopped. Rew had met several men and women who knew the secrets of taming the wild creatures of the world, but only one of them had the ability to travel quickly from the Northern Province to the Eastern. He cringed at the thought and forced it away.

Zaine drew herself up, smacked her fist against her chest, and cried, "As you command, Senior Ranger."

He shook his head at her antics and started walking without comment, the others falling in behind him. Rew reminded himself that she was young and brimming with the vinegar her harsh life had filled her with. She didn't understand. She wasn't ready for… Rew grimaced, thinking of what Anne had said the day before. The empath had been right, of course. The children weren't ready for what was coming. He didn't agree, though, that there was anything to be done about it. The Investiture was happening now, and it was already too late to prepare.

They hiked on, the road easy, but the girls were wheezing and blowing after another hour, unused to the constant, relentless pace. Even Anne began flagging, her soft-booted feet dragging in the dirt. She had demanded he push them to the brink, and he'd conceded the logic of doing so, but from the labored sounds of breathing, he judged the women weren't far from that brink. He decided to call a halt. A couple of hundred paces off the road, toward the river, he'd spotted a giant willow that would provide them excellent shade and cover. If the towering, puffy white clouds drifting above the willow brought rain in the night, they would appreciate shelter. The willow was close to the river, and all of them could use a dunk to wash off the dust from the road as well. Finally, the low, gently-swaying branches of the willow would help to contain the light of their fire. It was the best spot to camp that he'd seen so far that day, and it would be foolish to pass it by.

The girls collapsed like grass in a thunderstorm as soon as they made it beneath the branches. Grinning at each other, Anne and Rew made a rough camp and started the campfire. It seemed they weren't the only ones who'd recognized the attractiveness of the site, and there was already a well-used fire pit bounded by fist-sized rocks. In moments, Rew had a merry blaze growing in the circle, and he stood and stretched.

He looked to the girls, raised an eyebrow, and asked, "You don't think we're done for the day, do you?"

"Done?" asked Zaine, pointing at the fire. "If we're to keep hiking, why'd you build a fire?"

"Not hiking, no," Rew acknowledged, "but I think it best if we keep up your arms and spell practice. Yesterday wasn't enough. You need to practice daily. We don't know what we'll find in the days ahead, but the danger isn't over. Alsayer warned me, remember? But I don't need that traitorous bastard's word to know you're still at risk from the princes, the thieves' guilds, and I can only imagine who else."

Zaine swallowed and then cursed. "King's Sake, the thieves' guild. I didn't even think of them. Surely they'd..."

Rew snorted. "They'd be understanding that most of the Falvar guild is either captured or dead? In Spinesend, they knew your mission, lass. I don't think you ought to expect a hug and a warm bed when we arrive there."

Grimly, Cinda staggered to her feet. She looked down at the thief. "He's right, Zaine. Whatever is ahead of us, we're better off if we can defend ourselves."

Groaning, the slender thief rose, and Rew led them out into the grass between the willow and the river. There was a log there where a tree had fallen during some long-ago storm. Rew went about collecting branches and sticks and then stuck them down into the soft, half-rotten wood. In moments, he had a dozen tiny targets.

"We'll start at twenty paces. See what you can hit," he said.

"Those sticks are the width of my finger!" protested Zaine.

At the same time, Cinda complained, "I haven't thrown a spell half that far!"

Tucking his thumbs behind his belt, Rew told them, "Survival isn't going to be easy, so your practice shouldn't be, either. For today at least, I don't much care whether you hit the target or not, but I want to see you trying. Maybe you miss them all, Zaine, and maybe you still can't cast that far when we're done tonight, Cinda, but work at it until you can do a little bit better than you could this morning. Tomorrow, we'll strive for a little bit better than today. I can't make you experts at your craft in only a few days, but we can start you on the journey."

Grumbling under their breath, the two girls began trying to attack his sticks. Zaine was right; her aim wasn't near good enough to hit the slender targets, and Cinda's first attempt at casting barely made it three paces past her own feet before a shower of hot orange sparks fell on the lush turf, but the important thing was that they were trying.

Rew offered pointers to Zaine on how she was gripping her bow and where she should be aiming. He encouraged Cinda, and then Anne arrived and began giving more specific instruction. As the sun set, it cast their shadows in front of them, and the small targets became even more difficult to see.

Zaine released her bowstring, and her arrow flew half a dozen paces wide.

A raucous laugh sounded, and the party turned to see a narrow ketch floating down the river. Its sails were lowered, and the current was carrying it at a leisurely pace. A man, a long, floppy boatman's cap on his head, loose trousers on his legs, and a thick tuft of dark hair sprouting from his open vest, called out,

"Nice shooting, lass!"

Zaine scowled at him and nocked another arrow. She fingered it but didn't raise her bow.

"You can't shoot a man for having a jest at your expense," said Rew quietly.

"Hope you trained them better in the bed than you have with that bow, my man," crowed the boatmen, turning to a companion who was slumped in the front of the craft, cradling an open jug. "Hey, now, there's two of us, and you've got three women. What say we come ashore for a bit and give y'all a little entertainment. Six coppers a tumble?"

The man at the front of the boat cackled, and Zaine flushed with anger. She did raise the bow now, and Rew pulled it gently from her grasp.

"I don't lay on my back for anyone!" snapped Zaine. "That man needs to be taught a lesson."

"It's the way things are, sometimes," murmured Rew. "I'm not saying you have to like it, just that you can't shoot a man over a comment."

"Yes, but six coppers?" gasped Cinda with a chuckle. "He ought to be offering Zaine gold!"

The boat was floating down directly next to them now, and the standing man called again, "Hey, armsman, you can't possibly need all of that woman-flesh, and we're on a strict timeline. How 'bout you rent us one of the lasses? We'll drop 'er off down the river in Umdrac. I'll let you name your price for that, and she'll be in good enough condition once we're done. Though, I can't promise she'll be able to sit right for a few days after. How about the dark-haired girl? She looks like she'd do it free of charge and pay for our drinks in the village as thanks."

Cinda's mouth dropped open, and Zaine chortled at the noble-woman's expression.

Rew raised the bow, drew back the string, and let loose an arrow. The women gasped. The arrow zipped out over the river-bank, and before the boatman man could react, it flashed over him, tearing into his floppy knit hat and ripping it from his head. The arrow and the hat splashed into the water on the other side of the ketch, and the boatmen stumbled, falling onto his companion, cursing and spitting.

His companion pushed him off and flung his broken wine jug to the other end of the ketch. His stomach was stained purple, and from the look of things, he was demanding the first man buy him a new jug of wine.

Rew watched the ketch float downriver until the current took the boat around a curve and out of sight. He murmured, "Zaine was right. The man needed to be taught a lesson."

"That shot!" exclaimed the thief.

"Confident," said Anne, shaking her head. "Over confident. You could have hit the man in the head if you'd missed even a little."

"Maybe hitting him in the head was what I was trying to do," retorted Rew.

Anne rolled her eyes and turned to go check on their supper.

Rew handed Zaine her bow. "I can protect you from rude, randy boatmen, but I can't protect you from everything. Each night, you'll practice until you can make that shot yourself. Cinda, the same goes for you and your magic. I'm afraid strangers acting as pigs is going to be the least of your worries."

"Understood," mumbled Cinda.

Zaine simply nodded, her bow gripped tight in her hands.

The ranger followed Anne back to the camp while Cinda and Zaine turned to make use of the last few minutes of daylight and squeeze in some more practice. Behind him, Rew heard them whispering, and he grinned. It had cost an arrow, but it'd been worth reminding Zaine and Cinda what was possible if they put in the time and the effort. And besides, that boatman did deserve it.

3

T he next day, they found another of Raif's cold, lonely camps, but instead of quickly assessing it and moving on, Rew stayed there, studying the confusing evidence he'd found or, more accurately, the lack of evidence.

"What?" asked Cinda. She pointed to a track of bent grass that led from the road to a man-sized flattened patch. "Even I can see this is where he slept. What's the problem, Ranger?"

"Yes, that's where he slept," agreed Rew, "and over there are his tracks to get here from the highway, but where are the tracks going back?"

Cinda blinked at Rew. "Maybe he could have walked the same path?"

"What are the odds your brother would follow his exact foot-steps from the night before when he returned to the road in the morning?" asked Rew. "The odds are nearly impossible unless he was very carefully making the effort to retrace those steps, but why would he do that? The signs he left through the grass to get here are obvious enough, and even you can see he spent the night in this spot. Why the sudden turn to stealth? And perhaps more specifically, is your brother someone who has ever tried to hide his passage through this world?"

"But it could be random chance, right?" asked Zaine, though she didn't sound confident. "If that's the quickest way to and from the road…"

"If he didn't walk back to the road, where'd he go?" wondered Anne.

"Exactly," said Rew, glancing at the forest in front of them that Raif had camped beside.

Without speaking to the others, he walked along the edge of the trees, studying the ground, but quickly, he saw there was nothing. Raif walking into a forest without leaving signs was even more unlikely than him retracing his footsteps back to the high-way. Rew looked toward the road and the trampled trail Raif had left coming from there. Was it possible the boy had followed his own footsteps back?

Nothing Rew knew about the nobleman suggested he would be proceeding with that kind of caution, and if he was, then he'd done a terrible job and left obvious signs of his passing. Rew clenched his fist and turned back to the forest. The nobles had been confounding him since he'd first seen them in the jail cell, and after a month of them in his life, the ranger was… He frowned, rubbing his scalp.

The women shifted uncomfortably, and Cinda toed a rock, nudging it out from the dirt. They were anxious, perhaps unsure of what he was thinking but not wanting to interrupt him.

Rew stepped toward the forest again. The nobleman hadn't left the jail cell on his own. He had been carried out of it. The ranger walked along the edge of the forest again, studying the same area he had before, and again saw nothing. He smacked his fist against a tree. Something was amiss, but he couldn't put a finger to it. He knew that if he ignored his instinct and they started along the road, they could miss some point where Raif had turned away, and then they would never find the boy until he arrived in Spinesend. It would be too late, then.

Rew put his arm on the tree and rested his forehead against it. If he couldn't trust his instincts, what could he trust? What good was he? The ranger stood back up and brushed his hand off, shaking loose the bark that had stuck to his palm when he hit the tree trunk.

He frowned. The boy had been carried from the jail cell. The river otter. Could another animal... He began walking along the edge of the forest again. Finally, directly next to where Raif had made his bed on the grass, Rew saw a scuff on the bark of a tree. He looked up and found a thick branch just above his head. He reached up and pulled himself into the tree.

Climbing slowly, Rew studied the bark and saw more scuffs, more marks, and then, twenty paces above the ground, a few strands of coarse hair. Around the hair there were half a dozen scrapes on the tree as if a one-sided struggle had taken place. Rew pulled the hairs from the bark and rubbed them in his fingers. He sniffed them and then climbed back down to the women.

"What is it?" asked Anne, picking up on his expression.

"I believe," replied Rew, "that Raif was abducted by a large animal."

"What!" exclaimed Cinda. "How? Why? Do you think it was some sort of Dark Kind?"

"Not Dark Kind, no," said Rew. "They're not known for abductions, for one. Besides, aside from a valaan, none of the Dark Kind have the intelligence or strength to do something like this. You saw the narjags and the way they behave. It could be a conjuring, like the imps I fought in your father's throne room, but I don't think so. Imps rarely have the intelligence for such a feat, either, and they don't have hair like this." He held up the strands he'd plucked from the tree. "This looks natural. Native to our world."

"What creatures could lift a man Raif's size and carry him into a tree?" questioned Anne.

"A simian, for one," replied Rew.

Cinda gasped and covered her mouth with her hand.

Quickly, Rew added, "I don't think it sought him as prey, for what that's worth. Simians don't carry their catches back to a lair. They eat where they kill."

"Are simians common around here?" wondered Zaine, peering into the forest. "I'd never heard of anyone seeing one until we were in the wilderness with you."

"No," responded Rew. "They're not common here. Not at all."

"S-So…" stammered Cinda, dropping her hand. "What does that mean?"

"I don't know," said Rew, glancing into the forest. "I—I don't want to speculate."

"You have to tell me what you're thinking," protested Cinda. "One of those things we saw may have my brother!"

"The northerners have learned to train river otters and other small animals," said Rew, "but I know a man who has taken it further. It doesn't make sense, though. There's no reason for him to be here. He shouldn't be here."

"Who is he?" asked Cinda.

Rew shook his head and did not reply.

———

TRACKING THE PATH THROUGH THE UPPER BRANCHES OF THE FOREST proved to be a difficult and painstaking process. The creature, which Rew decided was indeed a simian, was moving twenty paces above the ground and making leaps between trees that Rew could not duplicate. It meant he had to follow from below as best he was able, looking up into the canopy and guessing the most likely path of his quarry. Periodically, he would climb up a tree and look for signs that they were going the right direction. Fortunately, it seemed Raif was not going quietly, and more than anything, Rew found himself following the marks of the boy's struggles.

As they progressed, Rew became certain he'd made the right decision. If it wasn't Raif they were following, he couldn't fathom what else it would be. Someone was being carried by the simian, and they were fighting every moment of it.

The trees were old and sturdy, but in several places, Rew spied branches that had been cracked, areas that were disturbed by the passage of something large. There were marks that could have been boots kicking against tree trunks or branches that might have been grabbed by a captive as they passed. Raif, despite being a terrible woodsman and an impetuous fool, was a fighter. He wasn't giving up. There wasn't much blood, though, which was a relief.

As the sun set, they hadn't found Raif or anyone else, so Rew called a halt. At night, the subtle signs of an animal's passing through the upper forest would be impossible to follow even for him.

"A fire?" asked Zaine, slinging off her pack and rolling her shoulders. "I know we didn't cover half the distance, but weaving through these trees was a great deal more effort than travel on the road. I could use a good meal."

Rew shook his head. "No fire."

"You're worried the simian will smell it?" asked Cinda.

"Not the simian," said Rew, shaking his head. "I worry about its master. It's likely they don't know we're on their trail, and we don't want to give ourselves away. If he's—If there is someone controlling a simian, we cannot be too cautious."

Anne tended to the girls, granting small healing and then laying out a simple, cold meal. The empath carved off hunks of salted ham, cheese, and then shared the last of their bread. It was already getting stale, and it would be best to eat it before it turned.

"With no fire…" mumbled Zaine in complaint. Then, she stopped and sighed. "I suppose no one said it'd be easy."

"We did not," agreed Anne. "You're doing the right thing, though."

The thief nodded curtly, and Cinda reached over and put a hand on the other girl's leg. "After we find my brother, we'll go to

Spinesend and find my father. We can't do it without you, Zaine. We need you, and I'm glad you agreed to come."

Her eyes shining in the faded light of the sunset, Zaine nodded. "Of course."

That night, Anne took the first watch after putting the girls to sleep. Rew napped a few hours before she woke him. It wasn't enough sleep, and his steps would be a fraction slower the next morning, but he didn't trust the girls to watch over them while they were pursuing something that could snatch Raif off the ground and barely leave a sign.

As Anne tucked her bedroll around her, Rew shivered at the chill autumn air. It was heavy with moisture but carried a clean scent. He inhaled deeply and decided it wouldn't rain, not that night, at least. He started a series of stretches, forcing blood to pump through his body, warming himself and chasing away the stiffness from a few hours of sleeping on the ground. In the distance, he heard the calls of night birds. Otherwise, it was quiet.

The hours stretched long, and Rew's thoughts trudged down narrow, gloomy lanes, taking a meandering path to every conceivable culprit but largely avoiding the one he suspected. He didn't know why the man would be involved, didn't like to consider what it meant if he was, but one by one, as the hours passed, Rew considered and dismissed every other possibility.

Bandits would have slit Raif's neck and left his body where it lay. Enemies of Baron Fedgley would have likely done the same. It's not as if they could offer the boy back to the baron for ransom, given the baron's own predicament. It could not be random chance, which meant Raif had been taken because of the Investiture and by someone who had knowledge Raif was traveling from Falvar to Spinesend. But even then, it wasn't clear why.

Despite his pedigree, the boy had no high magic to call upon, which Rew thought anyone would know if they were close enough to have learned of Raif's flight. With his father in captivity, it was true Raif effectively had the rule of Falvar, but he'd left the city. To prevent Raif from issuing commands to his army, a foe could have simply let him carry on his way.

What did the boy's capture accomplish?

The truth was, Raif was of little use to any of the serious players in the Investiture, which meant he must have been taken as leverage or for interrogation. With Baron Fedgley taken and the boy's mother dead, the only person Raif's capture would concern was Cinda. Rew glanced at the sleeping girl. She had potential, but she was untrained. What could Raif's kidnapper hope to make her do?

He ran his hands over the short stubble on his head, wishing they could have started a fire to warm him on the cold, long night. Perhaps the boy had been taken for an interrogation. Raif was nearly useless for any other purpose to the serious players in the Investiture. Did Raif's captor want to know what had happened in Falvar or where Baron Fedgley had been taken? Did the man want to learn more of Cinda?

Grimacing, Rew shoved his boots out in front of him. It was the thought he'd been avoiding all night. Had the man somehow deduced the reason Fedgley had been captured by Alsayer and followed to the conclusion that Cinda would be a threat as well? It might not be the case, but if it was…

Rew sighed and stood from the rock he'd been sitting on. He stopped halfway to his feet. Turning his head slowly, he looked at the trees surrounding them. He thought he'd heard a subtle thump, a flap of wings. The tracks of a river otter, the simian, and now this. He stood the rest of the way and watched the trees, waiting patiently.

It took a quarter hour, but finally, he spotted what he was looking for. Twenty paces from their camp, halfway up the trunk of a leafless oak tree, was an owl. Rew met its bright-eyed stare. The bird blinked, raised its wings, and fell off the branch to drift away silently.

"Blessed Mother," grumbled Rew.

WHEN THE SUN ROSE, AND THE GIRLS AWOKE, BLINKING SLEEP-clouded eyes and cracking their jaws with exhausted yawns, Rew was already cooking their breakfast.

Zaine stood and looked down at the campfire he'd started. She asked him, "I thought you said no fire?"

"I know who we're tracking, and he knows we're coming," said Rew. "There's no point hiding."

"If they snatched Raif, are they not a danger to us as well?" wondered Anne, returning from making her morning ablutions.

Rew scratched his beard. "I said there's no reason to hide because they know we're here, not because they are no danger to us."

"Why would these people kidnap my brother?" demanded Cinda.

Rew shifted then admitted, "I am not sure."

"Well, what do you know?" asked Anne, exasperated. "What could have possibly happened while we were sleeping that's given you such miraculous, but limited, insight!"

"I saw an owl, and it made sure I saw it before it flew away." Taking out a thick hunk of bacon and carving off thin slices, he told them, "I believe the otter, the owl, and the simian who took Raif are working for Vyar Grund."

"You saw an owl—Wait, the ranger commandant?" asked Anne, surprised. "Why?"

Rew shook his head, laying the final slice of bacon onto their pan and setting it on the coals of the fire he'd been stoking while the others slept. "Vyar Grund has learned the secret of communicating with animals. He rarely travels with his menagerie and even less often tells others what he's capable of, but he can do it. Amongst those with that rare talent, I can't think of anyone else who could possibly bring the creatures here and be waiting for us. I'm certain it's him."

"All of this because you saw an owl?" asked Zaine skeptically.

"That and the tracks of the river otter," commented Rew.

The thief rolled her eyes dramatically.

"Doesn't the ranger commandant know how to portal?" wondered Cinda. "Why would he task a simian with this? He could have taken my brother himself, could he not, and then been away where we'd never be able to find him? Why would Vyar Grund even be out here, roaming the wilderness, directing these animals to whatever ends you think he's directing them to? Surely the ranger commandant is no enemy of my brother or our family."

"I looked in the owl's eyes, and I am certain it was Vyar's," said Rew. "It wanted to be seen, which means Vyar wants us to follow these tracks deeper into the forest. I don't know why. I don't know why he wouldn't just come to us himself, but it's him."

Cinda grunted and looked away. Under her breath, Rew heard her muttering, "I hope you're right."

Rew knew he was right, but he didn't think Vyar Grund's involvement was a good thing.

The girls moved off behind the trees to take care of the necessaries, and Anne squatted next to Rew. "What does all of this mean?"

Rew did not respond.

THAT AFTERNOON, THEY FOLLOWED THE TRACKS OF THE SIMIAN TO A giant pool of water. It was fifty paces wide and was formed from a waterfall roaring down a ledge high above it. The basin below the waterfall was ringed in rhododendron and dark, green-leafed magnolias. The plants filled the area with the heady scent of their white blooms, and in autumn, they were a stark contrast to the bare branches and brilliantly colored leaves they'd been passing beneath.

Rew found a scuff on the ground where he believed the simian had descended from the trees, but he lost the tracks amongst the flat rocks that surrounded the pool.

"I don't understand," said Cinda.

Standing still, the ranger let his gaze rove around the open space. He barely hid a smile when near the bottom of the waterfall he saw a small, dark head pop up from the pool. Sleek fur dipped beneath the water, and then, the head remerged. The otter twitched its whiskers and dove again. Rew saw it was headed beneath the waterfall.

"Come on," he said, and led the party toward the cold mist that sprayed up where the water crashed down into the pool.

When they got closer, they saw the rock behind the waterfall was carved into a deep cave. The otter sat on the bank and scampered into the earth when it saw them coming.

"King's Sake," muttered Rew, looking into the dark, damp cave.

Cinda held up her hand, and around her fingers, a subtle glow sprang alight.

Rew blinked at her.

"Anne and I have been working on my control," said the young spellcaster, and she proceeded into the cave. "I can't cast it more than a few paces away, but I can hold it, and that's enough to light our way."

"Wait," said Rew, scrambling across the wet rocks after her.

"If you think my brother may be in here, I'm going in," said Cinda, not looking back at him.

Growling, Rew followed the noblewoman, and Zaine and Anne followed him.

They walked up a shallow rock slope that was slick with moisture and thick, green moss. Water trickled down it, coming from some source that was lost in the darkness ahead. Rew could feel the air moving sluggishly past them, the thick mist curling deeper into the cave. It had to be escaping into the open somewhere ahead. He sniffed and detected the metallic tang of copper on the air.

"There's an opening ahead," he murmured, glancing nervously into the darkness around them. "Keep your eyes open. Vyar Grund is close."

"What?" asked Anne. "How do you know?"

He shook his head, not responding. Copper was known to interfere with high magic. It obscured the sight of farseeing, for one. Many a noble had a room somewhere within their keep made of the material for secretive conferences, but why would Vyar Grund take Raif to such a place...

Zaine, stalking carefully beside him, trying not to slip on the dangerous footing, held her two daggers in her hands.

Ahead, Cinda moved steadily, her arm raised, the flickering, pale glimmer from her spell lighting their way until three hundred paces into the cave they saw the glow of daylight. The tunnel they were following opened into a much larger gallery. It reeked of copper, and Rew scuffed his boot across the rock as they entered, seeing a thick vein of the metal snaking through the stone.

He stepped beside Cinda as they reached the end of the tunnel. Light spilled down from an oval-shaped opening in the ceiling of the cave, illuminating thick spikes of rock that dripped down from the roof of the gallery and sprung up from the floor like a bed of needles or the yawning teeth of some ancient monster. The air was thick with cold moisture. Heavy mist obscured the half of the cavern that lay beyond the opening in the ceiling. Rew waited, letting his eyes adjust to the gloom.

"There," he said quietly, pointing to a bed of sand that lay just outside the shaft of light that beamed down from above.

Cinda raced to where Rew had spied her brother.

Raif was laying on his side, his legs bound, his arms tied behind him. A dirty cloth was wrapped around his face, gagging him. His eyes were open, and they gleamed with reflected light as Cinda crouched beside him and began sawing through the bindings with her belt knife.

Rew drew his longsword and waited. Anne knelt beside

Cinda, checking over Raif, who was cursing and grumbling. Rew listened as the boy described being jerked out of his sleep when some creature took him. Breathlessly, he related the harrowing journey through the treetops as the simian swung into the night. Before dawn, he'd been deposited in the cave and had been assaulted by a man he couldn't see. He'd been tied up and left there for a day with no food and only the water he could suck from the damp rag tied around his face. He hadn't heard the man return, and Raif claimed he'd been left in the cavern alone.

Rew had heard enough and barked, "Show yourself, Vyar."

A deep voice chuckled, the sound of mirth bouncing and echoing around the huge chamber. A cloaked figure stepped from the shadows. A dark, leather mask hid the lower half of his face, and his hood was pulled up over his head. His hands were gloved with soft, doe-skin gauntlets that extended to his elbows. Over his shoulders were two polished wooden hilts of the man's wide-bladed falchions. The ranger commandant looked to Rew but didn't have time to speak.

Raif, freed by his sister and helped to stand by her and Anne, charged across the sandy soil at Grund. The ranger commandant watched the boy come and then moved casually to the side, tripping Raif. The big youth sprawled forward onto his face, scrambling away and springing back up.

Cinda, her hand still glowing, flung her light toward Grund, releasing a hissing stream of sparks that mostly fizzled out long before they reached the ranger commandment. Those few that did reach him were easily batted away. Zaine stepped forward, but Rew caught her arm. He and the thief watched as Raif struggled back to his feet and then swung a devastating hook at Grund. The ranger leaned back, and Raif's fist swung by his face harmlessly.

Stumbling off-balance, Raif shouted wordlessly. He spun and charged, his arms windmilling, his fists flying at Grund like he was trying to beat the man into the ground.

The ranger commandant leaned out of the way, letting the fists fly by him. Then, suddenly, he changed tactics and blocked the attacks before slapping his palm against Raif's chest, knocking the big fighter back where he landed on his bottom.

"That's enough," called Rew. The masked man turned to face the ranger. Rew asked him, "What are you doing here, Vyar? Why'd you take the lad?"

The ranger commandant laughed again and said, "I took the boy because that scoundrel Alsayer was so interested in him, and now I find you are as well. Why is that, Rew? What about this family has attracted so much attention?"

Rew shrugged and did not respond.

Vyar Grund began walking around the sandy floor of the cavern, his eyes darting between Rew and the others. "Baron Fedgley is a skilled necromancer, of course. I know what he's attempting with the wraiths. The boy has no talent, but let me guess, the girl does?"

Rew eyed his superior and did not respond.

"Where are you going, and why are you escorting them, Rew?" asked Vyar Grund. "You belong in the wilderness near Eastwatch."

"I do," agreed the ranger. "I met them as they passed through Eastwatch. I promised to see them home safely, but it turned out that their home was no longer safe. I'm just trying to keep them out of harm's way. That is all."

The lower half of the ranger commandant's face was hidden behind his mask, but his eyes glittered with suspicion.

Rew frowned at the man. "Why this cavern, Vyar? I saw the copper. Who are you worried would be spying on you? Alsayer, someone else?"

"What is Alsayer planning?" questioned the ranger commandant, ignoring Rew's question.

"I don't know," answered Rew.

"He abducted Baron Fedgley," said Grund, standing motionlessly. With the mask over the lower half of his face and the heavy mist around him, it seemed as if his voice was coming from nowhere, as if he was a ghost. "You're going to rescue him, aren't you? I couldn't care less about the backstabbing and treachery of the nobles and that spellcaster, and neither could you. Why are you involved in this? Why are you helping this inconsequential baron and his family?"

"I told you," snapped Rew. "I just want to see the children to safety."

"Why didn't you return to Eastwatch after depositing them in Falvar?" growled Grund. "The younglings were safe enough there, if they'd stayed. Don't tell me you grew so attached to them you decided to follow them to Spinesend and rescue the baron out of the goodness of your heart?"

"How do you know Baron Fedgley is in Spinesend?" asked Rew quietly. "How do you know we're going to rescue him?"

He felt a shiver down his back, and it had nothing to do with the cool air rolling up from the waterfall out of the tunnel. The mist curled and boiled above them, rising on the cold draft from the waterfall, pushing toward the opening in the ceiling of the cavern. It cast undulating shadows across the floor and Vyar Grund. Still the ranger commandant did not move. Did not look as if he could.

Grund did not respond, so Rew asked again, "How do you know where Baron Fedgley is being held?"

The ranger commandant stayed silent.

Rew glanced at Raif, but the boy shook his head, as if to say he wasn't the one who'd told. Rew snarled, "You searched his mind, did you? The same way you control your animals. You told me you could not do that, Vyar. Does the king know? He's outlawed such things."

"I'm the ranger commandant, Rew," responded Grund. "I am the one who reports to the king, and I'm the one asking the questions here. You turned your back on what you could have been, and now you are nothing more than my ranger. Answer me. Why are you involved with Baron Fedgley?"

Rew snorted and shook his head.

"You're off your territory, Ranger, and it seems you're getting

yourself into the thick of political matters," said Grund. "You
know we are to avoid the Investiture. You, in particular, are meant
to be free of it."

"I am free of it," muttered Rew.

Grund raised an eyebrow.

"How did you know Baron Fedgley was captured by Alsayer?" asked Rew. "What are you doing in the Eastern Territory?"

"I ask the questions, remember?" chided Grund.

Frowning at his superior, Rew shook his head. It made no
sense. Why was the man there, and how had he learned what had
happened? King's Sake, why had he kidnapped Raif? Grund
claimed he was working to foil Alsayer, but why did he care what
Alsayer was up to? Why...

"You don't know, do you? He doesn't know."

Grund blinked at him. "Who do you mean, Rew?"

"You're not here on behalf of the king. You came because one
of the princes—ah, Valchon, of course—you came because
Valchon sent you. He wouldn't come himself, but he knew you
would do his dirty work."

Grund paused and then replied, "What are you talking
about?"

"You were always close to Valchon," murmured Rew. "Too
close, the king thought. What did he ask you to do? What did
Valchon task you with?"

Grund crossed his arms over his chest, and he stood a long
moment studying Rew. Finally, he said, "I don't know what
you're talking about. The king instructed me to eliminate the
House of Fedgley. He told me to start with the baron and to work
my way down. I didn't know where the baron was, so I took the
boy. I learned from him that Fedgley is in Spinesend, and that you
were assisting him in recovering his father. I sent back my friends
to check for you, Rew, and learned you were on our trail."

"The king doesn't even know you're in the east, does he?"

"Don't be ridiculous, Rew," snapped Grund. "If the king had
not instructed me to do this, why would I tell you such was the

case? If I was lying, all it would take was you opening your mouth to the king and I'd be finished. Now, as we're both the King's Rangers, and we've sworn to follow his commands—like them or not—let us finish this. The boy knows no more of his father's whereabouts than you do, so he's of no use to us. I'm guessing it's the same for the girl. Let's end them. Then, we can portal together to Spinesend and find the father."

"Vyar, no…" said Rew.

"We work for the king, Rew," declared Grund. "It is not up to us to question his orders. Come on, now. You've done worse in service to your king."

"No," said Rew, suddenly certain. "You're not working for the king in this, Vyar. I know you are not. If the king knew what was happening here, he would have come himself."

"You should have stayed in the wilderness, Ranger."

Rew lifted his longsword and did not respond.

"I'd prefer not to do it this way," said the ranger commandant with a sigh, "but orders are orders, and I cannot allow insubordination."

Grund reached behind his shoulders and drew his two broad-bladed falchions. The steel gleamed in the low light in the cavern. Grund began spinning them, the metal whistling softly as the blades sliced through the air.

"Anne," said Rew. "Get the children out of here. Take them—take them anywhere but Eastwatch or Falvar. Don't go anywhere he can find you."

"What…" she spluttered, staring at the ranger commandant, wide-eyed. "I don't understand. Why would—"

"He's not working for the king, Anne. He's doing this for Prince Valchon. Don't let him have the children or they'll die," snarled Rew. "Blessed Mother, we all will. He can't leave any of us alive after this."

Grund laughed, nodding as if to admit that what Rew said was true, and then he sprang forward, his falchions singing as they cut through the mist toward Rew.

The ranger danced away, the reflection of Grund's swords seeming to hang in the air, drifting away on the mist.

"Something's wrong with his swords!" cried Zaine.

"They're enchanted," growled Rew. "Everyone, get out!"

Wordlessly, the ranger commandant attacked, his weapons carving out swathes of air. Rew fell back, trying not to engage with his superior, trying to buy time for the younglings to flee, but they didn't. Instead, Raif charged, his arms spread wide as if he meant to bear hug the ranger commandant. Grund spun, sweeping both his falchions at the nobleman.

Cursing, Rew leapt forward, swinging his longsword to knock aside one of Grund's falchions and chopping at the man's other wrist with his hand. Grund took the blow on his arm and then snaked his leg behind Rew's. He smashed against the ranger with his shoulder.

Rew felt his legs fly out from underneath of him. He arched back, one hand reaching over his head to the wet, sandy soil. He allowed the momentum to take him, and he cartwheeled away. Grund pursued him, and Rew barely found his footing and raised his longsword in time to block a deadly strike from his commandant.

Backpedaling, Rew furiously defended, weaving his longsword in front of him while Grund struck over and over with both of his enchanted falchions. Behind the ranger commandant, Raif stood still with his arms held wide, his eyes wider. His mouth was open as he watched the two rangers fight. The cavern filled with the ring of steel against steel, and Grund pursued Rew across the sandy soil but then slowed.

"You've an enchanted blade?" he asked, pausing to catch his breath from his furious attack. "You never told me. I'm not the only one with secrets, it seems. What are its properties? Why aren't you using it?"

Rew grunted. "Because I don't need it, Vyar."

Grund shook his head. "That's a lie, Ranger. What else have

you been keeping from me? What other secrets are lurking in that head?"

Rew didn't respond. Instead, he attacked, aiming a blow at the commandant's legs and at the last second swinging his longsword up.

Grund caught the blow and diverted it. The commandant unleashed a blistering counterattack with his other weapon.

Rew stepped into the man's guard so that the commandant's arm smacked against his side but the blade missed. Rew swung his head forward, catching Grund on the bridge of the nose with the crown of his skull. Bone crunched, and Grund fell back, dragging his falchion along Rew's upper arm as he did.

Rew spun away and ducked, narrowly avoiding Grund's second falchion as the commandant brought it back, trying to trap Rew between the razor-sharp edges. Blood streaming from his shoulder, Rew staggered clear.

Grund stood, shaking his head. He wiped at his mask with the back of his wrist, and Rew saw the man's blood glistening on the back of his doe-skin gauntlet. "Not bad, Ranger, not bad. I thought perhaps your time in the wilderness had made you slow, but—"

A string snapped, and an arrow flew at Grund. The ranger commandant whipped a falchion around and knocked the arrow aside.

"Run," hissed Rew to the others. "Run, you fools!"

Then, he was backpedaling again as Grund charged, swinging both of his falchions in alternating, lightning-fast attacks.

Cinda's sparks flashed at the man again, but Grund ignored them, plowing toward Rew, who darted behind a stalagmite and then ran around several more of the mineral formations, heading deeper into the cavern. He was trying to buy himself time to think.

Grund stayed on his heels, though, his falchions whistling a pace behind Rew.

Rew ducked behind a thick stalagmite that rose twice his

height then spun, swinging back behind him with his longsword, putting his entire weight into it, trusting to luck the commandant wouldn't expect the attack.

Grund, coming around the spire of rock, was startled and barely raised his weapons in time to block Rew's powerful blow. One of the enchanted blades was jarred from the man's hands and went spinning off into the darkness of the cavern, but instead of panicking, Grund raised his palm toward Rew and unleashed a torrent of roaring fire.

Rew threw himself away, rolling across the ground and behind another stalagmite as the blistering flames followed him across the cavern floor. Cursing and batting at his cloak where it was singed by flame, Rew stalked silently away, heading toward where he'd knocked Grund's weapon.

But before Rew could find the blade, there was a scraping sound, and the enchanted falchion flew into the air, its silver edge reflecting the lonely shaft of light that spilled from the ceiling as it soared through the cavern's mist and slapped back into Grund's open hand. Rew spun, raising his longsword, and saw Grund behind him, both of his blades in hand, blood dripping from the bottom of his leather mask.

The men eyed each other, but neither spoke.

Rew stalked forward. Grund sidestepped behind the rocks and into the darkness, mimicking Rew's flight earlier. Rew went after him, knowing the commandant meant to lose himself amongst the stalagmites and darkness and attack from behind. Rew knew he was playing into Grund's hands, but it was better than letting the ranger commandant have time to formulate a better plan. Vyar Grund was an expert with his two falchions and had a deadly command of high magic as well. He could call upon fire, as he'd already demonstrated, and—

Cursing, Rew spun and sprinted back toward his companions.

Standing in the center of the cavern, in the light from the hole in the ceiling above, they all looked surprised as Rew came flying out of the forest of rock formations. He dropped his sword and pitched himself forward, rolling and reaching down to his boot to yank loose his throwing knife as he did. When he tumbled over his shoulder and back to his feet, he flung the blade.

Cinda squeaked, and Zaine cried in surprise. The bright steel flew between them and thunked into the muscular body of a simian that had been standing right behind them. The creature howled, its fur-covered paw reaching to clutch at the hilt of the knife in its chest.

Rew grabbed his longsword and lunged to the side as Vyar Grund burst out of the darkness and swung at him with one of his falchions. Rew turned as the falchion whistled overhead, but he couldn't avoid the second blade that cut across horizontally, drawing a thin line of blood across his chest.

The simian roared; Grund attacked silently, and Raif cried out in elation. The boy had found his gear, and the greatsword of his ancestors, on the sandy floor of the cavern. He was raising it above his head in triumph.

The clang of steel continued, Grund pressing Rew, smashing down with one of his blades, forcing Rew's longsword into the sand. The commandant whipped the other blade around and swung it at Rew's head.

Rew leaned back, barely avoiding decapitation and gaining a stinging cut across his cheek. He flipped his longsword up from the ground, digging the point through the sand and sending a shower of the fine grains into Grund's face.

The ranger commandant snarled, blinking his eyes to clear the grit, and suddenly was on the defensive. Rew came after him, slashing and hacking, both hands on his longsword, trying to overpower Grund's defense through sheer force of will.

The man was wielding two blades, but with only one hand on each, he couldn't match Rew's strength. Still blinking sand from his eyes, he couldn't trust to finesse, either.

Raif, rushing at the wounded simian, raised his greatsword. The creature lunged at him and caught the big fighter in a tight embrace.

Roaring in pain, Raif brought down the pommel of his huge weapon onto the ape-like creature's face, bashing it over and over until the simian released him.

Rew feinted a blow to Grund's head then jabbed with his longsword into the man's stomach, catching Grund with a few finger-widths of steel then snapping the blade back out and cutting along the inside of the commandant's forearm.

The simian released Raif and fell back, covering its face with its hands. It didn't see the boy wind up and deliver a sweeping attack to its torso. The greatsword cleaved into the creature and buried in the simian's chest.

Grund stumbled back, trying to find cover in the formations of stalagmites again, but Rew was relentless, keeping after his commandant, not giving Grund a breath to steady himself.

Snarling, Grund threw himself forward, trying to force Rew back, but the ranger was ready and hacked down into Grund's leg, carving a hunk from his thigh. The commandant grunted in pain and dropped a falchion, thrusting his palm behind himself.

Rew pressed him, and the commandant stumbled away, but as he retreated, a brilliant purple, gold-streaked vortex appeared behind him. The moment it opened, Grund backed through it. Rew crouched, preparing to jump after his commandant, but he hesitated. If he went to wherever it was Grund had portaled to, he'd have to leave Anne and the children behind.

Slumping against a wall on the other side of the portal, Grund held up his hand, and his enchanted falchion flew into the air from behind Rew and through the vortex. The opening winked shut a second later.

Rew stared at the empty air then staggered back out of the rocks to where his friends were clustered tightly together. He rasped, "Everyone all right?"

Raif, taking a tentative breath as if to test his lungs, said, "I think so. It felt as if that thing was trying to crack me like a nut, but somehow, I don't think it broke any bones. I've had worse in —Are you all right?"

Rew snorted, shifting his stinging shoulder and touching his bleeding chest with his hand. "I'll live." Blood ran down his chin from his cut cheek, and he wanted to dab it away, but he kept his longsword in his hand, looking around the cavern. "We need to leave this place."

"Not until I see to those injuries," declared Anne.

"Not yet," said Rew. "Vyar portaled out of here, which must have taken some effort with all of the copper in the rocks, but he might have strength to return still. We can't risk it. We have to get out of here so he can't pop out right behind us, maybe with more friends the next time."

Anne nodded. "Fair enough."

"Would he be able to fight if he returned?" questioned Zaine. "He appeared badly injured."

"He's tougher than you can know, lass. Trust me," said Rew, suppressing a groan as he adjusted his grip on his longsword, "we don't want to face him again now that he's angry, and we definitely don't want to find out what other allies he has."

Rew looked meaningfully at the dead simian, and they all nodded agreement.

They started back out the way they'd come, Cinda again lighting the way with her glowing palm. The party remained silent until they emerged from behind the waterfall and were within the thick growth of the forest. Zaine glanced over her shoulder at Rew and asked, "So, that was your boss?"

"He was," replied the ranger, and he left it at that.

4

Three leagues of quick-paced, strenuous hiking later, they paused to catch their breath. The younglings drew ragged, gasping lungfuls of air, and Anne slumped against a tree. For the first time on the journey from Falvar, she did not immediately offer her healing. Rew paced anxiously, wanting to put more space between them and the cavern, but he knew there was no point running the others until they dropped. If he overtaxed the group, they would be no good the next day. And the next day, they had to keep moving. They had to put more distance between themselves and where Vyar Grund would know to look for them.

The ranger commandant would have little difficulty following them through the forest, but distance meant they might have a warning before he arrived, and distance meant Rew may have an opportunity to obscure their trail. When they made it to the highway, even the ranger commandant would have trouble discerning their footprints from the hundreds of others. First, though, they had to gain some distance.

"Can someone," rasped Raif, "please explain what just happened?"

"You're welcome, by the way," said Cinda, reaching up and

gripping her older brother behind the neck. "I was worried about you."

Raif snorted. "I was fine, I think. At least, he hadn't done anything to me yet. I got wrenched around and banged up when the simian took me, but nothing broken, nothing badly bleeding. They roughed me up a little, then threw me down on the ground and left me there. It felt like I was dreaming, drifting in and out of consciousness. It was cold but no worse than I've felt on winter hunts through the barrows. I am famished, though, if we've time for a bite. I haven't eaten a proper meal, in, ah… I didn't pack well, and then Grund had me tied up for a day…"

Rew nodded to Anne, and she dug into her pack, pulling out a pouch of salted meat and a wedge of cheese for the boy. Raif fell on it ravenously, and Anne knelt beside him, putting her hands on his shoulders to assess just how bad his bumps and bruises were.

While her back was turned, Rew prodded at the cuts Vyar Grund had given him. The blood was congealing already, the tacky liquid making his clothes stick to his skin. They hurt something awful, and they'd caused a mess, but he decided they were shallow enough. He would survive, and rather than delaying, he figured he could keep going until nightfall. Then, a few stitches would sort him.

Cinda was watching Rew. "My brother had a good question. What just happened?"

Rew grimaced and kept pacing. He answered, "That man was Vyar Grund, the ranger commandant."

"Doesn't he work for the king?" questioned Zaine. "Why did he… Did he say was going to kill, ah, all of the Fedgleys?"

Clenching his fists at his waist as he walked back and forth in front of the younglings, Rew admitted, "That's what he said, and I think he meant it."

"The king?" questioned Anne. "Grund claimed the king ordered it, didn't he?"

Rew shrugged. "That's what he said, but men are known to lie."

"Tell us what you suspect," insisted Anne. "The king is the one who started the cycle, isn't he? The entire point of the exercise is that through backstabbing, betrayal, and outright battle, one of the princes proves themselves worthy, right? If the king is weighing on the scales, it seems... Well, I suppose calling something unfair in all of this isn't right, but that's what it seems like, doesn't it?"

"I doubt the king is trying to change the outcome of the Investiture," murmured Rew.

"What is it, then?" asked Anne.

Rew glanced at her again and kept pacing. The empath's face was serious, and he could sense she wouldn't be turned from her line of questioning. He couldn't think of a way to distract her, so he decided he had to tell her something.

"I think Vyar Grund is probably in league with Prince Valchon," said Rew, his voice barely above a whisper. "It could be why he brought Raif to that cavern. The copper in the walls would make it difficult for someone to farsee what was happening, even for the king. The other possibility—which I don't think is true—is that the king has become worried about necromancers."

"Why would the king fear necromancers?" asked Anne. "He is the most powerful one, is he not? Could Fedgley, or someone else, unleash something the king could not control? Is he worried what will happen to the princes?"

Rew shrugged uncomfortably. "Vaisius Morden is the most powerful necromancer the world has known. He has no fear of any summoning another necromancer could call upon. And believe me when I say the king cares little for the fate of his children and nothing for the damage they'll do to the common people as the princes contest with each other. He'll let the Investiture play out, and he won't interfere if the princes unleash wraiths or do any other despicable things I imagine they've planned. It's not ghosts that others may call which the king worries about."

"Worries about? So the king does fear necromancers?" asked Cinda. "Is that why Father was taken? Was the king behind it?"

"I don't think it was the king," said Rew. "That's not how he works. He'd be right to fear, though, what the princes may have planned with Baron Fedgley. I suspect Heindaw or Calb are behind the capture of the baron, and Vyar Grund is working with Prince Valchon, trying to figure out what is going on."

"Why would the ranger commandant kill Raif and Cinda, then?" asked Zaine. "This has nothing to do with them, does it?"

"High magic passes through the blood," explained Rew, glancing at Cinda then looking away, "from parent to child. When both parents have a talent for it, the child is always stronger. We've discussed it enough. Baron Fedgley is a talented necromancer."

Zaine blinked then turned to Cinda.

The noblewoman's jaw dropped, and she sat there, stunned.

"Cinda's not a necromancer!" barked Zaine. "She's not. She's, ah…"

"I'm an invoker," murmured Cinda. "We've been practicing invoking. Mother is—was—an invoker."

"Your father kept you isolated in the Duchy of Eeron," said Rew, still pacing, speaking his thoughts aloud. "He taught you no necromancy, which, by all rights, you should have a natural talent for. It's your family's legacy after all. I saw the wraiths he called in Falvar, and I am sorry, but I saw what your mother was capable of as well. Your father was the stronger, both in talent and practice. Alsayer claimed Fedgley was the most talented necromancer outside of the royal line, and maybe that's the truth. If it is, why did your father not teach you what he knows? Why did he not guide you to the power that resides in your veins? Instead, he gave you the theory, lass, of a skill you've little natural affinity for. He let Baron Worgon handle your instruction, what little of it there was. Why would your father do that?"

Rew stopped, looking down at Cinda where she was slumped against the trunk of a tree, her chest still rising and falling with the strain of the hike, her face flushed from that same exertion and from the torrent of ideas and emotions gushing through her.

"He didn't teach you," guessed Rew, "because he meant to protect you in his own way. He knew what was coming. The baron guessed he'd be a target in the Investiture, and he sought to prevent you from becoming one as well. As long as you remained ignorant of what you are capable of, the princes have no reason to pursue you."

"B-But..." stammered Cinda.

"But they don't know you are incapable of the feat they expect your father to perform," said Rew. "That was the baron's fatal miscalculation. He kept you in the dark to hide your abilities from yourself and from others, but everyone knows high magic passes through the blood, and the princes haven't been to this duchy in a decade. I doubt the king has even left Mordenhold in that time. None of them know you haven't been trained as a necromancer. As far as any of them know, you are your father's better." Rew turned to Raif and offered a grim smirk. "You as well, lad. High magic passes through the blood, but it doesn't always find fertile ground. With the way your father isolated you two, the princes couldn't know you have no magical talent."

"And Vyar Grund?" asked Anne quietly.

"Loyal to the king but also a friend of Valchon's since they were boys," muttered Rew. "Grund is the one who was tasked with teaching the young princes woodcraft. He taught them a bit of low magic and swordplay, as well. Maybe even a bit of invoking, though they had more talented tutors for that. Valchon latched onto the ranger, which I suspect is why the king assigned Vyar as the ranger commandant—an apolitical position by design. Vaisius Morden wanted Vyar away from his eldest son. He didn't want the boys gathering allies until it was time. I suspect Vyar is playing both sides now, still serving his duties as commandant but assisting Prince Valchon in the Investiture on the sly. I cannot be certain, but it fits."

"How do you know all of this?" questioned Zaine. "Did

Grund tell you? I don't think we should put much faith in the words of that man."

Rew shook his head. "No, my source isn't Vyar. I—Rest assured, I know what I speak of when it comes to the Mordens."

"What does it all mean, then?" wondered Raif.

"The princes, and maybe the king himself, are hunting your family," said Rew. "Vyar Grund is likely doing the bidding of Prince Valchon, and Alsayer could be working for Prince Heindaw or Calb. Duke Eeron or at least one of his arcanists… Ah, we need to learn more. He's probably in league with Heindaw or Calb as well, but is he on the same side as Alsayer, who knows?"

Grim-faced, the party sat in stunned silence.

"One thing makes sense now," mused Rew. "Before he took your father through the portal, Alsayer asked me to look after you. He must have known others were coming for you, and he wanted me to protect you until he could come back and snatch you himself."

"I… Oh my," murmured Cinda.

"What does this have to do with Father?" asked Raif.

"He's with Alsayer," said Rew, scratching his beard. "Maybe all of this explains why the princes are using the spellcaster. Everyone knows that treacherous bastard will flip sides as easily as we'd roll over in our beds. If one of the princes hired my cousin, it'd be difficult for the king to guess which one. That makes me think we have a bit of time. If Vyar Grund is stalking through the forest looking for us, it's because whichever prince has your father hasn't acted yet. That is one positive, at least. They're waiting for their moment."

"We've got to find Alsayer," declared Raif. "Time or not, Father is in grave danger."

"Lad," said Rew, "have you not been listening? At least two of the princes are seeking you and your sister. The king himself may be involved! Some of them mean to use you. Others merely want you dead."

"They're dangerous, we know, but those are the people who have Father," growled Raif. "We cannot leave him in their hands. That's why I left Falvar without you. I knew you wouldn't understand, that you wouldn't agree. I will not stop, Ranger. I am going to rescue my father."

"I understand," said Cinda. "I'll go with you, Raif, and together, we'll find Father and free him."

The boy nodded at his sister, clenching his fists at his side and not looking at Rew.

Cinda added, "You should have waited for me. We are family, Raif. We're better together."

Coughing and rubbing the back of his hand across his lips, Raif admitted. "You're right. I was burning hot, ready to fight. I wasn't thinking. I grabbed the sword, and I left. I... You're the strategist, Cinda, and I'm the steel."

"We're together now," she said, reaching out to grasp her brother's arm. "We will not leave each other again."

Flushing, Raif nodded in agreement.

"If you walk into Spinesend, you'll be captured or killed!" cried Rew. "Didn't you hear everything I just said? This is madness."

"He's our father," said Raif. "We will not leave him in the clutches of Alsayer, Prince Valchon, or anyone else. We will not turn our backs on our family, no matter what you say."

"I'll help you, if you'll have me still," interjected Zaine.

"Of course," said Cinda, squeezing her brother's arm to stop him from protesting. "We need you to identify the arcanist, and I'll be glad you're by our sides."

Giving a wan smile, Zaine shoved her arms beneath her cloak and sat back.

Rew threw up his arms in frustration.

"I'll accompany you as well," offered Anne.

"Anne!" shrieked Rew.

"You honor us," said Raif, inclining his head to the empath. Rew stared at Anne. She looked back, unblinking. Under his breath but loud enough they could all hear him, Rew repeated, "This is madness."

"It's, what, four or five more days to Spinesend?" asked Anne. "That's plenty of time for you to come up with a plan, Rew. I will not leave the children alone until it's over."

"Until it's over?" he growled, staring at her aghast. "Do you even know what you're saying, Anne? It's not over when they get to Spinesend. It's not even over if they did somehow recover their father from Alsayer. It's not going to be over until the Investiture is done and a new king sits upon the throne."

"We won't leave them until it's over," insisted Anne.

"I didn't say I was going," snapped Rew.

"You just fought the ranger commandant, Rew," reminded Anne. "You can't very well go back to Eastwatch now, can you?"

"Not Eastwatch, but we can go somewhere. Almost anywhere will be safer than striding into Spinesend."

"I'm going," said Anne. "You can come with us or not, but at least let me see to your injuries. You're bleeding all over your cloak."

Shifting, feeling the sharp aches on his shoulder and chest where Grund's falchions had cut him, Rew waved a hand dismissively.

"Rew, I insist," said Anne. "Like it or not, I'm going to care for you."

She stood and moved toward him. He took a step back.

Anne frowned at him, but she did not back down.

The party was silent, watching the ranger. Finally, he let out an explosive breath and said, "Fine. I'll accompany you to Spinesend."

"Good," said Anne. She raised her hand toward him again.

He stepped back and shook his head. "No healing."

"You speak of our madness but refuse healing when you're standing there dripping blood onto the dirt?" questioned Anne. "I can heal you. It's a small burden for me, Rew. Do not accuse us of

AC COBBLE

taking risks when you refuse healing. That is real madness, Ranger."

"Stitches when we stop tonight. I can make my own poultice. No empathy," said Rew.

"Why not?" retorted Anne. "Why not accept my healing?"

Rew shook his head and looked west toward Mordenhold, where the swirl of the Investiture was spinning like a giant, continent-spanning whirlpool. It was pulling at him, trying to draw him in. It was like swimming against the strongest current he'd been in, his entire body—his soul—striving to avoid the pull, and he was failing. The Investiture was scouring him, dragging him down into the depths.

He looked back, meeting Anne's eyes. Her eyes, the eyes of his oldest friend, but it was the face of the Investiture as well. The old magic was subtle; it was strong. Anne, the children, the magic, it was all part of a whole. Rew was failing, and he shuddered to think of the cost to him, to them, to all of Vaeldon. His head dropped to his chest. He was failing, unable to fight it, and he couldn't allow her to be bound by that connection, by that failure, as well.

He told her, "I'll go with you to Spinesend. I'll help rescue the baron. No empathy."

THEY HIKED WELL INTO THE EVENING UNTIL THEY MADE IT TO THE highway. With the moon overhead, Rew started a fire, and the younglings slumped down exhausted and spent. Anne prepared a rough supper, and everyone ate quietly. Both Cinda and Raif fell back onto their bedrolls, not needing Anne's help to pass quietly into the land of dreams, but Zaine scooted around the fire to sit close to Rew.

"Is traveling along the road wise?" asked the thief. "If we're worried Vyar Grund is going to be tracking us, isn't this exactly where he'd look first?"

Rew shrugged. "He may look for us on the road first, but he'll have a more difficult time tracking us here. The man is the ranger commandant, remember? If we blaze a trail through the wilderness, he'll have no problem following it. Perhaps I could move stealthily enough, but…" Rew gestured at the sleeping forms of Raif and Cinda. "On the highway, not even the ranger commandant will be able to separate our footprints from all of the others."

Zaine nodded, shifted nervously, and then asked, "Do you think he'll come after us again?"

Rew grunted and picked up a thin stick from their pile of firewood. "Yes, he'll come after us again. Him and others. I think there will be no rest, lass, until the Investiture is over or until our hunters are successful." Zaine had no response to that. Rew told her, "It's not too late to turn from this journey. You could flee to Yarrow or even Eastwatch. I can give you a note for Blythe in the ranger station. She'll take you on as an apprentice. You've the natural talent for it, lass, and you wouldn't be the first to find refuge in the wilderness. Anne and I can shepherd the nobles. We'll make sure they're safe—as safe as they can be, at least."

Zaine shook her head. "I couldn't do that."

"Couldn't?" asked Rew. "I think you could. You've little training, true, but you've a grace about you. With time under Blythe's guidance, you could move as silently as—"

"Rew, she means she couldn't abandon Raif and Cinda," remarked Anne from across the fire. "Zaine is part of this group now, a part of us. We all are. We're in this until it's over. I can feel the bond between us, Rew, and it has grown solid, even between the rest of us and you. Fight it as much as you want, but you, me, the nobles, and Zaine—we are all tied together now as a family."

"I'm not a part of anything," grumbled Rew, though he knew Anne was right. Defiantly, he claimed, "We'll get to Spinesend, recover the baron, and I'll be done with it."

"Done? I don't think so," said Anne. "Like it or not, you are a part of us. You can run, and you can hide, but that will not change what is true."

Rew stuck the end of his stick into the fire and did not respond. They sat quietly for a long time before Zaine retired to her bedroll. Rew and Anne were left on opposite sides of their little campfire.

"You can feel the bonds between us?" he asked the empath once he heard Zaine's breathing settle and was certain she was asleep.

Anne nodded.

Rew wondered, but could not ask, if it felt the same as the pull of the Investiture. Were the ties that bound him to the group like those that bound him to the king? That old, natural magic? Were they not just the same only on a different scale? He cringed at the thought and instead asked, "Have you always felt the bond?"

"Between the siblings, of course," she said. "Between them and I, as soon as I healed the lad back in Eastwatch. Between Zaine and the nobles, it was tentative, but it has grown strong since we left Falvar. The bond between you and I, always."

"Between you and I," responded Rew, looking up to meet her gaze.

"I'm going with them, Rew," declared Anne. "Wherever this journey takes them, I am going with them. So are you."

"Why?"

"They've the size and the age of adults, but in the wide world facing Vyar Grund, Alsayer—the princes, for King's Sake—they are like children," she said, "and children need looking after."

"They're not our—your, children," he argued. "They have parents. Well, they have a father, still."

"They were not born from my loin," she replied, rolling her eyes at his scramble to avoid mentioning their mother or that their father was currently in captivity, "but they are mine, and I am theirs. The bond between Raif and Cinda and their father is a legacy, only an echo. They are no longer of him and his line. I am going with them, Rew, and there is nothing you will say to convince me otherwise. Whatever they face, I will face. So will you."

"That's unfair, Anne," he protested.

"Life is rarely fair," she agreed. "None of us foresaw what was coming when we left Eastwatch, but when we did, our choice was made. All that is left is paying for it."

"Taking them to Spinesend is dangerous," hissed Rew. "If their safety is your concern, then we shouldn't be encouraging this. Help me take them somewhere the princes won't look for them."

"Their safety is my concern, but not my only concern," responded Anne. "If we spirit them away to some far-flung edge of the kingdom, what good will that do them? Perhaps they'd live a bit longer, but they wouldn't live the life they were meant to. Going on this journey, wherever it takes us, is what they are meant to do."

"Don't give me any mysticism about the Blessed Mother, Anne."

She smirked at him. "It is all connected, Rew. The Blessed Mother, the Cursed Father, the king, me, them, you, the world all around us. You can call it low magic, or natural magic, the priests call it prayer, but it is all one. You can feel it. Don't lie to me and say you do not. You just choose to ignore that which you do not like."

"I've never felt the pull of the Blessed Mother," he muttered.

Anne shrugged. They'd had that conversation before. Many times. Long ago.

"You're taking advantage of me," complained Rew.

"You don't have anything else to do, Ranger. So you may as well come with us. I've told you already I'm going."

"I won't be responsible for their foolish plans," retorted Rew.

"Feel responsible or not, but we are going to Spinesend, and if you think their plan is foolish, then guide them to a better one."

Rew snapped the stick in his hands and tossed both pieces into the fire.

"I'm tired, Rew," said Anne, "and you are as well. We can go back and forth all evening, but we both know that wherever this road takes those children, we will be beside them. Like it or not, whether you meant to make the choice when you left Eastwatch or not, you've a responsibility to this party now. I know you well enough to be certain you won't turn from it. Spare me your whining, at least for tonight."

He rubbed at his face with both hands, thinking that was a bit harsh, but all he said was, "Get some sleep, Anne. I'll wake you when it's your watch."

"Have a good night, Rew."

He grunted but did not respond.

5

Dawn broke, and Rew tossed back the flap of his bedroll. He stood and stretched. Anne was sitting cross-legged by the campfire, feeding sticks into it, building it back up from the embers it had died down to. Thick smoke from the damp firewood billowed up as it crackled and caught flame. Rew eyed her skeptically, thinking she looked rather chipper. He wondered if she'd stayed awake throughout her watch. He shook his head. There was no use chiding her about it now if she had dozed off, but it was worth remembering. On the other side of the camp, the three younglings still slumbered. They were wrapped tight in their bedrolls to block the cold air, and he couldn't see much more than their hair spilling out like feathers from the top of a quiver. He rubbed the stubble on his own head and yawned.

Moving quietly, Anne started laying out dried meats, cheeses, and a hard heel of bread. She gestured to a pile of empty waterskins beside the kettle she'd boil their coffee in.

Rew nodded and collected their waterskins. He walked from their camp to the dirt highway that led between Falvar and Spinesend, their nearly empty waterskins bouncing at his side. He would have paid gold for some of the fluffy eggs, crisp toast, and pots of rich honey that Anne served back at the Oak & Ash Inn, but on the road, fleeing from Alsayer, Vyar Grund, and the princes, he supposed it could be worse. At least he was getting coffee.

The road was quiet so early in the morning, and he didn't see another soul stirring when he looked each way down the highway. Even after other travelers began to move, they probably wouldn't see anyone coming from Falvar. It was too soon after the attack by the narjags, and the citizens and merchants of that place would be afraid to venture out. From Spinesend, the flow of traffic would be steady until those travelers paused at the tiny towns and roadside waystations and heard of what happened. Then, they would either turn around or rush toward Falvar, depending on how many family members and commercial interests they had in the city.

Dew-damp grass clung to his soft boots as the ranger strode across the road and down the gentle slope to the slow-moving river. So early, it was half-hidden by thin strands of mist, swirling a pace above the surface with the same lethargy as the water… and of the ranger, for that matter, he thought with a grin.

He reached the edge of the riverbank and knelt, dipping the waterskins into the cold stream. The lazy curls of mist and the subtle ripples of the current were only motion that he could see. A few birds called from back within the forest, but they remained hidden, and otherwise, it was silent.

As he was finishing filling their waterskins, he saw a sleek-furred head poke up from the center of the river. Rew watched as tiny waves followed the otter as it swam upstream, turned, and coasted on the current back past him. The otter's big, black eyes blinked at him as it drifted by. Rew fingered the knife sheathed in his boot.

Vyar Grund's otter, left in the eastern duchy when its master fled. Its head was probably still filled with instructions to watch out for their party, to report to its master when it found them. Rew wondered if the ranger commandant would come back for the otter and what the animal could communicate if he did. But instead of drawing his knife, Rew collected the full waterskins and stood. Perhaps he would regret it, but he'd let the otter live. There would be enough death in the world soon enough, and he'd wait as long as he could before adding his share.

He returned to the camp and found the younglings awake. He mentioned, "It's just two days back to Falvar, you know."

"We're going to find Father," insisted Raif.

"Leave it, Rew," said Anne. "We made our decision last night, and I can't handle you bringing it up every morning from now until this is over."

Sighing, he squatted beside the fire and set the waterskins by Anne. He rubbed his hands over the heat to chase away the chill from the river then told the group, "Four days to Spinesend if we push hard and follow the road, but when we get there, I recommend we stop and evaluate the situation from outside of the city. We should take the time to ensure we don't stumble into something. I'm certain there are more conspirators than just the arcanist, but we don't know how far it goes. If Duke Eeron himself is involved, then we need to worry about the guards at the gates, spies placed in crowds, and of course what we'll face in the keep."

The group was silent as they ate, and when they were done, the younglings performed their morning ablutions and began to pack the camp. Anne boiled water. Rew sat and thought. It was a morning for quiet contemplation as they began the next leg of their journey.

"Coffee?" asked Anne, breaking the stillness.

Rew nodded. He told the group, "I've been thinking about it. Even if Duke Eeron is not directly involved, we suspect Alsayer fled to Spinesend, and Vyar Grund could portal there just as easily. They may be cautious about acting openly if they're not in league with the duke, but high magic can be subtle as well as loud. There is risk in all that we do, but it will be highest when we cross the threshold of the gates and expose ourselves. We should plan our entrance carefully. The rest, we'll have to consider once we get there and feel the mood of the city."

The younglings nodded in between asking Anne for their coffee and lamenting the lack of sugar.

Rew warned them, "The risk is highest at the gates, but every moment we're in Spinesend will be dangerous."

"There is danger anywhere we go," challenged Raif. "If we flee, they'll still look for us, won't they?"

"They will," admitted Rew.

"What do you suggest, Ranger?" asked Cinda. "We have to go into the city because we aren't certain which arcanist holds our father, and the only way to figure that out is to let Zaine get eyes on them. Once she identifies the culprit, we can follow them and find out where they're keeping Father, or we can take the arcanist and force them to tell us, I suppose. For any of that to work, I don't see a way of doing it without going into Spinesend."

"We could send a message to Kallie," offered Raif.

Rew frowned at him. "Your sister?"

The nobleman nodded.

Scratching his beard, Rew admitted, "I hadn't thought of that."

"Surely she doesn't know where your father is being held," interjected Anne. "If she did…"

"She may not know, but she could help us from the inside," said Cinda, "and even if she cannot help, we can't leave her in Spinesend if we take Father from under Duke Eeron's nose. She'd be in incredible danger, wouldn't she?"

"She would be," conceded Rew. "You're right. We cannot leave her there, but we know Duke Eeron and his minions are plotting against your family, so it stands to reason they'd have your sister watched. We might put her in even more danger if we raise the alarm before we can extract her."

"We all agree we cannot leave her, and I think the ranger is right about the risk of sending a messenger into the city," said Raif. "She ought to be easier to find than Father once we're there, and if she's not, we'll deal with that when we learn of it. For now, getting inside the gates has to come first."

"Exactly," said Rew. He drew his hunting knife and cleared a space in the dirt beside their fire. "Spinesend is larger than Falvar and Yarrow combined, but that doesn't mean it's any easier to slip into. For centuries, the city has been built up with an eye toward defense." He began scratching rough marks in the dirt. "You've been to Spinesend, yes, but it's been some time?"

"It was years ago," replied Raif. "We passed through and spent a few days there on the journey from Falvar to Yarrow."

"I recall some of the city but not any details that would be helpful to us now," added Cinda.

Zaine offered, "I'm familiar with the poor areas of town, but I've never been into the keep before. It was all time with the thieves, you know? They never let me go to the wealthy areas. They have guards in those places. That sort of thing was carefully managed by the guild so we didn't draw undue attention."

"The city sits tight in the foothills at the tail of the Spine," said Rew shaking his head, trying to ignore Zaine. He drew the tip of his knife through the dirt to show them what he was talking about.

"Hence the name," said the thief, grinning.

Rew rolled his eyes but did not look at her. "Hence the name. There are steep hills around it and a lake which laps at the foot of the city walls. There are a few gates, but I think we have to assume those will be watched."

"Will they be looking for us?" wondered Cinda. "Even if Duke Eeron is involved, he may not suspect we'll come for Father, and anyone who doesn't have a finger in the plot probably won't even know what happened in Falvar until after we've arrived in Spinesend. Surely no one is traveling with more urgency than us."

"If Alsayer fled to Spinesend as we suspect, he'll have alerted whatever compatriots he has in the city," explained Rew. "We don't know who those people are or how far their reach may extend. We cannot risk walking straight in the gate where they could spot us. Believe me, it will be easier to recover your father if no one is aware we're within the city walls."

"That makes sense, but how do we get in?" questioned Raif.

"There are the sewers," murmured Rew, tapping the tip of his hunting knife on the drawing where the city met the lake. "Far less likely to be actively guarded if the conspirators are constrained by manpower, and once we're in the sewer system, there are countless places we can surface in the city. We run little chance of accidentally running into someone who will alert Alsayer or the duke to our presence—any people who travel the sewers aren't likely to have connections in the upper echelons of the city, of course."

Zaine snorted. "Of course."

Anne grimaced. "The sewers?"

"It's the safest way," responded Rew, slapping the bare blade of his hunting knife against his palm as he looked over his diagram.

"I don't think so," said Anne. "Come up with another plan."

Rew frowned at her.

"Do you have any idea what sorts of disease and illness are spread through that much waste?" asked Anne. "Sewers are hotbeds of infection." She prodded his shoulder just below the cut Vyar Grund had left in his flesh. "With an open wound, you're certain to catch whatever is floating around down there. Don't be expecting me to heal you, either. If you drag me through such filth, I'll happily repay your kindness by respecting your wishes and granting you no empathy whatsoever."

"The King's Ranger, felled by feces," said Zaine, her mouth tight to stop herself from laughing, her eyes twinkling with mirth.

Rew worked his mouth, trying to find the words to respond, but he had none.

"I have to say I agree with Anne on this," said Cinda. "Certainly there is another way into Spinesend which does not involve wading through rivers of human waste?"

"It's well known that during wars, disease kills more men than cold steel," added Anne.

"That's true," said Raif, vigorously nodding. "In the war against the Dark Kind fifty years ago, my tutors told me more men were lost to illnesses they caught carousing with…" the boy looked around the group sheepishly. "They were lost to disease, and we'll leave it at that. I agree with Anne on this."

"Very well," muttered Rew, stabbing his blade down on the other side of his diagram. "If not the sewers, then on the mountain side of Spinesend we could scale the walls. They're twice the height of Falvar's, heavily guarded, and none of you are adequate climbers, but—"

"We could take the thieves' entrance," suggested Zaine.

"What?" asked Rew.

Zaine pointed to a corner of the crude map he'd drawn in the dirt. "There's a small community of foresters and fishermen here. They don't enjoy the protection or the services of Spinesend, but their hovels are built right up against the city wall, and in the back of a tavern the thieves burrowed through. I don't think anyone watching for us will know of the place."

"You're sure?" asked Rew.

Zaine nodded. "It's how Fein and I left Spinesend for Yarrow just, ah… seems like it's been years ago instead of months. I was blindfolded for most of the trip, but I know I'll recognize the tavern outside of the wall. It's the only one in the village. The tunnel was operational then, and unless something big changed within the city, it still should be. It must have taken years to dig through that wall with no one noticing. The thieves would be reluctant to give up their access."

Rew stared at the dirt near Zaine's finger.

"Is it guarded?" asked Cinda.

"By thieves," responded Zaine, "Might be a bit of work getting through, but I think we can trust they won't go running to the duke's soldiers, eh? No matter what we have to do to get in, the thieves aren't going to want any more attention from the duke than we do."

Raif reached down to pat his family's greatsword that he'd laid beside his bedroll. "We'll get through, whatever it takes."

Rew tugged on his beard for a moment then nodded. He

sheathed his hunting knife and stood. "It's settled. We'll go through the thieves' gate."

Anne stood as well. Rew chose not to hear what she was muttering under her breath and instead he turned to finish packing their camp.

THAT EVENING, A THIRD OF THE WAY FROM FALVAR TO SPINESEND, they made it to the village of Umdrac. It was a small, humble settlement that had grown in between the highway and the river. The village was the final stop before the two paths diverged, the road hugging the base of the Spine, the river slicing through it. Umdrac subsisted on tariffs at its tiny port that serviced the river trade where bargemen would hand off their loads to wagon drivers. Its sole businesses seemed to be the transfer of goods and serving travelers looking for a hot meal and a cold drink. But because of the thirsty nature of bargemen and wagon drivers, Umdrac did significantly more business in that regard than its remote location implied.

Before they came upon the village, Rew told the others of it. He mentioned, "It's quite possible we'll find spies there. It's an easy place to station someone to watch the road between Falvar and Spinesend, and if someone is looking for us, I'd bet gold that's where they'll be."

"Should we avoid the village then and travel through the forest west of it?" asked Anne. "It's not easy going, and I've heard the forest is filled with bandits, but..."

Rew nodded. "We could travel rough, but that will delay us, and if there are spies, it might be best to find them here and away from the city where they could call in more resources. I don't mind a tussle with some common thug, but I'd rather avoid confrontations with both Vyar Grund and Alsayer at the same time in the middle of the city. At least if we run into trouble here, we'll have a better idea of what's ahead of us."

"I thought rangers relied on their stealth," said Zaine.

Rew touched the wooden hilt of the longsword hanging on his back. "Walk quiet and carry a big sword."

"You just want an ale, don't you?" accused Anne.

Rew protested, and while it was clear that Anne did not believe him, she finally conceded to stopping in the village. He might have exaggerated the luxury of the bathing facilities in Umdrac during the exchange, but they were a far sight better than cold river water, and he spent the rest of the walk to the village thinking of excuses in case Anne tried to tell him otherwise.

Soon, the scent of woodsmoke filled the air, and the sounds of village life joined the stomp of their boots. When they rounded a bend in the highway and saw Umdrac clinging to a low point in the riverbank, Cinda remarked, "Not much of a village."

"I'm not suggesting you settle down in the place," said Rew, "but if we learn something of what lays ahead, it will have been worth the stop."

Cinda shrugged, and Rew led them to the village and through the muddy streets to one of the village's two inns. It was the more expensive of the pair, and he usually stayed in the other because they served the same ale, but after quick glances at Anne and Cinda, he decided it was worth the price.

The people of Umdrac, used to travelers passing through their village, paid the party little mind. Rew kept an eye out, studying people's clothing, their boots, looking for anything out of the ordinary, but most of the people appeared to be locals. Those that were not had the look of seasoned travelers. A few of the bargemen and wagon drivers paused to glance over Anne and the girls, but they paid Rew and Raif less attention than even the villagers. Their group made it to the inn with no trouble, and while Anne immediately crossed her arms over her chest and tilted up her chin, it looked fine to Rew, so he paid for two rooms and five meals.

"Just two rooms," hissed Cinda in his ear as the innkeeper left to fetch a girl to show them around.

"They probably don't have many more," explained Rew. He gestured around the common area. "The workmen will sleep here tonight. Give it a few hours, and after the music and the drinking die down, they'll all settle on the benches, the tables, and the floor if they're really sotted. The wealthiest travelers, like you normally would, will have an entourage who will stage a camp outside of the village. It's only the successful merchants and perhaps high-ranking servants of nobility traveling on official business that will take a room. Even two rooms may draw suspicion. Any more will make us the talk of the inn."

Cinda, eyeing the filthy dirt floor strewn with fallen bits of half-eaten food and spilled ale, looked as if she would be sick. Anne had closed her eyes and appeared to be trembling.

"I've stayed in worse," remarked Zaine, slinging her pack off her back and stretching.

Rew slapped her on the shoulder and said, "That's the spirit!"

The innkeeper arrived back with his girl to show them their rooms. Rew and Raif took one and the women took the other. Rew slung his pack onto the floor and found a pitcher full of water and a wash basin sitting on a table between the beds. He bent over and began scrubbing his face in the lukewarm water.

"Not going to the baths?" questioned Raif.

"We'll be back on the road tomorrow, and there's no time to see a proper barber," said Rew. "I'm just trying to wash enough that my beard stops itching."

"They'll have a razor in the baths," suggested Raif. "You could shave yourself."

Rew stood and turned to the boy, water dripping from his face. "Have you ever shaved yourself, m'lord?"

"Never mind," muttered Raif, rolling his eyes and turning to sort through his pack.

Rew glared at the boy's back. Raif had a lush mane of hair that fell thick on his shoulders, though he barely had a wisp of it on his chin. Rew rubbed at the stubble on his head and resisted the urge to recommend Raif take the razor to his own scalp.

The boy removed his cleanest pair of trousers and a fresh shirt from his pack and cast a disgusted look at what he was wearing. "I don't suppose they'll have laundry?"

Grunting, Rew turned back to the wash basin.

"I'll meet you in the common room," said Raif.

Rew didn't bother looking up, but he did when he heard Raif cursing and then a loud scrape. The boy was dragging his greatsword free from the tangled straps of his pack. Rew asked him, "You're taking that giant sword to the baths?"

"Spies you said, right?" replied the boy. "I won't be caught unprepared again."

Rew picked up a towel and dried his face off to stop himself from shaking his head. "If you're wanting to avoid notice... Pfah. I'll be in the common room."

Raif walked out the door. Rew started toward it, but then he paused, turned, and picked up his longsword.

———

IF THE INN HAD A NAME, REW HADN'T SEEN IT ON THE SIGN, BUT THE ale was cold and the fire was hot. He'd found a table big enough for their party and had laid his longsword across it, reserving space for the others. He ordered an ale from the serving woman and waited, studying the room.

It was half-full, and in the corner, a lutist was twanging discordant notes, tuning their instrument. Rew wondered if the room was only half-full because the locals knew better than to come listen to the musician, or if it was because they didn't bother until the man was actually playing.

He took a long draught of the ale when it arrived and found it was crisp and clean. He was quickly on his second. There was no sign of the women or of Raif. He suspected they'd all take their time in the inn's baths. Rew hurried to finish his ale, knowing that once Anne arrived he'd have to slow his drinking. He ordered a third.

Halfway through it, Rew was feeling mellow and enjoying the first strumming of the lutist, even though it was obvious the locals had heard the man play before and weren't interested in hearing it again. Still, it was more entertainment than Rew had enjoyed since they'd left Eastwatch. He cradled his ale, kicking his toe in time to the fumble-fingered tune. When the serving woman passed by again, he raised his voice and ordered a fourth ale.

"Rew? The King's Ranger?" asked a man, jolting Rew out of a daze.

His foot stopped kicking and Rew turned from the lutist to see a tall man standing before him. The man was clad in an ochre tabard. Duke Eeron's livery. Beneath the tabard, he wore a quilted leather gambeson, and his hand was resting on the steel pommel of a broadsword. The soldier wore riding boots covered in the splatter of thick mud, though it had not rained in Umdrac for days, and his cheeks were reddened from a day out in the weather.

Rew did not recognize him, but he noted the soldier had two days' worth of stubble on an otherwise clean-shaven chin. With that and the mud, it wasn't much of a stretch to guess he'd come from Spinesend, traveling hard and fast on horseback.

The man stared down at him, beaming. "It's Rew, right?"

"Who's asking?" mumbled Rew, cursing himself for letting the soldier walk up to him unnoticed. An amateur error, like the nobles would make. He then decided his initial response had been stupid as well. It was the kind of thing people said in poorly written plays when they were hiding something. It was the kind of comment that immediately and unwittingly answered the soldier's question. Rew sipped his ale and then frowned at it. He set the ale down.

"Rodger, of Duke Eeron's Forward Scouts," declared the man. He shifted and then added, "I spoke to you some years back about joining the king's rangers in Eastwatch. You said you'd think about it."

"Ah," said Rew. "Of course, Rodger."

The man joined him at the table, casually pushing Rew's longsword aside and stretching his legs out in front of him. He sighed. "That feels good. I've been on horseback for the last two days. I've barely had time to stop and water the grass, you know?"

Rew scratched at his beard. Maybe he should have gone to the baths. He glanced at Rodger and tried to inquire casually, "Oh, really? If I can ask, where are you headed in such a hurry?"

"Falvar," replied the man, raising a hand toward the serving woman and calling for an ale. "Where else would I be headed on this highway?"

Rew grunted and did not respond.

"Speaking of which, what are you doing here, Ranger?" wondered the scout. "A bit outside of your territory, isn't it?"

"Just passing through," replied Rew, picking his ale back up.

"Well, keep a sharp lookout," said the scout, accepting a tankard of ale from the serving woman. He lowered his voice and leaned close. "We've had reports of banditry in the forest, and that's just the start of it. It's going to get bad around here, Ranger."

"Bad? The bandits, or…"

"The suspicion is that the bandits aren't operating independently," confided the soldier. "Believe me, they've got an agenda beyond just snatching a few coins out of your purse. Word is they've even got eyes right here in Umdrac. Watching for travelers, maybe. More like political targets, if you ask me. There've been reports of Dark Kind too, like you see out in your wilderness, though I don't believe that myself. It's been fifty years since anyone's seen a narjag along this road. Still, it's a sign of what's to come. It's a sign of trouble, Ranger."

"The Duke sent you to deal with it, then?"

The man shook his head. "That's not the fire we're cooking over, my man."

Rew fiddled with his ale. "What's that supposed to mean?"

The scout quaffed his ale, wiped the foam from his mouth with the back of a hand, and let out belch. "Just that the road between Spinesend and Falvar is going to get a bit hot, Ranger. No one's got time to deal with the bandits unless they stumble into them, and there's even less interest in a wild chase through the forest looking for Dark Kind. Out here alone, you need to watch your back. If I was you, I'd get over to Eastwatch as soon as you can. Dealing with those monsters out in the wilderness is going to be a damn sight safer than what the nobles have brewing in the duchy, that's the truth."

"Rodger, what does Duke Eeron have brewing?"

The scout winked at him again and finished his ale. He thunked the tankard down on the table and stood, stretching. "Gonna be a cold one tonight, Ranger, but I've got to get back on the road. Put my ale on the king's tab, will you?"

"I like that work ethic, Rodger," said Rew. "Sit a bit longer and let's talk. I'll buy you another ale. I've an opening in the ranger ranks, you know? We've been looking for a good man to fill the vacancy."

"Couple of years back, I would've leapt at that offer, Ranger," said the man, "but I'm afraid I've moved on. I've been doing well with the duke, and it seems it's finally going to pay off. With everything that is happening, he needs a man with my skills. I've been promised ample rewards once it's all settled."

"Once what is settled?" hissed Rew.

"Sorry, Ranger. I've got to ride," responded the man. "Keep your eyes and ears open while you're on the road. Another day we'll talk again? You can find me in Spinesend in the southern barracks if you want, once it's done. Could be I'll be looking for a change then. Maybe something a bit slower-paced would suit my retirement just right!"

The man laughed, offered a wink, and turned to go. He stopped. Halfway between the soldier and the door was Raif, staring open-mouthed at the scout's ochre tabard.

"A-Are you…" stammered Rodger. "King's Sake, you're Raif Fedgley!"

The scout's hand dropped to a pouch and he fumbled with the drawstring before yanking out a small slip of paper. He held it up, looking from the paper to Raif.

Rew leaned around the scout's back and saw the paper was a well-sketched picture of Raif and Cinda, though in the drawing they appeared a few years younger than they were now.

"I can't believe it!" exclaimed the scout. "Here, in Umdrac!"

"Ah..." mumbled Raif, trailing off, unsure what to say in the situation.

From the door of the inn, a man called over the sound of the lutist, "Rodger, are you in here drinking? We're to be outside of Falvar by tomorrow midday, man! Hold on... Is that Raif Fedgley?"

"I think it's time to go," murmured Rew, rising to his feet.

Raif blinked at him, confused. Rew hefted the heavy ceramic tankard his ale had come in and then smashed it across the back of Rodger's head.

"Get the women, get our gear, and get out of Umdrac!" barked Rew, stepping over Rodger's unconscious body.

"What about you?" asked Raif, turning and eyeing the handful of men wearing Duke Eeron's livery who were shoving their way through the crowded room. "Where will we meet you?"

"Don't worry. I'll find you," growled Rew. The soldiers were shouting at the other patrons of the inn to take Rew and Raif. None of them seemed eager to get involved, but more soldiers were pouring into the doorway. Rew shoved Raif in the back. "Go!"

Four men were working their way closer. The drunken, confused patrons were the only thing saving Rew from a rush of armor and steel. Like the scout, Rodger, they were wearing leather gambesons and carrying heavy broadswords. The four soldiers drew their blades, and the crowd panicked.

Rew, knowing he could flee in the confusion but realizing he needed to give Raif and the others time to escape, jumped onto a table and held up his longsword. He stared over the heads of the milling patrons at the four soldiers and made sure they saw his blade.

The soldiers slowed, waiting for the room to clear. Once the people had scattered, they began to advance again. They spoke no words because none were needed. Even if he hadn't been traveling with Raif, the soldiers had just witnessed Rew strike one of their own on the back of the head. For men of violence, there was only one response to such a thing.

Rew waited until they were close, and then he took two running steps down the table and leapt into the air, lashing out with his boot to kick a startled man in the face. The soldier's head snapped back and his broadsword fell from limp fingers.

Crashing to the floor, Rew slipped on the food-strewn, ale-damp surface and tumbled into another table. He rolled over it, flopping down on the opposite side, banging his hip against a bench, and then springing back to his feet.

The three soldiers who were still conscious stared at him in shock. Evidently, they hadn't expected someone to charge right at them, so he did it again.

He jumped back onto the table and launched himself into the middle of the men, bashing one with the hilt of his longsword, kicking the legs out from another and slamming his head against a table, and then grappling with the third, wrapping an arm around the soldier's neck and locking it under the man's jaw. The soldier flailed, dropping his broadsword, grasping at Rew's forearm with desperate fingers.

They wrestled, the soldier kicking against tables, trying to shake Rew's grip. The ranger held on tight, one arm snaked around the soldier's throat, the other holding his longsword, ready to deflect any attack the man tried to swing back.

Cursing, banging into the furniture, Rew almost didn't hear the stomp of boots at the doorway, but he did hear a man cry, "We're under attack!" Then, he heard the distinct ring of steel being drawn. Rew swung the man he was throttling around to see that six more soldiers had come in the door.

"King's Sake," he growled. He shoved the soldier away, and the man fell to his knees, coughing and clutching his throat.

Rew turned and ran, the six new soldiers hot after him. He couldn't face six of them without killing a few, and as far as he knew, these men were innocent of anything worse than following orders from their duke. In other times, Raif and Cinda would be protected by the soldiers of their liege, and if they recognized him in a crowded tavern, those men wouldn't hesitate to raise a tankard with the King's Ranger. No, if he could avoid it, Rew wouldn't kill the men.

He slowed. Had Raif and the others had time to get out of the inn and away from the village yet? Were they smart enough to find another exit from the inn, or would they be coming down the back stairs and out through the kitchen, the same way Rew was now leading the soldiers?

Swerving, cursing under his breath, Rew started heading around the corner of the room, hurdling the lutist's stage, stepping around benches and chairs that had been flung haphazardly when patrons fled the room, and jumping on and over tables.

"Get him!" snarled one of the soldiers, though his companions were already doing their best.

One of them, evidently slightly wiser than the others, split from the party and ran toward the front door where Rew was headed. The other five circled behind the ranger, trying to outrun him.

Rew charged toward the door and the man attempting to block it. The ranger swiped his longsword at the soldier's broadsword, smacking it aside. Not slowing, he drove the point of his elbow into the soldier's forehead. The hard bone of his arm cracked into the soldier's skull, and the man flew back, bounced off the wall, and slumped to the floor.

Bursting from the inn into the wide, dark street that ran through Umdrac, Rew skidded to a stop. Standing beside their mud-speckled, snuffling horses, were another dozen of Duke

Eeron's men. It looked as if they'd just dismounted and were coming inside to see what the commotion was about.

Raising his voice, Rew pointed down the street and cried, "He went that way!"

The soldiers stared at him, disbelieving.

Behind him, one of the five soldiers who had been chasing him in the inn came barreling out and swung a wild strike at the back of Rew's head. The ranger ducked it easily and smashed his fist into his attacker's chin, nearly lifting the man from his feet as he was flung back.

"Keep him alive!" shouted a voice from the doorway. "You, all of you, take him!"

Rew sheathed his longsword and ran.

Behind him, he heard some of the men mounting their horses. Others were pounding after him on foot. He knew he'd be more nimble footed and quicker than the armored men, but even the slowest warhorse would outrun him with little difficulty on an open stretch.

He jagged right, darting between a grocer and a bakery, coming out behind the shops and turning to run along the outside of the village. There was a gentle, grass-covered slope that led north along the river on his right, the village was on his left. The soldiers were crashing between the buildings and stumbling out into the open, already falling behind. He heard the thunder of the horses as they ran down the center of the village, and in half a dozen buildings, he saw the mounted men would come around the corner of Umdrac between him, the highway, and the expansive forest beyond.

Snarling, Rew realized he had no chance of making it to the forest with mounted men coming after him. He turned into the village, squeezing between two fieldstone houses to appear back on the street.

The soldiers on horseback were wheeling outside the village already, trying to head him off, not realizing he'd cut back behind them. The soldiers on foot, struggling in their leather gambesons, sounded a good fifty paces away.

Outside the village, past the soldiers on horseback, Rew saw four shapes running to the forest. It was dark, so they weren't immediately visible, but there was no cover until they reached the trees. If anyone happened to look that way…

He groaned. Then, Rew shouted at the top of his lungs. "You'll never catch me, you fools!"

Startled, a soldier on horseback turned, saw Rew, and began calling to his companions.

Rew ran deeper into the village, eyeing the shops as he ran, looking for—He saw a brewery with its windows flung open, likely to cool down the room after cooking wort all day. Rew put on speed, pelting down the road. He ducked behind another home. Using the cover of it and the building next to it, he scrambled up the side of the fieldstone wall. He reached up, caught a handful of thatch, and hauled himself onto the roof. Placing his feet carefully, he moved across the weather-beaten grass, glad it wasn't fresh thatch that would catch his boots as they sank into it.

On fingers and toes, distributing his weight as evenly as he could, Rew scrambled like a cat over the peak of the roof to the other side. Looking around and seeing no soldiers in view, he leapt across to the adjacent rooftop and crawled over that one as well. He made it across two more roofs, both times having to duck and flatten himself against the thatch while soldiers raced below. Then, he dropped in between buildings next to the brewery. He clambered up the wall and squeezed through the open window.

Inside, he saw vats where wort was being cooked, sacks of barley and hops, and racks of barrels where fresh brewed product was stored. There was a cart near the doorway stacked with a huge barrel that could have been for the inn and several jugs that may have been for citizens of the village. Rew picked up one of the jugs, walked to the racks of barrels, and climbed to the top of them. He clambered to the far corner and plopped down on top of a barrel. It was an hour after sunset and near pitch black inside of the brewery.

With the jug in his lap, Rew crossed his arms, gripping his opposite elbows in his hands. He closed his eyes, slowed his breathing, and pulled the darkness around himself in a fog of concealment. Breathing in and out, he gathered the shadows like a thick blanket and covered his body, starting at his legs and drawing the darkness higher. He could feel the shadow clinging to him, heavy, like a quilt of spiderwebs, and he felt the energy leak from his body as if his vigor was pouring out of a sieve. When finally he felt he could barely move, that the blanket of darkness was so heavy it threatened to suffocate him, he stopped and opened his eyes.

The room looked normal to him, just a hint of shadow in his peripheral vision, but for anyone coming inside, unless they came close with a lantern or a torch, the back corner he sat in would appear utterly black.

Rew unstopped the jug and took a sip. The ale, cool in the evening air from the open window, slid down his throat like nectar.

Outside, he heard the shouts of dozens of soldiers, their horses stamping and snorting. They were banging on doors, demanding entry. One by one, they started to search the buildings of Umdrac. Eventually, they entered the brewery and spent some time poking around, looking beneath the racks of barrels and behind the vats of wort. Twice more throughout the evening, soldiers came in and searched for him, but whenever their gaze roved toward the top of the barrels, they saw nothing but darkness.

Rew sat in his spell-crafted cocoon and sipped his ale, waiting until the soldiers stopped their search. Shortly after the village grew quiet, he fell asleep, his head resting in the crook of two stone walls in the corner, his bottom on top of a giant ale barrel.

6

Rew raised a fist to cover a yawn and sat up, wincing at a terrible crick in his back. A weight shifted in his lap, rolled, and then dropped. The half-empty ale jug bounced off a barrel, clunked against a rack, and then shattered on the floor of the brewery.

"King's Sake," muttered Rew, glancing around the dimly lit room.

The first strands of dawn were leaking through the open windows. He could hear birds chirping outside, the lowing of cattle waiting to be milked, the bray of a donkey, and little else.

The recollection of the previous evening seeped through him like hot water through coffee grounds. He decided it was past time to go. He climbed off the barrel and dropped into the center of the room. He took a moment to stretch, working the blood back into his muscles, knowing he might have to move quickly. Wiggling back out the open window, he peered around but saw nothing amiss.

Stalking like he was on a hunt in the forest, Rew crept to the street that ran down the center of Umdrac and glanced each way. He could hear the whinny of horses, but they sounded like they were in the stable behind one of the inns. There were signs that a few residents of Umdrac had risen, but only a pair of men were at the far end of the street. None of Duke Eeron's soldiers were in sight. All the same, Rew went to the backs of the buildings.

Eyes darting around, he crouched and hurried into the grass, keeping low, placing his feet with care to leave minimal trace. Like the wind, he weaved through the dew-damp emerald blades. When he got to the edge of the village, he spotted two, ochre-clad soldiers standing on the side of the road. They were speaking in low voices to each other and stomping their boots, trying to keep their toes warm.

Rew considered sneaking up behind them and bashing them over their heads, but decided it would be best if he left no evidence at all that he'd still been in the village. He watched and waited until it was clear the pair were spending little time looking around. They'd been on duty for hours, he guessed, and with the pre-dawn glow, they knew their watch would be over soon.

Rew scampered another hundred paces down the road to cross. With a backward glance at the soldiers to ensure they weren't chancing a stray look his way, he sprinted across the dirt tract.

Moving carefully and keeping low, he slithered away through the grass from the road to the tree line of the forest. When he got there, he stood, covering himself behind a thick trunk, and breathing a sigh of relief. He paused for some time, making sure there was no pursuit, and then he moved deeper into the autumn forest, stepping carefully on the leaf-strewn ground, hoping the bare branches gave him enough cover.

Finding the trail left by Anne and the younglings took only a few moments. They'd snapped dead branches as they brushed by trees, left scuffs in the dirt from careless boots, disturbed fallen leaves, and kicked over rocks, marking a path as easy for Rew to follow as the highway between Falvar and Spinesend.

As he walked, he tried to obscure the signs, pushing rocks

back to where they had rested, snapping branches in other directions, shifting leaves over boot prints, but there was only so much he could do. If Duke Eeron's scout, Rodger, was worth a position as a ranger in Eastwatch, he'd have little difficulty finding the trail. Grimacing, Rew left off his efforts to hide the signs and hurried ahead. Stealth wasn't an option, so he may as well hurry.

Shortly, he found Anne and the others just barely waking in a rough camp behind a tangle of fallen trees. The empath gave him a curt nod, and Cinda exclaimed, "Good, you made it!"

"I did, and now it's best we're away," advised Rew. "There is a score of Duke Eeron's men back in the village, and they'll be waking soon. It won't be hard for them to find us if they put any effort into it."

"Do you think they'll do that?" wondered Zaine. "Raif said they recognized him, but…"

Rew, looking over his shoulder the way they'd come, said, "Yes, they will search for us. They were headed to Falvar, but the man had a picture of Raif and Cinda on him. It's not the city they want. Come on. A child could follow the trail you left last night."

Standing in a clatter of rustling metal, Raif asked, "Do we run, or do we fight?"

Rew blinked at the boy. "Where did you get that?"

"Get what?" replied Raif.

"You're wearing armor," said Rew, gesturing at the boy. Raif wore articulated, steel pauldrons with an iron-studded brigandine underneath, gauntlets, and leather-covered greaves. Steel plates covered his thighs, but he wore no helmet. It was entirely ridiculous attire to be trooping stealthily through the forest while Duke Eeron's soldiers chased them. "Where did you get armor?"

"I snatched it on our way out of the village," said the boy, shifting the steel plates on his shoulders. "Left some coin behind to pay for it. Figured I might need the protection. It fits well enough, though I do regret sleeping in it."

Rew rubbed his face, considered arguing with the young noble about it, but decided it'd take the boy half an hour to remove all of that steel, and they didn't have time.

"We head due west and then we'll curve south. We can stay within the forest until we get close to the Spine. Once we're outside the city, we'll find this thieves' gate Zaine spoke of."

"Won't traveling through the forest delay us?" argued Cinda. "We don't know how much time Father has until… until something bad happens."

"If Alsayer wanted the baron dead, he would have killed him in Falvar," stated Rew. "No, we'll—What was that?" The ranger looked around and then gestured frantically. He whispered, "Move, move, but quiet."

They started off quickly but not at all quietly.

Rew led them deeper into the forest with a creeping sense of dread crawling up his back. He'd heard something, and it hadn't been an animal. Someone else was out there in the forest. Was it one of Duke Eeron's scouts? If so, why weren't they under attack? If a scout had found them and had gone back to get reinforcements, Rew thought he would have heard that. The bandits Rodger had warned him about? Vyar Grund? But the ranger commandant wouldn't hesitate if he'd found them; he'd certainly attack. Who else could it be? What were they waiting on?

Behind him, the rest of their party came along, sounding like a peddler's cart trundling over a rickety, iron bridge. Cinda's robes kept snagging on branches and bushes; Raif banged against tree trucks like the clanging of pots. Rew was pretty sure Anne and Zaine were making their share of noise as well, but it was difficult to tell with the racket the other two caused. If someone was out there, they'd have no trouble hearing where the party was walking. Rew kept them moving, kept them going for half an hour, until he saw a small clearing and a little hillock. The hairs on his neck were standing up.

Someone was following them. A dozen people, more? It was difficult to tell. They kept behind the trees several hundred paces away, but Rew had no doubt they were out there. And whoever it was, they were skilled in the woods. Rew had the uncomfortable feeling that the only reason their hidden followers had not shown themselves was because the party was walking exactly where their pursuers wanted them to go. It wasn't the Duke's men, he decided, but he didn't know if that was a good thing or a bad thing. Bandits wouldn't drive them deep into the forest just to question them.

"There," he said, "get up on that hill and put your backs to each other."

"What?" asked Raif.

"Get ready for a fight," instructed Rew.

That shut the boy up, and the group assembled on the short, grassy hill.

"Fight what?" wondered Zaine, drawing an arrow and nocking it.

"Wait," said Rew.

He could hear them now. Not just a few followers, but several. More than a dozen. They were still out of sight, but he sensed that the party was being encircled. He still had no idea who it might be.

After a moment, Cinda whispered, "What are we waiting for?"

"Them," said Rew. He drew his longsword and gestured at the cluster of cloaked men who were appearing from behind trees and surrounding them.

"W-Who…?" stammered Zaine.

"Draw your weapons," hissed Rew.

She raised her bow. Raif unslung his greatsword from his back. Cinda raised her arms, and her hands began to crackle with pale blue light. Even Anne held her belt knife.

The men surrounding them were covered in dark cloaks and had hoods over their faces, but they all held bare swords and axes that left little question about their intentions. The men moved closer, creating a tight circle around the party. Rew studied them, searching for weaknesses in their line or some clue as to who they were. Subconsciously, he sized up their foes and decided which were most likely to fall back if he charged, but then, Rew grimaced. He couldn't simply charge out and attack. If he did, he'd have a chance of breaking out of the circle and escaping into the thick woods, but Anne and the children would never make it.

There were no bows or crossbows facing them thankfully, but there were at least thirty of the cowled figures surrounding them. Too many, if they knew the use of their weapons.

"What do you want?" Rew called.

"Just the children," said a woman, stepping to the front and pushing back her hood. Dappled sunlight sparkled on sharp steel that adorned the woman's leather bracers. From the end of the bracers, gleaming claws rested on her wrists. Rew had seen the like in the south and knew with a twist, those claws would slide out and extend past her knuckles. The sides of the woman's head were shaved, and the rest of her blonde hair was bound into a tail at the back of her head. On her bare scalp, he saw intricate, blue tattoos scrawled over her ears. He'd seen tattoos like that before as well, but not in the south, he didn't think. He didn't have time to consider it.

"Mistress Clae," hissed Zaine.

The woman's head tilted. "Yes, though few know that name. Who are you?"

"If you don't know who we are," muttered Rew, "why do you want the children?"

"I know those two," said the woman, gesturing with her clawed wrist at Raif and Cinda. "I don't care who the rest of you are."

"Perhaps we should, Mistress," mumbled a man near her.

The woman glanced at him.

"That's the King's Ranger, Mistress."

"Is he?" said Mistress Clae, turning to study Rew. "What are you doing here, Ranger?"

"Everyone asks that," complained Rew under his breath. Louder, he said, "I'm an agent of the king, and I'm allowed to leave the territory, you know. As an agent of the king, I ask that you step aside and stop interfering with my travel."

"Allowed to leave your territory, certainly, but that doesn't mean you're allowed in my territory," declared the woman with a wink, "and unfortunately, I've already fallen afoul of the king's law. It pains me, but I don't think the old chap is going to forgive me even if I do spare his appointed ranger. My target isn't you, though, so give us the children and be on your way."

"I can't do that," said Rew.

"There's no reason for violence," claimed the woman. She tapped her lips with one finger, putting her claws dangerously close to her nose. "I have no quarrel with the king or his ranger. What if I paid you for those two? We have gold, and if you twist my arm, perhaps an enchanted artifact or two that one such as you might make use of."

"These children are my responsibility," said Rew, shaking his head. "If you mean to take them, you'll have to kill me first."

He felt Anne shifting at his back, and he wanted to turn and scowl at her, but the tattooed woman held his attention.

"Very well," said Mistress Clae.

"You'll have to do it quick, too," said Rew, raising his voice to be sure all of Mistress Clae's men could hear him. "Duke Eeron's soldiers should be here soon enough."

"What?" asked the woman, laughing at the claim. "That's a ridiculous ploy, Ranger. Surely you can—"

"Mistress," called another of the men.

She turned to the speaker, glaring at him.

"I hear horses," claimed the man. "When I left Umdrac to report last night, I saw some of the duke's soldiers enter the village…"

"Stay here!" shouted Rew to his companions. Then he charged off the knoll, headed directly for Mistress Clae.

She shook her arms, and three claws extended from each of her bracers. Rew swung a wheeling slash at her face. The woman brought up her claws, deflecting the blow, and then attempted to strike at him with her other hand, as he'd anticipated. Rew stepped in and grabbed her wrist. He twisted it, spinning her until her back was to him. Then, he began dragging her back to the knoll, his longsword in front of her, poised to drag across her throat.

Her men had been rushing him but pulled up in skidding stops.

"Stay back!" warned Rew.

"Rew," shouted Zaine from the knoll. "I hear the horses too!"

"Stay back!" cried Rew again, moving his longsword closer to Mistress Clae's neck to slow her men who'd started advancing again. Calling over his shoulder, Rew said, "When Duke Eeron's men come into the clearing, no matter what happens, stay on my heels."

"Wait, the duke's men really are in the forest?" snapped Mistress Clae, suddenly ceasing her struggles. "Why are—"

"There!" barked one of her thugs.

Crashing through the trees, a trio of mounted soldiers burst into view.

"Attack them!" demanded Mistress Clae.

Rew spun her around and drew back the fist holding his longsword, intending to smash her in the face and knock her out, but the woman allowed herself to tumble away, rolling clear of him. Mistress Clae's men, thinking there were just three of the duke's soldiers, rushed at the horsemen, swords and axes raised. The soldiers began shouting orders, wheeling their mounts and drawing their blades to slow the attacks. In seconds, more of the ochre-liveried men began appearing through the trees.

"Now we run," said Rew to his companions.

He led the party down the short hill, smashing his shoulder into one of Mistress Clae's thugs as he did, tossing the cloaked man back onto his bottom. The clearing exploded in chaos as more of Duke Eeron's scouts burst into the open space and were engaged by Mistress Clae's bandits. The two sides, stunned at the presence of the other, were soon fighting tooth and nail in a nasty, bloody brawl.

Mistress Clae started after Rew and the others, but a soldier on horseback came charging across her path, the man swinging a wild blow with his broadsword. She ducked, and while she was down, Rew and his party disappeared into the trees.

The fight had already spun out into the underbrush, and they almost immediately ran into a soldier and a bandit engaged in furious combat, both raining blows against the other, both their weapons fouled by the thick vegetation, neither one able to gain an advantage. Muttering an apology, Rew came in from the side, and with two quick thrusts, he killed them both.

"Hate to do that," he said over his shoulder, "but we can't have them telling which way we're going."

"Where are we going?" asked Cinda, glancing west where they'd been headed.

"Back to Umdrac, around the back of the place, and onto the water," said Rew.

"What?" questioned Raif. "How are we going to reach Spinesend on the water?"

"Lad, you're not getting to Spinesend on the road from Falvar or through these woods, either," said Rew, looking around cautiously as he found the path Duke Eeron's soldiers had taken through the forest. Following it, he hoped the crashing of the armored men and their mounts through the brush would leave a confusing enough trail that their party would be impossible to track. "On the highway, we ran into Vyar Grund, one of the most talented rangers in a generation. We've seen Duke Eeron's soldiers, and Mistress Clae—whoever she is. All three groups were independently looking for us, and they all knew we'd be on this road. If we stay on the highway, they're going to find us again."

"B-But..." stammered Raif.

"There are too many of them," said Rew, "and we've been lucky to survive as long as we have. In just three days on this road, you've been abducted, we've had to flee in the middle of the night, and if it wasn't for two of our hunters running into each other unexpectedly, we'd be... King's Sake, I don't even know who Mistress Clae is or what she wanted with you!"

"She's an affiliate of the Spinesend thieves' guild," offered Zaine, "but she's not much of a thief. I guess you'd call her an assassin."

"An assassin, see?" replied Rew. He cringed, glancing over his shoulder at the nobles. "An assassin from Spinesend, out here searching for you two?"

"Don't look at us," said Cinda. "I've never seen her before."

"Rew is right," said Anne, her calm voice cutting through the babbling protests of the younglings. "If we continue on the road, we won't survive the journey. If we don't survive, your father has no chance. The... what'd you say, Rew, the water? It's our only hope."

Rew offered her a curt nod.

"If we can find a suitable vessel," argued Cinda. "All I saw were river barges. They could catch up to us swimming if we're in one of those."

"Barges and the ketch those boatmen hailed you from," remarked Rew. "Those two looked thirsty enough, so I think there's a good chance they and their boat are still in Umdrac."

"Ah," said Zaine, a grin spreading on her face. "I'm liking the way you think, Ranger."

"Let's quiet down," he told them. "I don't know how long those two groups will be tangled up behind us, but let's not make it any easier for them. We can all agree it's best we get as far away as we can as quickly as we can, right?"

No one disagreed with that, and so wordlessly, they moved through the forest, Rew pushing them along the path the duke's soldiers had taken, hoping no one was talented enough to follow their trail.

THEY HIKED AT A RELENTLESS PACE FOR TWO HOURS, TAKING advantage of the path smashed through the forest by Duke Eeron's scouts and their mounts. When they reached the edge of the wood, Rew called a halt, and the younglings and Anne breathed heavily behind him. He peered between the final branches and tree trunks, over the road, across the grass, at the village of Umdrac.

Without the soldiers, it appeared peaceful, sleepy, as if the events the day before hadn't happened. Rew tapped his fingers against a tree, thinking.

"We could turn down the road," suggested Raif. "Those soldiers, if they survive the encounter with the bandits, may be hours behind us. The way between here and Spinesend could be wide open."

"We don't know what other watching eyes will be out there waiting," retorted Rew. "Besides, even if there's no one else, horsemen will have little difficulty catching us on the highway. It's days to Spinesend, remember?"

"Could we fight them?" questioned the nobleman.

"I'd rather avoid that," said Rew. "Fighting men like that isn't the same as narjags or ayres."

"They're bigger, aye, and have armor and better mounts," said Raif. "I know they will have some skill, but between all of us, if the bandits thinned them out…"

"I meant that killing a man is different than killing a Dark Kind," said Rew. "It's not something you want on your conscience."

"You killed that soldier and bandit when we were escaping," argued Zaine, "and the thieves when you rescued me. And, ah, the other time you rescued us, too."

Rew nodded. "I killed them, aye, but I didn't enjoy it. If we can avoid a fatal encounter with Duke Eeron's soldiers, we will. Unless anyone has any more objections, we're going to pass through Umdrac, find the boat Cinda and Zaine's suitors arrived on, and escape on the water."

"Suitors?" asked Raif.

"The river flows to Yarrow," interjected Cinda. "I don't like it. This entire journey has been about leaving that place. Baron Worgon won't welcome us back with open arms. Our father is not there, and—"

Rew held up a hand.

"What?" asked Cinda, frowning at him.

"Quiet," he responded.

"Thunder?" asked Cinda after a moment.

"Marching," said Raif, his face pale in the afternoon light. He swallowed, the apple in his throat bobbing like a man on a noose. "That's the sound of men marching. An army of them."

Rew nodded, peering down the road toward Spinesend.

"They must be headed to Falvar," said Raif. "We have to go back. We have to warn Commander Broyce and help protect the city."

"You lost half your soldiers in the scuffle with Alsayer and the Dark Kind," reminded Rew. "You don't have the men in Falvar to stand against Duke Eeron if he's coming in force."

"We have to do something!" retorted Raif.

"If they're marching to Falvar, it's because they're coming for you and your sister," said Rew. "The best thing you can do for your people is to not be there when Duke Eeron's men arrive. Commander Broyce is no fool. If your liege demands to see you, and you're not there, he'll show them around and then send them on their way. Broyce will avoid a fight, but he can't if you're standing atop the walls."

"That doesn't make any—"

"He's right," said Cinda, interrupting her brother. "If Duke Eeron is sending an army, we can't fight them. The best we can do is not to give them a reason to attack. Commander Broyce knows why we left, but he's as straight an arrow as they come. He won't instigate a conflict with Duke Eeron. Falvar is safer without us."

"I disagree," muttered Raif, though he offered no solution of his own.

Rew stepped from the forest, looking down the road. "That army is coming this way. We have minutes at best before we're in view. Come on. We need to get to Umdrac."

"We haven't agreed on the plan!" complained Cinda.

"No, we haven't," said Rew. Then, he started walking across the grass toward the village.

Anne shushed the mumblings of the younglings and led them after Rew. They might not like it, but the forest was full of enemies, and the road had an army marching down it. The river led to Yarrow, and while that wasn't their destination, it was the only place they could go.

"Rew," said Anne as they approached the village, "if we walk through there, won't the soldiers know exactly where we went?"

Rew, not answering, led them to the edge of the village to an abandoned hovel he'd run by the night before. He put his hand on the ancient thatch and whispered a hushed incantation. Beneath his fingers, the thatch began to blacken, and slender tendrils of smoke drifted up.

"How are you doing that?" exclaimed Cinda. "Is that high magic?"

"It's not. Quiet, don't draw attention," said Rew, taking his hand from the smoldering thatch and watching as tiny flickers of light grew into dancing flames. "Come, walk down the street, and let's be away from here before anyone notices the fire. With a little luck, this will distract them, and no one will realize we've passed through. Duke Eeron's men will likely assume we fled toward Falvar. If they don't know where we are headed and why, that's the only logical place you would go."

He led the party into Umdrac, encouraging the others to pull the hoods of their cloaks up and for Raif to hunch down, so it wasn't so obvious they were the ones the soldiers had been searching for. They walked slow, taking their time, heading toward the inns as any freshly arrived travelers would do. In the distance, the rumble of marching feet grew closer, and Rew glanced over his shoulder, wondering when someone would notice the growing flames atop the empty home.

"What's that, eh?" asked a man beside them. He had a stack of linens thrown over his shoulder and was speaking to a potter who was sitting in the open door of his shop.

"What's what?" asked the potter.

"Sounds like thunder," murmured the other man, glancing up at the clear blue, afternoon sky.

The potter stood from his stool, wiping his hands on his apron to clear them of sticky clay. He stepped into the street. "That ain't no thunder, that—Fire! At Garl's old place. Fire! Fire!"

All around them, villagers began rushing into the street, gathering buckets and filling them with water. There was little organization at first, but like any small community, they were all aware of the risk fire posed to the village, and they were all rushing into place to stop it. Rew, their party, and the other strangers in the village moved out of the way as a bucket line was formed from a well beside the blacksmith's shop.

Rew gestured to his companions and led them farther into the village, passing the inns and the long warehouses that braced the docks, then out to where a ketch was tied to the wharf. It was a small craft, but it had a short mast with a rolled sail and a pair of oars. It'd be a little tight with the five of them, but they'd all fit, and it'd be a damned bit faster than the pair of barges that were the only other vessels tied to the dock. Besides, if they had to steal from someone, Rew felt a lot better stealing from the two lechers who'd harassed the girls. Drawing his hunting knife, Rew crouched and slashed through the ropes that kept the ketch tied to the dock. Everyone boarded. With his boot, Rew shoved them clear.

"Raif, man the oars," he instructed, glancing up at the sail above them. "I don't suppose anyone knows how to work this?"

"You don't?" asked Cinda.

"I can't believe you stole a boat," remarked Zaine in an appreciative tone, "though you probably should have taken one you knew how to sail."

"Anne, you grew up near the sea," said Rew.

"Decades ago," she muttered, reaching up to fiddle with the sails. "I was a girl, then."

"You were old enough to—" began Rew, but he stopped when the empath shot him an icy glare.

"I'll do what I can," said Anne.

Grunting, Rew took a seat on a bench beside Raif and nodded for the boy to take an oar. Raif, watching Rew, leaned forward and dipped his oar into the river. Leaning back together, they propelled the narrow craft away from the dock and into the current.

Back in Umdrac, shouts were filling the street, and villagers were rushing to extinguish the fire that had spread all along the roof of the abandoned hovel. The villagers that weren't engaged in fighting the fire were watching as the first wave of ochre-liveried soldiers marched down the road from Spinesend. At the head of the column, in front of a company of cavalry, Rew saw a trio of men and women bedecked in plush robes. One in black—the attire of an invoker—led the army. It appeared, like the common soldiers, that the three spellcasters' attention was fixed squarely on the burning hovel and the villagers' attempts to fight the fire. None of the three high magicians moved to help.

"Put your back into it," muttered Rew, digging his oar into the water again, watching as the soldiers slowed their march, staring curiously at the scrambling villagers and the fire.

The highway hugged the river for another league before it curled away and the river plunged into the foothills of the Spine. A league where they'd be completely exposed to the marching soldiers.

"Keep your hoods up," instructed Rew, hauling on his oar in time with Raif. "Anne…"

Between frantic whispers to the girls as they tried to unfurl the sail, the empath shushed him.

Rew, pointedly not looking at the long line of soldiers that snaked from the village down the road, hoped Anne would figure out how to work the sail, and he hoped that no one thought to question why a ketch was speeding furiously away from the village moments before the soldiers arrived.

❧ 7 ❧

The river that flowed from Falvar to Yarrow and then far beyond to the sea, was a broad, slow-moving current north of the Spine. The water, brown near the village, gradually cleared as they moved away from the settlement. The sediment in the water that was stirred up by the activity near Umdrac fell to the bottom, and looking through the water was like peering through a thick piece of glass. Fat fish swam below, and pale rocks and rotting tree trunks marked the bottom.

Beside the water, the highway hugged the riverbank for a league before it peeled away, leaving only tall grass and willow trees dotting the bank. Beyond those, they could see the treetops of the forest, but eventually, those disappeared from view as well. On the other side of the river, they passed a narrow tributary, and then, the chalk-white walls of the Spine began to rise around them, the water curling through the foothills, taking an easy path into the rising stone.

At first, they were glad of the cover, leaving the bristling line of soldiers behind. Those men had paid little attention to a small boat on the water when there was the excitement of the fire in Umdrac ahead of them, but just the same, it gave Rew some comfort that they'd vanished from view without an alarm being raised.

Had they been noticed, they weren't the only craft on the river, but there weren't many others. Barges trawled the route between Falvar and Umdrac, and south of the village, they'd seen flat-bottomed boats where one or two fishermen would sit, casting nets for bait and lines for supper. They did not see any pleasure craft, and it seemed there were few sailing vessels akin to the ketch they'd stolen. So far from Falvar and Yarrow, that was to be expected. The villagers in Umdrac could not afford to keep a vessel that served no purpose but leisure, and they had little need of the speed the ketch offered.

It seemed the previous masters of the vessel had taken everything with them when they spent the night in the village. Rew guessed the two had been employed ferrying messages or high-value goods. He wondered if some merchant in Falvar had hired the pair to quickly share news of the battle against the Dark Kind, hoping to gain a trading advantage by using the quick-moving ketch to beat competitors to Spinesend's markets.

Whatever the reason the ketch had sailed to Umdrac, it had been a good choice for the party. Once they passed the last of the soldiers, it felt like they were on a pleasure cruise. Anne had managed to drop the sail, and it had filled with the gentle wind that blew along the river. They glided across the water with no need of rowing. With adjustments to the sail and the tiller that knifed into the water behind them, they had an easy time keeping to the center of the channel and coasting as fast as a trotting horse. It was cool on the water, but the sun shone bright, and with his cloak pushed back, Rew found it quite pleasant.

The sun dropped below the horizon. The moon shone bright on the cloudless night, and the stars twinkled above them, mirrored by the sparkling reflections on the surface of the river. Gaining confidence in her long-unused sailing skills, Anne had the younglings help her raise the sail back up, and they let the current carry them. Rew leaned against the tiller as they floated downstream, the water lapping peacefully against the wooden hull of the vessel.

From their packs, they produced a simple meal, and Rew remarked, "An ale wouldn't be amiss."

Anne snorted. He grinned at her.

"Boating on an evening such as this, we'd have flagons of pinkwine if it was a real pleasure cruise," said Cinda, "though, I never drank much of it myself."

"You were too young," declared her brother.

She reached over and punched his arm. "At least I didn't make a fool of myself like you did on Worgon's spring cruise. You were leaning over the gunwale and it sounded like you were coughing up the entire river."

"I think a river's worth is about how much of Worgon's wine I drank," admitted Raif sheepishly.

"There's no shame in that," mumbled Zaine, and they all laughed, recalling how sluggish she'd been moving after the night they'd spent in the miner's tower.

"In truth," said Cinda, "Raif is right. I was a child of fifteen winters this spring. Old enough to sneak a bit of wine with my friends but not old enough to drink it in front of Baron Worgon. Not old enough to inherit or to protest my father's instructions to stay in Yarrow. He said it was so I could find a suitable match, but everyone knew there was no one of my age and station in Yarrow. I should have questioned why he kept us there. I should have wondered why my father put us in that place at all. If he hadn't, if we'd been by his side in Falvar, maybe we would have been ready to help..."

"You didn't know. No one suspected your father..." said Anne. She looked as if she meant to say more, but she stopped herself, and glanced at Rew.

"What?" asked Raif, his eyes darting between the ranger and the empath. "Suspected our father of what?"

"Nothing," muttered Anne.

"What?" demanded Raif, turning to face Rew.

"Why do you think your father sent you to Yarrow? You're meant to rule Falvar one day, right? Wouldn't it have made sense for you to be raised there where you could learn the land, the government, and the people?" asked Rew. He turned to Cinda. "Why would Fedgley not keep you close and ensure you were getting proper training in high magic? As you say, there were no suitable matches for you in Yarrow, and no one with your father's skill in high magic. What good was fostering you there?"

The two nobles frowned at him.

"Well," said Cinda slowly, "at the time—"

"At the time, you were both children," said Rew. "You never had reason to question why, never had reason to suspect something was amiss, but now, you are no longer children."

Raif cracked his knuckles. "What, exactly, are you accusing our father of?"

"Nothing," said Rew, "I'm merely asking questions."

"It sounds like you believe he's guilty of something," growled Raif. "Out with it, Ranger."

Rew shook his head. "I'm just asking questions. It is up to you if you want to answer them. No opinion I have on the matter is any more valid than your own. All I suggest, do yourself the service and think it over."

Raif drummed his fingers on the gunwale of the ketch, looking as if he meant to offer a retort, but he couldn't think of one.

"Why do you believe we were fostered in Yarrow?" Cinda asked Rew, shushing her brother as he objected.

"I think your father meant to shield you from what is happening now," replied the ranger, propping a leg on the bench in front of him and leaning back against the rear of their boat. "I think he was misguided, but perhaps he thought by keeping you ignorant of your potential, he could free you from the pull of the Investiture."

"That's not all," said Raif. "Tell us what you suspect."

Rew's lips twisted. He waited a moment, but finally, he added,

"If you were fostered with Worgon, no one would suspect that Fedgley was plotting against him."

"Our father is a good man," retorted Raif.

"I'm not saying he's a bad man," responded Rew. "Tell me, based on your three years with him, is Worgon a good man?"

Raif frowned.

"He's as good as anyone," murmured Cinda.

"I don't like the way this conversation is going," warned Raif.

Rew held up his hands. "I am simply asking questions. If the questions are offensive, it's because you don't like the answers."

Raif snorted.

Cinda turned to her brother. "It's a valid question, why did Father foster us in Yarrow? We've much to think about, and much to talk about, but not here."

The nobleman eyed Rew, then Anne, and then Zaine. "Yes, not here, not now."

Rew reached back and trailed his fingers through the cold, black water. Overhead, the stars twinkled. The riverbank alongside them was a mass of shadow. "When we get to Yarrow, we all agree we should avoid Baron Worgon and his minions? We pass through the city and attract as little attention as possible?"

Raif nodded curtly. "Yes, we're agreed on that, at least."

"How long until we reach the city?" wondered Zaine.

Cinda shook her head. "Should we reach the city? I mean to say, would it not be better to disembark north of there and travel cross country to Spinesend?"

Rew grinned, thinking that finally, the girl was recalling the maps she'd seen. He told her, "The hills of the Spine encroach on Yarrow. If we were to abandon this skiff there, it might be commented upon, and moving cross country will be rough travel. Most importantly, though, we didn't get a chance to resupply in Umdrac. We've little food for a journey all of the way to Spinesend. I won't go as far to say docking in Yarrow will be safer than abandoning the vessel north of there, but I do think it will be a more comfortable journey."

Cinda pursed her lips.

Rew continued, "Besides, we want to move quickly, right? The roads will be twice as fast as traipsing through the mountains, and it's possible we may find our way into a carriage which will shave days off the trip."

"Worgon could have guards looking for us," warned Raif.

"You escaped the place over a month ago," reminded Rew. "I think it unlikely that any of the city guard will still be looking for you, and while those in the palace know your faces, we'll stay far away from there. Remember, Worgon has no reason to think you'd be passing back through his gates."

"Do you know of any secretive thieves' roads through the city?" Cinda asked Zaine.

The thief shook her head. "None that I suggest. Like the keep itself, I think it best we avoid the thieves."

Raif shrugged angrily. "If it's fastest, we dock in Yarrow. We've lost too much time as it is, and we can't afford more days climbing and hiking in the mountains. I've hunted there, and it's as the ranger claims—rough travel."

Rew eyed the boy, suddenly realizing that even after they had to rescue him, Raif considered this his party, and that he was the leader of it. Typical nobility.

Anne, evidently guessing Rew's thoughts, quickly declared, "It's settled, then. We dock in Yarrow and we take the road to Spinesend." She clapped her hands and added, "I suggest we rest while we're on the water. There's little danger to us here, and we may have slipped our pursuers back in Umdrac. With smooth water, we can—"

Rew coughed into his hand.

"What?" asked Anne and Cinda at the same time.

"You know this river goes through the Spine, right?" asked Rew, gesturing at the shadow-shrouded stone they were passing through. "The Spine is a mountain range. It's rocky, the river narrows, and we'll drop significantly in elevation in a very short time. I've never taken this way, but I know it's no easy passage.

That's why we don't see many other craft out on this water. If it was easy, the river would be the main route between the two cities. As it is, vessels only rarely travel south and never north. It's impossible to make your way upriver through the passage in the Spine."

"That sounds familiar," complained Cinda.

Rew shrugged. "You were the one who wanted to cross the Spine last time, and this certainly wasn't my plan when we first left Falvar. What would you have us do? Go back where Vyar Grund can find us? Mistress Clae? Duke Eeron's army? Taking the river was no one's first choice. It was the only way we had."

Cinda scowled at him.

"I hate to admit it, but the ranger is right," declared Raif. "Cinda, we have to reach Father. What other direction could we have gone? Once we saw Duke Eeron's army on the road, it was pretty obvious we weren't going that way."

"Not to mention," said Zaine, waving her hand around them, "we're on the river, and if you haven't noticed, the mountains are already rising around us. If there was a choice before, we don't have it now."

"Get some rest, everyone," suggested Rew. "By dawn, you're going to need it."

THE HULL OF THEIR KETCH THUMPED AGAINST A BARELY SUBMERGED rock, and the younglings' eyes blinked open. Deep between the chalk-white rock of the cleft in the Spine, it was still dim, though it was two hours past dawn. Rew had allowed the others to sleep because he was going to need them rested if their slender ketch was going to make it through the difficult rapids ahead of them.

For a brief moment, after the first rays of sunlight crept down the walls of the mountain around them, Rew had regretted the decision to find a watercraft. But, as they'd discussed the night before, there really hadn't been a choice. Dangerous or not, it was the path that they were on.

"What time is it?" mumbled Raif, looking around confused.

"Two hours past dawn," replied Rew. "Soon, I'm going to need one of you to grab an oar and stand at the prow. Be ready to push us off anything that looks bigger than a dog."

"What?" asked Zaine. Then, she jumped as the hull of the boat scraped against another rock.

"Sorry," said Rew, leaning hard on the tiller. "Not all of the rocks rise above the surface."

Cinda, wide-eyed, glanced over the edge of the boat into the clear water racing below them. "Should we be worried?"

Rew shrugged. "A little bit."

The noblewoman blinked at him.

Their craft picked up speed as the walls of the Spine narrowed around them and the water was forced through at a higher velocity. Cold, damp air gusted over Rew's scalp, and he could feel the spray misting against his skin when the water poured over rocks, tumbling and churning its way through the heart of the mountain.

Deciding it was best to assign tasks rather than waiting for the younglings to volunteer, Rew asked, "Zaine, can you grab one of those oars? Sit at the front of the boat and put out the handle. If we're headed for a hard collision, try to deflect us."

"I-I think I can," she stammered.

"Deflection is the key," advised Rew. "Don't slam the oar straight into the rock, or it's going to pop right out of your hands. Just push enough that the keel doesn't crash straight on. We're lucky this boat is well-built. It can survive a few scrapes, but we don't want to risk a direct collision at speed."

Swallowing nervously, Zaine freed the oar with Raif's help and then scampered to the front of the boat where she nestled the oar in the crook of her arm like one of the knights of old atop a charger facing down a jousting lane.

Rew grinned, shaking his head at the image of the slender thief ready to stand between their fast-moving boat and the immovable rocks. He'd seen a spare oar along the floor of the boat, which helped. If she lost that one or it shattered, they had a backup.

Anne began passing out breakfast to the younglings and asked Rew if he wanted to be relieved at the tiller. He smiled at her and shook his head. He was tired, having stayed up the entire night guiding them down the channel, but the chill air and the cool spray from the river was keeping him awake. It felt good to be facing the challenges of nature rather than those of men.

After the nobles ate, Raif took Zaine's place at the front so the thief could break her fast. Anne moved to the back and offered Rew a bite of green-veined, white cheese. He let her feed him, keeping his hands on the tiller, steering them clear of the rocks that he could see over the prow.

Raif, taking to his duties at the front with zest, banged his oar against submerged rocks they were in danger of striking, as well as ones Rew had already steered them clear of. The oar was going to be cracked and worthless once the boy was done with it, but it was a stolen boat, so Rew supposed it shouldn't concern him. Bouncing and jostling, they floated down the river, carried on the swift current as the walls of the Spine rose overhead.

"How many passes are there through this mountain range?" wondered Zaine, looking up at the sliver of sky above them.

"There's a reason it's called the Spine," responded Rew, leaning against the wooden tiller, steering them wide of a giant hunk of rock that stuck two paces above the water. "When you consider the entire expanse of the mountain range there are quite a few low points. If you could see the entire stretch at once, it would look like vertebra."

"Vertebra?"

"Have you ever felt the curve of a lover's back with your fingers?" asked Rew.

"No," muttered Zaine.

Rew blinked then said, "Ah… good. That's good. Well, you will one day, won't you? When you do, after you're old enough, you'll feel that their backbone is segmented. It's actually made up of about thirty individual bones, all stuck together with distinct ridges."

Zaine frowned at him.

"Feel your own back now," suggested Rew.

"I've felt my own back, Ranger," responded Zaine crisply. "I do bathe, you know."

He grinned. "Those bumps you feel look a bit like this mountain range. That's one of the reasons why they call it the Spine."

"And the other?"

"Because the stone has the look of old bone," said Rew. "It's as if some giant fell across the land, the flesh rotted away, and the mountain is what remains."

Turning to look at the wall of chalky rock they were passing, Zaine grunted.

"It's more of a finger, isn't it?" asked Anne. "The three major ranges in Vaeldon are like the fingers of a giant. That's the way I heard it, as if a creature of old slapped down a hand and died there, forming the bones of this kingdom."

"Slapped a hand down or clenched it, trying to gather up the soil of this continent," said Rew.

Anne looked at him curiously.

"I've never heard that," said Cinda. "It's funny, the stories people invent to explain the unknown."

Rew kept his eyes ahead and did not respond.

THE WALLS OF THE SPINE ROSE, AND THE SPEED OF THE RIVER'S current increased. They saw a few other vessels, mostly slow, narrow barges reinforced with heavy wooden spars and armored with thick rope bumpers. Rew eyed the bumpers, frowning. He'd forgotten that the ships that made the journey south did so with protection.

Uniformly, those other vessels were new wood, hastily assembled into something resembling a boat, and then shipped down-river where they would be disassembled in the south. That, or they were old crafts making their final journey. None of the boats would be returning north against the rapids after the trip through the Spine, and as they got farther, Rew saw that disconcertingly, there was plenty of evidence many didn't even make it to the south.

There were shattered beams sticking up from beside rocks, and the strewn wreckage of vessels washed up on the sides of the channel. Flotsam, most of it weathered and old, scattered in various points where the force of the current couldn't rip it free. The eyes of their fellow travelers on the river as they passed the slower barges and the concerned looks they got did little to salve Rew's nerves, but none of the people they saw spoke. On the river, it seemed it was every craft for itself.

"You're sure this is safe?" asked Cinda, her voice cracking as her brother thrust forward with his oar, leaning into the blow, jolting his shoulder and knocking their boat off course where it swept a hand's-span away from a massive, looming rock.

The water flowed over the white stone like a bubble bursting from beneath the river, a kraken raising its head. Pouring around the rock, the water shot them along a slide at terrific speed. Rew clung to the tiller, trying to steer them, but the water took their craft where it wanted.

"The rocks are smooth from the constant rush of water," he offered, a grin plastered on his face. "It could be worse."

"Are you enjoying this?" asked Anne, her face a little pale, her knuckles stark white where she clutched the gunwale of the skiff.

"No, of course not!" protested Rew, glancing ahead to where the water jetted between two towering boulders. "I suggest you hold on tight for this next bit."

Anne spun, looking ahead and cursing.

"You always told me not to say the Blessed Mother's name in vain," called Rew over the roar of the water.

"I'm offering her a prayer," snapped Anne.

"Didn't sound like a prayer," mumbled Rew.

Anne raised a hand and made a rather rude gesture at him without looking. If she added a comment, Rew couldn't hear over the growing roar of the river. She slapped her hand back down, holding on tight as they flew into the gap between the rocks. Suddenly, she and the younglings shrieked. They dropped several paces on the torrent of churning water and they flew ahead like they'd been launched from a crossbow.

When the roar of the river subsided, Rew laughed, thinking that none of the words still pouring from Anne's mouth sounded anything at all like a proper prayer.

❧ 8 ❧

Anne leaned against the tiller, hardly having to touch it as the craft wallowed downriver. The banks were wide and the current swirled in lazy eddies, sluggishly propelling them forward. Above, their sail flapped listlessly, the wind only slightly stronger than the drag of the river.

Sweat pouring down his brow and cheeks in the autumn air, Rew bent again and filled the cook pot. Water sloshed in the bottom of the boat halfway up to his calves, and for a brief moment, he tried to guess if it was rising or if he was keeping up with it. He grunted, lifted the cook pot, and poured the water over the gunwale.

"I think you're losing the battle, Rew," remarked Anne coolly.

Not responding, he bent again, filled the pot, and dumped another load out of their slowly sinking ketch.

"That trip through the rapids wasn't so fun now, was it?" asked Anne.

"We made it," replied Rew.

"We made it through the rapids," retorted Anne. "I'm not certain we'll make it to Yarrow at this rate."

"Another few hours," said Rew over the splash of another pot-load of water dumping into the river. "Maybe half a day. You think… the sails?"

"What do you expect me to do with the sails when there's no wind, Senior Ranger?" asked Anne. "If the wind blows, we'll catch it, but until then, we've only the current to carry us since we shattered all of our oars. We might be halfway to the river bottom by the time we see the walls of the city."

Rew kept bailing and did not respond.

Sitting on the sides of the vessel, Zaine and Cinda looked on grimly at the ranger's work. Raif crouched in the prow, his head in his hands, his back heaving with laborious breaths. Water was up to the boy's knees, but he looked as if he didn't notice. For hours, he'd been bailing as well, but the young fighter's spirit was fading beneath the relentless leak of water coming into their craft. It was a well-made boat, but they were not skilled sailors. The run down the rapids through the heart of the Spine had finally taken its toll, and they'd sprung several leaks in the bottom of the boat. Rew had tried stuffing the gaps with their clothing, but it'd been no use, so they had started to bail.

The girls had helped for a time, trying to relieve Rew and Raif, but constantly lifting the heavy pot-fulls of water had quickly worn them out. They'd discussed Anne's healing to sustain them, but while she could take the pain from sore muscles, she couldn't replace the energy they had expended, and it was dangerous to push too hard while her healing masked the damage being done to the body.

Rew felt like he was close to collapse as well, but their boat was leaking and someone had to dump the water out. He kept his back bent, lifting pot-fulls of water and pouring them over the side. For several more hours, he kept at it, struggling to keep up with the leak. When they could, Raif or the girls would get a spurt of motivation and assist, but quickly, they'd wear out again.

Finally, Rew felt the stir of a breeze, and the northern wind caught their sails, flapping the canvas above his head, and shoving their boat forward, the keel plowing stubbornly through the water like a pregnant sturgeon. With the wind, Rew felt his hopes rising, and it gave him the motivation to prevent the water from doing so. Splash after splash, he kept them afloat, and with the wind at their backs, it wasn't long before they cleared a final, ten-story tall outcropping of pale white rock to round a bend and see the sprawling mass of Yarrow.

The city was the size of Falvar, but where that place had been built for defense against the nomadic people in the north and the wraiths that followed after the great wars, Yarrow had been built for commerce. As the easternmost city of any size and with its position on the river south of the Spine, it traded enough to be a major force in the region, though it was no Spinesend.

The walls served more to hold the mass of the city together than to provide an adequate defense. They rose only a third the height of Falvar's, and behind those walls, they could see the wooden beam and mortar homes and shops of Yarrow. The roofs of the common places had cedar shingles, while the palaces and guildhalls were topped with slate. The clatter of people, animals, and a decent-sized port reached the party even from a league distant on the water. It seemed peaceful enough from afar. There were no legions of soldiers manning the walls, no smoke or other signs of warfare, and no patrol boats darting out from around the port to assess the new arrivals.

Rew paused his bailing and scratched his beard. Patrol boats. He should have thought of that. He held a hand above his brow and scanned the vessels around the dock, but saw no cause for alarm, so he bent back to bailing.

"Where are we going, Rew?" asked Anne, pushing hard on the tiller to try and aim the water-logged craft toward the city.

"Left side of the port," gasped Rew, hauling up another pot-full of water. "That's where the wealthy merchants and nobility dock."

"Baron Worgon's pleasure cruises always departed from there," confirmed Cinda.

"Should we, ah, avoid that area, then?" questioned Zaine. "Surely the rich folk will have their boats guarded."

"It's all guarded," grunted Rew. "If we hold our noses high enough in the air, the guards won't give us any bother. Over on the commercial side, the port master will be on us like a dog on a bone until we pay wharfage fees and explain who we are and why we're arriving in a sinking boat."

Zaine glanced at Cinda.

The young noblewoman shrugged. She told the thief, "I wouldn't have phrased it like that, but as long as we act—"

"Arrogant," interjected Rew.

Cinda sighed and continued, "As long as we act like we belong, the guards will probably give us no bother. They'll be more concerned that we actually are nobles and that they might offend us than whatever we're up to. No one else will be stupid enough to dock a sinking vessel at Worgon's private dock unless they have permission."

"That's right, no one but us," declared Rew.

All four of the others scowled at him. He winked back.

When they did arrive at the dock, right next to Baron Worgon's own pleasure barge, three soldiers appeared to question them.

"This is a private dock," called one of the men.

"We're here for Baron Worgon's fête!" exclaimed Cinda. "His seneschal Kaleb invited us to dock here."

"Kaleb..." muttered the soldier, looking at his companions. "I don't know of any fête..."

"Of course not," said Cinda, stumbling as the boat crashed into the side of the dock. She looked back at Anne. "Really?"

Anne shrugged. "It's been awhile since I've brought a boat to dock."

Snorting, Cinda hefted her pack and then stepped onto the dock, pushing the soldiers back with her presence. "Can you tell me, have the tents been set up on the south lawn yet? I was told by Kaleb the party will spill out there from the ballroom. I mean to sneak in through the conservatory to avoid Worgon. That's the quickest way from the docks, is it not? The way the baron himself comes and goes without causing a fuss amongst the commoners?"

The soldiers looked at each other, raising their eyebrows, evidently surprised this pugnacious girl knew the details of the keep so well.

"Ah... m'lady," said one of the soldiers. "Your craft appears to be in some amount of disrepair."

"Yes, yes," said Cinda, bowling over the man's words. "I've already had words with my captain about it, and rest assured, he'll be strapped at the earliest possible convenience. Now, as I'm certain you must have been told, the fête is meant to be a surprise for the baron, so I insist you keep our arrival secret. We've come all of the way from Carff, and it'd be a shame if the surprise was ruined."

"Well, actually..." began the third guard.

Cinda waved a hand in his face. "Ask your questions of Kaleb. It's that fool man's job to answer such queries, after all. I simply do not have the time today."

Clambering from the vessel behind her, the rest of the party stood on the dock.

"Boy," said Cinda, turning to her brother and giving him a wink, "attend to my luggage."

Smirking, Raif scooped up Cinda's canvas rucksack and bowed his head.

The girl strode toward the soldiers. They scrambled away to prevent her from running into them, and with three open-mouthed soldiers behind her, Cinda led the party down the dock and into the city of Yarrow.

YARROW WAS A CITY OF MUD AND TIMBER WHERE FALVAR WAS OF stone and iron. The streets were paved in an endless procession of bricks, the buildings constructed of massive, milled beams and clapboard siding or stucco. Rew thought stone would have been a more sensible material to build with. It didn't burn easily, for one, but it was heavier and more difficult to maneuver. It seemed to him that the people of Yarrow took the shortcut of easier construction, knowing it wouldn't last as long.

They passed busy workmen on nearly every block, putting up fresh sand and mud plaster on the walls, raising a new frame, or repairing the brick streets that had been cracked by heavy wagons or turned up by the passage of innumerable feet. The city rang with the sounds of the work, and Rew remembered how much he disliked the place because of it. The wood of the buildings was a constant reminder of the wood in the forest, and in Yarrow, he was always aware of how much he'd rather be somewhere else.

His companions must have felt the same. They cut nervous glances down every cross street and into each darkened shop. The people of Yarrow paid them no mind, though. They were passing through the poor quarters of the city, and after several days of hard travel and panicked flight, the companions looked as if they belonged.

All of them were eager to pass through as quickly as possible and find the open road beyond, but it was foolish to ignore the chance to resupply and to rest. A single good night in a bed could do wonders even for a ranger who had no qualms about sleeping beneath the stars. That, and Rew wouldn't mind an ale or two.

"What about this place?" asked Rew, nodding at a humble building they were passing. "I've taken a meal there, and while it was simple, I remember the food being hearty and fair priced."

Raif shrugged. "May as well. We can't go to any of the places I've been. They'll be filled with people from the keep."

"Have you ever stayed at this place?" asked Anne, eyeing the low-slung building skeptically. "It looks like it's no more than a tavern. Are there even rooms inside of there?"

"There could be," answered Rew.

"Rew…"

"If there are no rooms, we'll find somewhere else, but we have to start trying somewhere," said the ranger with a wink.

Around them, the current of foot traffic continued, and Rew gestured for the party to move to the side of the street. No sense in forcing people around them and drawing attention.

"Maybe we should sleep somewhere we know it will be clean," muttered Anne. "That's a better place to start from, don't you think?"

"The inns where the rangers stay will know me on sight," said Rew. "I don't think Worgon or his minions have any reason to be looking for me, but it's best if we move through Yarrow unnoticed, so Anne, unless you happen to know of a good inn in this city, we have to start somewhere, and it may as well be here."

Sighing, Anne looked up and down the street, as if somewhere in the poor quarter she would find a nicer place to stay.

"There's a grocer we passed just a block down and a general goods store across the street," mentioned Rew. "We can pick up all of the supplies we need without having to traipse all over Yarrow. I know it probably won't be to your standards, Anne, but we cannot hike for hours trying to find the cheapest, cleanest inn that none of us have been to before. If we want to be safe," he waved a hand around them, "we have to stay somewhere we wouldn't normally stay."

Reluctantly, Anne agreed, and Rew led them into the smoke-filled common room of the inn. He made arrangements for rooms, which fortunately, they did have. They settled in, and Anne and Zaine went out to collect additional provisions for the final leg of their journey to Spinesend. They'd all agreed, the empath and the thief were the two least likely to be recognized by someone in Yarrow.

While the women were out, Rew purchased parchment from the innkeeper and scrawled a note to Ranger Blythe. She would be expecting him back soon, and it was clear enough he wouldn't be going back. Not now, likely not ever. He grunted. If Vyar Grund really had been working for the king and not one of the princes, then Rew wasn't going to be welcome anywhere anytime soon.

Still, he owed it to Blythe to tell her what he could and to warn her. Grund knew that she was Rew's favorite, and that meant she would need to step carefully around the commandant. She'd also need to find her own recruits to replace Tate and Jon— and himself, Rew supposed. It was about time to begin requesting funds from the capital for the next year, and... He laid down the quill and scowled at the note. There was so much to tell her. Too much for the few sheets of parchment he'd gotten from the innkeeper, but Blythe was as good of a ranger as he could hope for, and Ang and Vurcell would support her in whatever ways she needed. He hoped it'd be enough, because it would have to be. The other rangers were on their own, and there wasn't a thing he could do about except scrawl down a few brief bits of advice.

Rew bent back, finished his letter, and left it with the innkeeper to post the next morning. He ordered an ale. He drank it down but stopped at one. The memory of how easily the scout Rodger had approached in Umdrac was still fresh in his mind, and if they'd found trouble in quaint Umdrac, Yarrow was only going to be worse.

Rew waited in the common room until the two women returned. Then, he took advantage of the inn's baths. His muscles screamed with protest from the bailing he'd been doing all day to keep their ketch afloat, and as he sank into the steaming hot water, his legs trembled like over-cooked noodles. He slumped down in the wooden tub until only his head and his knees poked above the surface of the water.

Steam enveloped him, and he blinked at the moisture, unable to see the rest of the room. He wasn't worried. There was no one but him in the chamber, and he trusted his senses to alert him if someone else entered. After a while, though, he caught himself falling asleep, so he pushed his body up and grabbed a bar of harsh soap sitting beside the tub. As he scrubbed, he tried to recall the details of the layout of Yarrow and the easiest route out of there in the morning. If they wanted to make good time, there was no way to avoid the western gate, but that was where the greatest risk was. If someone was indeed looking for them, they would be posted at that gate.

Rew finished his bath, toweled off, dressed, and went to meet the others in the common room. He found the four of them hunched over a table in the corner of the room, half-empty ciders and wines in front of them. An untouched plate of pickles and bread sat in the middle.

Taking a seat with his back to the door, Rew glanced at the others. It would be better if he were in position to watch the room, but he didn't want to deal with the fuss of arguing with them about it.

The party sat silently. The only topics they wanted to discuss were too sensitive for the crowded common room. To entertain himself while he waited for their food, Rew ordered a pitcher of ale, pretending it was for the table and forgetting he'd planned not to drink. Waiting for his ale, he crunched on the sour pickles.

Behind him, he could hear the din of steady conversation. It sounded like locals and a scattering of other travelers, all leaning in close over their drinks, discussing the weather, the abundant crops coming in from the south, and how it was forcing down the prices for local farmers to the point the dirt-tillers didn't have a spare copper to spend in the city. There were rumors of Dark Kind somewhere out in the countryside, though no one seemed to know anyone who'd actually seen them. Rew heard a vigorous debate about whether the favorite horse from last season would perform nearly as well at the races in the next weeks or whether it was time for the knackers. Then, he heard talk of Duke Eeron.

"Aye, I know Baron Worgon is his bannerman, but the baron won't stand for such treachery."

Rew tapped on the table quietly and tilted his head to the left, indicating the others should try and overhear the conversation happening at the adjacent table.

"What's Worgon going to do?" argued a second voice. "Eeron's got four times the men, ten times the spellcasters, and he's the duke, for King's Sake!"

There was a sharp snort, and a woman's voice silenced the two men. "Worgon has the support of Prince Valchon. Eeron is nothing more than a roach beneath the boot of the prince. When it comes to it, the soldiers Eeron can put in the field, his pathetic spellcasters, they'll be swept away like summer wheat. The prince'll back Worgon's play. I know it."

"You know it," cackled the first man. "You don't know nothin'."

"I know the prince has personally requested Worgon's assistance locating the children," snapped the woman. "I overheard it yesterday when I was escorting Seneschal Kaleb. Worgon was like a father to those two. Remember, they fostered here in Yarrow the last three years."

Rew's gaze turned to Raif and Cinda. The two nobles shuffled back into the corner, Raif raising his hood over his head, Cinda picking up her mug and shifting behind Rew's pitcher of ale as if to hide.

"Aye, they fostered in Yarrow," admitted the first man. "Everyone knows that. It doesn't mean Worgon's got any more chance to find them than anyone else. King's Sake, woman, if they wanted anything to do with Worgon, they wouldn't have fled!"

"I know what I know," declared the woman.

The second man spoke, his voice quieter than the other two. "You don't know any more than anyone knows in any tavern on any street in this city. It's true, Fedgley's children fostered with Worgon. It's true, more like than not, blood will be spilled between Worgon and Eeron. Whether Prince Valchon truly supports Worgon and would take action against Eeron, no one knows 'cept the prince himself. Not even Worgon knows that. It's why he hasn't marched yet. And whether those children will shelter here in Yarrow after what Eeron did to their family... It all depends on what they believe. I mean, it's no more than rumor that the duke was behind the attack on Baron Fedgley, right? I've heard every wagging jaw in this city talking about it the last two days, but I ain't heard Duke Eeron confessing to it. The children fostered with Baron Worgon, but the duke is their liege. Don't be so sure they'll listen to the tavern gossip."

The first man chuckled. "Aye, fair enough. There's no telling what the children know or the mind of the prince."

"Prince Valchon wants those two," insisted the woman. "He wants them, and the safest place they can find right now is inside of Baron Worgon's keep. Maybe they know that, maybe they don't, but I'd bet gold if they do know, they'll come here and they'll seek shelter. If they do, I'd bet the rest of my gold that Prince Valchon comes and supports the baron."

"You don't have any gold," retorted the second man.

Ignoring him, the woman continued, "It'd be something, wouldn't it, to see one of the princes in battle? If he comes, I mean to march with the rest of 'em. I've heard stories of what high magic is like, and I'd be pleased to see a bit of it before I'm buried."

"If you see the prince's high magic, chances are you'll be buried then and there," cried the first man. "Pfah. If the baron decides to march against the duke, I don't plan to be around for it."

"You'll desert?"

"I'll retire," responded the man. "I've put in my years. War ain't worth the trifle pay they give an old-timer like me."

Rew heard the clunk of an empty mug on the table, and the woman said, "You're a coward, you know? If the baron marches, I aim to be on the first rank, and I'll be telling my children and their children about what I see."

"You ain't got any more children than you do gold," cackled the second man.

A chair scooted, and someone stood. The woman declared, "I'm tipsy enough. Let's get on with it and finish our patrol. Another hour and we're off duty, and I don't mean to earn any extra time tonight, lads."

"Going to see Johan again, eh?" asked the first man, standing as well.

"Only way I know of getting children," said the woman, bursting into a drunken chortle.

They moved away from the table, and Rew risked a glance to see the backs of three soldiers wearing the ochre livery of Baron Worgon. He turned to the others, picked up his ale mug, downed half of it, and asked, "Well, what do you think of that?"

9

Rew waited while the two nobles sat in confused shock. Finally, well after the soldiers had left the inn, Cinda stammered, "But... But Worgon was plotting against Father? We heard it. We know he was!"

"Those soldiers thought you might come running to Yarrow," said Rew. "They don't believe the baron was plotting against your family. It didn't sound like they'd ever been tasked with trying to hunt you down, either."

"Father was working with Prince Valchon, too, wasn't he?" questioned Raif, scratching his head in confusion. "How can the prince be allied with Worgon as well? They must be mistaken."

"The Investiture," murmured Anne. "It makes for strange bedfellows."

"If Worgon is opposed to Duke Eeron, but we know it's the duke who took Father..." murmured Cinda, her face scrunched up as she worked through the problem. "We overheard Worgon plotting against—"

"Did you overhear Worgon himself?" questioned Rew.

"Well, not the baron himself, but his close confidants," responded Cinda.

"How close?" pressed Rew. "Seneschal Kaleb?"

"Kaleb's too careful for that," interjected Raif. "He…" The young noble was staring at Rew and Anne, who were sharing an uncomfortable look. "What?"

Neither the ranger nor the empath spoke.

Cinda leaned forward on the table. "What are you hiding from us?"

Rew looked down into his ale mug, hoping Anne would speak, but she gestured for him to explain.

"Ah," started the ranger, "from what we understand, it wasn't Worgon plotting against your father, but instead it was your father plotting against Worgon. Baron Fedgley himself planted those rumors and arranged for you to see what you saw. He meant to pit Duke Eeron and Baron Worgon against each other, which seems to be working, except Duke Eeron moved against your father before he did Worgon."

"What!" cried Raif, half-standing.

Zaine caught his arm and tried to pull the big lad back down into his chair.

Cinda stared at Rew and Anne, her eyes narrowing.

"I don't believe it!" exclaimed Raif, his voice harsh with the strain of keeping it from a shout.

Rew shrugged in response.

"Where did you hear this?" asked Cinda.

Rew turned to Anne again, but she shook her head. She told him, "You heard it, not I."

Grimacing, Rew admitted, "Your father told both Alsayer and I when we first arrived in Falvar that he was behind the plot. He said he'd planted the rumors, he'd arranged it all. He wanted it to appear that Worgon was betraying him. Raif, Cinda, it was your father who was planning to turn on both Duke Eeron and Baron Worgon. His downfall was that he didn't think the Investiture would start so soon, and he didn't foresee Duke Eeron striking first."

Cinda sat back, crossing her arms over her chest.

Raif clenched his fist on the table and hissed, "Ranger, if we weren't in hiding, I'd jump across this table and smash your face."

Rew stared back at the youth, unsure of what to say to that.

"Now, now," said Anne, attempting to play the peacemaker. "Rew is just relaying what—"

"You knew?" asked Cinda. "You knew and said nothing?"

Wincing, Anne replied, "I knew, but there wasn't a time when—"

"Is this why you tricked us into coming to Yarrow?" demanded Raif, glaring at Rew. "You hoped if you could get us here, you'd drive us into Worgon's arms? Are you working for him?"

"No!" hissed Rew. "Of course I'm not working for Worgon. I didn't want to come to Yarrow any more than you did. We were forced here by Duke Eeron's soldiers and the assassins in the forest, remember?"

Raif snorted, shaking his head in disbelief, his body trembling.

"I'm not trying to direct you toward Baron Worgon," added Rew. "Think about it, Raif. Haven't I been saying we should leave immediately, that we should avoid the keep? Worgon wasn't behind the plot against your family, but that doesn't mean he's your friend. Prince Valchon is not your friend, either. You're best off running away from all of this, but if you insist on going to Spinesend and trying to rescue your father, then our plan should remain the same. Ignore Worgon, let's slip from Yarrow unnoticed tomorrow morning, and we'll do what we can in Spinesend. You shouldn't trust any of these nobles."

"Don't trust the nobles!" snapped Raif. "I'm a noble, or have you forgotten?"

"That's not what I meant," muttered Rew, wincing.

"And what do you mean, our plan to go to Spinesend?" barked Raif. "At every turn, you've tried to talk us out of it!"

Rew threw up his hands. "I'm trying to help you, lad."

"Yes, help us," snarled Raif. "Help us do what? Turn from our mission, move farther and farther from where we're supposed to be? We shouldn't trust any nobles, should we? Pfah. I see where you stand, Ranger."

"You've moved farther from where you should be well enough on your own," growled Rew. "Unless you've forgotten how we met in the first place, or how I rescued you from Vyar Grund?"

"Ah, yes, the ranger commandant," scoffed Raif. "Your boss, you mean? As far as we know, you're in league with the man."

"King's Sake, lad," growled Rew. "You watched me fight him. You saw the cuts he left on my body."

Smacking a fist down on the table, Raif declared, "I'm seeing things for what they are, now. Eeron, Worgon, and even the rangers. You're all working together, trying to drive us where you want us to go."

"What possible reason would I have for any of that?" asked Rew, gritting his teeth in frustration. "I had you locked in a jail cell. Grund had you bound on the floor of that cave. If either of us had wanted to take you somewhere, we would have!"

"Locked in a cell," said Raif, his jaw bunching. "Thank you for reminding me of that. I've been stupid, haven't I? It's been apparent since we first met you."

"You were locked in the cell because you attempted to steal from Anne!" snapped Rew. "What, are you also accusing me of forcing you from Yarrow and taking up a life of crime? That was your choice, lad, and I had nothing to do with it. I didn't even know you existed until I found you in that cell, and I'm the one who rescued you after you were taken from there—by Worgon's thugs, lest we forget. Over and over, I'm the one pulling you from the burning buildings you keep walking into."

"Aye, you didn't put us in the cell, and you rescued us when we were taken from there, but you didn't let us out of the cell, did you?" argued Raif. "Maybe those thugs didn't work for Baron Worgon at all. Even you said that a few days back, didn't you? Maybe they—Cinda told me they never said who they were working for. Could have been you, for all I know!"

Rew snorted. "Maybe they didn't work for Worgon. You're

right, we all just assumed that, and I know you were unconscious lad, but think about it. Why in the Blessed Mother's kind earth would I hire a gang of thugs to kidnap you from my own jail?"

"To gain our trust," declared Raif, glancing away, as if even in the midst of his outrage, he knew that sounded ridiculous.

Cinda put a hand on his shoulder, but he refused to look at his sister.

"Raif, you're letting your anger cloud your thoughts," warned Anne.

"None of what has happened has been my choice," said Rew, forcing himself to be calm. "I only want the best for you, lad. What reason would I have for any sort of conspiracy?"

"You tell me what reason, Ranger," snarled Raif, brushing Cinda's hand away and glaring at Rew. "You're the one who keeps speaking about how the princes are interested in us, how everyone will come for us. Why is that? What value do we hold for—Ah. Ah yes. It's obvious, isn't it? You want us for yourself. What, Ranger, will you sell us to the highest bidder? Use us for… for the same thing they would?"

Rew could only shake his head. "I don't have any agenda except for helping you and your sister. I've risked my life for you, which you'd see plainly if you thought about it. Surely, with all we've been through, you know I'm here to help—so let me do it!"

Raif shook his head. "I think I'm just about done with your help, Ranger."

"You're being foolish," said Anne, "and you're going to get yourself and your sister killed."

"Am I?" said Raif, his nostrils flaring, his face flushed. "Am I being foolish? What good has following any of your advice done me? If we did everything you said, we'd be leaving Father to die. Wasn't that your advice?"

"Raif," said Cinda, putting her hand back on her brother's shoulder, "they're not our enemy."

"I'm not so sure," stated the boy, picking up his cider and quaffing it in three large gulps.

"They are right, Raif. If it wasn't for their help, you'd be in the hands of our true enemies," reminded Cinda. "I watched the ranger carry you three leagues down that road to Eastwatch, and I watched the empath heal you. I watched it more than once, Raif! If it wasn't for them, we could have died from that attack the spellcaster launched in father's throne room. We witnessed Rew fight the man who killed Mother, remember? And if it wasn't for them, the Dark Kind might have overrun Falvar. I spoke to the soldiers after you left. Rew is the one who led the defense of our city. He fought for us and our people. He killed... You saw the imps in the throne room. You felt the spell Alsayer unleashed against us and saw what he did to Mother and Father. Rew didn't plan this, Raif. He didn't want us to leave Falvar. It was you who left in the middle of the night, alone. Rew followed because I asked him to. He fought his own superior, and he's still healing from the wounds he took! Rew is not plotting against us, Raif. If he meant us harm, he could accomplish it by simply letting us go our own way."

"Thank you," murmured Rew, nodding appreciatively to the girl.

"You may mean well for us, Ranger, but you are keeping secrets," said Cinda, turning back to glare at the ranger and stabbing a finger toward him. "You haven't told us the whole truth, have you?"

Rew winced. She was right, and there wasn't much he could say to argue against it.

"Are you both committed to helping us still?" asked Cinda, looking between Rew and Anne.

"Of course," said Anne. She leaned over and elbowed Rew in the ribs.

"Yes," said Rew, studiously ignoring Anne.

"Then let us discuss this matter between ourselves, and we'll tell you what we decide to do," said Cinda.

"What you decide?" questioned Rew.

Cinda nodded.

"Well, that doesn't make any sense," argued Rew. "We'll help you rescue your father, but not—"

"Come on, Rew," said Anne. "Let's give them time to think this over."

Grunting, Rew picked up his ale mug and the pitcher. The pitcher was empty, so scowling at the table, he sat it down and left with Anne. Behind them, he heard Cinda telling Zaine to stay. Muttering under his breath, Rew followed the empath to the bar and settled his back against it with both elbows on the counter.

"Another pitcher," he said to the barman. He glanced at Anne. "And a wine for the lady."

The barman walked off to fill their orders.

Rew leaned toward Anne. "They're being foolish."

"Are they?" asked Anne.

"What do you mean?"

"We hadn't told them about their father and about Worgon," reminded the empath. "That's important information, Rew, and we'd been keeping it from them. I see now we should have told them what we know. If we want them to trust us, we have to show we're trustworthy."

Rew shook his head. "They know now, and see where that is getting everyone? It's just confusing them. This entire exercise is foolish, dangerous. It will only be worse if we let the children decide what the next steps are."

Anne snorted. "It's their lives. It's their father we're trying to rescue. We have to let them decide what to do. That's for the best, Rew."

"Best for who? They've abandoned their barony, their people. What about those folk!"

"And if they'd stayed in Falvar as you wanted, then what? When Duke Eeron's soldiers arrived there, do you think it would go better or worse for the people if the Fedgley children were behind the walls? Would Raif and Cinda have turned themselves over to a man they suspected of kidnapping their father, or would they have fought? Fleeing Falvar might have been the smartest decision any of us has made since this started. By leaving the city, they gave themselves a chance, and they likely prevented open warfare and saved hundreds of lives."

Rew frowned at her. The barman returned with their drinks, and Rew refilled his ale mug. He drank, and Anne let him think. After half of his mug, he conceded, "We had no way of knowing that Duke Eeron was on the march. Of course, if we'd known he was coming, my advice would have been to flee. The duke has no ill will toward the people of Falvar, just its leaders. As long as they aren't there, there is no conflict. You're right about that, at least, but—"

"So the children made the right decision, did they?" interrupted Anne.

"That's unfair!" claimed Rew. "We didn't know what was coming."

She poked him in the ribs again with a finger. "Aye, and they didn't know about their father's plotting and how Worgon may not be their enemy. If more information would have helped you to make the right decision, then why wouldn't it help them do the same?"

Rew tilted up his ale mug, hiding his face with it.

Anne lifted her wine and turned to study the room.

Flummoxed, the ranger set down his mug and said nothing.

"It looks like they're arguing," said Anne, looking toward the youths in the corner.

"What if they decide to go to Worgon?"

"Then we'll accompany them."

"I have responsibilities in the territory," muttered the ranger.

"And responsibilities here," said Anne. "We've committed to helping the children, Rew. Besides, I know you already wrote to Blythe. What'd you tell her, that Vyar Grund tried to kill you and you'll be resuming your duties just as soon as you can get rid of the nobles? Come on, Rew. You made your choice, and it's sealed in blood now."

He didn't reply.

"You told me, they're at the heart of it," continued Anne. "It's not just about them. If Prince Valchon or one of the others gets their hands on Cinda, what will they do with her? I know you have your suspicions."

He didn't respond.

"Wraiths let loose in a major city, or is it worse than that, Rew?" wondered Anne. "A necromancer is a powerful pawn in the game of the Investiture, but I worry... What do you know? What are you not telling even me?"

Rew looked away.

"Didn't we just talk about keeping secrets?" demanded Anne.

"I can't," he said. "I can't tell you."

"There is more, isn't there? You know why the princes want Baron Fedgley and Cinda, don't you?"

"I have a suspicion," whispered Rew.

"Then tell me," insisted Anne.

"I can't."

Anne snatched up her wine mug and turned to go back to the younglings. "You frustrate me, Senior Ranger."

"I know."

"Whatever they decide to do, you will help. Whether it's leaving here at dawn or going to see Worgon in his keep, you will help," declared Anne. Then, she left him alone at the bar.

Rew didn't reply as she walked away. Whatever the children decided, he was certain that it would be foolish, just as the entire enterprise was foolish. But she was right; he would help. He had to, now. He could feel the pull of the Investiture on his soul, dragging him down, deeper into the whirlpool. There, at the bottom of that swirling maelstrom, was the reason that the princes wanted Cinda and her father.

He'd help, but he worried about how many might die because of it.

Leaning on the bar, Rew drank his ale in silence.

THE MUD AND TIMBER STRUCTURES OF YARROW ROSE AROUND THEM as they marched down the wide boulevard, keeping as close to the center as they could. The streets were bricked, but it had poured rain the night before, so the gutters beside the paving were filled with refuse washed from the alleyways and behind the homes and the shops. It smelled dank, the stench lying over the city like a blanket.

Rubbing her delicate nose, Cinda murmured, "Up in the keep, the air felt fresher."

Rew nodded. "That's the way it is with nobility. Sit up in your towers, divorced from the filth and the stench that washes below you."

"You've made your point, Ranger," responded the young noblewoman crisply.

"Not well enough, it seems," groused Rew.

"Baron Worgon is allied with Prince Valchon," said Cinda. Without waiting for a response, she continued, "And our father was also allied with Prince Valchon. That's what you told me. I understand your concern about the princes and the risk involved with becoming known to them, but the choices have already been made! Our family—and Baron Worgon who you think we can trust—are supporters of Valchon. Whether the prince will ignore us or use us, we can at least be certain he wants us alive! Can we say the same for whoever stands behind Duke Eeron? You were right all along, Ranger. We cannot face Duke Eeron alone, so what better ally than a prince?"

"It's not so simple," complained Rew. "I did not say you can trust Baron Worgon and you certainly cannot trust Prince Valchon. Bah, it's the Investiture, lass. Allies, enemies, they're not all that different! You shouldn't trust any of them."

"Maybe not," allowed Cinda, "but if we can tell Prince Valchon where our father is, then perhaps the prince will rescue him. We're not trusting the prince to do the right thing because it's the right thing, but because his interest aligns with ours. Is that a worse plan than going to Spinesend and trying to rescue Father ourselves? Don't you see what I mean?"

Rew grunted and did not respond. He saw what she meant, and he understood why the nobles had decided as they had, but he didn't agree with their decision. Just because they hadn't actually heard Baron Worgon plotting against their family didn't mean he never had, and freeing Baron Fedgley would not be the end of their problems; it would only create more of them. Whichever prince was behind Duke Eeron wasn't going to simply forget about the baron once he'd been sprung free. But Rew couldn't find the words to explain himself to the nobles. In their view, family meant supporting each other no matter what, and he wasn't going to be able to talk them out of it. It didn't matter that the world simply did not work the way they wanted it to.

"I'm glad you're with us," said Cinda, "even if we're not taking your advice."

Rew offered a bitter smile and rolled his shoulders. Several blocks ahead of them rose Yarrow's keep, the seat of Baron Worgon. Right or wrong, that was where they were going, and, terrible idea or not, he'd agreed to help.

"You don't talk much, do you?" pestered Cinda.

"Not when I can help it."

"Then let us do the talking when we get inside," instructed the noblewoman.

She strode to the front of their party, and she and Raif led the way to the gates of Baron Worgon's keep. Half a dozen guards stood there, and through the open doors, Rew could see dozens more moving about, ferrying supplies, training, and preparing for battle.

Now that they were next to the keep and past the clangor of the rest of Yarrow, they could hear the constant ring of hammers on steel as blacksmiths rushed to fashion more weapons or repair old ones. A group of boys ran by the open gates, bundles of recently fletched arrows on their backs. The battlements above were well-patrolled by armored soldiers, and Rew judged by Raif's low whistle that none of this was normal for Yarrow.

On the river side of the city, they'd noticed nothing out of place, but now Rew wondered what they would see on the western side. That side faced Spinesend. Were soldiers staging there, preparing to march, or did Worgon have them working to shore up the city's defenses? It was clear from the little activity they could see through the open gate that Worgon was aware of what was happening elsewhere in the duchy and he was doing his best to prepare.

"No one inside unless you have official business," called one of the guards in front of the gate.

"I am Raif Fedgley," declared the boy. "I am here to see Baron Worgon."

The guard looked him up and down. His voice—his entire demeanor—dripping with doubt, the guard asked, "You're the son of Baron Fedgley?"

"I am," confirmed Raif, puffing his chest out and nearly standing on his tiptoes trying to draw himself up.

Rew glanced at Anne and rolled his eyes. Nobles, without their velvets and silks, without their embroidery and sparkling jewelry, looked much the same as everyone else.

"I'm his sister, Cinda Fedgley," declared Cinda. "We fostered here not long ago. Surely one of you recognizes us?"

The guards shifted, the men looking at each other as if they wondered whether it was possible the two, travel-stained youths in front of them could possibly be nobility. They must have been weighing that chance against the trouble they would find if they brought the worn-looking pair in front of a senior officer.

Finally, one of them took the initiative and spoke. "I'm sorry, but if you're Baron Fedgley's children, why are you dressed like that? I've seen Baron Fedgley's brood, and they dress just as fine as any other noble. Pardon the thought, but you two look like you've been swimming in pig mud."

Cinda coughed, and Rew grinned, imagining how bright red her face must be.

Raif reached over his shoulder and wrapped his hand around the hilt of his family's enchanted greatsword. "We are who we say we are, and if I hear you insult us again—"

"Boy," warned one of the guards, his hand moving to his own sword hilt, "don't think to draw steel on us."

Raif did not draw his blade, but he didn't let go of it, either.

Anne leaned toward Rew and shoved him on the back. Sighing, he stepped beside the two nobles.

"I am Rew, the King's Ranger," he said. "I request an immediate conference with Baron Worgon."

The soldiers eyed him up and down. Their leader asked, "Are these two who they say they are?"

"They are," confirmed Rew.

"Very well, then," responded the soldier. "Fall in. I'll take you to Seneschal Kaleb, and he'll either grant you an audience or not."

Rew nodded and followed the soldier as he took them through the gates, across the busy courtyard, and into the keep.

"King's Sake," muttered Raif. "Why'd he let you right in when he was ready to throw us down the street like a pair of snot-nosed pig farmers?"

"Men see what's in front of them and rarely any deeper," Rew replied back in a whisper. "I'm dressed like the King's Ranger, and I carry myself as such. You've the attitude of a noble, but right now, you're wearing the uniform of a snot-nosed pig farmer."

Behind them, Anne laughed, and Raif offered a sheepish grin. The big youth brushed his clothing, little more than tattered rags after their time on the road, and then he reached up to pull his hair back behind his head. He claimed, "Perhaps my attire is that of a pig farmer, but this is the face of nobility."

Despite himself and the seriousness of their situation, Rew chortled and shook his head. "A visage all snot-nosed farmers would be jealous of, m'lord. Never again shall I imagine you in the muck, tending to pigs."

His grin faltering along with his bluster from earlier, Raif looked ahead to the massive doors of Baron Worgon's throne room. "No, but maybe being a farmer wouldn't be so bad, would it?"

"Not bad at all," agreed Rew. He reached out and squeezed the young noble's shoulder before letting go and looking ahead as they walked into the keep.

At a delicate desk perched right outside of the throne room sat Seneschal Kaleb. The slender man looked up, saw the party crossing the expansive foyer, and leapt to his feet, accidentally spilling a jar of ink across the documents he'd been working on and tipping his chair over backward. He didn't give the mess a second glance.

"M'lord, m'lady, Senior Ranger," he babbled. "What are you— ah, come with me. The baron will want to see you."

10

"You're back," murmured Baron Worgon, peering at Raif and Cinda over steepled fingers. He wore a doublet covered with thick embroidery and topped with a waterfall of lace that spilled from beneath his jowls. The garish ensemble did little to hide his protruding belly and the white of the lace only served to contrast how red the man's cheeks were. Purpled veins swarmed around his nose, like a map to the ravages of too much drink and not enough exercise.

You can have one, but not both, Rew had always believed.

"We are back," acknowledged Raif, his voice tight.

The big youth shifted his feet, and Rew wondered if the young noble was reconsidering the decision to announce themselves to Baron Worgon. It was too late now.

"Why did you leave so quietly in the night?" wondered the baron. "My men spent days looking for you. I sent my best scouts and trackers, but they found nothing. It was as if you vanished into the air."

"W-We…" stammered Raif. "Ah, we heard of a plot against our father, so we rushed to Falvar to warn him. We got there in time to see him but not in time to foil the attack upon our city and our family. Have you heard what happened?"

AC COBBLE

"Rumors and outlandish tales," said Baron Worgon, nodding slowly. "I've pieced together what I could. I knew Duke Eeron was plotting against your father. I sent messengers to warn Fedgley, but I don't know if they got through or if when they did, it was already too late. You mentioned you were present and could not stop the attack, yet it seems you're in good enough condition now. Tell me, what did you see?"

Raif worked his jaw, chewing over what they could tell the baron.

Cinda spoke up before her brother had the chance. "M'lord, our father was taken by a man we believe to be a minion of Duke Eeron. We have intelligence that our father is being held in Spinesend by one of Duke Eeron's arcanists."

"Intelligence?" asked the baron.

Cinda nodded at Zaine, who was standing near the back of the party as if she hoped not to be noticed.

"The girl is trustworthy?" asked Worgon, leaning over to peer at Zaine.

"Ah, yes," mumbled Cinda. "Yes, of course she is."

Rew forced himself to keep his face blank and not roll his eyes at that.

"And you, Senior Ranger, what is your role in all of this?" asked Worgon.

"I'm here to see to the safety of the young nobles," stated Rew. "They appeared in Eastwatch after leaving Yarrow, and I took responsibility for them. Their well-being is the only reason for my presence in Yarrow."

"They speak the truth of what occurred and that their father is being held in Spinesend?"

Rew nodded. "I was in Falvar when the attack happened, and we're confident the baron was moved to Spinesend. I think it likely he's still there, being held for when he's needed."

Worgon studied him, bobbing his head slowly, his loose jowls shaking with the motion. He opened his mouth and sucked on his white mustaches, a disgusting habit thought Rew, but he remained quiet, letting the baron assess him.

After a moment of watching the old toad gnaw on his hairs and ponder, Rew added, "I have no interest in the Investiture, Baron, except for seeing Raif and Cinda through it."

"I see," rumbled the baron. He stood, putting a hand on his bulbous paunch, and asked, "Care for a pipe?"

Rew shook his head. "Too early for me."

The baron did not make the offer to the children or to Anne, which was just as well since they would have said no, but the baron didn't let his guests' declination stop him from enjoying his own pipe. Worgon waddled in front of a small, crackling fire in his study and retrieved his leaf box from the mantle. They waited while he thumbed a long pipe full of leaf and then lit it. He turned, puffing thick, white smoke.

"You've broached the subject, so I think there's no harm in speaking openly," said the baron. "The Investiture has begun, and risks are all around us. I am sorry to hear about the attack on Fedgley. I truly thought he meant to do as I and hide behind his walls, but it seems he had more ambitious plans. Hiding and staying uninvolved is how both of our baronies made it through the last cycle undisturbed. Of course, we didn't increase our holdings during that period, either. Some men cannot be content with what they already have."

"Duke Eeron means to take the entire duchy," growled Raif. "He's not content with Spinesend. He wants Falvar and Yarrow as well!"

The baron gestured at Raif with his pipe. "Lad, he already has Falvar and Yarrow. Both your father and I are his bannermen. Duke Eeron is not acting because he wants the lands we control or even our people or our gold. If that's all he wanted, he could raise our taxes, and we'd have no recourse. The duke could maneuver us into a corner and force us to grant him whatever he desired, if his wants were so simple. He's our liege, and we owe fealty to him. You think the king would have an open ear for us protesting against the man he appointed to rule the Eastern Territory? Vaisius Morden is no fool, and the last thing he wants at any level in this kingdom is a vassal complaining about his liege."

"Why is Duke Eeron attacking, then?" asked Cinda. "He abducted our father!"

"Aye, so he did," murmured Worgon, taking another draw on the pipe and then slowly releasing the smoke. It drifted up, wreathing his head, blending with the wild fringe of white hair that stuck out above the man's ear and looped around his head. "I can only surmise Duke Eeron wants something from your father that no man owes his liege, so it must be taken by force."

"Are we speaking openly, Baron?" asked Rew.

"Of course," responded Worgon.

"Then you know very well why Duke Eeron took Baron Fedgley," stated Rew, thinking to test the man, to see how he reacted. "It's the same reason your patron allied with Fedgley. It's the same reason your patron is after Cinda."

Worgon stuck his pipe in his mouth, his jowls flushing, the smoke puffing quickly from the lit bowl in his fingers.

"Let us lay our cards on the table," continued Rew. "I have little patience for the games of nobility. Raif and Cinda want to rescue their father. I aim to protect them, no matter who attempts to harm them. What is it you and your patron want, Worgon? Do you mean for the Fedgleys to trade one captor for another?"

"Ranger, all I want is to survive the next months with my head on my shoulders and my barony intact," claimed Worgon.

"Why did you ally with Valchon?"

"I didn't," grumbled Worgon, shrugging uncomfortably, hot ash spilling from his pipe as he did. "I told you the truth. My plans were to lie low and solicit no notice from the players in this grand game. The prince came to me just a week past. He portaled right into my throne room. I'd never met the man, but I suppose you have. He demanded my assistance and instructed me to use my relationship with the young Fedgleys to earn their trust. If I was unwilling to perform this task, he strongly implied that my son Fredrick would be more than capable of doing so when he took my place on the throne. It was left unsaid that Prince Valchon could snap his fingers and make that happen. He was here only a few minutes, and that was it."

Rew grunted in response. If he took the man's word for it, then Worgon truly did know nothing of what was occurring. That was all they could hope for.

"Exactly," continued Worgon, acknowledging Rew's grunt. "It wasn't my choice, but it seems I've been pulled into the whirlpool, and there is nothing to do but try and swim the current. I don't know what Duke Eeron's plans are for Baron Fedgley, and I don't know why Prince Valchon wants the children." The baron turned to Raif and Cinda. "He demanded my assistance earning your trust. That is all he told me. I will say, he is an ally of your father, and has always been a friend of the Fedgleys. In times like these, you cannot do better than to join with him."

"Your assistance earning our trust?" asked Cinda, her jaw tight, her eyes flicking between Worgon and the rest of the room. "How do you plan to do that?"

"By telling you the truth," replied Worgon. Raif and Cinda looked nervous, but Worgon waved his pipe to calm them. "Don't be afraid, lass. The Investiture is a scary time, there's no doubt, but victory is secured through loyalty, not betrayal. I know that. Prince Valchon knows that. The prince with the most loyal followers will gain the crown, as they always have. Loyalty is what this kingdom is built upon, and there's no reason we should not follow the same path. You fostered with me. You know me. I've come to know you as well. What say we trust each other?"

"Trust each other with what?" growled Cinda.

"Your father and I both pledged our support to Prince Valchon," continued Worgon, gesticulating with his pipe but not meeting the young noblewoman's stare. "He swore before I did, but lass, we're on the same side. Your ranger friend here says you plan to rescue your father, and I can help with that. Once Fedgley is free, we can all give Prince Valchon what he wants. We have a history together, and we share the same goals. It's as good a foundation for trust as any."

Nodding, Raif remarked, "I can see it the same way."

"That's only if what Prince Valchon desires is also what we desire," retorted Cinda, shooting her brother a warning look.

"The first thing we must do is rescue your father," said Worgon to Raif, ignoring Cinda's comment. "I won't lie to you, lad. That will not be easy. Duke Eeron has more spellcasters than I and far more men. Unless he does something foolish, I'm afraid—"

"His men are marching to Falvar," said Raif. "We saw them on the road. They'll be over a week before they return to Spinesend."

Worgon's hand dropped, threatening to spill the embers of his pipe across his carpet. "What?"

Raif turned to Rew. "How many of them were there, Ranger? Two thousand, I think you said?"

Sighing, Rew agreed. "Could be. Those men were marching to Falvar, but we're not certain—"

"King's Sake, that's our opportunity!" declared Worgon. "How long ago was this?"

"Two days," muttered Rew. "We saw them in Umdrac two days ago."

Baron Worgon's eyes burned with excitement.

Rew held up a hand. "They were marching to Falvar, Baron, but we don't know if they kept on or turned around. They were searching for the young nobles. We escaped, but—"

"How did you get away?" interrupted Worgon.

"On the water," mumbled Rew, grimacing. He knew what the baron was thinking.

Worgon frowned. "Did they see you escape?"

"We don't think so."

He hated to tell the bulbous baron the truth, but he wasn't sure lying would be any better. Could they gain Worgon's assistance while keeping Prince Valchon out of it? Rew thought frantically, but there was too much he didn't know, too much he'd have to guess at. In the end, in the face of uncertainty, he decided it was the truth that would serve them the best. Deceit and treachery were the games of nobles, not his.

Worgon raised his pipe to his lips and drew a lungful of smoke. He exhaled and said, "Where would Duke Eeron and his men believe the children fled, except to Falvar?"

Rew didn't respond. Raif and Cinda were going to insist upon going to Spinesend, with or without Baron Worgon's help. If they slipped out of Yarrow again, the man would forget whatever loyalty he professed to the younglings, and he'd hunt them just as assiduously as Duke Eeron. Now that they'd presented themselves, the safest way forward was beneath Worgon's wing. And if they wanted that wing to fly toward Spinesend…

Worgon raised an eyebrow at him, waiting for a response.

Rew grunted. "We escaped unnoticed, and we do not believe Duke Eeron's men know the full scope of our plans. You're right, Baron Worgon, they would have assumed we fled to Falvar and the safety of its walls."

"Two days ago?" asked Worgon, rubbing his hand with his face. "From Umdrac, hrmph, they'd still be a day from Falvar, then? Two thousand of Duke Eeron's men, now a week from Spinesend? They'll search Falvar once they get there. Of course they will. They have to. Even with two thousand men, conducting a thorough search to determine the children are not there… Duke Eeron's captains won't risk returning to Spinesend unless they're sure."

Rew frowned but nodded.

"Spellcasters, war hounds?"

"There were spellcasters," said Rew. "We weren't close enough to see any details, but there were at least three men in robes at the head of the column."

"What color?"

"The leader wore the black of an invoker," said Rew. "I saw blue and green as well."

"Duke Eeron only has one invoker of any talent," murmured Worgon, staring into his fire. "Cavalry?"

"Yes, the cavalry was on the march," responded the ranger. "Two hundred, I'd guess. Plus what had to be his elite advanced scouts."

"Interesting," said Worgon, raising his pipe back to his puffy, purpled lips. "The duke still outnumbers us, but without his elite troops and his most skilled casters... Perhaps we could bring surprise onto our side. I've a thought that's been nagging me ever since Prince Valchon appeared in my throne room, but I couldn't risk it with so many men around Spinesend. Certainly not while Duke Eeron kept his cavalry close."

The baron moved to a wide table at the other end of his study and began shuffling through maps and arranging documents covered in rows and columns of figures. Whispering to himself, he would read a line and stab a fat finger onto the map, seeming to lock some imaginary factor into place, then go back to his charts. The party watched him quietly, unsure what he was calculating and not wanting to interrupt the portly man's thoughts.

Finally, Worgon looked up and declared, "I think it may work."

"I'M CAPTAIN GRAEWALD," DECLARED THE MAN, HIS GRUFF VOICE booming in the stone room. "I'll be responsible for your safety while you are in Yarrow."

"I don't recall seeing your face around the keep before, Captain," remarked Raif.

The big man drew himself up and explained, "I spend most of my time out in the field, m'lord. I find life in the keep doesn't suit me."

Rew studied the man, frowning. A seasoned campaigner as he claimed, no doubt. He had wavy, blond hair that hung over his ears. Rew thought it could have used a trim, though he suspected that was the way the man preferred it. Graewald had a short beard, also blond, that did little to cover the pale white scar rising along one side of his jaw or the knotted pucker on his other cheek. Rather than hiding his old wounds, the beard seemed to show them off.

Ignoring Rew's scrutiny, the captain turned, glancing around the tower room they'd been deposited in, and nodded appreciatively at its defensive nature. He gripped the leather-wrapped hilt of a wide-bladed broadsword on his hip. Beneath the man's gloved hands, Rew could see the hilt of that sword showed evidence of use, but without seeing the blade, he couldn't tell if it was from battle or from practice. The man's chain hauberk looked in good enough repair, as if he rarely took a strike to the body, and his boots were in great shape, though Rew doubted they were the ones the man wore in the field.

It was the captain's trousers that gave away his profession. The seat of his pants and the insides of his legs were worn from contact with the leather of his saddle. Graewald embodied a typical cavalry commander. A simple look identified him as a man used to sitting on the back of his horse, dishing out death as he rode high above it.

Rew had never trusted cavalry men.

If you meant to fight someone, you should fight them standing on your own feet. Worse, while cavalry were always eager to brag about how quick they were into a fight, they never seemed to mention how quick they were away when it turned against them. They enjoyed blooding their swords and then trotting off before the fighting got hot. Cavalry, more often than not, were men who made sport of war. They were always wealthy, as no one else could afford the horses that gained entry into the divisions. Third or fourth sons of nobility or first or second sons of the wealthiest merchants. The nobility because their parents had no place for them in the keeps, the merchants because valor on the battlefield was amongst the few ways to earn one of those keeps. Cavalry were men who sought glory but were never the ones you trusted to plant boots and hold a line.

Graewald was returning Rew's study, eying the ranger up and down skeptically. Rew asked him, "Related to Baron Worgon, are you, Captain?"

The man shifted, a slight frown curling his lips down and pulling at the scar on his cheek. "No, I hail from Spinesend, and since you're about to ask, I am a cousin to Duke Eeron."

"You're a cousin of Duke Eeron?" asked Raif, suddenly losing his fawning look and replacing it with one of shock and anger.

"I've no loyalty to the duke, lad," stated Graewald. "He had no place for me, and I left when I was young. Baron Worgon has taken me in and given me all the opportunities a man could ask for. I've risen to captain in his most prestigious unit, and that's more than I ever hoped when I arrived in Yarrow."

Raif nodded, satisfied, but Rew wondered. Nobles were rarely content with their lot in life. They always wanted more. Unless Graewald simply enjoyed spilling blood, which Rew admitted was quite possible, then he doubted the captain had all that he truly hoped for.

But Worgon had trusted their safety to the man, and despite his reservations, Rew had to acknowledge Graewald was an experienced and capable seeming sort. The captain had quickly surveyed the chambers they'd been assigned to. He'd commandeered more men to post outside of the rooms, and he'd given the two young nobles specific—and firm—instructions on where they could go and when. Graewald had requested that if they needed to deviate from his schedule, they should clear it through him first. The man had left nothing for Rew to complain about, except that the captain had also lumped the ranger into his instructions.

As Graewald finished explaining the restrictions, Rew bit the inside of his lips, trying to stop a smile as he watched the faces of Raif and Cinda.

"Captain," said Cinda, drawing herself up, "we lived in

Yarrow for three years, you know. We were safe then, and I've no doubt—"

"Lass," said the Captain, "when you lived in Yarrow, was Baron Worgon preparing for war with Duke Eeron? Was your father a captive of the duke, and did you think that Duke Eeron hoped the same for you?"

"Well, no…" replied Cinda, her voice trailing off.

"We are to be part of this battle as well, Captain," declared Raif. "Duke Eeron has our father, and we're going to make him pay. The duke will regret ever starting a fight with the Fedgleys."

"Will he, now?" asked the captain, setting his fists on his hips. "If it wasn't for Baron Worgon and our army, what would—"

"Enough," said Anne.

The captain turned and blinked at the empath, surprised at the interruption.

"Thank you for showing us our rooms, Captain Graewald," said Anne. "Please let the servants know we'd like some refreshments on your way out, will you?"

The captain opened his mouth then closed it. He offered a shallow bow to Anne and a nod to Raif and Cinda. He avoided looking at Rew again, and he'd been ignoring Zaine since the moment he saw her in the corner. Turning on his heel, the captain marched out of the room, and the door banged shut behind him.

"That man is insufferable," said Anne the moment the captain's crisp bootsteps faded from hearing.

Rew grinned at her, and the younglings nodded agreement.

"What do we do now?" asked Zaine.

"We wait while Baron Worgon assembles his men," said Rew. "Shouldn't take more than a day. In the meantime, I hope the serving staff will bring ale."

"No ale," said Anne.

"What?" exclaimed Rew.

"Worgon is preparing his men to march, and we should prepare as well," said Anne. "You men clear the furniture from the center of the room. Cinda and I will practice her casting. Then,

Rew, you take Raif and Zaine out onto the balcony and start arms training."

The rest of the party looked at each other before, as a group, they shrugged. There wasn't much time, but they had nothing else to do, and no one could argue the sense of preparing themselves for what was to come.

Rew and Raif bent their backs to move all of the furniture in the room to the sides, and then the two of them, followed by Zaine, stepped outside.

They were halfway up a tower, high in Worgon's keep. Their living quarters opened onto a large balcony that was the roof of a room below. It afforded plenty of space to practice and an excellent view of the town of Yarrow and the land beyond.

Raif and Zaine glanced out over the land to where they could see Baron Worgon's troops, mustering into their units, readying to march. Row after row of tents were staked neatly down, and huge depots had been set up for supplies. Wagons and livestock were on the fringes, carts filled with weapons and women were being unloaded for the soldiers' use. Baron Worgon had been preparing, Rew saw.

Rew looked between the two youths and called for their attention. "We'll take turns. First, Raif."

The big nobleman pushed back his hair, looked around, and said, "We've no practice blades, no sparring armor, and no dummies for striking. What are we doing, Ranger?"

"We'll use our swords," said Rew, and he drew his longsword. Raif frowned at him.

"Come on, lad. We don't have much time."

"Hold on," said Raif. "You want me to attack you?"

"Yes."

The big youth blinked at him uncertainly.

"You won't hurt me," asserted Rew.

"What if you trip, or something gets in your eye, or…" began Zaine. She shook herself. "Before, you told me not to practice like this. Do you remember? By the river, you said—"

"Practicing with real blades is a foolish idea," growled Rew, "except when it's an emergency. If you insist on this path, you should understand that it is an emergency. More people than I care to think of want you dead. If you want to learn to defend yourselves, we'll have to dispense with caution and common sense. It's the path you've taken."

"I'm not insisting on any path," protested Zaine.

Raif reached behind his shoulder and unsheathed his greatsword. "Ranger, this blade is enchanted. If I swing hard, it will shear through your steel like I'm hacking into stale bread."

"No, it won't," said Rew.

The big youth frowned at him in consternation. "Ranger, I haven't had time to test the properties of the enchantment, and my father made efforts to ignore that part of our family history, but this is a powerful blade. I've used it enough to know that common steel cannot stand against it."

Rew walked to the edge of the balcony where there were several large planters. In the spring, they would hold blooming flowers, but in the autumn, they were empty. Grunting, Rew dragged one closer to another and laid his longsword down across them.

He turned to Raif. "Strike my sword as hard as you can."

Shaking his head, the nobleman complained, "Your longsword will shatter with the impact."

"If it shatters, I can buy another," said Rew.

Raif glanced at Zaine, as if he wanted her to protest as well, but the thief merely looked on in interest. Finally, Raif shrugged and stepped forward. He raised his greatsword above his head and swung it down. Not with all of his might, but hard enough.

The two blades clanged together. Rew's longsword bounced with the impact, and Raif's greatsword was jarred from his hands when he was caught by surprise at the resistance from the other blade. The two weapons fell to the tiled balcony with a clatter. Raif stared open-mouthed at the lengths of gleaming steel. There wasn't a mark on either one.

"I don't understand," said Raif.

"Your sword is enchanted!" cried Zaine, pointing at Rew. "I remember now. Vyar Grund said the same! What can it do?"

Rew winked at her without answering, walked around Raif, and picked up his blade. He moved back into the center of the balcony and said, "Let's begin."

Raif collected his sword, hefting the giant weapon that was nearly as long as the big youth was tall. He turned and eyed Rew's blade. "Do you know the properties of the weapon?"

"Of course," responded Rew.

"Tell us what they are?" asked Zaine from the side of the balcony.

Rew shook his head and settled his feet in front of Raif.

Raif grunted, tentatively approached, and swung a strike at Rew. The ranger didn't move, didn't bother to defend. Raif's blow whistled by half-a-pace away from him.

"You can do better," he told the nobleman.

Raif swung a few more desultory strikes, and Rew began to parry them, not speaking, letting the confidence of his movement communicate that he was prepared for more. Slowly, the force and speed of Raif's attacks increased.

Rew continued to comfortably defend. He did not attack; he just waited as Raif swung at him. It was no real sparring practice, and it would teach the boy little, but Rew wanted to understand what the youth was capable of. So far, he'd only seen Raif in action during the brief moments they fought the narjags, and it was little evidence of the boy's training.

Raif, perhaps frustrated with the ease Rew defended his attacks, began to strike with more force, and Rew began to see yawning gaps in the youth's style. The nobleman struck with vigor, making good use of his strength, but he did so with all of the grace of a blacksmith hammering against an anvil. Raif tried to use the weight of his blade and the muscle behind it to batter Rew into submission. Perfectly adequate when striking an unmoving object like a practice dummy, but Rew had little difficulty shunting the blows aside and leveraging his skill to keep himself well out of reach of the greatsword. In a short time, Raif was panting and wheezing, exhausted by the strain of lifting and swinging his huge weapon. Rew let him continue for a moment longer and, not wanting to waste all of the boy's energy, called for a rest.

Raif put his blade point-down onto the tiles of the balcony and leaned against the cross guard. Between ragged breaths, he said, "I don't understand."

"Don't understand what?" asked Rew.

"With that effort, I could have shattered two dozen wooden practice dummies," rasped Raif. "I could have beaten half a dozen sparring partners into submission. You look as comfortable and as rested as when you stepped away from the table after breaking your fast this morning back at the inn. What magic is this, Ranger? Is it a property of your longsword?"

Rew shook his head and waited while the big youth gathered his breath to continue.

"You're the better swordsman. I knew that," admitted Raif, "but even a veteran soldier would have collapsed under the strain of defending those strikes."

Rew nodded. "You, and I suspect those you've sparred against, use your strength and the size of your weapon to hammer an opponent. It's not a terrible strategy when facing a single, heavily armored, slow-moving, and slow-thinking opponent, but it's an awful way to combat someone like me. I didn't meet your attacks. I merely let them slide to the side, which is far less exhausting."

Raif frowned.

"I'll teach you. For now, understand we have much to do and much to unlearn," said Rew. He saw the protest in the boy's eyes, so he added, "I didn't bother to swing back, Raif. I didn't even try. It was your own efforts which have worn you down. Think about that while you rest, and we'll practice more later. Now, it's time to assess Zaine."

"Same plan?" asked the girl, sliding off the edge of the balcony where she'd been sitting.

Rew frowned at her. "What, ah, what's on the other side of that railing?"

Zaine turned and looked down. "The courtyard before the keep's gates."

Rew shuddered at the thought of sitting on the railing with his back to such a great fall. He took a couple of steadying breaths then raised his weapon. "Attack."

Zaine moved toward him with none of the fervor or the anger that Raif had. It made her more dangerous, but it was quickly apparent she didn't have the boy's training or anything like his strength. Before long, she stopped.

Rew grinned at her. "With those two daggers you're at an extreme disadvantage to my longsword. If I'm ready, the only way to approach me is to knock my blade aside with one of yours and try to get inside of my guard with the other. You have to learn to use the two blades in tandem. You'll never beat an opponent with a longer weapon as long as they can keep the pointy tip aimed at you."

"Knock it aside?" questioned Zaine.

Rew nodded.

She swiped at his longsword, and her dagger clanged off of his steel.

"Harder," he encouraged.

She swung again, ringing his blade with hers. Over and over, he instructed her to attack, and she struck several more times before he stopped her.

"Now, instead of striking my sword," he instructed, "place your dagger against the tip and try to force my weapon out of your way."

Doing as he asked, she put her dagger against the mid-point of his longsword and tried to shove it away. Nothing happened.

"Right at the end, lass."

She moved her dagger toward the tip of the longsword, and as she pushed on it again, he allowed the sword to waver, letting her shove it aside.

"See," he explained, "the further from my grip you put your force, the easier time you'll have turning my weapon from your path. It's the simple physics of leverage. I mean no offense, but you'll never be stronger than me or many of the opponents you face. You'll have to use your speed and your wits. Of course, that doesn't mean you shouldn't try to get stronger. You should, but learning to use that strength effectively is how you'll survive."

"How do I get stronger, then?" asked Zaine.

"Practice," said Rew. "First, I'm going to teach you both some simple exercises we'll use to begin our day. This will build your muscles as well as endurance in your heart and lungs. Every day, until this is over, we'll begin with these exercises. After that, Zaine, you will start work on a sparring dummy if we can borrow one from Captain Graewald—or some of Baron Worgon's furniture if we cannot. You'll practice aiming your strikes and putting your weight behind them. Raif, we'll work on your positioning and your dexterity. Against a slow, weak opponent, you'd do quite well. Against a fast, skilled opponent, you'll be dead."

"That's unfair," muttered Raif. "I survived the narjags."

"With Anne's healing," reminded Rew.

"He's got a point," chimed in Zaine.

Raif rolled his eyes at her and then turned back to Rew. "Fair enough, Ranger. You've proven you're a superior swordsman, and since we're not going anywhere right now, I'll do as you say."

Ignoring the boy's haughty tone, Rew nodded and told them to put aside their weapons. "First, we're going to get your bodies working. Drop onto your bellies and put your hands flat on the ground. You're going to push yourselves up. No, no, keep your body flat as you do. You want to feel it in your chest. That's… Well, not that awful. Do twenty more."

11

For three days, they'd been languishing in Yarrow. Each morning, Rew would walk out onto the balcony outside of their rooms and look over the sluggish preparations of Baron Worgon's men. The encampment beyond the city walls had the look of the beginnings of a major military endeavor, but as men and women occupied the rows of tents, new provisions arrived, and the numbers swelled, they never actually lined up to march. It was a source of frustration for all of them, so they communicated it in looks and guttural grunts. They all felt the simmering need to do something, and no words were necessary to give their emotion shape.

The waiting did give them time to train, though. Rew set Raif and Zaine a series of exercises designed to build their strength and stamina. They cycled through the movements each morning, and then they'd work on combat skills, erasing the bad habits the pair held and replacing them with effective theories of how to defend oneself and how to kill. In the afternoons, they practiced what they'd learned in the morning until the younglings dropped from exhaustion.

It wasn't enough to turn them into expert warriors. That would take years of repetition and experience, but Rew hoped he could lay a foundation to build from. Back in Eastwatch, he would spend months training his rangers, and it was years before they were considered adequate, but he simply did not have that much time with the younglings, so he did what he could.

Indoors, Anne taught Cinda as best she could. Fortunately, the girl had some of the theory from Arcanist Ralcrist and the other tutors she'd been exposed to. She knew what to do but didn't have the strength to do it. That changed when Rew suggested they stop invoking and begin necromancy. The girl's mother had been an invoker, but it was her father's blood and his talent that surged through Cinda's veins.

Anne had scowled at him. He realized the thought had already occurred to her, but as an empath, she had a natural aversion to necromancy. He understood, but Anne had dragged him along for the journey, and while he was there, he would do the best he could. He insisted they give it a try.

From that point, instead of sending pathetic charges of energy or wobbling balls of heat across the room, Cinda began practicing the cold chill of death. She could not yet call to the spirits, and it was too dangerous to practice in a crowded city, but Anne found the girl could draw on the power of the departed, and so they began practicing that.

Late the evening on their third day confined to the tower, after the younglings had fallen limply on the couches, worn from the day of training, Anne spoke to Rew out on the balcony. "It feels wrong, teaching her these things."

He shrugged. "It is who she is."

Anne pulled her shawl tight around her shoulders. "That doesn't make it right. It's the antithesis of all that I've practiced in my career. Besides, necromancy is what got the Fedgleys into this mess. Why take the same road trying to get out of it?"

"Necromancy is what got everyone into this," acknowledged Rew. Anne's head twisted to the side, and he saw the reflection of her eyes as she looked at him in the dark. Quickly, before she could ask what he was alluding to, he added, "How is Cinda holding up? Raif is going mad at the delays. He's ready to storm out and command those soldiers to march."

Anne looked past the walls of the town below them and out to the fields where Worgon's soldiers were camping. During the day, they could see a hundred tents spread out around the road that led from Yarrow. At night, they could only see the campfires. The fires flickered like a reflection of the stars above, except they burned an angry red-orange in the black of the night.

"Cinda is ready to leave as well," said Anne. "She's fuming that Worgon has left us out of his councils and that all we know is from what we can see standing on this balcony. I think if Captain Graewald says one more time he's only sharing what we need to know, Cinda's going to strangle the man. That, or we'll find out what she's really capable of."

Rew watched the campfires below, not responding.

"Why hasn't Worgon marched?" wondered Anne. "When we first arrived, he was cackling about the element of surprise, but every day we sit and let his army mull about is another day for Duke Eeron's spies to report and for the duke to respond. If Duke Eeron has called his men back from Falvar, we may have already lost our advantage. Three days… It's been too long. I'm no tactician, but even I can do the math. If we wanted to arrive outside Spinesend before Eeron's men returned, we should have left already."

"He claims his son, Fredrick, is conscripting more men from the countryside," replied Rew. "I'm not sure why you'd want untrained louts instead of the element of surprise, but Worgon seems convinced it's the better path. He thinks the duke's men will spend days in Falvar looking for the children, and if so, there's still time."

Anne frowned and Rew could only shrug. He wasn't an experienced tactician either, but Worgon's son had whispered in the baron's ear, and the man wouldn't listen to any suggestions otherwise.

"How can he be so confident?" questioned Anne.

"Worgon is waiting for Prince Valchon to arrive," said Rew. "He has to be. It's the only explanation of his confidence."

"What will the prince do when he comes?" asked Anne, looking sharply at the ranger. "What does he want with the children?"

"I don't know, Anne," replied Rew. It was true. He only suspected. "The moment we walked into Yarrow's keep and asked to see Worgon, we set a course for a meeting with Valchon. It's the only reason Worgon's interested in us and the only reason he's putting his army in the field. If it wasn't for Prince Valchon's support, Worgon would never even consider this mad plan of his. Instead, I imagine he'd be hiding behind his walls and offering his allegiance to the duke."

"What do we do?" murmured Anne, leaning forward to put her arms on the balustrade, staring into the darkness and the campfires below.

"I don't know," replied Rew. "I've explained this until my tongue's gone numb, sagging like a dog's in summer. The children say they believe me, but they don't understand. To them, Prince Valchon represents the height of nobility. His lineage, his power, it's what their family—all of the noble families—is working for. They don't know the man or how empty his heart is. They can't fathom that this hierarchy they're a part of, nobility's rule of Vaeldon, is such an—ah, it doesn't matter. They don't know because they can't know. For them to understand, they'd have to confront their role in all of it. They'd have to acknowledge the blood and gore that paved the highway their ancestors walked to earn the title."

"Tell me of Prince Valchon," said Anne.

Rew rolled his shoulders, taking a moment to consider how to explain the man. He scratched his beard and then said, "Valchon is the oldest of the brothers, though only by a few years. If you met him, I suspect you'd like him. He's gregarious, attractive, long of body, and dark of hair. He likes to jest and loves his entertainments. His court is filled with music, art, and women. It's well known that Valchon employs the best cooks in the kingdom. To a favored visitor, there are few places in Vaeldon more pleasant that Valchon's keep in Carff."

Anne remained quiet beside him.

Rew continued, "His strength is not that of arms or even magic, though he is talented. His true strength is his charisma. He draws people to him, and they trust him. Each of the princes will collect allies, both true and false, but those who follow Valchon will do so because they want to. He's an easy man to like."

"It sounds like you know him well," remarked Anne.

"I do," agreed Rew. "I did, at least. Prince Valchon thrives on being around people, and it was common to see him in Morden-hold. Later, I visited him several times when I was in Carff for, ah, on the king's business. There's a way about Valchon, where he draws you in and makes you promises. Shockingly, for one in his position, he actually follows through and does what he said he would do, but no one ever considers what will come due from that, what they owe him in return. Now that the Investiture has begun, Valchon will be calling in favors, assembling those he thinks he can rely upon. When Valchon moves against his younger brothers, he'll do so with scores of allies at his side."

"Allies like the two barons and Alsayer?" scoffed Anne. "Every time I've heard Prince Valchon's name, it's because someone is betraying him."

"True allies," said Rew with a shake of his head. "No, I'm afraid the Baron Fedgley and Cinda are not meant to march beside Prince Valchon. They're for... they're for later, when some of the pieces have been removed from the board. I cannot say more."

"Rew..."

"I cannot say, Anne," he told her. "Rest assured, he means to use the Fedgleys, not to help them. It's best if we keep Cinda from that man's grasp. Best if she never sees him."

"We should tell her."

"Tell her what?" asked Rew. "That Valchon has plans for her

which I cannot reveal? That he means to use her and her father? Raif and Cinda know all of these things, Anne, and unlike some of what we've told them, I think they believe it. They want Valchon to need them because that is their leverage. It goes both ways. They need him, they think, so in turn they must be useful to the man. It's the sort of arrangement nobility thrives upon, though they do not understand that the Investiture is different, that the royal family is different. I don't know how to explain that to them, Anne. I've tried."

Frowning, Anne didn't respond.

"I've been warning everyone about this," reminded Rew.

"I know, I know," she said. "I thought that Worgon... I expected him to... Ah, I don't know. I expected him to help, I guess. He fostered these children for three years, yet he treats them as no more than pawns on a game board. They are no more important to him than Graewald, or Graewald's horse, for that matter."

Rew remained quiet. It was true, but he'd said as much before. He'd said it often enough he knew the words had lost their meaning.

"Do you think we should get the children away from here?"

"I didn't want us to come in the first place," replied Rew sardonically. "If you recall, I said presenting ourselves to Worgon was a terrible idea."

"That's not helpful, Ranger. If we want to leave, how would we?"

"The same way Zaine took the younglings out last time, I suppose. If it worked before, then it could work again. The bigger challenge will be convincing the younglings."

"I'm not sure," argued Anne. "We've been sitting in this tower for three days now. Another day or two, and the waiting will teach them more of Worgon's intentions than your words ever could, than your words have, I suppose I should say. I think after several days sitting here watching the baron squander the element of surprise, they'll be willing to change course and leave. Sometimes, all it takes is time to think things over."

Rew grunted.

"Will you talk to them?" asked Anne.

"I think it best if it comes from you," he told her.

"I don't like interfering in these matters."

Rew laughed.

Anne sighed. "Very well. I'll talk to them."

THE NEXT MORNING AT BREAKFAST, ANNE SPOKE TO THE YOUNGLINGS, and to Rew's surprise, they began making plans.

"I'm not ready to scamper out of here today," Raif had said, "but after three days locked in this tower, it's worth thinking about, isn't it? We should at least discuss our options, in case..."

The big fighter had stuffed a mouthful of food into his mouth and had not finished his statement. He hadn't needed to; they all understood.

Over platters of sausages, breads, beans, and roasted tomatoes, they reviewed how Zaine had snuck the younglings from the keep and out of Yarrow the last time. From the keep, the trio had worn disguises and joined a traveling minstrel group that had played at a banquet for Baron Worgon earlier in the evening. The guards' eyes had been on the group's dancers as they'd walked out, and besides, no one had been expecting the Fedgleys to leave. They'd escaped before anyone would have been watching them. Once in the city, they'd left the minstrels with a purse full of silver and instructions to travel quickly the first few days out of Yarrow. Then, they'd changed into plain attire that Zaine had procured in the city and had secreted themselves in the empty bottom of a yam farmer's wagon underneath a pile of burlap sacks. The man had sold his wares in the market and was leaving Yarrow back to his farm. He'd paid his duties when he'd entered, and the guards at the gates hadn't given a second look at his empty wagon.

Sneaking out in a yam wagon had been effective, though not particularly inspired, thought Rew. The minstrels with the dancing girls sounded more titillating, but in the midst of Yarrow preparing for war, there were no entertainers in the keep, and he doubted many in the city at all. Rew frowned, shaking his head. Yams?

"I figured it was a bit more… ah, creative," said Rew after hearing of the plan for the first time. "Perhaps a secret passage or an explosive distraction? Maybe the girls with the minstrels could have put on an impromptu performance near the gates to draw the guards away? I think that would have been more effective."

Zaine shrugged. "My plan worked."

"It did," said Cinda. "Ranger, you heard Worgon. He said it was like we vanished into air."

Rew frowned and scratched at his beard. "Unfortunately, security is a lot tighter now. It's no great guess to think that while Yarrow is marshaling for war, the guards at the gates will be searching everyone who comes and goes looking for spies. We can see from the balcony that they've already stopped all traffic heading west. Disguised or not, no one is going to let us travel that way openly."

"The soldiers are going that way," said Zaine. "I've watched them while you and Raif spar. Scouts, maybe, heading off down the road. Perhaps we could join them?"

Rew glanced between Cinda and Zaine. "I don't think we'll have much luck draping a chainmail shirt on you two and convincing the soldiers you're in the army."

Cinda flexed her arm with a wink.

Zaine suggested, "We could get fake beards and stuff extra clothing beneath the chainmail to look bulkier. If we stay behind you and Raif, then maybe it could work."

Rew frowned at her. "Do you have a fake beard?"

Zaine shrugged.

"What about…" started Raif, but he trailed off, shaking his head as if quickly realizing his idea wasn't going to work.

"Where soldiers go, so do ladies of the night," offered Anne. "The girls would have no problems passing in the right attire. You and Raif could serve as our guards or, perhaps even better, customers taking them out into the town. I—"

"You could pass," said Rew, nodding sagely. "Hike those skirts up a little, undo a few laces of your blouse..."

Anne frowned at him. "I was going to say I could leave separately, posing as a healer."

Rew shrugged. "You could, but where's the fun in that?"

"I could pretend I was distributing herbs to all of the diseased men and women in the keep. Maybe even give the guards a little education about the consequences of pulling down their trousers every chance they get," said Anne. "That might be fun, eh?"

"There are female guards, too," said Rew with a wink. "Don't blame it all on the men."

Anne snorted.

"It wouldn't be my first idea," said Cinda, "but if you think it could work, I'm willing to try. I, ah, I don't have much experience with such women, so maybe if you..."

Rew, still grinning, shook his head. "No, I don't think it will work. We're trying to avoid notice. Parading a pair of scantily clad young women in front of a group of bored guards is going to get us the opposite."

Anne pursed her lips. "I suppose that's true."

They sat around the table, picking at the remains of their meal, thinking. No one had come up with a suitable solution when a heavy fist pounded on the door. Rew opened it and found Captain Graewald standing outside.

The captain glanced in and saw them at the table. "Bit of a slow morning?"

Rew shrugged. "We have nothing to do and nowhere to go, Captain. Perhaps if you allowed us out of this room..."

The big blond man grinned. "You're in luck, Ranger. Baron Worgon has instructed the army to march. It will take them some time to get organized, but by mid-morning, they'll be on the road.

The baron has requested you accompany his cohort. Take an hour, say, and I'll be back to collect you?"

"Certainly," said Rew.

Graewald looked around to Raif and Cinda. "Cheer up, you two. We're going to rescue your father."

———

WITH THE ARMY ON THE MARCH AND HEADED THE SAME DIRECTION they wanted to go, Captain Graewald coming back in an hour, and broad daylight outside, they all agreed they'd lost their opportunity to escape. There were no plans they could conceive of that might get them out of the keep and out of the city before Worgon realized something was wrong and locked the place down. That left them with only one choice, to accompany the baron and his army to Spinesend, though the younglings' faith in the man had been shaken by the delay getting his men started.

"Well, at least we're headed in the right direction," said Raif. "I didn't intend to sit in Yarrow for so long, and I can't help wonder what the man has been up to, but maybe it's for the best. We've got an army with us now."

Rew grunted but did not respond. They had an army and had completely blown any element of surprise. There'd be no sneaking into Spinesend with Worgon's men camped outside of the walls. Not to mention, getting away from the baron, away from all nobility, would have been the best. That was hard to explain to a noble.

Nervous but eager to be leaving the tower chamber that had been their prison for the last three days, they walked down the stone stairwell to the courtyard where the baron's elite troops were assembling. Worgon himself was standing outside, overseeing the preparations and furiously flapping a paper fan in front of his face. The day was cool, but in the bright sun, the rotund baron's face was red as an apple. Rew thought he might have been well served to stuff a little less lace into his collar, but the fashions of the nobility weren't any more sensible than anything else that they did.

"Overseeing the preparations," boomed Baron Worgon, gesturing around the courtyard at the scurrying servants, none of whom seemed to be paying him a bit of attention. "It's dreadful out here, but a leader must show their face in times of war. That's what I've always said."

"Of course, m'lord," murmured Raif, looking skeptically at the baron.

"Father," purred a slender man. His face was narrow and sharp, like he'd been drawn on a blacksmith's anvil. His clothing was fine, but it was dark and embroidery- and lace-free. His hands were bereft of jewels, and at first glance, he couldn't have been more different than the baron. At second glance, it was obvious that without the extra weight and years on the baron, this man was his son. "I'll be taking my leave now. Cousin Appleby is still here, and we owe him our attention."

Snorting, the baron nodded.

"Appleby has inquired about—"

Worgon waved his son away, his jowls wobbling like a drunk's legs.

"Should you have need of my council, I can be there in—"

"If I have need of your council, lad, I'll ask for it," snapped Baron Worgon. He rubbed two pudgy fingers at his head, mussing his wispy, white hair. The baron turned from his son to stare at a squad of veterans who had no need of the baron's scrutiny.

The younger man glared at Baron Worgon's back and then shoved his long hands into his coat pockets. "Best of luck on the campaign, Father. Do try to listen to your commander, won't you? His council could keep you out of trouble, if you accept it."

The baron did not turn to face his son, and with a wicked smirk on his lips, the younger man turned on his heel and strode back into the keep.

"My son," explained the baron, "he fancies himself a grand general."

"Is he not?" asked Rew.

Baron Worgon snorted. "Don't jest with me, Ranger. My son hasn't lifted a sword in years, and he's tragically poor at invoking. His contribution to my court is snide japes, lecherous behavior which scandalized his poor mother until her final days, and simpering intrigue. Believe me when I tell you, that boy would like nothing more than seeing me fall on the field of battle. It's why he wanted to accompany us. I'm sure of it."

"The baron and Fredrick don't get along," whispered Cinda into Rew's ear. "They can't be in the same room for more than a quarter hour without a fight breaking out."

Rew raised an eyebrow in mock surprise, and Cinda rolled her eyes at him.

"Pfah," coughed Worgon, "I can guess what you're saying, lass. My son's proclivities are well-known in the Eastern Territory. He'd prefer us to manage the barony with the tip of a quill rather than the tip of a sword, but before he'd do either, he'd sit a serving girl on his lap and show her the tip of his—You don't have much of the type in the wilderness, Ranger, but the courts in the cities are full of them. My son is a craven, and worse, he conspires behind my back. Fortunately, his cowardice runs so deep that I haven't been bothered to do anything about it. It's the Investiture, a time for war, and the boy spends his days filling the post's carriages with his letters. For days, he counseled me to wait, to gather more forces before we marched. I did, though not because he advised it. I think that's what has emboldened him today. What, does he think Duke Eeron wants—to conference with us? No, it's a time to fight, and it's men like us who were made for times like these."

"Not everyone can enjoy your vast experience in battle, m'lord," responded Rew.

"Your jests are as transparent as the finest glass," chided the portly Baron Worgon. "I'm no swordsman, Ranger, not like you, but I've seen my share of violence. I've done what I needed to do to keep this barony in order."

"He's an invoker," whispered Cinda as the baron turned his back, peering at the carriage his servants were packing. She leaned in closer. "Though one of small talent and no control. I suppose it doesn't matter when one has no care for what damage one causes. A clenched fist swung by a blind man. At least, that's what Father said of him."

"It will be some time before things get exciting," said Worgon, his attention on the activity around them. "With the army in our train, the journey should be four, five days before we reach Spinesend. We may take another day to prepare our attack."

"I'm worried, m'lord," warned Captain Graewald, emerging from the crowd of soldiers around them and overhearing the last of the baron's comments. "Duke Eeron's spies have had time to report our activity. We should have left sooner, no matter what that fop Fredrick said. Duke Eeron is going to be ready for us now. We should be prepared to engage the moment we come within sight of his walls. I can have my men—"

Baron Worgon waved a hand at Captain Graewald to silence him. "We had to give Duke Eeron time, Captain. I didn't wait just because my idiot son asked me to. You know that."

"A day, two at the most, would have been plenty of time," muttered Graewald.

Rew frowned. "Time?"

The baron winked at him.

The ranger stepped closer to Baron Worgon. Captain Graewald shuffled in between them. Rew asked again, "Time?"

"Time to flush out any mousers the duke had in our ranks," explained Baron Worgon. "I'm sure his spies have been thick in my court for months now, but I didn't know if any were prepared to pounce. It seems they were not."

"None were ready with the authority to act or the skill to portal, that is," remarked Captain Graewald, shaking his head. "We'd be foolish to think spies were not on horseback the moment the Fedgley children appeared in the throne room."

"A trap!" exclaimed Rew. "You kept us in that room as bait for Duke Eeron's spies? That is why you haven't marched yet?"

"You were not bait, Ranger, but the children, yes," admitted Baron Worgon, brushing at the lace spilling over his doublet. "I'd hoped if anything, you'd be able to supplement the security we put around the room. I've heard stories about you, Ranger."

"Wait, what?" cried Raif. "We were bait?"

"Don't worry, lad," said Worgon, waving a hand to shush him. "If Duke Eeron had moved against you, we were prepared to stop him. It would have been easier that way, in fact. I could have snared him or his agents here in Yarrow instead of having to march, but such are the things we must do, eh? It's not always comfortable being a leader, and the spoils of war always come at a steep price."

"You kept us here for three days thinking some spellcaster spy would report to Duke Eeron and he'd come after us?" asked Cinda, her eyes wide, realization dawning on her face. "But... but what if something had gone wrong?"

Baron Worgon shrugged and then gestured to his waiting carriage. "I can see you're upset. Let's discuss it inside of the carriage. I think that's better than out here in the courtyard in front of everyone. I'll have my servants pour us a couple of glasses of port. That will settle your nerves."

Dragging their feet as if they were on their way into a jail cell, the younglings mounted the steps to the carriage and sat inside. Anne followed them, Zaine slipping silently in after, and then the baron, with the assistance of a footman shoving the round man through the narrow door. Captain Graewald gestured for Rew to enter as well, but the ranger shook his head.

"I'll walk," said Rew.

"The carriage is horse-drawn, Ranger, and the escort will be mounted," warned Graewald. "We'll be moving quickly. You certain you want to walk?"

Rew nodded, catching a glance of the nobles piled into the compartment of the carriage. "I'm certain."

REW TROTTED BESIDE THE CARRIAGE AS IT RUMBLED THROUGH THE brick streets of Yarrow and then out into the country beyond. Around him, the baron's mounted guards kept the way clear, shouting ahead that the baron was coming and for the citizens to get out of the road. The people were quick to do so. Whether it was due to the guards' shouting or because the team of horses pulling the carriage did not slow when they came upon someone, Rew didn't know.

Either way, the people cleared the road, and the carriage trundled along at a brisk pace. When they passed through the city gates and into the country, the buildings and citizens were replaced by units of Baron Worgon's army. The men were arrayed in ranks, their camps finally packed, their supplies organized by the quartermasters into long trains that were already on the move. Those wagons were pulled by huge, lumbering oxen, and they moved at half the speed of the men and a quarter that of the carriage. Each morning, the wagons would start before dawn, and each evening, they'd arrive after the sun set. Feeding a large army on the move required careful planning and dedicated teams handling the logistics. It seemed Baron Worgon was well-prepared. Better prepared than he should be with only three days' notice. Despite Worgon's assurances that he'd planned to hide behind his walls, it seemed he'd already been readying the army to march.

Rew observed all of this as he jogged beside the carriage, studying the faces of the soldiers as well as the state of their supplies. The older men looked nervous, the younger men eager. The elders might have seen combat before, and they knew the horror they faced. The younger contingent had not yet been blooded, and their heads were likely still filled with the recruiters' promises of loot and women. Rew wondered how many of them, the nervous and the eager, would survive the next weeks and months. It could be most, or it could be few. There were assumptions one might make when it came to conventional battle, but there was no predicting what would happen once high magic was released upon the field.

When they passed the ranks of men and began down the open road, Captain Graewald's mount fell in beside Rew. For a long time, the captain said nothing. Eventually, he asked, "You can keep this pace all day, Ranger?"

"I can," said Rew, his breathing even, his strides long as he jogged next to the carriage, letting it set the pace but keeping near the front so the clods of dirt and dust kicked up by the horses did not foul his way.

"How'd you get involved with these nobles?" inquired the captain. "I'd heard your kind had never taken sides in an Investiture."

"We don't take sides. The children came through the Eastern Territory when they fled here, and I ended up feeling responsible for them. I'm just making sure they find a safe place from all of this, though I'll admit, it's gotten rather more complicated than I originally thought," replied Rew, figuring there was no harm in sharing that bit of information. Before Graewald could probe further, Rew asked, "How did you get involved with Baron Worgon?"

The soldier laughed. "Same as I told you several days ago. I left Spinesend with nowhere to go. When I unexpectedly found an opportunity to join the baron's service, I did."

"Surely it's not so simple," challenged Rew.

"I'm no spy," said Graewald, "if that's what you're thinking."

"I didn't say that, but you haven't told me the whole truth yet, Captain."

"I enjoy a fight, Ranger," said Graewald, his fingers tapping on the hilt of his broadsword as he rode, "perhaps more than I should. I didn't so much leave Spinesend to find adventure as I was chased out of Spinesend after killing a man. I'd been drinking, and it seemed I'd begun a conversation with the man's girl. As things do, it escalated from there. I told you, I'm a distant cousin of Duke Eeron. I'm not close enough to get away with what many witnesses described as a murder, but I'm close enough that I had time to slink away before I saw the magistrate or the inside of a cell. That's the whole truth of my departure, Ranger. In Baron Worgon's service, I found an outlet for my baser needs, and he found a man willing to do his dirty work. I'm not ashamed of what I am, and I've no need to lie about it."

"I believe you," said Rew, and he meant it. There was no deception in the captain's tone or his face, though Rew didn't like what he saw there.

"I've seen you sparring with the younglings," said Graewald. "Perhaps you and I could cross blades one day? Only for practice, of course."

"Of course."

The captain laughed. "Am I making you uncomfortable, Ranger?"

"All of this makes me uncomfortable, Captain," replied Rew.

"You know what's coming, then," said Graewald. He lifted a hand from the hilt of his broadsword and waved behind them. "None of them do. The baron knows, and he's told me. I understand your fear, but I live for this, Ranger. Ever since that first drunken night when I tasted another man's hot blood on my lips, I've found nothing so thrilling as pitting myself against an opponent, knowing only one of us will walk away. We've lived to see great times, Ranger, but only some of us will live to see the end of them."

Rew did not respond, and the captain rode beside him without speaking. After a quarter hour, Graewald said, "I need to ride back and check on the men. If you tire, but you can't stand the thought of riding with the nobles, we can spare you a mount."

Running alongside the road, Rew shook his head. "I don't ride."

"I'll see you tonight, Ranger," said Graewald. Then, he slowed and turned his horse around, going back to check on the long train of soldiers who were strung along the highway behind them.

❧ 12 ❧

Baron Worgon's carriage stopped with two hours of light left in the day. The vehicle moved several times faster than the marching men, but there was no point in outpacing them and arriving at Spinesend before the army got there. The quartermasters had gone ahead and identified a campsite, and the baron's forward guard had already set up a command tent and the baron's personal tent. It occupied a low hill that oversaw the road for a league ahead and behind them, and there was a sumptuous buffet of cold meats, cheeses, and fruits laid out. Decanters of wine were held in the hands of liveried servants waiting to hear the baron's preference, and there were promises of a more extravagant feast later as night fell.

As the only other landed nobles of significant lineage tagging along with the army, Raif and Cinda were invited to join Baron Worgon. Rew, Anne, and Zaine were not invited but joined anyway. The baron could not refuse an agent of the king, so he was polite to Rew, but he chose to ignore the additional women, studiously incurious as to who they were.

"Your son, Fredrick, is in charge of Yarrow in your absence?" asked Rew. "What about his younger sister? Did she stay as well?"

"In charge," snorted Baron Worgon. "I suppose that nominally he is, but my administration knows which of his commands to take and which to ignore. The boy's sister, though not quite as hopeless as my son, does not have the temperament for a military campaign. It's a relief, really, letting my son prattle on to someone else for a change. You wouldn't believe the madness he's been advocating for recently, Ranger."

Rew nodded but did not respond. Several of the baron's soldiers and servants could overhear the man disparaging his heir, and not one of them looked comfortable doing so.

Raif and Cinda looked nervous as well, perched on the fronts of their camp chairs, their hands in their laps. Rew frowned at them, thinking that they'd spent years around Baron Worgon, and even if it made them uncomfortable, they would have heard the man's opinion on his progeny before. Rew wondered what had transpired in the carriage with the baron during the ride. He probably should have accompanied them, but earlier that morning, he couldn't stand the thought of being locked in a small, jostling box with so many nobles.

The baron waved to his servants, and they filled a crystal glass of wine. The corpulent noble sampled the cheeses and meats that had been set out for him and looked back over the road they'd marched down as the first ranks of his soldiers appeared. At his shoulder, Captain Graewald kept watch as well.

"A bit slow, aren't they?" mumbled Worgon around a mouthful of pungent cheese.

"They're out of shape, m'lord," responded the captain. "Most of those boys have never been on campaign and have never seen combat. I'll be honest, m'lord, I worry about that."

Worgon waved his hand. "It's no matter, Captain. We don't need them to win the battle. We just need them to keep Duke Eeron's men off me long enough that I can release my spell."

"Spell?" asked Rew, but the baron ignored him.

"Captain," suggested the baron, "why don't you give us some entertainment? I'd like to see you spar with the ranger."

Graewald turned to Rew, his face blank. "I hardly think that fair, m'lord. The ranger was running alongside your carriage all day today. He must be exhausted."

Rew frowned. The captain's face was like stone, but his eyes burned. He couldn't read the look in the other man's eyes, but it gave him a shiver.

"What about the lad, then?" asked Worgon, gesturing toward Raif.

"I'm not sure—" started Graewald.

"Do it, Captain," instructed Worgon, his tone suddenly cold.

Raif looked to Rew, and Rew shook his head to warn the boy, but instead of declining, Raif winked at the ranger and turned to the captain. He declared, "Unlike the ranger, I spent the day resting in the carriage. A little exercise will be good for me."

"Fetch the lad's armor from the carriage, and find him a helmet somewhere," called Worgon to his waiting servants. He stood and began directing others to set up posts and string them with rope. He then whispered into the ear of his captain.

Rew leaned toward Raif. "I don't know what he's playing at, but you shouldn't do this. Don't let him get what he wants. It sets the tone of who is in command. Your father shares a rank with Worgon, and you're of age now. This man is not your superior, and you ought not to be his entertainment. You have no reason to impress him and don't need to do what he says."

"What are you worried about?" scoffed Raif.

"I'm worried the captain is going to beat you into the ground as easily as those men are pounding in those posts," said Rew, nodding toward the servants who were marking off a square for Graewald and Raif to spar within. "Worgon didn't suggest this simply to give you a little exercise."

Shrugging off the ranger's concerns, Raif moved to where Captain Graewald was donning heavy, steel armor.

Rew, eyeing the captain's broadsword, stayed next to Anne and the girls. The young nobleman was impetuous and arrogant.

AC COBBLE

There was nothing Rew could do outside of making a terrible scene that would stop this.

"Are you worried the captain will hurt him?" asked Cinda.

"I'm not sure," responded Rew. "Something isn't right with Worgon. He's not acting like his normal self. How did he seem in the carriage? Did he strike you as unusual?"

Cinda brushed a strand of hair behind her head and responded, "He did, but these are unusual times. He was eager for the coming conflict, and he shared with us his vision of what this territory could become. Worgon is normally reserved, and he's never before shared such things with us, but we've never before been in the Investiture. There's never been an opportunity to improve the standing of either of our houses, he said, not like there is now. What do you suspect?"

"I don't know," admitted Rew, watching Raif and Captain Graewald prepare to spar. "This plan makes less sense the more I think of it. Even with the element of surprise, Baron Worgon would be at a disadvantage to Duke Eeron. Without surprise on our side… it doesn't make sense at all. And then why the sparring? Raif fostered in Worgon's keep. Surely if the baron was interested in your brother's talents, he had plenty of chances to see the lad on the field. I don't think Worgon would be so reckless to seriously injure your brother while we're watching, but… You should talk to him, see if you can convince Raif to stop this foolishness."

Cinda casually walked to Raif and pulled him down so she could whisper in his ear. Her brother shook his head, and Rew didn't need to overhear to know what the elder sibling was saying. When he collected the helmet Worgon's servants had provided and donned it, Cinda returned to the others on the low hill.

She told them, "If anything, I think trying to talk him out of it is only making him want to do it more. He's not going to back down from sparring unless we tie him up and hide him in the tent. My brother can be rather stubborn, particularly when his pride is involved."

"I've noticed that," said Rew, watching as Raif adjusted the helm and then slid down the visor to protect his face.

The boy was clad in a steel breastplate and pauldrons. His arms were protected in steel as well, his hands covered in articulated gauntlets. The metal gleamed dully in the waning light of day. It was the armor he'd stolen in Umdrac, with a few extra pieces like the helmet provided by Worgon. There was no steel below his belt. There, Raif was only protected by thick padding and his boots. Evidently, he and Captain Graewald had agreed to avoid strikes below the waist.

"Why is he doing this?" asked Anne, staring at Baron Worgon.

The baron was sitting at the table, popping a small green fruit into his mouth and cradling a glass of wine in his hands. His attention was fixed on the upcoming combat, but Rew sensed the baron was well aware of what the others in their group were doing and perhaps what they were saying. Rew frowned and moved to stand beside the rope enclosure.

Raif and Graewald had final adjustments made to their armor by the servants and then squared off against each other, both raising their swords in salute. With no referee, the captain's voice called out from within his helmet to ask if Raif was ready. The youth responded that he was, and they both advanced.

Captain Graewald swung a tentative blow, and Raif met it with his greatsword. Again, the captain struck, and again, Raif met the blow. Graewald stepped to the side, circling the younger man, and Raif launched a powerful stroke. Graewald caught it easily on the edge of his broadsword, and Raif's greatsword slid away. The captain stepped forward and put his heavy shoulder into Raif's chest, knocking the youth stumbling backward. Raif raised his blade again and swung with all of his might.

Again, Graewald took the blow and directed it away. The series repeated itself several more times as if the captain was waiting for Raif to show any hidden skill, but when Raif did not,

Graewald made him pay by ramming the pommel of his sword into the side of Raif's helmet. Staggering, Raif held his greatsword in one hand and reached toward his head with the other, leaving his side unprotected.

Graewald bashed the youth in his steel-covered ribs with the edge of the broadsword. It wasn't a terribly strong blow, but Raif wasn't prepared, and he was sent flying off his feet. He landed heavily in a pile of crunching, clanging steel.

"Apologies, m'lord," called Graewald loudly. "An amateur blow. I thought you'd be prepared for it."

Rew cringed. It seemed the youth had forgotten everything that he'd been taught over the last several days. As Raif struggled back to his feet, using his greatsword to help push himself up, Rew saw it was only going to get worse. Through the slits of Raif's visor, the youth's eyes blazed with outrage at Graewald's poorly concealed taunt. As soon as they were set again, Raif charged, swinging his greatsword like a housewife chasing a fly from a fresh-baked pie.

Rew's eyes flicked to Baron Worgon and then back to Raif. Captain Graewald met Raif in the center of the square and swung a powerful horizontal blow. It caught Raif unguarded on his shoulder, bounced off the steel pauldron, then rang against Raif's helmet. The youth was spun, and the captain gave him a hearty blow to his backplate for good measure.

Raif stumbled, confused and shaken. Captain Graewald advanced, raining blows on the youth, harrying him about the practice square. None of the strikes were delivered with Graewald's full strength, but they were hard enough to keep the younger man smarting and off-balance.

"Raif is not acquitting himself well, is he?" worried Cinda, "but at least he's still on his feet."

Rew shook his head. "Only because Graewald wants him to be. He could have finished your brother at any time during this contest. He's playing with him."

Cinda frowned, but there was nothing she could say. It was

clear Graewald was the superior swordsman, and while she wanted to cheer her brother, it was obvious he was a nail to Graewald's hammer.

Raif collapsed to his knees, and Graewald stepped back. Rew saw the man's helmet turn toward Baron Worgon. Shooting a glance over his shoulder, Rew saw that Worgon was barely watching the fight. Instead, he was watching their group. Cinda? Or… no. Worgon was watching Anne. Rew turned to the sparring match. Raif had managed to rise again, though his greatsword was trembling in his hands.

"Surely a big strapping lad like you isn't done yet?" called the captain. "When I was your age, I'd spar for hours."

Unable to bend his pride, Raif attacked, and Graewald was waiting for him.

The captain met the blow, except instead of letting the blade slide past him, he held his steel strong and then shoved Raif away with a pointed elbow. Raif struck again and again, and Graewald failed to meet him with his own blade. Instead, he absorbed the blows on his shoulder and arm. Before a third strike, he reached up with a hand and put it on Raif's chest. He pushed the youth back. Raif flailed, nearly flopping onto his bottom, but when he regained his feet, he charged at Graewald, sensing a weakness that was not there.

"Raif!" shouted Cinda, worried her brother might hurt the man, but Raif did not listen.

The captain held his sword low, the sharp point toward the ground. As Raif came close, the captain retreated, raising his blade to where it was waist level with the youth. With his vision obscured by his visor, Raif couldn't see the sword, and that it was pointed just below where his breastplate ended, at his unprotected groin.

"Mother's Blessing," cried Rew.

Without thought, he leapt over the rope barrier, and in three long strides, he arrived in time to shove Raif off his path, sending the boy crashing onto his side.

"What are you doing?" exclaimed Captain Graewald, suddenly standing straight and uninjured.

"I saw what you tried," growled Rew.

"I don't know what you're talking about!" complained Graewald. "Just a friendly sparring match, Ranger. A friendly match, and the lad was getting the best of me! Quite an energetic pup, isn't he? He's worn me out."

"Was it friendly?" asked Rew, turning to look up the short hill where Baron Worgon sat.

"Maybe the ranger cares to spar?" asked the baron loudly. "If I'm not mistaken, that young man was about to trounce my captain. Surely you'll grant Graewald an opportunity to redeem himself?"

"No," said Rew.

Armor rustling, Raif clambered slowly to his feet. "What was the meaning of that, Ranger? I wasn't going to hurt the man."

"I know," snapped Rew.

"Step back. Let us finish," said Raif. "I think I was finally figuring him out. Perhaps some of that training you gave us was paying off, eh? Out of the way, Rew. Let us continue."

"No."

Raif reached up and raised his visor. He stared at Rew in consternation, but he didn't argue.

"The boy's not afraid. Why are you?" asked Captain Graewald.

"I saw what you attempted, Captain," warned Rew. "If I see something similar again, we won't be sparring."

"What—" started Graewald, but he saw the look on Rew's face, and he stopped.

"Give him a go, Captain!" shouted the baron from the hill.

"I don't think he's interested, m'lord," replied Captain Graewald.

"It's an order," replied Baron Worgon.

Captain Graewald shrugged, and then he raised his broadsword.

Rew didn't bother to object. Worgon had given his order, and Graewald wasn't one to ignore a chance to fight. Instead of arguing, Rew reached over his shoulder and drew his longsword.

Before Rew had time to settle his feet, Graewald charged. Rew was unarmored and facing an armored soldier who'd spent over a decade in the baron's service. There was no pretense it was anything other than it was, so Rew didn't bother to hide.

He leapt at Graewald, whose eyes widened behind his visor.

Rew crashed his longsword against the side of the captain's broadsword, shoving the blade away. Then, he kept his momentum until he was toe-to-toe with the bigger man. Graewald swung his head forward, attempting to headbutt Rew with his helmet.

Rew leaned back and then wrapped his free arm around Graewald's, trapping the man's wrist and his sword out of position. Rew stabbed his longsword point-down into the dirt, reached up, and gripped the rim of Graewald's visor.

The big soldier raised his free hand, his gauntleted fist reaching blindly for Rew, unable to see because Rew's hand was in his visor, but the ranger moved quicker. He released the captain's arm with the broadsword and drew his hunting knife. Rew turned, keeping out of Graewald's grasping reach, and shifted his hand to allow room before the soldier's eyes. He put his hunting knife into the gap, the point resting on Graewald's cheek, just a fingernail below the man's eyeball.

Graewald froze.

"I told you I saw what you attempted," whispered Rew, "and you should know, the next time you try and harm the lad or his sister—anyone in our party—I'm going to bury this blade in your skull. I answer to the king, Captain, and him alone. Your baron, the duke, neither of them will say a word if I have to kill you, so before you take another order from that man, think about what it will mean for you personally."

"I've no choice, Ranger," hissed the soldier. "Disobeying the baron means my death."

"Maybe," said Rew, "but who do you think you've got a better chance of getting away from, the baron or me?"

Rew shoved the soldier back and hooked a foot behind the captain's ankle. Graewald fell flat on his back, but before he'd even struck the earth, Rew had turned, pulled his longsword from the dirt, and was pacing quickly to the rope barrier. He hopped over and went straight up the hill to Baron Worgon.

"Try it again, Baron, and I'm not going to spare your man," declared Rew.

"What are you talking about—"

Rew flipped over the table, sending the contents to the side in a shower or crashing crystal and silver. He slapped a palm into the baron's chest, knocking the portly man over in his chair. Rew knelt beside the fallen baron, resting his hand on his longsword, putting the steel point-down in front of the baron's face.

"When we first met in your throne room, you asked me why I was with the children," said Rew. "I told you I'm protecting them. I know you instructed Graewald to injure the lad. Why?"

Baron Worgon's eyes flicked over the hill, and Rew turned to follow the look. Anne was standing with Cinda and Zaine. All three had their arms crossed over their chests in nearly identical, nervous poses. Worgon said, "In war, more men and women die of disease than steel, Ranger. Common soldiers, spellcasters, even the commanders are susceptible to all manner of illness. Nobles like me have died when they did not need to. I told you I've heard rumors of you, and I've heard rumors of your empath as well. A good healer, Ranger, could be worth two or three of my best spell-casters."

Rew snorted.

"The battle with us and Duke Eeron may be quick, but the war after will be long," said Baron Worgon, trying to rise, but Rew held the corpulent man down, flat on his back. "I'd like the empath to join my service, but I wanted to test her skill first."

"She's not going to join you, Worgon," hissed Rew. "You try and injure one of us again, you look at or even think of Anne, and

I'll kill both you and your man." Rew put his finger on the baron's chest, just below the billow of lace at the man's throat. "And don't bother with your high magic, Worgon. I've got a nose for it."

Spluttering, flopping around on his back like a flipped-over turtle, Baron Worgon shrieked, "I've a whole flaming army marching up that road, you fool! I'm the Baron of Yarrow. These are my lands, and you're in the middle of my army. I get what I want here, Ranger. You cannot touch me!"

Rew moved his hand up and grabbed a fistful of the baron's lace. He tugged the portly man off the turf. "Test me, and I'll slit your fat throat, Worgon. It's true that you're the baron of Yarrow, but I'm the King's Ranger."

13

They ate supper in awkward silence.

Rew had directly threatened Baron Worgon and Captain Graewald, but both men knew they deserved it. They'd risked Raif's life to determine just how capable Anne was with the foolish conceit she might consider joining them. It was the sort of thing Vaeldon's nobility did in the secure confines of their keeps, surrounded by stout walls and steel. It was the sort of thing that they rarely suffered for. Suffering was the burden of others, the commoners. But rare did not mean the same thing as never, and any noble of Vaeldon was aware their actions could come back to bite them, and when they did, they were prepared to tuck their tails like cowed dogs. Pride bowed before the need to survive.

Typically, such a comeuppance would be at the hands of a more powerful noble, but every now and then, it came from sharp steel and determination. Both Worgon and Graewald realized that Rew was capable of slaying them and that he was willing to face whatever consequences he faced for such an act. Which, the truth was, may be no consequences at all. He was the king's agent. Against such resolve, there was nothing they could say, nothing they could do, so they did neither. Instead, they ate, and they drank.

Rew scowled across the table at the baron, who was studiously avoiding his gaze. The man was a scoundrel, but even Rew had to admit he wasn't any worse than the rest of them. Sighing, Rew lifted his wine and took a slow sip. Not a big sip, not as much as he wanted, but enough to take the edge off, to slow his heartbeat, to still his hands that twitched, wanting to grab his sword.

Raif, it seemed, was unsure about what had happened, and the boy sat quietly, confused, his eyes darting between Worgon and Rew. During the incident, his vision had been blocked by his visor, and he hadn't noticed Captain Graewald's sword rising to impale him. The women had been watching the fight, but during the heat of the engagement, they weren't experienced enough to have caught Graewald's move. They'd all seen Rew threaten both Graewald and Worgon, though, and they'd been shocked by it. Shocked, until the baron didn't demand Rew be locked in manacles and imprisoned. Worgon had done nothing except to call for his servants to right the table and bring a fresh selection of food and drink.

The children didn't understand the game that was being played, but they'd seen enough to know that they didn't understand, so they kept their lips sealed.

"The Investiture, you understand?" the baron had asked Rew once he'd stood and his servants had brushed off his clothing. "No hard feelings."

"I meant what I said, Worgon," Rew had replied.

The baron had waved off Captain Graewald, who'd been loitering about as if unsure whether he was supposed to continue the fight with the ranger or join him for a glass of wine. The big man had exhaled a sigh of relief when the baron offered Rew a glass. After that, Graewald had disappeared into the camp.

The party joined the baron at the newly set table, and they watched with him as his men streamed into the camp, spreading out, erecting tents, and crowding around growing fires to chase away the autumn chill. Ale barrels were rolled out to strategic points in the camp, and the men clustered around to dip their ration.

Baron Worgon's servants appeared with thick, fur blankets for the women and the baron, but Rew and Raif declined. Night fell, and an extravagant dinner was served to them. All around their table, the sounds of joviality rose from the camping soldiers. The men, just one day outside of Yarrow, still had heads filled with empty promises of loot at the end of the road. It seemed the ale barrels were doing the trick and keeping the illusion going.

Throughout the evening and after a long period of uncomfortable silence, Worgon regaled them with tales of his youth when he was last on campaign. By his telling, it was a lot less comfortable then and a lot more dangerous, though the stories were of stamping out small rebellions or dealing with localities under his domain that had refused to pay their taxes. During the last Investiture, Worgon had been in power, but he'd been a much younger man and firmly beneath the shadow of Duke Eeron. The duke had avoided the swirling fight of succession, and the Eastern Territory had largely been uninvolved.

Rew knew that Worgon hadn't had anything to do with the previous Investiture, which the rotund man only spoke about in hints and innuendo. It seemed to Rew that Baron Worgon had not a concern in the world. There was only one reason he would be so confident, and Rew decided in the face of the man's odd, buoyant mood, he'd challenge him on it.

"Where is Prince Valchon?" asked Rew, breaking his silence after several hours of not speaking.

Worgon gave him a tight smile.

"You don't know," asked Rew, "but you believe he will assist you?"

Nodding, the baron pinched off a piece of sweetbread from his dessert plate and popped it into his mouth. Around the delicacy, he mumbled, "The prince will meet us outside of Spinesend."

"And he'll fight with you to topple the duke?" asked Rew.

"He won't need to," claimed the baron. "I have a plan. We're going to draw Duke Eeron's men outside of the walls where we will crush them. That spellcaster you saw at the head of his forces marching to Falvar is the duke's strongest invoker. The duke himself is a powerful enchanter, but there's nothing he can do to stop my own magic. The man you saw, he is the only one under Eeron's banner with strength to deflect my spells. With him out of the way, no one can stop me."

"If the invoker hasn't returned to Spinesend," remarked Rew.

Worgon shook his head, his white hair waving in the cool wind. "We've days yet, Ranger. The man won't risk returning to Spinesend until he can be certain the children did not flee to Falvar or the lands beyond. That will take time. When he finally hears we are marching, it will be too late. The man, talented as he is, does not have the strength to portal. Only Duke Eeron has developed that skill, but he doesn't have strength to open a portal for more than himself and one or two others. By the time they realize what is happening, it will be too late for Duke Eeron's army."

"The duke won't portal to Falvar to collect his invoker?" pressed Rew.

"He won't," declared Worgon. "Running for help would be an admission that his bloodline is failing. You're not of a noble house, Ranger, but you've been around us enough to know how horrific Duke Eeron will find that thought."

Rew grunted and then asked, "You've strength to take on thousands of Duke Eeron's men?"

"I do, but my magic is wild and unfocused," explained Baron Worgon, twirling a half-empty wine glass. "If Duke Eeron holds his men behind the walls of the city, I cannot risk unleashing my power. There would be too much damage to the structures and the people of Spinesend. What would be the point of conquering the place if its wealth is destroyed in the process? Or worse, if Baron Fedgley is caught in the conflagration. That's the prince's point of view, at least, and I'm his humble servant. He'll be there, and he will see how useful I am. Worst case, Ranger, if Duke

Eeron surprises me with something unexpected, Prince Valchon will slap him down."

"Why are you so certain that the duke will come out to meet you in the field?" probed Rew. "The walls of the city will give him an incredible advantage."

"I told you. He'll look weak if he does not quickly confront us," said Worgon. "During the Investiture, there is nothing worse than looking weak. What would any of the princes think if Duke Eeron did nothing about a hostile army camped outside of his walls? What sort of ally would that make the man if he's afraid to protect his own lands?"

Rew shrugged. In his view, there was far worse than merely looking weak, but he thought it fruitless to mention that to the baron because he did have a point about the way the nobles thought. Clearly, the man was swimming on a tide of confidence, and it would be futile arguing with him. Glancing at Raif, Rew's lips twisted. All of them were overconfident, striding into dangers that they could not conceive.

"And if the mere presence of my army doesn't incite the duke to attack," declared Worgon, gesturing at Raif and Cinda, "then certainly the presence of these two will. How could he not come after us?"

"Bait, again," muttered Cinda.

"Indeed, my dear," admitted the baron, "but for a good cause. You do want your father back, don't you?"

"They're just children, Worgon," said Anne, speaking up for the first time that evening. "You gamble with their lives."

"A small gamble," claimed Worgon, "and my own life will be just as much at risk as theirs. If I was not completely confident we have the better of Duke Eeron, I'd still be barricaded in Yarrow, hoping he would expend himself against Falvar, Prince Valchon, or in some other far away conflict. And if he did not injure himself elsewhere, then I would support him. I'm a proud man, but not too proud to kneel when I'm beat! We've got an opening, though, so we shall take it. When we're successful, the young Fedgleys will be reunited with their father, and I will secure the seat in Spinesend for House Worgon. In months, when Prince Valchon ascends the throne, we'll all be swimming in more spoils than we ever could have imagined."

Raif and Cinda looked hopeful as the baron continued to describe the future of the eastern duchy with him at its head and the Fedgleys restored to their proper place in Falvar. It was obvious Baron Worgon had become enamored with his own sparkling vision of what the future could hold.

As Rew sat and watched the man, his worries began to grow. The backing of Prince Valchon would be significant, but the fact was, the prince was not with them. Perhaps he'd promised to meet them outside of Spinesend, but Baron Worgon was experienced enough to be doubtful. It was as if he'd completely thrown caution to the wind, which did not match with what Rew knew of the man's history or what he'd seen the last decade they'd been neighbors. It was simply unlike Baron Worgon to proceed so recklessly and expose his own neck.

Hours after full dark had fallen across the camp, the soldiers around them continued to revel. Rew stood and waved Anne over to join him at the edge of the candlelight around Baron Worgon's table.

"Tired of his buffoonery as well?" she asked in a low voice.

"Baron Worgon has always been a rather staid man," said Rew. "He struck me as practical on the occasions I had an audience with him, and the younglings described him the same way. Does this... ranting sound like the voice of a practical man to you?"

"The Investiture remakes us all," said Anne.

Rew shook his head, scratching at his beard. "I've been thinking these last hours... Could it be a glamour?"

"What?" Anne laughed.

"I'm serious," said Rew. "Could someone have cast a glamour on the baron and he's now seeing a future which has no chance of coming to pass? Do you think someone could have bewitched him strongly enough to draw him out of Yarrow and onto the road to Spinesend?"

"A glamour that powerful would be highly unusual," said Anne. "I'm sure the baron takes precautions against such. Any man in his position would have a skilled low magician in the court." Anne frowned. "His son, in fact. That man we saw, Fredrick. He's rumored to have incredible skill at low magic. It's why the baron has never loved him, I was told. Worgon believed Fredrick's mother laid with a commoner and that's how he never obtained the same skill as Worgon himself. I'm not sure how he explains their similar appearance... Whatever Worgon's disappointment with Fredrick, though, it'd be unlike a noble not to make use of any available resource. It was clear Worgon does not like him, so there must be a reason he hasn't sent Fredrick away."

"How do you know this?" wondered Rew.

Anne smiled at him. "I wasn't always an innkeeper in Eastwatch."

"But is it possible?" asked Rew, frowning. "Can you determine if it was done? If Fredrick is the one who watches for such chicanery, and he isn't here..."

"When showing a man what he wants to see, even massive illusions are possible," admitted Anne. "Such a glamour would have taken time, though, Rew. It would take weeks, if not longer."

"But it can be done," said Rew, looking back at the table where Baron Worgon was gesticulating grandly. "Can you tell..."

"To be certain whether or not the baron is affected by a glamour, I'd need to establish a bond with him. With a man of his talent, it's likely he could sense something of me just as I gain a sense of him. It's risky, Rew. Even drunk, I think he'd realize what I was doing."

Rew grimaced, thinking how desperately far the baron was willing to go to assess Anne's skill. "Too risky, then."

"What would even be the point?" asked Anne. "Baron Worgon assembling an army and marching must be the last thing that

Duke Eeron wants to happen, and it may very well play out to our advantage."

"Unless Duke Eeron has the exact same plan as Baron Worgon," argued Rew.

"You think Duke Eeron means to catch Worgon in the open?"

Rew shrugged and did not respond.

They returned to the table and watched as Baron Worgon steadily worked his way through a second carafe of wine. Rew and the rest of the party had begun drinking, but as the night wore on, they all stopped. Rew couldn't shake the feeling that something was wrong, and the others picked up on his nervousness. After the scene earlier with Captain Graewald, all of them had already been on edge. Around them in the camp, the last of the soldiers had arrived and were still dipping their rations from the ale barrels. Singing, shouting, and blustery laughter was rising like a tide around them, nearly drowning out their own conversation.

"How much ale did you give the men?" asked Rew, frowning at the dark, smoky camp around them.

Worgon burped and shrugged. He patted his prodigious belly. "I gave them plenty. It's the last night of fun some of them might have. Our plan is a good one, but in war, there are always dangers. Not all of these lads will make it home, Ranger, so let them have their merriment. It's a few days of hard marching after this and then the serious business of conquest. Maybe if you had a little drink yourself, you'd loosen up. It is the Investiture, but that doesn't mean it has to be all darkness and gloom."

Rew did not respond.

Baron Worgon poured himself another wine and then reached over and filled Rew's glass to the brim. Rew scowled at him, and the baron winked, evidently forgetting about the nastiness earlier in the evening.

Down at the base of the hill the baron was camped on, a fight broke out amongst the soldiers. It was lit only by nearby cook fires, and it was over quickly as other men jumped in to pull the combatants apart.

Raising his glass, Worgon bellowed, "That's the fire we need, lads!"

He chided the soldiers below to let the two men back at it, but either they could not hear him or they were ignoring him. Amidst the chaos, it could have been either way. The revelry continued, and Rew began suggesting it was time to retire. Worgon nodded, his jowls trembling with the motion and yelled for his servants to set up a tent for the party.

Rew opened his mouth to object, to claim they could do it themselves or, even better, sleep out in the open, but he settled back and sighed. The camp around them was a swirling mass of noise and smoke, and there'd be no falling asleep in that chaos anytime soon. And with so many drunken soldiers about, it was only sensible for the women to have a tent.

Anne looked across the table at him and shrugged.

In the distance, Rew heard a thin wail and peered out over the camp. The soldiers were stumbling amongst the tents, raising their ales and toasting each other. Thick clusters of them glommed around the ale barrels. Rew saw no disturbances, but given his earlier suspicions, he was nervous. "You hear that, Baron?"

"The men are getting excited," said the baron with a wave of his hand. "Spirits are high before a fight, and hungry dogs are going to bite, Ranger. Mix in enough ale and there's always a scuffle that goes too far on campaign. The captains and my commander will sort it, and if necessary, I'll sit in a quick judgement tomorrow. Could be a good lesson for the rest of our march. In my years, I've found it's best to let the men blow off a little excess steam before they settle down to the business of war. A wild night steadies the nerves."

"Done a lot of campaigning, have you?" retorted Rew.

The baron poured himself another glass of wine.

"How are we to sleep with all of this?" complained Raif, waving his hand around to encompass the carousing soldiers.

"Should have drank more wine, lad," said the baron, chuckling deeply. He raised his own glass. "I'll sleep like a baby tonight."

Captain Graewald suddenly emerged from the darkness like a lich stumbling out from some foggy moor. Rew reached for his weapon but stopped when Graewald scowled at him. The captain turned to his liege and said, "Baron Worgon, the men have had their fun, and I think perhaps we ought to stop up the ale barrels for the evening."

Worgon leaned back toward the dining table and grasped a nearly empty carafe of wine. His glass was still half-full, but he topped it off, shaking out the last few drops and then set the carafe down with a hard thud that threatened to shatter the thick crystal. The baron grinned at the captain and declared, "We've hard times ahead of us, Graewald. Let the men enjoy themselves."

"M'lord, I'm afraid we're going to have a difficult time getting the men marching tomorrow," worried the captain. "A lot of the men have gotten sotted already, and if we go much longer, we won't be able to stop the barrels without open warfare in our own camp. Let's batten down the hatches, so to speak, before it's too late."

"The men are ready to fight!" said Worgon, raising his glass.

Grimacing, the captain opened his mouth to reply when another shrill cry cut through the general revelry.

"See!" said Worgon, a grin plastered on his red face. "This is what we need, Graewald. That's the spirit we want boiling inside of these men as we face battle. I want them thirsting for blood!"

"You know I never back from a fight, m'lord, but these men are acting like they're marching to a tavern brawl," said the captain. "Passion is good but keeping your wits about you is better."

Worgon drank his wine.

Graewald shot Rew a glance and raised his hands as if to ask for help. The ranger shook his head. He certainly wasn't going to assist the belligerent captain.

"Do you have physicians in the camp?" Anne inquired.

Graewald nodded, but added, "Of course, if they're as drunk as the rest of the men, I'm not sure how useful they'll be."

"Maybe I should go…" began Anne.

Rew reached over and put a hand on her arm. "No. We stay together."

"You heard that scream," said Anne. "Someone out there is hurt. They could use my help."

"Your help, eh?" slurred Worgon. "I'll stab one of 'em myself just to see what you're capable of, Empath." He winked. "I want to know if the rumors are true. My physicians don't believe it, but I… I'm a…"

Rew glared at the baron, whose sentence had trailed off half-forgotten. The portly man was swaying slightly and had a sly grin on his face.

Another cry rose on the night air. From down below them, Rew heard a nasty laugh as someone thought it amusing a peer had been injured or killed. It was madness, the drunkenness happening around them. So many men, all of them heavily armed, allowed to get so intoxicated… Even if they weren't marching to war, it was terribly irresponsible. It'd happened so quickly, as the sun had set, gone from… Rew frowned, looking around at the camp.

There was another cry, and Captain Graewald bit off a strangled curse. The big blond man glared balefully at the baron. Fortunately for the captain, Worgon was too far gone in his own cups to see the disgust in the captain's stare. "M'lord, if this continues, we won't have men left to fight for us when we reach Spinesend."

Baron Worgon, his wine cup at his lips, waved a hand dismissively.

Rew clambered onto the table, turning slowly, looking out past the hill they were situated on.

"Ranger!" barked the baron, trying to sound angry as Rew's feet disturbed his plates, but a giggle spoiled the effect.

"What is it?" Captain Graewald asked Rew.

"I don't know, but this night is not right," replied Rew. "Can you feel it?'

Graewald gripped his broadsword and clenched his other fist. "I don't know what you're talking about, Ranger, but I know we're making ourselves trouble we don't need. King's Sake, I tried to find the commander, but he's nowhere near the tent, and he's not up here. If the Baron won't—What is it, Ranger?"

"A glamour," said Rew, looking from the baron and then out to the darkness around their camp.

"What?" asked Graewald. "I don't understand."

"Are you sure, Rew?" asked Anne.

"There are no stars," said Rew suddenly. "There are no stars, no moon, and I can't see a damned thing past the edge of our encampment. Graewald, what is the watch rotation?"

"Two dozen men rotating every two hours. Half of them posted, the other half walking in pairs in a circuit around the camp," answered the captain.

Rew grunted. It wasn't a terrible system, except… except someone had blocked the stars. Someone had cast a glamour over their entire camp. Before that, they'd gotten to the baron, drawn him out from behind his walls and into the night where the fool had allowed his entire army to drink themselves into a stupor. Grimly, Rew wondered if that had been part of the glamour, or if the man was simply an imbecile.

"Captain Graewald," said Rew, "I expect an imminent attack. Prepare your men."

"Hold on!" blurted the baron. "Hold on right there. These are my men, my army. You can't command them!"

Graewald, ignoring his liege, asked Rew, "What will we be facing?"

"I don't know, Captain," responded Rew, his voice tight with worry. "The only magic they've shown is low. It's of little use for offensive spells, but Captain, if they've cast a glamour wide enough to cover our entire encampment…"

Captain Graewald nodded and turned, shouting to the men below, looking for his fellow captains, and trying to find the horn player who should be stationed near the baron. When he found the man, a boy really, Graewald gripped him by the scruff of the neck and demanded the boy begin playing 'to arms'.

The hornblower, shrinking from the giant, heavily armored captain and looking nervously at the portly, drunk baron, quickly decided to comply with the captain's orders. Thin notes barely pierced the cacophony of the brouhaha down in the camp.

Rew, still on the table, watched as the closest soldiers laughed, thinking it was some joke or that their hornblower was drunk, too, until they saw Captain Graewald's face. Slowly, the nearby men began to scramble about, stumbling from the ale barrels as the captain charged into the thick of things, shouting encouragement. The men, feet clumsy from drink, careened about, falling against tents, scrambling for their weapons. Farther out, past the range of the captain's voice, the revelry continued unabated.

"It's too late," muttered Rew, jumping down off the table. "We're too late."

"Too late for what?" asked Cinda.

"Gather your things," instructed Rew, moving to the base of the hill where the servants had been erecting their tent. Luckily, they'd been invited to the baron's table immediately upon arrival at the camp, and none of them had taken time to unpack their things. Rew warned the others, "Weapons out. No matter what happens, follow me."

Nodding, the rest of the group gathered their weapons and packs. They stayed on his heels as he climbed back to the top of the hill. Even Raif, it seemed, had decided that for once, staying behind the ranger was a good idea.

Baron Worgon snapped at them when they reappeared, his jowls shaking with rage, his wine glass sloshing in his trembling fist. "What is the meaning of this, Ranger? Are you attempting to take over my army?"

"Any moment now, Baron..." said Rew, looking around and

realizing that not a man was coming to the baron for instructions. "Any moment now, we're going to be attacked."

Down in the camp, he could see the wave of activity that frothed in Captain Graewald's wake. There were other spots of loose organization where other captains must have heard the horn and begun calling to their men, but the bulk of the army was still lost in their cups and their amusements.

Around Graewald, some of the soberer soldiers began peeling off, headed to the outskirts of the camp, and the captain turned to go toward the command tent. Rew could see the large soldier's blond hair bobbing as he pushed his way through the men. At the command tent, a cluster of officers stood, arms over their chests, confusion on their faces as they looked toward the hornblower, who was still furiously blasting out the alarm.

"Worgon," said Rew, "your commander will need you."

"Need me?" slurred the baron. "He doesn't need me, Ranger! I'm the one who needs him."

Rew blinked at the baron, thinking that perhaps in his intoxicated state, the baron had just accidentally said the truest thing since they'd met him. Rew shook his head and pointed to the command tent. "He's down there. You should go to him."

Spluttering and stumbling to his feet, the baron hissed, "I'll do that. I don't know what you're up to, but—"

Rew gave the baron a gentle shove to the back to get him started, and the round man tripped over his own slippers, fell, and rolled down the side of the hill.

"Oops," said Rew as the baron flopped to a stop two dozen paces below them. Some of his guards bent to help him, but most of them cackled uproariously at the baron's flailing attempts to stand.

"Rew, what is going on?" asked Anne.

"You heard those screams? They were from far off, likely the scouts on patrol. I suspect they were taken out so a force could organize to attack underneath the cover of the glamour. Any moment now..." said Rew. He kept turning, studying the camp.

He pointed to the north, where the fewest number of soldiers stood between them and the darkness beyond. "There, I hope. When all breaks loose, we're going north. Stay on my heels and keep moving."

"Wait, how do you know—" began Cinda.

"Can't you see the glamour?" Rew asked, gesturing above them. "Not the spell itself but the effect. There were clouds above when we stopped for the day but not complete coverage. We saw the gleam of the moon on those clouds after the sunset, remember? Right now, there's not a trace of light from anywhere outside of this camp. Someone has cast a pall of darkness over us, and there's only one reason they would do that."

Uncomfortably, Cinda looked above them. She nodded curtly. "We'll be right behind you."

At the bottom of the hill, the baron had finally regained his feet, and he was admonishing his soldiers and telling them to run up and arrest Rew and the others. The soldiers looked hesitant, but they'd seen the baron tumble down the hill after a push from Rew. No matter how drunk you were, throwing a noble down a hill was illegal, particularly while inside of that noble's fiefdom. Watching the soldiers, Rew wondered if he might be able to claim it was king's business. The soldiers wouldn't believe that, but it might give them an excuse not to act rashly. Whatever was about to happen, Rew certainly didn't intend to face it in manacles. The prospect of fighting off these men wasn't much more attractive.

Reluctantly, the soldiers below started walking his way, but halfway up, they stopped. There was a clash of steel off in the distance, and screams of pain cut through those of mad glee. The baron's elite guard was soberer than the rest of their compatriots, and they were veterans. They understood what those sounds meant.

"I don't see anything yet," muttered Raif.

"The darkness is closing in," said Rew, pointing toward where they could hear the conflict. "The glamour is overtaking the edge of the battle."

"Should we run?" asked Zaine. Her bow was in her hand, and an arrow was nocked, but she had nothing to shoot at.

Rew shook his head. "Not yet."

"Why north?" questioned Raif, looking nervously all around them.

Rew shrugged. "If it is Duke Eeron attacking, then I suspect he'd have arrayed the bulk of his men to the south to cut off Worgon's escape. If they mean to eradicate the baron's forces, the first order of business is making sure the army can't run back to Yarrow."

"So what do we do?" demanded Zaine.

Rew drew his longsword. "Like I said, stay behind me, and we go north toward Spinesend."

"We know," muttered Raif, raising his greatsword. "Always stay behind you."

"Right," said Rew. Then, he was hit by a visceral wave of utter, bone-chilling, deathly cold.

❧ 14 ❧

R ew was flung backward. He stumbled into Anne as a torrential blast of bitter cold assailed him. He raised his arms in front of himself and tried to ground his body in the world, but they were far from his world, and instead of the peace of the wilderness, he found himself clutching at the chaos of battle erupting around them. He teetered, his body and soul scoured by the relentless blast of magic, until he broke through the madness and found the cool calm of the natural world outside of their camp. He clutched it tight and withstood the torrent of death.

For one hundred paces in front of him, a terrible path was blazed through the soldiers, leaving a carpet of dead, frozen bodies. Scores of them, lying twisted and in anguish, ice-cold.

From the darkness at the edge of the camp, a man emerged clad in scarlet robes. His hands were raised above his head, and swirling clouds of green-tinged white smoke churned around him. On his chest, a gleaming silver pendant shone in the light of the fires that still survived outside the path of destruction he'd wrought.

"King's Sake," growled Rew. "Necromancers. Zaine, can you shoot that man with an arrow?"

The necromancer strode forward confidently, his lips moving

as if he was intoning the words to another terrible spell, but they could not hear him over the screaming of the nearby soldiers who had escaped the initial blast.

"Zaine," barked Rew, "shoot him!"

No arrows flew from behind, and Rew didn't want to turn from the necromancer to look at the young thief, so he strode forward, taking advantage of the open space the man's magic had torn through the camp.

The necromancer saw the approaching ranger. Swinging his arms like he was raising a wood axe, the necromancer brought his fists around and flung a wave of freezing air at Rew. It was the breath of death.

Rew saw it coming this time. He crossed his arms and rooted himself to the earth. Like an icy stream, the spell rushed over him, breaking on the rock of his resistance. He took another step forward, and two more men emerged from the darkness behind the first necromancer. Both of them were adorned in the same crimson robes and were already clutching trailing fistfuls of vapor.

"Blessed Mother," snapped Rew. The second attack had not been strong, but three trained necromancers in the midst of a field of dead bodies was not something to trifle with. He glanced over his shoulder to see Zaine standing open-mouthed in shock, her bow forgotten in her grip.

Rew turned to the necromancers striding purposefully toward him. It seemed they'd seen him resist their spells. The breath of death swirled around the three of them, trailing in the wake of each spellcaster like a bridal veil.

"Cinda!" snapped Anne. "Death's grip!"

"W-What?" stammered the noblewoman.

"These men are weak, barely trained," cried Anne. "Use the death's grip spell. Draw your power from what they're holding. With necromantic high magic, the strongest caster controls the flow."

"I-I don't…" stammered Cinda.

"Now!" demanded Anne. "Take their power. Do not let them cast at us again!"

Rew kept trotting toward the necromancers, ignoring what was happening behind him. He'd seen the girl's pitiful casting, and he wasn't going to trust his life to it.

A howling wave of armed men emerged from the darkness fifty paces behind the necromancers. They were brandishing swords and axes, and they wore the ochre livery of Duke Eeron's army. They fell upon the stunned soldiers of Baron Worgon who were cowering in fear from the necromancers.

The glamour that encapsulated the campsite fell away. The shine of the moon and the stars felt like a brilliant dawn after the unnatural darkness, but it revealed a terrible truth. Worgon's surprised, drunken army was surrounded.

Duke Eeron's men charged into the fray, their weapons rising and falling on the stumbling, startled soldiers of Baron Worgon. In moments, gleaming blades were coated in gore, but even Duke Eeron's men avoided the necromancers, running wide around the three, spreading into the camp far away from those cold husbands of death.

"Death's grip, Cinda! Now!"

The three necromancers as one drew back their hands, then they flung the breath of death at Rew. He grimaced, holding up his arms, hoping that in the chaos of the battle he could anchor himself hard enough to survive the combined blast unscathed. Anne was right; they were poorly trained, but all three of them were focused solely on Rew, and the power of departing souls flowed to them like the tide.

Seconds before the twisting tendrils of the breath of death reached him, Rew felt the strange heat of death's flame building behind his back. He hurled himself out of the way, rolling across thawing bodies and shattered tents that had been caught in the first attack from the necromancers.

Above him, right where he'd been standing, a luminous, char-treuse tongue of fire lanced toward the necromancers, cutting through their breath of death and incinerating one of the hapless men in a blink. His flesh boiled and sloughed away, and before Rew could draw a startled gasp, only a skeleton stood in the place the necromancer had been.

The skeleton, animated by the power of the spell, teetered, the soul of the man bound to its old frame. The man's soul was not properly tied, though, and Cinda clearly had no idea how to direct it, so in the space of half a dozen steps, the skeleton collapsed, just one more body lying on the field of battle.

Rew sprang to his feet, and without looking over his shoulder, he charged.

The remaining two necromancers were staring in horror at the fallen skeleton of their deceased peer, and they didn't see Rew coming until he was on them. His longsword swept in a powerful horizontal arc, taking both of the men through the neck with one blow.

As the necromancers' severed heads thumped to the ground, Rew turned to see his companions hurrying after him, Raif carrying Cinda who appeared to have fallen into a daze. Zaine was looking around as if she'd finally decided to use her bow, but now she had no obvious targets. Anne was tight-lipped, but she wasn't putting hands on Cinda, so Rew had to assume the girl was healthy enough they could keep moving.

Around them, the clash of battle rose. Rew shouted, "Raif, pass her to Anne. I'm going to need you."

The big youth placed his sister's feet on the ground and draped her arms over the empath's shoulder. Cinda's head lolled bonelessly, but Rew thought he heard her mumbling something, and while her knees wobbled, they didn't buckle beneath her. Zaine took her other side, and awkwardly helped while still holding her bow. Supported by the other women, Cinda could stand.

Raif drew his greatsword and stood beside Rew. Ahead of them, the way was still open, filled with the devastation of the necromancers' initial attack. It would not last long. Already, rampaging soldiers had spotted them, and Duke Eeron's men were veering toward the party. Zaine fired an arrow at one of the men. It clanged off his helmet, snapping the man's head to the side. He shook it off, cursing.

"Raif," instructed Rew, speaking loudly over the cacophony of the battle, "you and I are going to smash a hole through their lines. We have to do enough damage to get them out of the way, and then, we keep moving. Remember, we're not trying to win this fight. We just need to open a path we can run the party through. Zaine, watch our backs. Use your arrows to slow them down. Tell me if they're chasing us."

"There have to be thousands of them," hissed the thief.

"We just have to get through this bunch," said Rew. He turned, looking at a pack of approaching soldiers bedecked in Duke Eeron's ochre, their swords coated in the crimson of Baron Worgon's soldiers' blood. "If we get into the countryside and have enough distance, I can cover our passage, but we have to get through first."

Rew and Raif led the way, headed toward a wall of Duke Eeron's steel. Hundreds of men were appearing out of the countryside, and Rew could hear that behind them, all around the camp, there were thousands more.

The soldiers were naturally hesitant about rushing into the site of the necromancers' attack, which helped Rew and the others move freely, but it also made them visible in the flickering lights of the campfires and the blazes that sprang up amongst the tents as men fought and scattered flame. The clear night sky cast a cool glow that was nearly blinding after the black of the glamour. Silver and orange illuminated the chaos around them. They charged through a hellscape of frozen, broken bodies, hearts racing, breath coming in tight, panicked bursts. Ahead, a squad of the duke's men broke off and ventured into the desolate patch Rew and the others were racing across.

"Knock them back on their heels, and I'll clean them up," instructed Rew.

Raif hoisted his enchanted greatsword onto his shoulder and trotted out to meet the soldiers. The boy was either too foolish to be afraid, or he was caught in a battle fervor. Whispering a prayer to the Blessed Mother, Rew hoped it was the second. They were surrounded in the midst of a battle, and their only hope was rash action. Luckily, that was Raif's specialty.

Five of the soldiers approached, showing no caution as around them, their army raged through the unprepared forces of Baron Worgon. Their leader's plan had worked, and the course of the battle was already clear. All that was left was completing the slaughter.

Raif didn't know that, though, and as the soldiers came into range, he swung with all of his might. It was an awful blow and a strategy that would surely result in his demise had Rew not been standing behind him.

The tip of Raif's enchanted greatsword cleaved through the limbs of two of the men, shattering the steel of one of their swords brought up to defend and lodging in the second man's abdomen, crashing through the chainmail that protected him. The soldier's eyes grew wide in shock that the blow had carried through his partner, and his senseless hands groped the steel of Raif's greatsword. The other three soldiers had leapt back, avoiding the powerful strike and stumbling on the uneven mass of dead bodies that had fallen in the necromancers' attack.

Rew flowed into the wake of Raif's swing. He struck at the men before they had a chance to recover, sliding one thrust over a man's chain hauberk into the soldier's neck. Another, Rew whipped his longsword around and clipped the man right beneath his helmet, sending the metal cap spinning away along with a shower of blood. The third soldier began to recover, swinging his sword wildly at the ranger. Rew ducked, and when he rose, he stabbed the man in the eye.

Raif, gaining his footing after his initial wild swing, lunged at another wave of Duke Eeron's men. The soldiers, having watched their five companions fall beneath the nobleman's and the ranger's blades, were not as eager to engage. They retreated, and Raif pursued, wheeling his greatsword in giant, sweeping strokes.

A soldier raised his own blade to meet the nobleman's, and the lesser steel shattered beneath the weight of the enchanted greatsword. Cursing, the soldier backpedaled, and Raif came after him. He hauled back to chop at the man, but a second soldier stepped in and thrust at the nobleman. Raif staggered, the blow landing solidly on his ribs, but not piercing the steel breastplate he still wore from sparring with Captain Graewald.

Before the soldiers could attack again, Rew was in front of Raif, forcing the men away, giving the nobleman time to recover. Rew caught a swing on the edge of his longsword, turned it, and swiped his weapon against the hilt of his attacker's sword, stripping it from the startled soldier's hands.

Rew punched the man in the face, then reached out, grabbed another man by the throat, and threw him to the side. He dodged as a soldier came charging at him and kicked the man's knee, cracking the bone.

Hundreds of paces behind them, near the command tent, a violent explosion roared, drowning out the sounds of fighting all around them. Rew felt the heat from the blast against the back of his neck. He spun. Debris and bodies flew through the air, raining around the camp like hail scattering before a sudden winter storm. Another detonation ripped the night, fifty paces to the side of the first, and men on both sides of the conflict screamed in terror, rushing away from the magical detonations.

The entire camp was turning into a massive, moving battle, as no one wanted to be near what was happening around the command tent. They kept fighting as they moved away, though, afraid to turn their backs to the high magic or to the enemy.

Knots of Baron Worgon's men found their peers and guarded each other's sides as they struggled to fight free. Duke Eeron's men, holding a huge numerical advantage but no longer the advantage of surprise, smothered Worgon's forces in some areas and were beaten back in others.

Rew led his party through the chaos. Tents and piles of supplies were burning; bodies littered the ground like branches after a tornado. Men, covered in gleaming steel, sometimes in blood, flashed in and out of the light of the fires, attacking or running.

Zaine held an arrow nocked, but she didn't fire at anyone, having difficulty telling which side was which in the smoke and the darkness.

Rew and Raif tried to keep the soldiers away from their party, but some would randomly stumble close, and they would fight. Most of the time, the soldiers were happy to avoid the small group that did not seem affiliated with either side of the battle. Every dozen steps the party took, another eruption would shake the camp, and they'd hear pained screams as men's bodies were torn apart.

Near the edge of the encampment, Rew held out his hand to stop the younglings and Anne. Thirty paces in front of them, half a dozen dark shapes darted across the ground, their chittering calls the only thing that had warned him of their approach. He called to the others, "Imps."

The imps passed them, eagerly streaking into the battle. Rew saw them tearing through the ranks of soldiers, headed toward the command tent. Some conjurer had sent his pets to hunt for Baron Worgon, guessed Rew, and he certainly wasn't going to stop them. The baron had to be the one responsible for the intermittent explosions. By setting them off in the heart of his camp, the man must be killing as many of his own soldiers as the enemy's. The baron, drunk on wine and fear, was lashing out wildly, not caring what devastation he caused.

"There!" said Rew, pointing in the direction the imps had come. The creatures, with their talons and teeth, had frightened Duke Eeron's men out of their way, and there was still a clear path where Rew and the others could sneak through the lines.

Rew shoved a soldier aside then had to pause and bury his longsword in the man's guts when the soldier tried to fight back.

Yanking his blade free, Rew stepped over the body and kept them moving. Near the edge of the fight, far enough away from the explosions that men weren't running in terror and close enough to freedom that Rew could smell the clean air, they were surrounded by half a dozen of Duke Eeron's soldiers.

Zaine released her arrow, and miraculously, the steel tip punched into a soldier's throat. He fell to his knees, and Rew nudged Raif forward to knock a hole in the ring of men where the one had collapsed.

The nobleman, twirling his huge greatsword above his head, began laying about with it. Anne and Zaine, still supporting Cinda, followed in Raif's wake, just far enough behind the big fighter that they avoided his greatsword.

Raif struck a soldier in the arm, crunching through chainmail to find flesh and shatter the bone. The man wailed, falling away, but another smashed his sword across Raif's back. Zaine rammed the end of her bow into the eye of Raif's attacker, and the party was clear of the soldiers, Raif leading them into the night.

Rew brought up the rear, defending furiously against three men who came after them. One thrust at him, and he stepped aside, gripping the man's wrist and hauling on it, directing the blow into the unprotected hip of another soldier. The ranger swung his longsword over the head of the man whose wrist he held, killing a third soldier, then brought his knee up, catching the trapped man on the nose. He let go, and the soldier slumped down, clutching his ruined face.

Seeing no one coming and no one paying attention to them in the insanity of the battle, Rew scooped up Cinda and started to jog away from the fight, taking the party past the road into the open land around the camp. With the shining moon overhead, he had no trouble seeing, though Anne and the others seemed to as they offered a constant litany of curses as they tripped and stumbled.

Cinda cradled in his arms, Rew began whispering a rolling incantation. He felt weariness settle into him, as if his strength was draining out with each of his steps. His magic, flowing out and around him, spread to encompass the party, drawing the darkness around them and clinging to the ground they walked across, obscuring the tracks that they left.

The fog of concealment would hold over their trail but not for long. Hopefully long enough that they could gain distance between themselves and the camp. If there were any decent trackers in Duke Eeron's army, they would have hell sorting through the mess of footprints that must be scattered all around the campsite. If they could somehow sort it out and began following the party across the countryside, well, then Rew and the companions would have a problem.

But Rew had no reason to believe the attack on the camp was directed at the younglings. Duke Eeron wanted them, certainly, but he might not have known the children were with Worgon. Planning the ambush and the glamours would have taken longer than the time the children had been in Yarrow. Of course, once Duke Eeron did learn they'd been with Worgon, Rew had no doubt the duke would set his hounds on their scent.

THEY RAN, TRIPPED, AND SCRAMBLED FOR TWO LEAGUES BEFORE Cinda finally began to stir in Rew's arms. She blinked up at him and worked her jaw, as if learning to use it for the first time. She pulled loose a hand and clasped her head with it.

Rew kept going, afraid to slow, terrified that if he stopped, he wouldn't get moving again. The strain of fleeing in the night, he could handle. Even carrying the slender girl was a burden he could shoulder for hours, but doing it while maintaining a fog of concealment around them was taking all that he had. It was as if he'd had to peel his mind in two, one repeating his incantation, the other focusing on putting one foot in front of the other and not stumbling in the dark, pitching both himself and the noblewoman onto the ground.

Finally, Cinda was able to croak, "I guess we escaped?"

"We're trying to," said Anne in a low voice, barely loud enough for Cinda to hear. The empath came to walk beside them and touched Rew's arm. "How are you holding up?"

He shrugged, lifting Cinda with the movement, but did not respond. He had to keep repeating his spell, or it would fail, and if Duke Eeron's men were close enough, the group would be exposed.

"Can you walk?" Anne asked Cinda.

"I—maybe in a little bit," responded the noblewoman, stretching her leg out past Rew's arm. She looked up at the ranger's face. "Sorry. My legs feel like cold gravy."

"You did well," said Anne. "That... that wasn't the death's grip spell I suggested, but it was good."

"I don't even know what I did," responded Cinda. "It was like I was shoving my hands into an icy stream, grasping for a bar of wet soap with frozen fingers. It kept slipping from me, but all of a sudden, a torrent of power surged through my body. It felt like it was filling my heart and lungs to bursting, pulsing out into the rest of me. My fingers were burning, and I had to get it away, so I cast it at those men."

Anne nodded. "Your family and Baron Worgon, through intent or incompetence, have done you a disservice. They attempted to train you as an invoker, like your mother, but it's clear you've an affinity for necromancy. That power you felt was the cloud of departing souls freed from their bodies during the battle. You were able to tap into their strength, wresting it from the other necromancers, and the results were obvious. You have talent, lass, and if we can teach you the skill to control it, you will be a potent force."

"The power of the departing souls?" whispered Cinda. "I— You're saying I made use of those men's souls? The dying soldiers?"

"You're a natural," said Anne, "and it's a good thing, too. I'm not certain we would have walked out of there so easily without you plowing the way for us."

"So easily?" hissed Raif from behind them.

"I didn't have to heal you this time," quipped Anne.

They trudged on, lost in the hours, until Zaine noticed, "There's a structure up there. A barn, I think. It looks dark, but that's a good thing, isn't it?"

"Rew," asked Anne, "shall we take a moment to rest? We have to pause sooner or later, and from up there, we'll have a clear view of the way we came. Dawn is just an hour or two away, and there's sense in finding a place out of sight where we can rest and watch to see if anyone followed us."

The ranger nodded but did not respond. Like a plodding beast of burden, he turned, shuffling toward the hill Zaine pointed to. He glanced up, seeing the silhouette of a building and nothing more, but he trusted the young thief's vision more than his own. He tried to gesture with his hands, shifting Cinda awkwardly.

Zaine asked, "You want me to scout?"

He nodded again.

Swallowing, Zaine looked at the others and said, "Stop five hundred paces short of the barn, and I'll find you there."

"If you run into trouble, shout," suggested Anne. "We don't want to give ourselves away, but if you need us, then we're already in trouble."

Wordlessly, Zaine flitted away, quickly vanishing into the gloom ahead of them.

❧ 15 ❧

R ew woke with a start. The air was cold and his cloak had fallen open as he'd slumbered. Around him, clustered in the corner of the abandoned barn, were Raif, Cinda, Anne, and Zaine. Rew frowned. The four of them were asleep, as he had been, which meant that no one was on watch.

Silently, he rose and moved to the cracked doorway that they'd slipped through in the hour before dawn. Drained from covering their flight with his magic and carrying Cinda, Rew had collapsed and almost immediately fallen asleep. He'd thought the others were discussing setting a watch, but he realized now, if he'd been that exhausted, they wouldn't have been in much better condition. They had no magic to maintain as they ran, but Cinda had cast plenty of her own during the battle. Raif had been in the thick of it, and none of their party had the stamina to continue hiking for very long after a sleepless night.

But no one had found them, it seemed, and as Rew peered with one eye through the gap in the door, he didn't see any throngs of soldiers covering the countryside. He didn't see any trackers following their path. He didn't see anyone at all.

He waited, listening and extending his senses. Even in the forest where his connection to the world was strongest, he could only gather vague impressions, but here, he felt nothing at all which could be construed as a threat. There was little plant life other than the grass that covered the low, sweeping hills. He detected no animal life larger than a bird or a mouse. Glancing at the others to see they still slept, he gently shoved on the ancient door, cracking it open a little more, and he slipped out into the sunlight.

It was cold, the weight of autumn fully upon them, but the sky was clear, and the sun hung huge and yellow overhead. Both appeared faded, as if they'd been scrubbed on the washboard too many times. The natural world had been drawn upon. Someone had pulled through their connection to the world to cast the glamour the night before. Rew shivered from the air and from the knowledge of how much strength it would have taken to pull so much from their surroundings. It implied both a sensitivity to the world and a mind-boggling power over it.

Rew turned from the sky and circled the abandoned barn. The grasses around them, not as lush as those in the barrowlands, were already turning yellow to match the pale glow of the sun. There were no trees nearby, just the grass and long rows of fallow fields that some forgotten farmer had dug into the infertile soil.

A league to the south was the road that ran between Yarrow and Spinesend. Several leagues to the north and in the west, the Spine stretched across the horizon, passing beyond his vision to the tip of the range, where Spinesend sat at the foot of the mountain like some brooding gargoyle guarding the entry to the Eastern Territory.

Pulling his cloak tight around himself, thinking he should have bought a warmer one in Yarrow, Rew circled the hill. The road and the Spine passed west and out of sight. Days from their position was Spinesend. Several hours behind them was the site of the battle. Considering what he'd seen as they'd fled, Rew was confident Baron Worgon's men had been slaughtered. It was possible a few had escaped, but since none of them appeared to be roaming the hills nearby, and there was no sign of the duke's forces hunting them, Rew guessed the survivors would be very few.

His magic had held; that was clear. If it hadn't, there would be pursuit. They hadn't stumbled far enough the night before to completely evade any patrols Duke Eeron sent after them. Rew's magic had obscured their flight and saved them, but it wouldn't keep the hounds away forever. Whether from captives taken after the battle or when Duke Eeron moved against Yarrow, someone was going to spill the story that Raif and Cinda had been in the baron's company. Would Duke Eeron expect them to be so bold as to continue their journey to Spinesend? Or would he think they'd go into hiding after seeing the duke's might?

Rew couldn't guess what Duke Eeron might think, but he knew what the children would want to do. Sighing, he turned back to the barn. Enough sleep or not, they had to get up, and they had to move. They might have no allies and no plan, but they had a mission.

When Rew returned to the barn, he bustled about, making enough noise to wake the others. Anne rose wordlessly and began checking on everyone's health, though Rew was certain she would have done the same before they'd all fallen asleep. Once she'd determined that no new injuries had somehow occurred during their slumber, she prepared a cold meal. There was no need to discuss whether it was appropriate for a fire. No matter how much Rew wanted a cup of coffee or the others wanted something warm in their bellies, it would be reckless to tear apart the barn and raise a plume of smoke signaling their position and leaving signs that they'd camped there.

The younglings remained quiet, but Rew suspected they had questions bubbling under the surface. When the shock wore off, when they could move past the horror of the battle, they would consider what was next. For now, their thoughts would be riven with images of bodies obliterated by magic and cut open by steel. He thought the night before had been the first time that any of the children had killed a person.

Rew could only recall some of the details of his first. It had been a long time ago, and while he hated to acknowledge it, killing got easier. He remembered even fewer details about the second, and at some point, he'd lost count. It shouldn't get easier. Death was the same horrible truth no matter how many times one brought it. A life, full of promise, was ended. The familiar sickening coil of guilt wormed through his stomach, but he'd learned to ignore it, or to live with it when he couldn't. If the children survived the Investiture, they would as well.

King's Sake, he could use an ale.

Rew squatted down in front of the younglings while Anne prepared the food. He told them, "It is not your fault. You did nothing wrong."

"I—I took the power of people's souls," whispered Cinda, staring down at her hands. "I used it to… I killed a man. I burned him. I—What happened to him? He—He was… animated."

"You saved us," said her brother, putting a hand on his sister's shoulder.

"I'm a necromancer!" exclaimed Cinda, her voice loud in the abandoned barn. "I held that man's soul. After he was dead, I kept him here!"

"You released the power," said Rew. "You did not bind that man to his corporeal body. You borrowed the souls of the others only and then granted them rest. You only killed to protect us."

Cinda shook her head, unable to meet anyone's eyes. "I felt that man lingering here on this plane. He was in pain, tied to his skeletal remains! Bound tightly or not, that is what I did to him. I kept him here. There are tales of horrible men and women who bound the souls of others, who—"

"You are just like Father," retorted Raif.

A tear welled in her eye and then dripped down Cinda's cheek.

"What?" asked Raif, staring at her. "What?"

"Like Father," she snapped. "I'm not sure that is a good thing. Why did Father keep the stories of our family from us if it's something to be proud of? I'd rather be some commoner with no magic at all than—I didn't mean it like that, Raif. I didn't—"

Raif stood, his jaw set, his eyes hard. He turned and walked to Anne. The empath handed him a roll of bread stuffed with cold sausage and cheese.

"You have power that can be used for terrible purposes," said Rew quietly, leaning toward Cinda, "but it is not what you are capable of that defines you. It is what you do. If you use necromancy to bind souls of your service, to steal power, to slaughter and bathe in the blood of innocents, then yes, you'll be like those terrible men and women you are thinking of. If you use your strength to help others, to fight atrocity, then you will not. The choice is yours. There are necromancers on both sides of history, Cinda. Both good and evil."

Cinda blinked at him.

Rew stood, stretching his back where it was sore from sleeping slumped over in the corner. "You have a choice. Always remember that."

"Duke Eeron was behind the capture of our father," declared Raif, gesturing with his roll from the other side of the abandoned barn. "He was marching against Falvar, and we can only imagine what he did there. He ambushed Baron Worgon and killed his men with no warning, no quarter. Duke Eeron is an evil man, and those who choose to serve him are evil as well. I do not feel any guilt for doing what we had to do last night, and I feel no guilt for what we'll have to do to free Father and secure the barony. I regret that violence is necessary, but it's men like Duke Eeron who make it so. It's not us, Cinda."

Rew glanced at Anne, and she shrugged.

It was more complicated than that. Duke Eeron had moved against his bannermen, true enough, but both of them had been plotting against the duke as well. They were equally guilty in Rew's view. All nobles were, but he wasn't going to tell Raif that. The nobleman just wanted to recover his father. He just wanted to return to what his life had been. It wasn't going to happen, but it wouldn't hurt the boy to keep dreaming. For a while, at least.

"Right," said Zaine, startling everyone. "How do we get out of this?"

Grinning, Rew picked up a sausage from Anne, and he pointed north then swung southwest with it. "That's the direction the Spine thrusts toward Spinesend. Assuming the nobles in our party have had no change of plans, that's still the place we need to go. Frankly, after what we've seen the last several days, I don't think it's much more treacherous than anywhere else we could set our path."

"We have not changed our minds," stated Raif.

"The roads will be too dangerous," said Rew. "There are far too many people looking for you, and we're not lucky enough to keep slipping away unscathed. That leaves travel across the open land, or we can move into the lower elevations of the Spine and work through the mountains."

"The Spine doesn't seem like it'd be easy travel," remarked Cinda.

"It would not be," agreed Rew.

"From what I recall of our flight last night," said Zaine, "there's nothing but grass and low hills for leagues around us."

"The terrain is quite flat, and there's almost no cover," acknowledged Rew.

"Slow travel or dangerous travel," mused Raif. "Neither choice sounds very good."

"It's all dangerous, is it not?" asked Zaine.

Rew, chewing on the link of sausage, swallowed his bite and responded, "It's all dangerous, but the simple fact is that there are too many people after us, and we have no way of knowing what's ahead. Speed could be an ally but not one we can trust. Stealth is the only way we can be certain we'll make it to Spinesend. We have to take the mountain route."

"I don't like the additional time it will take, but if you think the mountains are the most certain route, that's the way we'll go," said Raif, not waiting for the input of the others. Pointedly not turning to look at his sister.

Rew eyed the boy from the corner of his eye. Had the battle changed the youth's mind, and he was willing to accept Rew's leadership, or was he merely conceding common sense? Or, perhaps more likely, was he just being obstinate and refusing to discuss a plan to rescue his father?

Apparently seeing the look, Raif stated, "You're right. We've pressed our luck as far as we can escaping from our enemies while they face each other. I don't think any of us want to rely on that happening again. Freeing my father is too important to risk on electing an easier walk. No matter the difficulty, the mountains are the best way."

Rew nodded but did not respond.

AFTER NIGHT FELL, THEY SCAMPERED ACROSS THE OPEN, MOONLIT landscape like naughty field mice afraid of swooping owls. They followed a wending course between the low hills, keeping to the shallow valleys so their profiles would not be visible from a distance. Rew did not bother raising a fog of concealment around them again, but he did keep his senses attuned, reaching out and questing for any sign of pursuit. He felt nothing.

As they moved, he mulled over how Duke Eeron had managed to cast a glamour covering Baron Worgon's entire campsite. Had the same low magician that encompassed the campsite in darkness also cast upon the baron back in Yarrow? Since they'd walked into his court, Baron Worgon's actions had not made sense to Rew, but it would take someone in the baron's inner circle to have known about their arrival and been able to respond so quickly and effectively. And how had the duke surrounded the camp in a matter of hours with an entire army?

There was only one answer, and Rew hated to consider the implications of it. The only way the ambush could have been staged was with the assistance of powerful users of both high and low magic. The attack had taken more spellcasting skill than Duke Eeron retained in his court, and whoever had done it had remained hidden. The fledgling necromancers they'd faced had not been capable of either the glamour nor moving such a large army into place. A hidden set of hands had supported the duke, and that made Rew nervous.

There had been an informer close to Baron Worgon, and there had been resources arrayed to react quickly. The same person, different people? How had Worgon's son, Fredrick, not caught the glamour before his father left, unless he was involved? But the man they'd seen wasn't capable of high magic, was he? Rew sighed. He wasn't going to figure out who it was with the information they had available, but he could guess why they'd done it.

He looked back at the party and saw Cinda shuffling slowly behind him. She was still exhausted from the explosion of magic she'd unleashed the day before. The princes wanted Baron Fedgley's necromantic talent, and if they couldn't get it, they'd take his child's. It was the only reason they would turn their eyes to Eeron's duchy in the midst of the Investiture. Baron Fedgley and his children were in grave danger. The entire kingdom was, if they were found and forced to do the princes' bidding. Of course, the entire kingdom was in danger if the Fedgleys didn't do what Rew suspected they were capable of. Hissing in frustration, Rew kept walking. Danger surrounded them everywhere, and he didn't know which way to run.

Ahead of him, Anne glanced back, evidently hearing his violent exhale of breath. She raised an eyebrow, and Rew shook his head. He couldn't tell her what he suspected—what he knew —but seeing the empath's face gave him comfort. He understood what she would do if she had his knowledge.

The concerns of the entire kingdom were too large for her. It was too much, too great a burden to be adequately evaluated, but the danger to the children was not. They could do something about the children. They could help them. No matter the danger, no matter the pieces moving across the kingdom, Anne would help the children.

Raif joined him some time after that, and for half an hour, the two of them walked through the darkness without speaking. Finally, Raif acknowledged, "You were right. We shouldn't have gone to see Baron Worgon. We lost days cooling our heels as bait in the tower, and then we nearly died in battle. Duke Eeron was a step or two ahead of the baron the entire time, and if we'd listened to you, we'd be in Spinesend already. Maybe that was our opportunity to rescue Father. With Duke Eeron focused on Baron Worgon... But now, he'll know we're coming."

Rew didn't respond.

"Why are you helping us?" asked the nobleman. "It's not for any reward we can grant you, I know that. You're risking your life for us and our father, yet I see nothing in it for you, Ranger. Is it only because Anne asked—well, that's a polite way of saying it. Is it because Anne demanded you do so? Why does the empath have such sway over you? It's obvious you're a powerful man, and she's only an innkeeper and a healer."

"There are different kinds of power, lad," said Rew. He looked at the nobleman. "At first, it's true, I was only helping because Anne asked. I thought I could get you lot off my hands and return to the wilderness before the Investiture swept me up. I'm afraid that's not the way it worked, and now I suppose, I'm helping you because it's the right thing to do."

"You don't seem like a man who is afraid of much," said Raif, "yet you're afraid of the Investiture. Is it really so awful that it forced a man like you to hide away in the eastern wilderness for a decade?"

"I am afraid of it," agreed Rew, "terribly afraid, as anyone who knows anything about it should be. That's one reason I've stayed in the east, but not the only one. I always thought it best—Pfah. I suppose there's something about the three of you that's convinced me to face my past, to face what I am. There's only so long one can run, and while I worry what will happen when I stop running, I've realized that I have no choice. Maybe I never could have run far enough away from what I was—what I am—and it's time to deal with that."

"Your past," murmured Raif. "Do you mean your family?"

Rew did not respond.

"You're a bastard," guessed Raif.

Rew laughed. "Aye, a bastard."

"Sorry," mumbled the nobleman. "I didn't mean—"

"No, it's true," said Rew. "I'm a bastard. I know my father but nothing of my mother. I was brought into my father's house when I was an infant, though never as his son. I was not there as family. Instead, I was fashioned into a tool, a weapon that my father could use against his enemies. It was not a life that I chose, when I was old enough to choose, to keep living."

"And you ran."

"I ran," confirmed Rew. "I've been running since. I ran as far as I could while staying within the realm. I couldn't take that final step to truly leave. I worry sometimes why that was. Why did I not board a ship in Carff and leave Vaeldon behind me? Why couldn't I hike through the wilderness and find out what's on the other side?"

"Complicated or not, it's hard to turn your back on family," said Raif.

"That is true."

Raif was quiet for a moment, then he asked, "So you do have some noble blood in your veins?"

Rew snorted. "I do."

"You're not proud of it?" wondered Raif.

"As I told your sister," said Rew, "your blood doesn't make you who you are. Your actions do. I take no pride in being born to a nobleman. It's brought me no joy, and no good has come of it. No, I'd rather be judged on what I do. Will the world be a better place because I was in it, or will I simply scramble for more like everyone else? If I'm remembered at all, I'd rather it be because I did something, not because some nobleman rutted with a woman and neither bothered to dose her with moon tea." He laughed. "I suppose, in a roundabout way, that's the answer to your question, isn't it? That is why I'm helping you. Maybe—I think I'm just now realizing that myself."

"You've given me something to think about," said Raif.

"You and me both. That's all any of us can do, lad, because none of us have the answers. I do know this; there's nothing wrong with being born a noble or as a commoner," said Rew, "but your birth should be the start of your tale, not the end of it."

"It's on all men to be good in this world," agreed Raif, "no matter their station when they enter it."

"What good are you doing in the world, then?" Cinda asked, coming to walk beside her brother and looking around him at Rew. "What are you two talking about?"

Rew smirked at her and winked at Raif. "We're talking about life."

❧ 16 ❧

The familiar white chalk foothills of the Spine loomed around them, but instead of offering cover and comfort, the ridges they traversed felt like skeletal fingers curling beneath their feet. The party panted and gasped, constantly climbing up and down over ridges that jutted several hundred paces high. It was brutal travel, but it gave them a chance to hide if they were spotted, and it offered them the ability to look out from a height at the grass that spread around the base of the mountain range.

When they did, they saw nothing except scatterings of tiny villages where farmers and herders scrapped out meager existences away from the trod of the nobles and their cities. Peering through Rew's spyglass, they would study the villages and the animals they saw grazing there. They never saw soldiers or any other evidence that something was amiss. Life in those places seemed undisturbed and unconcerned with the battle that had taken place just days away. Far off the main highway that ran between Spinesend and Yarrow, Rew wondered how long it would take for those villages to find out there had been a battle.

"There's nothing to exploit for the nobles' games, I guess," said Anne, handing the spyglass back to Rew after spending a few moments watching one of the villages.

"Not all nobles are bad, you know," muttered Cinda, clambering up beside the empath and the ranger at the top of the rocky ridge they were standing upon.

"Not all," agreed Anne.

Rew didn't need to look at the empath's face to see that while she didn't think all were bad, she thought most were. She'd spent enough time in the world and seen enough of the injury such folk caused. It made Anne's insistence that they help the children even more curious. There were children everywhere that needed help, after all. There were probably some down in the village that would benefit from the empath's ministrations, but Anne never asked to go down so she could grant her healing to the common people. Instead, she kept with the party up in the foothills, assisting a pair of nobles fight against the plots of other nobles.

It wasn't like her.

Rew peeked through the spyglass himself, seeing nothing amiss, but in the distance, he spied the gleam of light reflecting on water. A river wriggled out across the plain. In the mountains, it might be no more than a trickle of a stream, but it was water, and where there was water, there was life.

He closed the spyglass and called out to the group, "I think we have a chance of decent hunting if we hurry. I see water we can reach a few hours before dark. I don't know about you, but I'd like to have some fresh game in the pot tonight."

"What are you waiting for, then?" asked Raif, starting down the opposite side of the ridge.

Rew stowed his spyglass and started after the youth, grinning. Raif had been quiet the last two days, focused on the difficult travel in the mountains, so it was good to see the boy taking an interest in something. After subsisting on what little rations they'd fled with from Baron Worgon's camp, Rew couldn't blame him.

"You want to take a turn with my bow?" asked Zaine, walking easily beside the ranger, her feet padding lightly on the rocky slope.

Rew shook his head. "I'll go with you and give you a bit of advice, but dinner is on you tonight." The thief scowled at him, and he winked back at her. "You're not a bad shot when you're in a hurry. It's only when you take time to aim that you have trouble."

"Maybe if a rabbit comes at us and threatens my life, you'll have something to eat, then," she retorted.

"You never know," said Rew, and he hurried up, pulling Raif away from the steep slope he was starting on. Rew pointed to the sheer wall at the top of the ridge and directed the boy to an easier path. Nobles. He shook his head, and they kept hiking.

———

LATER THAT DAY, UNENCUMBERED BY THEIR GEAR, REW AND ZAINE climbed higher into the mountains. Two hundred paces below them was a thin band of water that splashed and poured its way down into the grassy foothills where it spread into a proper river. Up high, it was deep and fast. Rew saw fish in some of the larger, calmer pools, and he decided he would try to rig a line and a lure that evening. He could wake up early, and as the sun kissed the water and the others slept, it'd be a good chance to try his luck.

But for now, they were searching for more difficult game. He'd seen signs of goats, which would make a great meal if they could track the spry creatures down. In the autumn, with any luck, they'd find a fat one that had spent the summer gorging, preparing for a long winter. Not to mention, in Rew's experience, the fattest goats were the slowest goats.

But mountain goats, even fat ones, weren't easy prey. They were agile and quick, and so close to the village they'd spied with the glass, the goats would be wary of people and would have learned to avoid them. If they hadn't, they would already be in some villager's belly.

"If you've time, it's best to craft a small shelter for yourself and spend a few days laying out food for the animals," advised Rew, leaping up onto a waist-high rock and then reaching a hand down to haul Zaine after him. She ignored his proffered hand and ascended just as gracefully as he had. "Goats, deer, hogs, any of the calmer sort of natural beasts learn where the food is and then start coming back. That's when you strike."

"And if you don't have days to build a shelter and train them to come to your food?" asked Zaine, breathing heavily, putting her hands on either side of a narrow chute of rock and pushing herself up it.

"Then you look for where they can find water, and you've got to get a bit lucky," advised Rew.

They scampered up the steep, rocky incline until they found a flat piece of land that overlooked a narrow valley. The valley was carved out of the mountain and was only fifty paces wide and five hundred long. It was flat and filled with sediment that had grown thick, shrub-like trees. The finger of water they'd been following ran through the middle of it, but around the water, the ground was obscured by heavy growth.

Zaine raised an eyebrow, and Rew nodded. If he was a goat living on this mountain, it seemed as good a place as any to find food and spend his day. The young thief nocked an arrow on her bow and pursed her lips. Rew touched her shoulder and pointed along the rim of the valley. If they descended into the thick bush, they couldn't see more than a dozen paces in front of them, and Zaine's bow would be useless. From above, though, they had a chance of scaring any animals out of the brush and she'd have a shot at them.

Rew leaned toward her and whispered in her ear. "You move quietly over to the other end of the valley, and I'll stay here. When you're in place, I'll rush in and flush out anything that's hiding."

Zaine, moving with the silent feet of a thief, circled the valley high on the rock face. She moved confidently for someone who had grown up in a city, but Rew supposed during that time, she'd learned to pass like an owl on the wind. Her parents dead, trapped with family who did not want her, surviving on the street, the thieves…

He shook his head and drew the two throwing knives from his boots. He hoped to scare any game rather than have to take it down with a knife, but it was wise to be prepared for anything when you couldn't see what you were rushing into, and the growth near the water was too tight for his longsword to be effective.

Zaine settled down on the other side of the valley, her bow held ready in her hands. She signaled to Rew and then drew her bowstring, waiting.

Rew began a low hooting sound and walked into the bush, kicking and stomping on anything on the ground he thought might make some noise. He kept the hooting going, directing his voice up the valley.

He was a third of the way through when he heard scrambling ahead of him, the crash of bodies, and the click of hooves running across loose stone. There were no calls from the animal, no panicked warning to others that he could identify, but something was fleeing ahead of him.

Rew pushed through the undergrowth quicker, wondering what it was he'd startled. A goat, most likely. Were there deer up in these mountains? He'd never spent time in this part of the Spine, and while he'd only identified scat from goats so far, it didn't mean nothing else lived there.

He thought about that and suddenly started to scramble. Goat or deer, maybe, but what else could be in these hills? Rock trolls, silver-breasted harpies, simians? Narjags or ayres? Shoving branches aside, cursing at the thick vegetation, he struggled ahead before deciding he wasn't going to make quick time at the base of the valley. He cut to his left, forcing his way out and scrambling up the rim of rock that surrounded the low-lying trees.

Zaine was standing at the far end with her arrow drawn back to her ear, evidently having heard something approach. Rew opened his mouth to shout, to warn her to run, when a tawny goat burst from the trees and bounded toward her. Zaine released her arrow.

The shaft whizzed off her bow toward the goat but flew half a dozen paces behind it. The goat, ignoring the missile, raced away with the dexterity of one born to the mountains.

Zaine nocked another arrow and pulled the string back to her ear.

Rew grinned when a second goat leapt into view.

The thief fired again, this time compensating for the speed of the animal, and her arrow thumped into the goat's side. It squealed and went down kicking.

Running along the rock face, Rew moved around the valley to the thief and her prey. She was still standing rooted in the same spot, looking open-mouthed at the goat she'd taken down. Rew arrived and saw the animal was still breathing. He put his back to her, knelt, and stabbed one of his knives into its throat, seeking its brain. His back still turned, he wiped the blade clean and slid it into his boot. Zaine didn't seem the squeamish type, but one never knew with children. He turned and grinned. "Well done."

"Did you see that?" babbled Zaine. "I—I shot the thing. I can't believe I actually hit it."

THAT EVENING, THEY RISKED THEIR FIRST FIRE IN THREE DAYS AND, over the course of several hours, roasted the goat on a spit.

Rew eyed the plume of smoke that rose from the fire into the night, but judged it worth it when he saw the grins and gleaming eyes of the younglings. So far from the wilderness and despite his momentary panic earlier, they'd have little concern from natural beasts in these mountains. There should not be any of the Dark Kind nearby, either. In the vicinity of Spinesend, the world was tame, compared to the wilderness Rew had come to call home. It was only human hunters Rew was truly worried about, and they were far enough afield that their little fire shouldn't attract any of those.

In truth, they were on just about the least efficient route they could have possibly taken to reach Spinesend, and that may be the one thing helping them. No one would expect them to be coming from the southern face of the mountains. Rew certainly never would have planned such a wandering path. Fortune, ill or fortuitous, had given them their most likely chance of arriving at the city unnoticed.

Rew was lost in his thoughts, musing about the bitter irony of tying his wagon to the nobles, helping those who were most entangled in the things he wanted most to avoid, when Raif cleared his throat.

"Cinda," the boy asked his sister, "would you care to sing?"

"What?" responded the girl, a flush creeping into her cheeks.

"You have a beautiful voice," responded Raif. "It's been months since I've heard you use it. It'd be nice to hear you sing again."

"It's been years since you've heard me sing," muttered Cinda.

"Not that long," claimed Raif. "Don't you remember when you and Worgon's niece stole that wine? You sang all night."

Cinda grinned at her brother and shook her head. "That doesn't count, and you shouldn't have been eavesdropping on us, even if she did fancy you."

It was Raif now whose face glowed a rosy red.

"I know a song," said Zaine. "It's, ah, it's a plain one. The men my father used to work with sang it, and the thieves knew it as well."

"I'd like to hear it, then," said Raif.

Sitting up, looking at the others over the fire and the roasting goat, Zaine began. Her voice had no training, but it was clear and sweet. The song wasn't so much of a song as a poem she recited, and it was quite filthy. By the time she finished, Rew was cackling, and Anne was scowling between him and Zaine.

Grinning, Zaine admitted, "I know it's a bit raunchy, but when

I first learned it, I had no idea. My father's friends thought it good fun to teach it to me. I think even my mother got a laugh out of it. She would never have admitted that, of course. That was... That was a long time ago. I can't believe I still remember it. Funny, what you remember, isn't it?"

"I don't understand," said Cinda, brushing a lock of dark hair behind her ear. "What does 'ride the mare with no care, when she's bare, pull her hair...' Oh. Oh, I do understand. That and— Oh my. That's just the beginning. It's all quite inappropriate, isn't it?"

Laughing, Zaine said, "It took me years to understand how bad it was."

"It's not about baking?" chuckled Raif, false surprise on his face. "'Kneads my loaf like she kneads her bread, no breath for talk while we're in her bed.'"

"That's enough talk about that," said Anne, giving Zaine a direct look.

Winking at the empath, Zaine said, "I've a few others, but perhaps another time?"

"I can give it a go," said Cinda, "though I don't know any songs as colorful as Zaine's."

Haltingly, Cinda sang a soaring hymn to the Blessed Mother that Rew guessed she must have heard the minstrels perform in her father's or Baron Worgon's court. It was meant to be accompanied by an instrument, but her rendition was as pure as snowmelt.

When she finished, the others clapped, and Anne sang a little rhyme for infants and then another Rew had heard when she was cooking or walking the forest looking for herbs. She forgot the words in the third stanza, but it was just as nice hearing her hum the remainder.

Raif offered a marching tune the soldiers would sing before they left on patrol. He stumbled halfway through when he realized he'd learned it from Worgon's men, but he soldiered on, forcing his voice into a deep, bellowing boom and raising his fist at the end in a mockery of the men's excitement. The others laughed at the performance, and he laughed with them, standing and offering a bow around the campfire.

"Rew?" asked Cinda, turning to the ranger.

"Rangers don't sing," he claimed.

"Ang and Vurcell do quite often," mentioned Anne.

"I don't sing," grumbled Rew.

"No hiking songs, eh?" prodded Raif. "What is it that rangers do around the campfire after a long day? Surely you're not always alone on an expedition?"

"Not always," replied Rew.

"What do you do for entertainment? What do you talk about?" asked Zaine. "Scary stories?"

"Sometimes," said Rew. He looked around at the others and then sighed. "Around the campfire at night, rangers tell each other true stories. History. The sort of history that isn't in the books, that isn't documented by the king and his scholars. We tell our history and of the rangers before us. It's the real history of Vaeldon, a history passed down by those who witnessed it."

"But you're the King's Ranger," said Cinda. "The king is your liege, isn't he? What sort of history would you tell that the king doesn't want recorded?"

"Rangers can be a miserable lot," chirped Anne, winking at him. "Give a man a little independence and look at what they do with it!"

Rew snorted.

"Tell us something," said Zaine. "Tell us one of these true stories."

"Yes, come on, Ranger," encouraged Raif. "Tell us of the history of this land."

Rew shifted uncomfortably. Perhaps telling them of the stories had not been wise.

"Tell us how the King's Rangers came to be," requested Cinda.

Rew lifted his eyes and saw the noblewoman looking at him, excited and innocent.

"Very well," he agreed. He stood and turned their goat over on the spit before he began again. "You're aware of how Vaisius Morden became the first king of Vaeldon?"

"Not really," remarked Zaine.

"Well," said Rew, "it's a long story. One we don't have time for this evening, but so you understand what comes after, you should know that after the wars with the Dark Kind and the conjurers who brought them to our world, these lands were in the throes of great turmoil. Mankind had beaten back the Dark Kind, but much had been lost in the war. King Vaisius Morden the First's reign did not begin in peace and prosperity. None of the official histories will admit it, but there was great dissension amongst the people of Vaeldon. Many were terrified of the threats they faced, and not all were happy with how the war was won or who had done the winning."

"Not everyone wanted to bow to the new king?" asked Zaine. Rew nodded.

"He was a great hero, though, wasn't he?" asked Raif. "I thought that after he led the people against the Dark Kind and won, it was more or less unanimous?"

"Unanimous, I suppose, but one could wonder if that's because Vaisius was a venerated hero or because his enemies knew better than to openly challenge the most powerful necromancer the world had ever seen," said Rew. "Few raised their voices in complaint, but many spoke behind their hands in whispers. Vaisius Morden did throw back the Dark Kind, and he did rescue our world from being swept beneath a horde of those evil creatures, but the cost was high."

Cinda blanched.

"A necromancer's power ebbs and flows on the tides of death," continued Rew, giving the girl a tight smile, "and Vaisius Morden took power from many of the dead. People's friends, people's allies. Rarely his own. Early in the war, he released the power of the lost as you did back at the battle, Cinda, but as the years passed and the fighting intensified, he held onto what he took. He claimed he needed the strength and that without it, all would be lost. Maybe, maybe not. He raised hordes of the undead to face the Dark Kind. The need was great, but... People's friends and family died in battle, and then rose again, dancing on the strings Vaisius Morden held."

"There were rumors that Morden used his influence to steer his enemies into harm's way, and it was they who suffered the greatest losses," continued Rew. "His power waxed and waned with the tide of the war. When mankind faced its darkest hours, he was the strongest, and when the Dark Kind were thrown back, he was weakened. You can understand that there was resentment and suspicion when he named himself king. Some of those whispers went further and speculated that perhaps it was Morden or his allies who had breached the ether between our world and the Dark Kind's, and that the new king had been responsible for the flood of evil that came through."

Raif chortled. Rew turned his eyes to him, and the boy said, "Well, that's impossible, of course."

Rew shrugged. "Is it? It's what some whispered when they thought they would not be heard. Of course, they were heard, and King Vaisius Morden the First began a new campaign, this time against those he felt did not offer true fealty. He purged the whisperers—or at the very least he tried to. Some families were more discreet than others." Rew stretched out his legs, looking at the party around the fire. "It was a time of great sorrow and great fear. Even the common people were aware of the machinations in the nobles' halls, and there were rumblings of a rebellion. The people were tired of war. They spoke of one last fight that would end it all. There was a movement to overthrow the nobility. The king and the other nobles kept their armies close, for their own protection, but that meant there was no one to face the remaining Dark Kind. It made the resentment against the ruling class bitter, but individually, the nobles were too afraid to send out their armsmen. No one trusted anyone. The entire kingdom was on the verge of utter ruin."

"Our tutors never taught us anything like this," murmured Cinda.

Rew smirked. "I am too humble to say it, but others have claimed that is when King Vaisius Morden had his most brilliant insight. The rangers were the answer. They were envisioned as a force independent of the nobility, free to enact the king's law, tasked with protecting the people of Vaeldon. They were men and women recruited from amongst the common people—no nobles— and they were selected because they were skilled at what they did. Birth, affiliation with a particular lord, none of it mattered within the King's Rangers. Units were assembled, and they were tasked with hunting the Dark Kind and the natural beasts terrorizing the villages. The rangers never interfered with politics. Their one mandate was to protect the people of Vaeldon. In a land raised on a tide of treachery, the rangers were the ones who brought trust and faith back to the people, and bit by bit, the rangers helped resettle a kingdom that had been nearly burnt to the ground. Each year, the rangers would push back the shadows that clung to these lands, forcing danger into the wild places and away from the king's people. Eventually, it was the King's Rangers who established Vaeldon's borders as we know them, and for the last fifty years, it is the rangers who have held those borders."

"I never knew that about the rangers," said Zaine with a low whistle.

"Have all eight of the Morden kings been necromancers?" wondered Cinda.

"They have been," confirmed Rew.

"Powerful ones?"

Rew nodded, meeting her gaze.

"The child is always more powerful than the parent," murmured Anne.

"Assuming the bloodlines are bred carefully," reminded Rew.

Cinda blinked. "But... Vaisius Morden... All of the kings have been named Vaisius, have they not? The princes... None of them are named Vaisius. Whoever triumphs in the Investiture will adopt the name?"

"They will."

"T-There's no queen…" stammered the girl, pushing her hair back again. "There are three sons. There are always three sons, but there has never been a queen, has there?"

Rew grinned at her. "Just now realized it?"

"That doesn't make any sense," claimed Zaine. "How could—"

"One queen would result in one bloodline," explained Rew.

"Each of the princes has a different mother!" cried Raif. "Blessed Mother, that's crazy. They're set against each other to prove which bloodline is the strongest. That's… that's terrible."

Rew nodded and did not respond.

"But why?" asked Cinda. "Does each Morden king care so much about their legacy that they are willing to commit to such an insane plan? Has there never been a son of the king who rebelled, who… I don't know… did something?"

"None that made it into the king's history books," replied Rew with a shrug.

"They'd have to turn their back on the throne, face their own father," said Raif, shaking his head. "How could they rebel?"

"They could do something," muttered Cinda, frowning at her brother.

"Maybe they have," said Zaine, watching Rew. "Maybe they rebelled, but they failed. It's only the winners that write the books, eh, Ranger?"

Rew shrugged. There were some stories the rangers told that the children weren't ready to hear yet.

Anne tsked at them and leaned forward, smelling the aroma of the goat. "Enough of this talk. We keep it up, and none of us will be sleeping tonight. I think this is done. What do you think, Rew?"

Rew drew his hunting knife and poked at the goat. The flesh was crisp on the outside and tender inside. He dug his knife deeper, feeling how firm it was and inhaling the scent of the cooking meat. He declared, "I agree."

"Hold on," said Cinda. "I have more I want to—"

"Not tonight," said Rew. "You asked for a true story, and I told you one. Let's leave it there. The deeper you delve into the history of Vaeldon and the Mordens, the more questions you will have. Trust me, there are no happy stories to be told from that dark history—in the books or out of them."

"I don't know why you expect me to keep my mouth shut after what you've told us!" exclaimed Cinda. "The king, the princes, they... It's awful!"

Rew grinned. "I cannot make you keep your own mouth shut tonight, but I can promise that no more words will come from mine."

Then, he began carving off hunks of the goat and dropping them into bowls Anne had already prepared with slices of tuber she'd found in the valley. She'd cooked the root vegetables on the embers of their fire. Flavored with the juices of the goat and the salt they'd had in their packs, it was quite good.

True to her word, Cinda continued to ask questions, but true to his, Rew did not answer.

❧ 17 ❧

After two more days of difficult travel through the mountains, they finally stumbled across a narrow, barely perceptible path. There were no signs of what it was used for, but Rew judged it worth the risk to speed their travel. Mountaineers or hunters who traversed the rough trail through the remote mountains were unlikely to be active spies in Duke Eeron's service. If they were like the wanderers who occasionally passed through Eastwatch into the wilderness, they probably wanted nothing at all to do with the party—or with anyone else—but as the party walked along the footpath, worn into the side of the mountain from decades of use, they saw no one. Whoever traveled this way and then disappeared into the wild wasn't doing so now.

Nearer to Spinesend, the bone-white stone of the mountain began to crumble, opening gaping ravines. Boulders scattered the slope where they had tumbled from above. Vegetation found better holds, and tough bushes and twisted trees sprouted up where before the terrain had been barren. The path they were on kept them clear of the worst of the obstacles, but there were several times they had to walk carefully around dangerous drops or climb over rock that had fallen in the way.

Even with the path, it was a tiring trek, but as they reached the end of the Spine, Rew had to admit it'd been just about the easiest stretch of the journey since they'd left Falvar. There'd been no secret attacks by the ranger commandant or bandits, no surprise encounters with soldiers, no capture by nobles hoping to use them in some deadly way. It was just them against the mountain, and that was the type of conflict Rew had learned to enjoy.

It was a pleasant diversion, working together to climb over and around the rocks, exhausting themselves hiking each day, collapsing in contented heaps in the evenings, and complaining about their unchanging menu. The challenge of their mission came crashing back when they finally crested a ridge and overlooked the city of Spinesend.

It was several times larger than both Yarrow and Falvar, and it had the imposing defenses of a seat of the duchy. Fifty pace-high walls encircled the city, and a deep, cold lake lapped at its foot. The city rose against the mountains of the Spine, some of the higher towers carved from the rock of the mountain itself rather than built of quarried stone. Soaring bridges spanned the open air from tower to tower at the tops of the city, and thick forest spread between the mountains and the lake. The desolate landscape they'd been moving across finally retreated beneath the surface of the land, covered by the fertile plain that lay beyond Spinesend.

Several leagues away, Rew knew that fields and farms lay like a patchwork quilt. Spinesend perched at the border between the harsh rock of the Spine and the cultivated soil beyond, but it was no mistake that the city had grown there, in the foot of the mountains, instead of where the crofters tilled their land. The founders of Spinesend hadn't been farmers. They'd been warriors, and the city was located in the mountains because it made it almost impossible for enemies to approach. Their party had Zaine's thieves' gate, though, and they could only hope it was still accessible.

"You're certain the duke won't be watching?" asked Cinda,

her voice tinged with worry now that she was faced with the enormity of what they were attempting.

"I can't be certain," replied Zaine, "but if the duke knew about it, surely he would have shut it down long ago? Before the Investiture stirred things up, I can't imagine the duke would be happy about thieves sneaking in and out of his city."

"You never know," said Rew. "There might be some benefit to being aware of the hidden ways and leaving them be. The duke has little concern for petty thievery, and by allowing the gate to continue operation, he could watch for true threats, like spies or hostile spellcasters."

"If he is watching the thieves' way…" mumbled Raif

"We have to risk it," continued Rew. "The main gates are certain to be watched, and we'd be staking our lives on any disguise we concocted. The walls are too tall for us to easily scale, so unless we want to revisit the sewers, I think this is the best route."

"It's been decided we'll try the thieves' gate," said Anne. "There's no use chewing over it now. Either it's watched or it's not. If we are to continue, we've all agreed it's the best plan we have."

"In that case," said Zaine, "we need to go down there."

The young thief pointed to a small settlement that was wedged between the walls of Spinesend and the lake that lapped at its feet. It was a place for fishermen who wanted to avoid the duties at Duke Eeron's wharf and for foresters who couldn't stand the thought of entering and exiting the city gates each day on the way to the woods. From afar, it was obvious it was a humble place filled with humble men and women. With any luck, it was beneath the notice of the duke and his minions.

Rew glanced at the sky above them. "Several hours of sunlight left. I think it won't take us more than a few to move around and get into position at the edge of the woods. I suggest we rest there, hidden in the forest, and then we enter the village under the cover of night. Zaine, I'm guessing the thieves are used to nocturnal visitors?"

"Of course," she said.

Rew looked around at the party, seeing nervousness reflecting in their eyes but determination in the set of their shoulders. "Let's go, then."

THEY'D MOVED SLOWLY THROUGH THE FOREST NEAR SPINESEND, taking the woodsmen's trails, moving closer as darkness fell, following the foresters who retreated from the trees to the comfort of hot suppers and beds back in the village. By the time the party reached the edge of the wood and peered out at the nameless village that housed the thieves' gate, full dark had fallen.

The village was lit sporadically with the glow of fires and candles that escaped through shuttered windows. There were no lights on the street. Not much of a street at all, really, and no lights from watchmen or from guards. The village was outside of the city's administration, which was a comforting thought to Rew.

High above the settlement, Spinesend's battlement rose like a cliff. There were braziers lit to guide the steps of the guards on patrol, but the light of those fires hardly kissed the thatch roofs below. Between the crenellations of the battlement, they could see soldiers walking about in regular circuits. Others were stationary, looking into the forest below or, more often, huddled close to their fellows in conversation.

The guards seemed relatively alert, which Rew guessed was unusual, but the Investiture had begun, and these men must know there had been combat several days away with Baron Worgon's forces. Even after a resounding victory by their side, it'd take some time for their comfort to return, for the worry of a retaliatory attack to fade.

From fifty paces above, though, looking out into a dark forest, the men would have almost no chance of seeing the small party as long as they didn't give themselves away with their own light. The celestial glow in the sky intermittently shone through sparse clouds. Thick thunderheads would have been better, but there was enough cover that they could time their walk across the open area between the forest and the village without the moonlight giving them away.

"Ready?" Rew asked, turning to look at the party.

The younglings were bunched tightly together, their cloaks swung over their packs, their hoods tugged forward to cover their heads. They looked like lumpy, wool-covered monsters. Anne had her hood back, as if she thought the chances anyone would recognize her were nil. Rew pantomimed her pulling the hood up with a wry grin. If some of their party was walking undisguised, it would only make the younglings look guilty. Consistency was key to appearing as if they belonged, and it was cool enough outside that no one should think twice about the hoods. Besides, any thieves' gate was likely to have regular nighttime visitors, so Rew was not overly concerned that someone would suspect anything was amiss. Getting to the village and into the tavern which housed the hidden gate should be no problem. Of course, once they got there…

Rew rolled his shoulders, winked at Anne after she pulled up her hood, checked his own, let his fingers trail over the wooden hilt of his longsword, and then started out of the forest, standing tall and walking at a steady pace. Crouching, the younglings followed. Rew glanced back and saw Anne walking behind them, her eyes twinkling with mirth at the youths' furtive behavior.

Rew led them to the village, his eyes restless, scanning back and forth from the crudely constructed buildings, to the darkened spaces between them, and then up to the battlement that rose like a terrible wave blocking the dim light that escaped the clouds. There was no alarm within the village at their approach, and no one called out from the battlement, though he supposed even if they were seen, maybe there would be no outcry. Unless someone identified them, there wasn't anything suspicious about a group of people walking into a village. Even after dark, people must occasionally come and go.

When they reached the village, a stray dog came out and began barking at them. A voice from inside a low hovel shouted at it to stop barking and be quiet. It didn't, but no one looked out to investigate. The windows and the doors of the village were shut tight to keep out the autumn chill, but many of them fit poorly and spilled enough illumination that Rew and the others could see where they were going.

At the end of the maze of low-slung buildings and sheds, they found one structure that was properly lit—the tavern Zaine had described. There were two torches framing a thin, plank door. There were windows covered in waxed paper that let out a warm glow from within, and gaps around the chimney bled light profusely. It looked as if the builders had found the drunkest mason possible to mortar the stones together. Smoke leaked out with the light, filling the street with the smell of burning oak and fat that sizzled as it fell into the cookfire. Rew wondered how much of the smoke actually made it to the top of the ramshackle chute.

The sounds of people talking spilled out as well, along with the thin timbre of a flute, but no rattling dice, no shouted revelry or singing like they might find at a popular inn inside of the city walls. This was a place for the locals to enjoy an ale and to catch up with their neighbors, and Rew guessed they couldn't afford to gamble away their pitiful earnings. As they drew closer, the wail of the flute grew louder, and he supposed they also couldn't afford any decent entertainment.

Leading the way, Rew pulled open the plank door of the tavern and stepped inside.

The place was as he'd expected. There were several tables that looked to have been cobbled together from the spare pieces of ancient fishing boats. The walls were adorned with the tools of that trade and, as far as Rew could tell, might have hung there since before the raising of Spinesend's towers. A few of the patrons might have predated even that.

A pair of geezers who had more fingers than teeth—and they didn't have all of those—looked to the party as they walked in. Their eyes slid past Rew and Raif to settle on the women, and their grins turned lecherous. The old men must have noticed enough about Rew and Raif, though, that they didn't make any comment. At the old men's age, experience was no longer an advantage when it came to a fight.

There were a dozen other men who looked to be fishermen of the sort that spent half their income on feeding their families and the other half on ale with nothing but debt left over. Rew would have gambled against all of that debt that they were spending the evening telling each other how years ago, things were easier. There was a young man perched on a chair atop one of the sturdier tables playing a simple tune on his flute with the kind of skill that wouldn't earn him a stage inside of the city, overseeing a floppy cap that was empty of tips. A pair of crones, who might or might not have been affiliated with the geezers and who might or might not have been sisters, cackled at each other, sharing jokes that would have made Cinda blush had she been paying attention. The crones and the geezers wore the only smiles that Rew saw in the room.

Commanding the space from behind a ramshackle bar was a middle-aged woman of prodigious bust with a nest of curly orange hair that stuck up from her head in defiance of everything Rew had ever been taught about the laws of physics. She leaned forward, putting her wares on display as soon as she saw the men enter. She might have shot the girls a jealous look, but it was difficult to tell as her face had been plastered with enough coats of powder and paint to cover the hull of one of the fishing boats tied to the posts along the lake.

Rew grinned.

The proprietress of the place was made up and posing like a trollop, but she was too young for so much makeup, and she didn't have the world-weary slump in her shoulders of one who had decided that spreading her legs for strangers was a better business than running her tavern. There was too much life left in her to be the owner of such a place. The sparkle in her eyes as she assessed them when they reached the bar confirmed Rew's hunch, and he was certain they'd come to the right tavern. Now, they only had to convince her to show them the gate and see them through.

"Let me guess," drawled their hostess, winking at Rew. "An ale for my mate here. For his lady, my finest wine, which I'm sorry to say is not very fine. No wine, but cider for the girls? And for the big, strapping lad, a mug of milk."

"Milk?" spluttered Raif.

"Aye, lad," said the woman, standing up and adjusting her top. "Milk."

"I haven't drank milk since I was a child," snapped Raif.

"Not that long ago, then?" questioned the woman.

Rew put a hand on the quickly reddening boy's shoulder and warned, "She's trying to provoke you."

The woman winked at him.

"Why are you trying to provoke the lad?" Rew asked her.

"Just having a little fun," claimed the woman. "No harm meant by it."

"You know why we're here," said Rew.

The woman rolled her shoulders, her bosom moving like the waves of the sea. "Aye, I'll dip your ale, and you can spare me the story about how far you've traveled and how you can't stand the thought of traveling even farther into the city. You're in luck, mate. Our ale is just as cheap and almost as good."

"That's not why we're here," said Rew quietly.

The woman raised an eyebrow, which was quite a feat, as the thing was painted on her face like wood glue.

Rew scratched his beard then looked at Raif. "Ah, I see. The milk. We'll take that milk."

"And?" asked the woman.

Rew hid a grimace behind his hand, still scratching his beard. A password. The woman was looking for a password, and none of them knew it. They'd discussed this problem on the journey to Spinesend, and unfortunately, Zaine didn't have a solution. She told them that when she'd come through, others had done the talking, and that if there was a password, it was likely changed frequently. The thieves hadn't burrowed all of the way through Spinesend's wall for interlopers. The fewer people they allowed to use the gate, the more valuable the way was to the thieves.

It seemed they'd already stumbled, and now the woman was just prodding them to see how much they knew. She would likely go report to her superior the moment they turned their backs.

Rew smiled. In a low voice, he told the woman, "I don't know the password, but I know there's a way into Spinesend through here, and I'd like you to show it to us."

"Ain't no way into Spinesend 'cept for the city gates, mate."

"We can't risk the city gate," said Rew, "so we mean to take the thieves' gate. We can pay."

The woman shook her head, her lips curling into a lazy smile, but her eyes glinted with intelligence. "I told you, mate, ain't no gate that I know of. Maybe if you loan me the big lad for half an hour, he can jar my memory a bit, eh? Could be one gate I'll let the lot of you make use of."

Raif raised a fist, looking at the woman curiously.

"That's not what she wanted to be jarred with, Raif," muttered Rew.

"He's as fresh as a daisy, ain't he?" cackled the woman.

"We have a message from Fein for the leadership of the guild," said Rew.

The woman's smile froze. "Who? I thought—I ain't heard of no man named... What'd you call him?"

"You've heard he's dead, then," guessed Rew. He nodded back

toward Cinda. "She's a necromancer. She's been in contact with his ghost. He has a message for the guild."

The woman stared at the ranger, her smile locked in place, her eyelids blinking slowly. She didn't know what to say to that.

"Get me the ale, the wine, the two ciders, and the milk, and we'll wait for your superior," said Rew.

"Three silver," said the woman.

"That's expensive milk."

The woman shrugged. "You said you could pay."

Rew dipped his fingers into his purse, made a show of shuffling through the coins, clinking them loudly against each other, and then finally pulling out three shining silver ones. He put them on the bar counter, and the woman scooped them up. She turned and dipped him an ale then got the others their drinks as well.

Scowling at the milk, Raif picked it up and followed Rew to a table. He declared, "I am not going to drink this."

Rew sipped his ale and winked at the boy.

"You can have my cider," said Cinda. She pushed it to her brother then leaned toward Rew. "Why did you tell her I'm a necromancer?"

Rew didn't respond. He was watching the proprietress, who ducked through a curtain at the back of her bar. He turned and looked over the rest of the patrons at the decrepit watering hole.

"Can necromancers really speak to ghosts?" asked Cinda.

"No," responded Anne. "Not like that."

"Then why did you..." started Cinda before becoming flustered and staring at Rew in confusion.

"Are you planning to follow her?" asked Zaine. "She must be going to get others. If we tail her, maybe we can slip away on the other side before she comes back, or at the least we can take her and force her to show us the gate."

"We'll wait until they return," said Rew.

"You'll talk your way through?" asked Zaine.

Rew nodded.

"That didn't work well last time," mentioned the thief. "Remember, you and I were almost killed, and Jon was?"

Rew sighed, thinking that was a bit harsh. "It won't go the same way this time."

"Won't it?"

He didn't respond.

Throwing up her hands, Zaine looked to Anne, but the empath only shrugged and sipped her wine. She spit it back into the mug and declared, "This is terrible."

"Poisoned?" worried Raif, looking down into his half-empty mug of cider.

"May as well be," complained Anne, pushing the wine away and sitting back, crossing her arms over her chest. To Rew, she said, "This had better work."

"It will work," said Rew. "There's enough truth to the story they have to consider if the more outlandish parts are true as well. It's not going to be the job of some low-level sentry to speak to us about it. It will be a senior guild member, and that's who we need to speak to. No one else will take the risk of letting us in."

Anne frowned at him.

"No one comes to this tavern for the wine," Rew told her.

"The cider isn't too bad," said Raif. He peeked into his sister's mug. "How's the milk?"

"In your lap unless you show me proper appreciation for sharing," she retorted.

"I'll be back," said Rew. He stood, looking around the room to see who was drinking ale and who was drinking wine. The trick of detecting magic, high or low, was to know that it was there. When you were looking for a specific spell, it made it that much harder for the casting to fool you. He sniffed the air and ambled across the room to the two crones who were still cackling madly at their own jokes. "This place is so dour. Mind if I join you?"

"You can join us, young man, though you may have trouble with our husbands," cried one of the old women, clapping and then gesturing to the two old men nearby.

"Oh, I think I'm no threat to them," said Rew, turning to look at two mostly-toothless grins as the pair of geezers gawked at him.

"You young ones are so modest. My husband wasn't half the man you are even before he got to be half the man he was." The old woman held up a finger and let it curl down toward her palm. "I've just been waiting for my opportunity. You want to take us somewhere private, or do it right here?"

"Right here," said Rew, sipping his ale.

The crone spluttered.

"What would happen if all of these people saw who you really are?" he asked.

"What are you talking about, young man?" asked the second crone, leaning forward on spindly elbows, her leather-like skin stretched taut across her skeletal face. Her teeth were yellowed and jagged, the half that were there, at least. Tufts of white hair stuck from her head like horns, and her bony fingers were laced beneath her chin, showing off long, claw-like fingernails.

"The change is a bit obvious, don't you think?" asked Rew. "When I walked in, you looked like my grandmother, but now, you look like one of the witches my grandmother used to make up stories about. If I wasn't convinced a moment ago, all you've done is show me that I was right." Rew grinned. The crone blinked at him. He asked her, "If I was to yank away that glamour, what would happen?"

"I'm not sure I know what you're talking about," responded the first woman.

Rew looked between the two of them. "Do you normally repeat each other, or just when you're nervous?"

The old women scowled at him.

"Look," he said, "my friends and I don't want to cause trouble. We don't want to make a fuss. We don't want to do anything other than pass through the gate. You'll never see us or hear from us again."

"Simply knowing about the gate is reason enough that no one should hear from you again," threatened the first woman.

The leader, guessed Rew, or at least the more experienced of the pair. He turned to the second one and told her, "Tell me of the gate, or I'll remove your glamour, and we'll talk face to face."

"You can't do that!" barked the visage of the crone.

Rew sat down his mug of ale and leaned across the table. "Yes, I can. I can pull off your glamour, and I can counter whatever low magic you throw at me. I can deal with however many thieves the barmaid is bringing with her. I am not afraid of you and your guild, and I will do what I have to do because the only thing that is important to me is entering the city unnoticed. If I have to kill a few thieves to do it, well, I don't think you'll be running to the city watch, will you? No one else in this rundown sty looks like they have friends in the city, either."

He watched them for a moment, and neither replied. They both kept their eyes on him, struggling not to react.

Rew continued, "Let's handle this like civilized people. I don't want violence, and I suspect neither do you. Let's settle this before the barmaid comes back and there's no choice but to fight. What does it take to gain entry to the gate?"

"Three gold coins for every member of your party," said the first crone.

"That's too much," said Rew. "I can give you one."

"The boy's greatsword, then," countered the crone.

"Two gold coins per person. That's my final offer."

The two women turned to each other and seemed to have a wordless conversation. Rew wondered whether they actually could. It was rumored to be an ability of some low magicians, but he'd never encountered anyone who could do it. It certainly would be useful for a watcher outside of a hidden gate.

Finally, the second woman stood and shuffled toward the back of the tavern.

"She's going to prepare the way," stated the first. "Pay me, and then she'll guide you through."

"If she betrays us, her death will be on your hands," declared Rew.

"She's my daughter," said the crone.

Rew nodded and dipped his hand into his purse. He sorted through until he found ten gold coins and slid them to the crone, covering the gleaming discs with his hand so none of the other patrons saw.

The crone grinned at him, her black gums and yellow teeth on full display. "Only one of us is holding a glamour. Did you know that?"

"I didn't," admitted Rew.

"How'd you guess then?"

Rew touched the side of his nose and did not reply. The crone frowned at him, but he ignored her and stood. He gestured to his companions and led them back behind the filthy curtain that covered a room behind the bar.

They saw racks of barrels, a pot of simmering stew over a fire, several wheels of suspicious-looking cheese, and a large tub where ale mugs were floating in a dark, murky pool. A cake of soap sat next to the tub, but if it had ever seen the water inside, Rew could not tell. Anne gripped Rew's arm at the sight, and he suppressed a shudder. He enjoyed needling the innkeeper about her penchant for cleanliness, but some things went too far... He'd just drank—He walked quicker, pushing aside a flimsy curtain and entering a narrow storage room.

"There," he croaked, nodding to another doorway.

They walked through the opening and found themselves in a long, narrow hallway. A middle-aged woman stood waiting for them. She had a shawl wrapped around her shoulders, obscuring most of her body. Her curly hair was piled high on her head, exposing a slender neck. Cheap bangles hung from her arms, and her ears were studded with dozens of piercings. She stared at them with no expression. The younglings gawked at her, probably noticing that her attire was identical to the old crone they'd watched leave the bar room. Without word, the woman picked a torch off of the wall and turned, walking down the hallway.

They followed, hurrying to stay close as darkness pressed around them. In a moment, they could no longer see the walls of the hallway, and everywhere was ink black. The woman walked on, unconcerned with the encroaching dark.

"If we got lost in here…" whispered Raif.

"Just keep walking straight," responded Rew. "There are no turns, nowhere to get lost."

"Is it another glamour?" wondered Cinda.

"They've painted the walls black and hung curtains or rugs above to muffle the sound," said Rew. "A special paint, maybe. See, it's absorbing the light from the torch and making it seem like nothing is there. Listen to our footsteps. We're still in the tunnel. Besides, our guide hasn't turned. Give it two or three dozen paces and we'll find the other end. My guess, most strangers in this passageway are given several more drinks before they're brought through."

The woman glanced over her shoulder at him, a curious expression warring with her forced somber one. Rew winked at her. True to his prediction, in thirty more paces, the woman pushed aside a black cloth that hung over a doorway, and flickering yellow light spilled through.

The woman told them, "We're in the back of a bathhouse. Through that door is a hallway that leads by a number of rooms and to the front. There may be people in those rooms or in the hall. They know nothing of this. Do not speak to them, and do not make eye contact if you can avoid it without looking suspicious. I'll walk you through the hall and take you to the exit. Turn left and go at least three city blocks before you change your course. From there, you are free to do as you please."

Rew nodded.

The woman continued, "If you give away the location of this gate, you and whoever you speak to, will be killed. Do not come sniffing around again, you understand?"

"We do," assured Rew.

The woman grunted, opened the door, and walked them through the bathhouse until they exited onto the streets of Spinesend. She looked to the left where she'd told them to walk, and then she stepped back into the doorway, watching them.

Rew led the others down the street, heading deeper into Spinesend.

❧ 18 ❧

The city of Spinesend was a warren of streets and stairways that twisted and climbed their way up the side of the mountain like branches of a barren, stone tree. There were beautiful vistas around some turns that looked for leagues out over the lake, the surrounding hills, and even the farmland beyond. Away from the main thoroughfares, there was no logic as to how the city climbed the side of the mountain, and one could be stunned by suddenly walking out almost off the edge of a cliff and then, at the next turn, thrusting deep into a grim cavern lit only by a string of smoky torches. Unlike many of Vaeldon's cities, Spinesend was not divided into quarters. There was no market district, no neighborhood designated for the tanners and the abattoirs, no place all of the bankers congregated, and nowhere the poor found refuge from the boots and the truncheons of the wealthy and their servants. Instead, it was like ingredients in a pot—dumped in, swirled about—but not so much that the lumps were stirred away.

Spinesend was confusing and loud, and at night, there were few areas that could be deemed safe. While word had been sent to the thieves' guild that they'd had fair passage through the gate, that didn't stop the cutpurses from tailing them looking for an opportunity. The denizens of Spinesend were savvy enough to wear their coin purses inside of their clothing, and they never carried packs on their backs. In the maze of the city, a cutpurse could be lost in the tangled streets and alleys in a blink.

Within blocks, Zaine had pulled her hood over her head and warned the others. "Watch for thieves. They've seen us, and we're perfect targets. Wealthy looking but not so wealthy we have guards."

Raif reached over his shoulder for his greatsword.

Zaine warned him, "You draw that, and we'll have people screaming at the sight of us. We can't suffer attention from the watch."

Grunting, the nobleman dropped his hand, and the group shuffled closer together, walking up the cobblestone streets, taking narrow staircases to climb higher toward Spinesend's keep.

They didn't mean to assault the place right away, but they wanted to get closer and find a base they could conduct reconnaissance from. They had to find the arcanist whom Zaine had seen meeting with the fixer, Fein. They meant to follow that man to see where he went, and they hoped he would reveal the location Baron Fedgley was being kept. They had to do it all without being spotted by anyone in Duke Eeron's service and without drawing attention that may alert Alsayer, Vyar Grund, Mistress Clae, or any of the other hunters who stalked them.

Mistress Clae.

Rew scowled at a scampering urchin who was looking at them a little too closely. An assassin in the thieves' guild, Zaine had called the woman. Did she have eyes and ears amongst the thieves, or did she consider herself above that? After several more blocks, Rew decided that if the woman did maintain contacts in the lower echelons of the guild, and if she had asked her informers to look for them, there was nothing they could do to hide. One could duck the guards and soldiers patrolling the city, one could hide from a few high magicians who would never deign to venture into the poor quarters, but one could not avoid the thieves. They were everywhere, like flies hovering around dung, and Rew could only hope it was simply interest in their coins and valuables which attracted the thin, pale-faced cutpurses.

He shook himself. The task ahead was daunting, but the first step was simple enough. They were looking for an inn that was close enough to the keep they could monitor movements in and out of the place, and it had to be an inn that Anne was willing to stay.

It couldn't be too close, though, or people from the palace may frequent it. Raif and Cinda were known in the duchy by other members of the nobility and their courtiers, and it was possible the children's description had been shared with the duke's soldiers. Rew might be recognized as well. He made an effort to avoid nobility when he could, but over the years, he'd made several appearances in Duke Eeron's court as well as the other cities in the Eastern Territory. As the King's Ranger, a man outside the normal chain of authority, a man who'd been to Mordenhold and had met the king, he'd always attracted a certain level of attention.

Zaine, on the other hand, couldn't be seen in many of the lesser sinks in Spinesend. She'd spent months around the thieves' guild hoping for acceptance into a burglary crew, and when that didn't happen, she'd survived amongst the urchins and the others hoping to become apprentices. She hadn't been a member, so most of the guild wouldn't recognize her face, but enough of them would that there was reason for caution.

Reluctantly, Rew had allowed Anne to take the lead when she'd claimed to know of a suitable place to stay. He worried about the damage her choice might do to his dwindling coin purse, but they couldn't go anywhere he or the others had stayed, so it was either allow Anne to have her choice or to wander aimlessly, hoping they stumbled across the perfect hiding spot. After a brief moment of staring at her that went on perhaps a little too long as her face had started to cloud, Rew nodded for her to take them to—

"There," said Anne. She pointed to a small stone cottage that crouched in the shadow of a soaring bridge. The cottage was backed into a switchback in the road, and as the road wrapped around the cottage and higher toward the bridge, it left raw stone at the tiny structure's back and a line of progressively larger buildings lining the street below it.

Rew guessed the land was too small for anyone to bother demolishing the cottage and building something more substantial. From the looks of the place, it had been built in a different era. Peering at the darkened building and the wooden sign hanging above the door, he said, "Anne, that's an herbalist."

"It is," she agreed.

She strode forward, raised a brass knocker, and smacked it down against the surprisingly thick wooden door. The knocker thumped again, but Rew couldn't hear a thing beyond the door. They waited, wondering if anyone was coming.

Zaine yawned. "Wherever we stay, I wouldn't mind finding a bed soon."

"We'll find one here," assured Anne, "assuming she's home."

She rapped the knocker against the door several more times for good measure before they heard a muffled voice leaking through the thick wooden barrier. There was the sound of a heavy bolt being drawn, and then the door opened.

"Been awhile," drawled a woman, looking Anne up and down.

"It has been," agreed Anne. "We could use a place to stay and something to eat."

The woman nodded and stepped back to allow them into the dark room. There were no lights inside, but from the moonlight that bathed the outside and the lantern that hung at the bend of the street, Rew could see the woman was close to Anne's age and dressed in the same type of flowing blouse and long skirts that the empath favored. Her hair was a tangled mess, but he supposed she'd been woken from her slumber. She wore no jewelry or shoes.

Anne walked inside, and Rew followed. As the sign outside proclaimed, it was an herbalist's shop. There were a row of floor-to-ceiling cabinets lining one wall and a row of shelves along the other. He could not see the details, but the cabinets appeared to be labelled with the esoteric products any herbalist hawked, and the shelves were lined with glass jars that held a variety of contents from flower buds to ground powders. There were other shelves with stacked bones, fat sticks of chalk, and a leering skull. He looked closer and saw gleaming emblems fashioned of more silver than a humble herbalist's shop should ever be able to display, and stoppered jugs which he quickly stopped reading the labels on after the first one.

Turning from the jugs and frowning at the skull, Rew walked carefully through the room. Behind him, Raif crashed into a table, stumbled across the room against the shelves, and barely caught a jar before it rolled off from the impact.

"A little light, maybe?" he croaked.

"Cinda," said Anne.

"What?"

"Cast us a bit of light, please."

"I don't think..." started Cinda, but she stopped. Instead of speaking, she held out her palm, and a pale glow emanated from her hand, reflecting green and white against the rows of glass jars, illuminating the scowling herbalist and the rest of the party.

The herbalist snorted, turned on her bare heel, and took them deeper into the cottage. Noises from outside vanished, the thick stone walls and heavy doors and windows of the cottage blocking out all of it. The herbalist's cottage was built like a castle, thought Rew.

Near the back, they found a cozy kitchen that had a large, leaded glass window that opened up to a surprisingly lush garden behind the building. Rew peered through the window, seeing in the moonlight that the garden was filled with row after row of planters, all spilling thick tangles of herbs and vegetables.

In the kitchen, the herbalist finally lit a handful of candles, and a golden glow bathed the room. Cinda let the eerie light in her palm dissipate. The kitchen held a fire, a hearth, an oven, a table with two chairs, and the customary pots and pans one would expect to find in a small but well-stocked larder.

"There's a cellar through there," said the herbalist, nodding toward a door set in a slant against the wall and the floor. "I don't consume animal products, but you should find meats and cheeses I've been offered in trade for my services. I dislike keeping that stuff here, but I can't stomach the idea of turning away someone who needs my help, and I hate to simply throw it away and waste what has been given. It makes me sick giving it to the poor—that's simply one beast of burden used to feed another. You may as well eat whatever you find and take what you cannot finish." She turned to Anne. "That is, assuming you haven't changed and still consume the flesh of animals?"

"I do," murmured Anne.

"You've never changed, have you?" asked the woman.

Anne shrugged, as if unsure whether it was a question or an accusation. She didn't answer either way. Instead, she gestured for Raif and Zaine to collect a candle. They took it and ducked their way through the cellar door. After an uncomfortable silence, Anne told the herbalist, "I've never had a reason to change. Have you?"

"What are you running from?" asked the herbalist.

"Why do you think I'm running from something?" wondered Anne.

"Because you never change," said the herbalist.

Anne laughed. "Well, maybe I have changed, then. We are not running from something but to something. We have a task that will take us several days to accomplish here in Spinesend, and we could use a discreet place to stay. You are still in that business, are you not?"

"For some," responded the woman coldly, turning her eyes toward Rew and giving him a flat look.

"We are traveling together," said Anne. "Would you turn us away?"

"You know I cannot," muttered the woman. She glanced at Cinda, who was shifting nervously in the corner of the room. "And what else is it you need, Anne? It has been a long time, and you ask much."

"I only ask for a place to stay," assured Anne. "I promise."

The woman, appearing only slightly mollified, nodded.

Raif and Zaine returned from the cellar hoisting a long string of short, fat sausages and a wheel of cheese. Raif lifted a jug and asked, "Is this ale?"

The herbalist looked away from the meat and cheese. She declared, "I shall leave you to eat." She pointed to a stairwell that led to a loft which extended over the front half of the cottage. "You'll find beds and blankets up there. There's a barrel in the garden for bathing. If discretion is necessary, I recommend you only go outside at night. The back is hidden from the street, but my neighbor is a widower who constantly monitors the guests that I have. If she sees a man, she'll squawk like a hen down at the tavern." The herbalist snorted. "As if I'd want an affair with a man. The woman's rumor-mongering does not concern me, but it may concern you if you mean to keep your presence quiet."

Without further word, the woman went through another door and shut it behind her.

"I'm starving," muttered Zaine, tugging a sausage free from the string that Raif was holding.

The big youth found a knife in the kitchen and began slicing off hunks of the cheese. Anne found a bowl filled with fruits and passed those out. They ate and drank from the jug of ale while they plotted until dawn.

When the herbalist returned at daybreak, she shooed them off to bed, telling them that many of her customers arrived early in the morning and that it would do none of them good to answer questions about why five adventurers were sitting in the kitchen getting drunk so early in the morning.

The excitement of arriving in Spinesend and safely making it through the thieves' gate had kept them all awake, but they hadn't slept in nearly a day. They needed rest. They stepped outside and splashed a little water on their faces to pretend for Anne they were getting clean. Then, everyone climbed the ladder into the loft. There were nearly a dozen low pallets piled with folded blankets and pillows. It was warm, tucked under the eaves of the cottage, and blinking heavy lids, they lay down fully clothed.

Rew, lying on a pallet beside Anne, whispered, "Odd, isn't it, having these beds up here?"

Anne grunted, her eyes already closed.

"Are you going to tell me what this is about, who that is downstairs? Is there anything we need to know?"

"She's an old friend," explained Anne, "and I'll tell you about it the moment you tell me why you refuse my healing."

Rew groaned and flopped onto his back.

"Not so nice when it's someone else keeping the secrets, is it?" asked Anne.

"I can't. Anne, I'd tell you if I could," he said, speaking to the thick beams of the ceiling a pace above his head. "Don't put us at risk because you're irked at me. I saw the supplies that woman hawked. I thought you had an aversion to necromancy?"

"I do," declared Anne. "The woman is no more a necromancer than you or I, and Rew, don't lecture me about putting the party at risk, unless you are willing to swear to me that the secrets you keep are not of the dangerous sort?"

He had no response to that, so instead, he closed his eyes and fell asleep.

THAT EVENING, THEY RECONVENED IN THE KITCHEN. THE HERBALIST wordlessly served them heaping bowls full of noodles and vegetables covered in a savory mushroom broth. Raif saw there was no meat involved and muttered about it, but once he'd tried the dish, he wolfed down his serving and gratefully accepted another. The herbalist left an ale jug on the table, but after a look from Anne, Rew declined, and the younglings followed his example.

Looking wistfully at the jug, he admitted to himself they did have a tricky bit of work to do that night. Perhaps it was for the best.

"Tell us what you're thinking, Rew," suggested Anne.

He cleared his throat then glanced at the herbalist, who was in the corner taking a hot loaf of sweetbread from her oven. She didn't look as if she was trying to eavesdrop, but it was a small kitchen, and she couldn't help but overhear every word that they said.

"She's trustworthy," assured Anne.

"Well," began Rew, frowning at Anne, "the problem with arcanists is that they're all old and studious."

Zaine guffawed, but the others listened patiently.

"If I recall correctly, Duke Eeron has six arcanists, and they all have chambers in the keep," said Rew. "They live and work there. I imagine they rarely leave."

"They have to leave sometime," said Zaine, "unless they're keeping Baron Fedgley in their own chambers. We just need to wait for them to come out."

Rew shook his head. "It's not so simple. Eeron's keep is several times the size of those in Falvar and Yarrow, and there are several public entrances. I can only speculate about private ones or secret passages, which is likely what the arcanist would use if he's sneaking about. Even if we split up and cover every public entrance, only Zaine knows what the man looks like. The rest of us have no way of knowing if the old men coming and going are the arcanist we seek or are... well, any other old man."

"We've got to go inside, then," said Raif, clenching his hand into a fist.

Rew shook his head at the boy. "Stealth, remember?"

"You have a plan," said Cinda. "Out with it."

"It's highly risky for us to sneak into Duke Eeron's keep, but what if we drew out the arcanists?" proposed Rew. "If we bring them into public where we can observe them, we can identify which of the men Zaine saw meeting with the thieves. If we know the man, we can begin putting a picture together of who this person is, where he goes, and how we can shadow him, or, even better, we might get a chance to snatch him off the street."

Nodding, Raif said, "That makes sense. We take him and force the truth out of him."

"We have to be careful, though," warned Rew. "If we take the man, we could bring attention to ourselves when someone comes looking for him. Worse, we may alert his conspirators that something is wrong. It's possible your father may be moved, and if we don't get any answers from the arcanist, we could lose our only clue. I suggest we watch first, and we formulate a plan once we have more information. If he doesn't quickly lead us to your father…"

Raif nodded and cracked his knuckles.

"We've made it here," said Cinda. "A few more days to gather intelligence is a worthwhile investment. If we can at least identify the arcanist, I think we'll have a chance of making it work."

"That's my thought," confirmed Rew. "Now that we're here, let's not be hasty and run out across thin ice."

"How will you bring them out?" asked Cinda. "As you say, these men are scholars, and if they're anything like Arcanist Ralcrist and Baron Worgon's man, they'll rarely leave their chambers except on a constitutional, and I suspect we could be waiting weeks to catch the man venturing into the city."

Rew nodded. "If men like them did not spend every waking moment studying, I'd call them lazy. It's unnatural, staying inside all of the time and reading so many books."

From the corner of the room, the herbalist snorted.

Grinning, Rew added, "Whatever their habits, arcanists are men of grand curiosity. They have a burning passion for their subject, and when presented with something they do not understand, they keep digging until they reach a conclusion, not that it is always the correct one. My point is, if we pique their curiosity, they'll come running. We have to find something that intrigues these men, and we have to stage it in a place they will come to. Most importantly, it has to be an area we can observe."

"A mystery that will intrigue a group of arcanists?" questioned Cinda. "I assume you have something in mind?"

Rew shook his head. "I hoped you would."

"What?" asked the girl, laughing. "I don't know what would interest these men. I've never met them, and I know nothing of them."

"What would draw out Arcanist Ralcrist?" pressed Rew.

Cinda shrugged.

"If we had the man's crystal, that would do the trick," mused Rew. "Whether they wanted to study it or to stop it. I don't think there's any arcanist in Vaeldon who would ignore a device that could interrupt high magic. It'd be worth a fortune in the right hands, and I'm surprised no one managed to take it—and your father's arcanist—out of Falvar already."

"The crystal was destroyed," reminded Anne. "Its secrets are lost."

"They could be," acknowledged Rew. "It still seems strange Alsayer wanted the device destroyed. I would have thought such an enchanted artifact would be an incredible boon during the Investiture for either him or his patron. People in power want to hoard secrets, not destroy them." He scratched his chin and glanced at Cinda. "Regardless, perhaps if Cinda made a large enough—"

"No," said Anne.

"She could do it!" argued Rew.

"I want this more than anyone, but I don't understand how I harnessed that power during the battle," said Cinda. "I'll try anything, but I don't think we should stake our chances on my blind fumbling. You and Anne told me it was made easier because so many souls were departing, right? If that's what it takes for me to achieve that kind of strength, then it's not very practical."

"Well," murmured Rew, "I was thinking—"

"No," said Anne, again.

"It could work!" exclaimed Rew.

"That doesn't make it a good plan."

Cinda glanced between the two of them, confused.

"The arcanists won't be able to resist a talent like Cinda," argued Rew. "That's what all of this is about, isn't it? If we draw them to us, it gives us the chance we need."

"Maybe it'd give us a chance," responded Anne, "but certainly it'd alert everyone to our presence in the city."

"They'll know soon enough when we extract Fedgley from the cell," claimed Rew.

"No," repeated Anne.

"What are you two talking about?" demanded Cinda.

"We're not doing it, Rew," insisted Anne.

He jabbed a finger toward the herbalist. "I've been paying attention, Anne. I know who your friend is. She could get us inside."

The herbalist kept working in the corner, ignoring them, but Rew detected a change in her posture. Her shoulders were tense, and she chopped her vegetables with the same vigor Raif used on the practice field. Rew nodded and turned to Anne, raising an eyebrow at her.

The empath scowled at him, shaking her head.

"I don't understand," said Cinda.

Sighing, Rew glanced at the noblewoman and explained, "There are extensive crypts beneath Spinesend. They're guarded and sealed by priests of the Cursed Father, but I believe we have a way in. I thought if…"

Anne made a sound deep in her throat, and he thought he heard a growl from the herbalist. Cinda blanched.

"It's worth thinking about," muttered Rew.

"I'm telling you no because it's the wrong thing to do," said Anne, "but in addition to that, we'd be trapped down there. There's one entrance and one exit, and the moment someone detected us, they could seal us inside. You do not want to cross the Cursed Father's priests, Rew. It is not worth considering."

Rew shot a look at the back of the herbalist, but the tension had dropped from her shoulders at Anne's words, and her chopping had resumed a less frantic pace.

"I know we dismissed it as too risky before, but should we contact our sister?" asked Raif. "Surely Kallie knows the arcanists in Duke Eeron's employ? Even if she can't match Zaine's description to the man, she'll have their names and will know where their chambers are. That's a start, isn't it?"

Rew shook his head. "It's too dangerous. Remember, we agreed we won't contact her until your father is freed, and then everyone can flee together. If he's interested in the two of you, then Duke Eeron will also be interested in Kallie. It's inconceivable he left her unwatched, and he'll have people reading every word of correspondence she receives. Think about it. Your sister is the first place Duke Eeron would expect you to go, which means she needs to be the last stop before we run."

"Aye, but what if we can't free Father?" questioned Raif. "With Kallie, at least—"

"It's too risky," declared Rew. "Surprise is the only advantage we have, lad, and we'll lose it the moment we speak to your sister."

"Is it riskier than Cinda raising bodies in the crypt?" barked Anne. "Harnessing necromantic power is dangerous, Rew, particularly without adequate training and in a stressful situation. You know that."

Rew crossed his arms and sat back, glaring at his bowl of noodles and vegetables. Under his breath, he muttered, "I could use an ale."

"No," said Anne.

Rew rubbed his face with both hands.

"Anything we try will be dangerous," added Anne. "Unless you have a better plan, Rew, then we're foolish to ignore the one ally we might have inside of the keep. She'll be watched, true, and any post we send her could be intercepted, but what if we find a way to contact her quietly or use some sort of code?"

Sighing, Rew sat forward and turned to the nobles. "How do we get in touch with Kallie, then?"

"That I don't know," admitted Raif. "It's been three years since we passed through Spinesend and saw her last. I recall which wing of the keep she had a room in but not the actual room, and there's no telling if that's still where she stays."

"I like the idea of a code," suggested Zaine. "We could send it to her in a letter. Even if it's intercepted, it won't do our enemies any good."

"What sort of code?" asked Cinda.

Zaine shrugged. "She's your sister."

"I've only spent a few hours with her in the last several years," reminded Cinda. "I was thirteen winters when we came through Spinesend and visited her. She'd been fostered here for years before that. We're sisters, true, but..."

Zaine frowned. "No code then. Maybe a straightforward message?"

"We've much to explain to her," replied Cinda. "She knows nothing about Father's capture and nothing about the people who've been plotting against our family behind her back. She's in a nest of vipers and doesn't know it. I think it's something we need to talk to her face to face about. If we did sneak her a letter, how would she even know it was really from us?"

"It's obvious we've got to get to her in person, but the problem is most of us could be recognized in the keep," mused Raif. "If they're watching her at all, they'll be watching for Cinda and I. We're putting a lot of faith in the Blessed Mother's luck that we won't run into someone who knows us."

"I could go," offered Zaine. "Even if Duke Eeron's people see me, they won't know who I am. We could hide in plain sight."

Four pairs of eyes turned to her.

"What?" she asked. "I've never even been inside of the keep, never met your sister before in my life. Duke Eeron and his minions will have no idea who I am."

"Alsayer would," argued Rew.

The thief shrugged. "The spellcaster must have better things to do than watch over Kallie Fedgley all day and all night. How much would he share with his spies? Would he have explained that they should look out for me as well? It's quite possible he thinks I'm dead, killed when Balzac captured me."

"I could go with her," said Anne.

Zaine shook her head. "I've spent years training to sneak in and out of places. It's what I do."

"I should come with you, then," said Rew.

Zaine rolled her eyes. "No offense, Ranger, but you've spent more time in Duke Eeron's keep than the rest of us combined. You may not want to admit it, but you are rather famous in the Eastern Territory. If anyone is recognized by the guards, it'll be you. No, no one will suspect me of anything as long as I keep my head down. Think about it. They have no reason to stop me, and even if the duke himself stared into my eyes, he'd have no idea that I was involved with the rest of you."

"Anne then," murmured Rew. "She'll go with you."

"What if I need to do a bit of serious skulking?" asked Zaine. She turned to Anne. "I don't mean to be rude, but if I need to scale a wall, move silently down a hallway…"

"I hate to agree to this," responded Anne, looking to Rew, "but she's right. There's no reason anyone should be suspicious of her, so she's in little danger compared to you and the nobles. If she finds something she needs to investigate stealthily… I think she should go alone."

Rew looked around the group, feeling his heart thumping at the idea of sending Zaine in without the rest of them, but what other choice did they have? It'd been his idea, but Cinda providing some excessive display to draw out the arcanists wasn't any safer. A message to Kallie Fedgley stood as much chance of getting intercepted as not, and they'd have no way of knowing until it was too late. There could be hundreds of people inside of the keep who would recognize the King's Ranger. If Alsayer, Vyar Grund, or others had left descriptions with spies, they'd have the most difficult time describing Zaine. Vyar Grund hadn't even seen the girl without Rew's sword in his face, and Zaine was right. Alsayer could very well believe that Zaine had been killed in Falvar by the thief Balzac.

"This is dangerous," said Rew, studying Zaine.

"I know," she said.

Cinda reached over and clasped the thief's hand.

"I hate it, but it's the only sensible solution," said Anne. "No one wants to protect these children more than I, but Zaine is right. This is what she does."

Rew, cursing himself for it, relented without comment.

❧ 19 ❧

Anne's herbalist friend was more than she seemed and, it turned out, more helpful than any except Anne had anticipated. They'd laid out their plans in her hearing, and when they'd finally settled on sending Zaine into the keep, the woman had broken her silence and spoken. She'd disregarded Rew's plan of Zaine climbing up the walls of the place and instead suggested they use a simple disguise.

"There are hundreds of staff who move in and out of Duke Eeron's keep every day," said the woman. "Some of them live there, but most live in the city with their families or in boarding houses supported by the duke's coffers. Several times a day, there are streams of men and women who come and go from the main gate. If the guards aren't instructed to look for her, the easiest thing is to just walk right in."

Rew frowned. "A disguise… It could work, but we'll need to find—"

"There's a flighty young lass who owes me a sum she cannot pay," said the herbalist. "I've been treating her for various ailments caused by… ah…" The herbalist glanced at the younglings. "The lass is friendly with some of the guards. It doesn't matter. She cannot pay for my services, and I cannot turn her away, so the poor thing has been accumulating debt that we both know she'll never have coin for. She's friendly to a fault with the men, but she's as honest as winter is cold. If we ask her, she'll help you, and she'll thank us for giving her a way to wriggle out from underneath the debt."

"Can we trust her?" wondered Cinda.

"She won't turn you in on purpose, but she's not one to keep her mouth shut," said the herbalist. "I'm sure you can concoct a convincing lie for her. She's not very bright, unfortunately."

"If she gives Zaine away..."

"If the lass can find as many quiet spots in the keep with the guards as she seems to, then I'm certain she can discreetly walk your thief in the front gate," assured the herbalist. The woman peeked outside of her window. "Her shift starts at midnight. If we hurry, we can catch her before she goes in."

"Tonight?" asked Zaine, swallowing uncomfortably.

"You're in a hurry, no?" replied the herbalist.

"Well, yes, b-but..." stammered Zaine.

"How will Zaine find Kallie's rooms?" asked Cinda.

"Let's ask the maid. Perhaps a solution will present itself," suggested the herbalist. She put down her knife and the vegetables she'd been chopping then gestured to the party. "Hurry up. Finish your meal and prepare yourselves."

REW PEEKED AROUND THE CORNER OF THE STONE WALL OF A PASTRY shop, looking at the backs of several dozen men and women who marched through the gates of Duke Eeron's keep. The space around the gates was well-lit with roaring braziers built high with fires and half a dozen lanterns hung on the wall, but outside of those lights, the city was dark.

They were high above the roofs of the city and even the peaks of the Spine as its final jagged thrusts tapered down and the towers of the keep rose in its place. Close to midnight, the sky was black with cloud, and even below, the luminous glow of Spine-send had dimmed as, one by one, people put out their fires and their candles, and the winding streets were filled with night. So high above the city and the mountains, the wind whistled like a slashing knife, keening as it blew around the stone of the keep, cutting through the wool and cotton of their clothing.

Rew tugged his cloak tight and kept an eye on the crowd of people entering the keep. Somewhere in that group was Zaine, though he couldn't tell which of the bundled shapes was the thief.

Half an hour earlier, they'd gotten into position, tucked between a pastry shop and a haberdasher, almost directly across a courtyard from the main gate of the keep. There were no lights near the shops, and they'd easily slunk in behind the buildings. Poking their heads out while staying deep within the shadows, they had found an excellent view of the gates. During the daylight hours, the courtyard would be filled with people bustling about on errands, but at this hour, it was completely empty except for the approaching crowd of men and women, their livery hidden beneath cloaks and jackets.

There were two dozen guards milling about the gate. They made little effort to stir themselves from before the fires to peer into the hoods and cloaks of those coming inside. Rew thought it made little sense to even bother having guards at the gate if this was all of the inspection they gave visitors, but on the other hand, it was a cold night, and their fires were warm. The servants entered and exited this way every night, and at midnight, it was unlikely any of the guards' senior commanders would be making a surprise inspection. The commanders, like most sensible people, would be abed.

Rew looked up at the passing clouds, obscuring the light of the moon and casting the towering keep in a cloak of black, though the top of its walls and the yawning maw of the gate flickered with fires to light the guards' way. From where the ranger stood, he could see nothing beyond the stone edifice, but he knew on the other side, the city fell away, dropping one thou-

sand paces before it reached the exterior wall and the lake outside
of it.

It was no wonder Spinesend had never been overthrown.

The legend of the place was that even when King Vaisius
Morden the First was consolidating Vaeldon, Spinesend had not
been taken. Instead, the rulers at the time had elected to bend the
knee for the good of the people. It was probably true they bent the
knee without a fight, but Rew doubted they were thinking of
anything other than their own necks. By the time Vaisius Morden
had reached the Eastern Territory, the king would have claimed
all of the rest of Vaeldon. Still, it was impressive that at least in
recorded history, control of the city had never been transferred
due to violence. Fighting one's way up the thousand paces from
base to peak, through narrow streets and easily defensible alleys,
would be a bloody, horrific endeavor.

"What now?" asked Cinda in a whisper as they saw the last of
the servants pass into the keep with no trouble.

"Now we wait," said Rew, shifting his cloak, wishing they'd
taken time for him to purchase a warmer one.

Behind him, the others retreated between the pastry shop and
the haberdasher. Clustered together, they tried to avoid the bitter
wind, but Rew didn't leave his post. He knew it'd be hours before
Zaine returned with word from the Fedgleys' sister Kallie, but he
had to wait. It made sense to send the thief in alone, but worry
gnawed at his belly, and it wasn't going to subside until she
returned. If something were to happen to her inside of the keep,
he wasn't there. He wouldn't even know. She could do this, he
told himself, but...

He stood at the corner, staying in the dark of the alley but
keeping his eyes fixed on the gate of Duke Eeron's keep. For a
while, Anne joined him, looping her arm through his and leaning
close so they shared the brunt of the wind. They did not speak,
and after a time, she returned to the others, whispering quiet
assurances all would be well and that they'd all known it would
take Zaine most of the night to work her way through the keep.

She had to find Kallie Fedgley's room, slip inside unnoticed, wake her, and convince her that her father had been captured by someone in Duke Eeron's service. They'd all known that would take time. They'd all known there was nothing they could do but wait.

At some point in the long night, Raif and Cinda fell asleep. They were burrowed in a pile of scraps from the haberdasher's shop, and with Anne watching over them, they'd succumbed to boredom and weeks of accumulated exhaustion.

Rew stayed awake, though, a sentry watching an empty gate.

He blinked, surprised, when he realized the sky was lightening. The keep was no longer a black monolith defined by the fires lit along its walls, but a silhouette with silky gray, pre-dawn gloom behind it. Rew glanced at the others and saw the children were still sleeping. Anne might have been. Her chin was cradled in her hand, and she was slumped over with her hair hanging down in front of her face.

Looking to the keep, Rew began to get nervous as the sun rose near the horizon. Pink and peach crept along the black walls, reflecting the striated clouds above. There was movement around the open gate, but he saw it was merely the guards changing shifts. A few individuals began to appear on the streets outside of the keep, taking quick steps through the cold morning, bodies bundled up, breath blowing clouds of white vapor like drake's fire.

A few jests and barks of laughter drifted on the air as one group of weary, chilled guards shuffled away and another took their place. A man dragging a rumbling handcart piled high with bulging sacks passed by, whistling tunelessly as he went to deliver his goods to some shop beyond where Rew could see.

In the building beside him, Rew noticed warmth emanating from the wall, and he realized the ovens must have been lit in the night. The heat was soaking through the thick stone. Soon, the bakers would be sliding pastries in and out of those hot ovens. He cursed himself for not hearing the people moving about inside. It was constructed stoutly, but he was the King's Ranger. He'd lost his focus, standing there in the cold. He shuffled deeper into the alley, gently stamping his feet and swinging his arms to get his blood flowing again. He leaned out so he could keep looking toward the keep.

From the open gates, he saw a pair of guards glancing toward him, and for a moment, he thought he'd been spotted, but he realized they must be eyeing the pastry shop, waiting for it to open. Troops of soldiers, servants, courtiers, and other palace visitors would soon be passing in a constant stream in front of his hiding place.

Rew grimaced. Someone had to wait for Zaine, but they couldn't do it there any longer. The bakers or the haberdasher might come to drop refuse in the alley. Any passerby could chance a glance and see them. If those people happened to call to the guards across the way, Rew and the others had no explanation for why they were lurking in the shadows.

He was about to turn and wake the others so they could use the last bit of predawn darkness to slip away when a bevy of servants showed up at the gate, the same ones Zaine had entered with, he thought, but now their shifts were over, and they were leaving for their beds and their families.

Rew waited, his eyes fixed on the three dozen liveried men and women. From a distance, he couldn't tell if Zaine was with the group or not.

Finally, as the servants cleared the gate and started moving to the different slopes and stairs that poured down the side of the mountain and through the city, Rew spotted her. Zaine's hood was up, but he could see her looking directly at him. She flapped her cloak, gesturing down a street, and kept walking.

With a sigh of relief, Rew turned to wake the others, and when another pack of servants arrived at the gates, they used the distraction to leave the alley and head in the direction he'd watched Zaine go.

"SHE'S SCARED," SAID ZAINE, TWISTING A STEAMING MUG OF DARK
coffee in her hands.

"Of course she's scared!" barked Raif. "Our father was taken
by these people and has been held captive for weeks. Duke Eeron
marched on our barony, and we can only guess what atrocities he
committed when his men got to Falvar. I worry that what
happened to Baron Worgon and his men is a bitter clue. If Kallie
wasn't scared, she'd be insane."

Shaking her head, Zaine responded, "No, that's not what I
meant. I mean she's scared of… of you. She says she doesn't know
where your father is, that she's heard nothing about him, and she
refused to meet with you. She told me that you should leave and
return to Falvar."

Raif snorted. "Never. Until we've rescued Father from Duke
Eeron, we cannot leave this place."

"She said you should go home after she suggested turning
yourselves into the duke, and I told her you wouldn't do it," said
Zaine. "Raif, she thinks you and Cinda are being foolish, that the
duke does not have your father, and that you're only going to get
yourselves hurt and damage your family's reputation. I worry
she's going to tell the duke you're in Spinesend. I made her
promise she would not and that you'd leave for Falvar, but—"

"What!" shouted Raif, shooting up so quickly from the table
that he nearly knocked it over.

Anne grabbed the big youth's arm and dragged him back
down into his seat. The empath glanced around the coffee shop
they sat in, smiling as if to cover the outburst, but no one seemed
to be paying them any mind. Patrons were downing their brews at
the counter and then quickly scurrying off on their morning
errands.

"Zaine, tell us what she said," requested Cinda. "Exactly what
she said."

"When I told her that you two were in the city," continued

Zaine, looking between the nobles, "she began trembling. She was... mad, I think. When I offered our help, she refused it. She was nearly shouting at me. I worried we'd draw the guards. She said it'd be best if you came to the keep and asked to see the duke. I argued that he was the one who'd betrayed your family. Then, she demanded I go and that I never speak to her again. She, ah, she said she only wants to see you if it's on the way to the throne room to see Duke Eeron. Kallie told me she believes the duke can explain everything if you talk to him, but if you refuse, then you're safer back home than in Spinesend. She's worried what you'll do here."

"That does not sound like Kallie," worried Cinda. "Are you sure you found the right person?"

Zaine stared back at the noblewoman blankly. She shook herself, and continued, "She barely let me describe the arcanist we seek, and I think it's possible even from my brief account she recognized the man, but she wouldn't tell me who he is, and when I tried to press her, she almost physically tossed me from her room. I tried, but I'm afraid it was of no use."

Crossing her arms over her chest, Cinda looked like a boiling kettle.

"It's been three years since you've seen her, Cinda," mentioned Rew. "Much can change in three years. Much has changed, it seems."

"We're family," stated Raif flatly. "She is one of us, and that has not changed. I think you were right, Ranger. We should have gotten our father first and then our sister. I hoped she'd be able to assist, but... We'll get him, and then we'll get her out of there as well. We should have suspected Duke Eeron would attempt to turn her against us. He's a powerful man and a talented high magician. With time, working against an unsuspecting mind... We're going to have to come up with another plan, quickly."

Rew grimaced, refraining from pointing out how much easier things could have been at numerous occasions had everyone just listened to him. Instead, he commented, "We're still stuck. We don't know where your father is, and if anything, trying to scout the keep and find him now will be even more difficult."

"Kallie did not give me a clue as to who the arcanist may be, but I think I have an idea where Baron Fedgley is," said Zaine.

Rew turned to her in surprise. Everyone quieted and leaned close.

"When I entered, most of the servants were free to go to whatever section of the keep they worked in," explained Zaine. "That floozy Anne's friend set me up with was one of them. No one spoke to us. We just started walking toward the senior officers' quarters where the girl works fluffing, and apparently warming, quite a few of the beds. She told me all about… Ah, before we passed out of sight, I saw there were two groups that the guards took particular time with. They stopped them, searched them, and seemed to be checking names off on a list. I asked my guide what was happening, and she said one of the groups served the duke in his private quarters, and one tended to the duke's guests. She gave me a little wink and told me she meant the guests that had not planned to stay. She said the duke keeps prisoners in a highly secure section of the castle. These aren't the same sort that are locked in the dungeons, apparently. She told me they are important people, so the servants take care of them rather than the guards. The girl claimed there's a spellcaster who has been there for several weeks, and they are taking extra precautions because of him."

"That must be Father!" exclaimed Raif.

Zaine shrugged. "Of course my guide could not confirm who was imprisoned there, and as I mentioned, I got nowhere with Kallie. I didn't want to risk sneaking in alone without giving you an update, and after meeting with your sister, I figured I needed to get out of there. It would make sense, right? How many captive spellcasters can the duke have? The extra precautions sound exactly like what I heard the arcanist discussing months ago."

The younglings all turned to Rew, and he nodded. "If he hasn't been moved off somewhere by one of the princes, then it makes sense your father would be held close because they'd want easy access to him. Unless Duke Eeron also captured Baron Worgon, I don't imagine there'd be another spellcaster worth the hassle of keeping alive."

"We have a plan then," said Raif.

"I'm not sure what we have counts as a plan…" protested Rew. He turned to Zaine. "Where is this secure section of the keep?"

Zaine nodded out the window of the coffee shop, and they all turned to look out over the vista. A tower thrust up from the edge of the city like a piece of the keep that had been built in the wrong place. It soared above the buildings below it, and Rew knew from past experience its shadow was used to tell time by the denizens of Spinesend. Connecting the tower to the keep was a thread-thin bridge that hung hundreds of paces above the city below. The sides of the square tower were sheer, worn smooth by masons when the tower had been built in some forgotten age. From a distance, the sides looked as flat as a piece of glass. Even if weather and time had done their work and left the stone pocked and broken, climbing it would require ascending a straight vertical with no breaks for five-hundred paces, and the entire stretch was in sight of the city below. Any climber would be visible in the light of the sun or the moon, and without light, the climb was utter suicide.

"King's Sake," muttered Rew.

"W-We can't… There's no way…" stammered Cinda, looking open-mouthed at the tower.

"Perhaps we could overwhelm the guards on the bridge," suggested Raif, his voice wavering between hopeful and crestfallen. "It's narrow… Ah, there can't be that many guards on such a small bridge, right?"

Rew shook his head. "With surprise and enough force, maybe we could get inside, but how would we get back out? If we fight our way in, it's certain to alert the men in the keep. There could be thousands of soldiers there, not to mention whatever spellcasters that the duke keeps in his employ. To leave that tower, we'd have to battle our way through all of them. No, stealth is our only hope."

"I don't mind a climb, but I don't think I could scale those walls," said Zaine. She glanced at Raif and his sister and didn't need to mention that it would be simply impossible for the nobles to make it.

"No, we can't all climb up that tower," said Rew. He was scratching at his neck, thinking absentmindedly that he needed a shave, staring at the tower and the bridge. "The tower itself is too visible…"

"What are you considering?" asked Anne.

"Let's go back to your friend's place," said Rew. "You and the children can get some rest. I'll go walk around for a bit."

"We're not children," complained Raif.

"Of course not," said Rew, standing and quaffing the rest of his coffee. "You all must be tired. Let's go."

"You won't tell us your plan?" asked Cinda.

"I've got to make one first."

❧ 20 ❧

The next evening, they stood at the backside of Duke Eeron's keep, in between it and the tower where they hoped Baron Fedgley was held. They all stared straight up into the sky at the soaring bridge that jutted overhead in two arches like a stone elemental skipping across the sky. The setting sun, just now hanging above the tips of the Spine, made it look as if the bridge was afire with orange and red.

"When you said you had a plan, I thought it'd be a better one than this," complained Anne.

"We cannot go across the top of that bridge and fight through the guards," said Rew, "and we cannot scale five hundred paces up the side of the tower while half of Spinesend is watching us. Duke Eeron will have warded the prison against portaling, so even if we recruited a friendly spellcaster with the capability, that's not an option. What other choice do we have?"

"We could bribe a guard," suggested Anne.

"With what?" asked Rew. "We'd have to bribe an entire shift of them, and my coin purse can't support that. We could try to visit a bank and draw on the king's account, but Vyar Grund may have already blocked my access, and that's a certain way to let anyone hunting for us know where we are. Maybe we could steal some coin, but even then, we're assuming the guards wouldn't just take our bribe and report us to their captains after. It's a risk we cannot take."

The empath grunted and pointed above their heads. "Not taking any risks, are we?"

Rew grinned but did not respond. He didn't like what was coming any more than she did, but what other choice did they have? Like so much of the journey, it was take the leap or flee. So close to their father, the children weren't going to flee. That meant the only thing to do was try to catch them when they jumped.

"Up we go, then," said Rew.

He glanced around, seeing that no one was nearby. Then, he started up the slope of the hill that Duke Eeron's keep was built upon. So far below the seat of power, opposite the main entrance to the keep, the neighborhood was comprised of slums and closed shops. There were few people on the streets, but those people paid no attention to anything but their own misery. Still, it was best to be cautious, so Rew crouched low and found cover where he could.

For three hundred paces, they climbed natural stone and scree, using small bushes and scrubby trees to haul themselves up. If it wasn't for the risk of being spotted, the climb was no more difficult than the hiking they'd done in the wilderness and crossing the Spine, and they were starting out well-rested. Without complaint, the younglings followed Rew, and within half an hour, they'd ascended to the base of the back of Duke Eeron's keep.

There was nothing there except a blank wall of stone that rose one hundred paces above their heads. At that point, narrow windows began to dot the side of the structure, and another hundred paces above that was the start of the first arch that supported the bridge to the tower. Rew glanced at the tower, a black obelisk in the evening sky, rising like a spear thrust through the lower sections of Spinesend. Climbing the slope beneath the keep got them half the distance to the top of the tower, and on the backside of it they'd avoided any watching eyes, but now they had the tricky part. They had to get to the tower.

Rew shook himself and looked around cautiously again.

There were no soldiers in the vicinity, as Rew had expected. He'd scouted the site earlier, but with such little time, he hadn't been completely sure. They were so far below the battlements and the bridge that he doubted anyone had ever tried to enter the keep from this direction, and if they had, they'd find the keep guarded by a score of armed men and a closed portcullis. Assailing the keep from this side would be virtually impossible by any but the most skilled climbers, but they were not going to the keep. They were going to the tower.

Rew, not wasting time and the little daylight they had, took a length of rope from Raif and settled it across his shoulders on top of one he already carried. He staggered under the weight and took a moment to settle himself. He grunted, guessing it was at least ten stone worth of rope, nearly half his own weight. Nothing to do about it, though. They needed all of it.

He picked up a bag of iron spikes and a small hammer and hung them on his belt. He took several deep breaths. The sun had finally set, and darkness fell across Spinesend.

"You sure about this?" worried Anne.

"No," replied Rew.

"If you fall from up there, I won't be able to heal the damage," she warned.

"I've been refusing your healing for months now, Anne. No reason to change that."

She shook her head, worry evident in her eyes, but there was nothing else to say about it. What he was going to attempt was incredibly dangerous, but she knew as well as he that the children wouldn't be dissuaded, and the best they could do was to give them a chance.

Rew knelt and dug up a handful of dirt. He rubbed it on his hands, wishing he'd thought to borrow a stick of chalk from the herbalist, but it was too late now. Besides, given the other macabre implements the woman sold, he worried about where that chalk had come from. Turning, forcing himself to focus on the moment, he put a hand on the rough, pitted stone of Duke Eeron's keep, and then, he found a toehold. He hauled himself up, gasping from the strain of climbing with the rope, the iron spikes, the hammer, and his weapons. It was like climbing with a small man on his back.

In moments, he could feel the chill from the stone seeping into his fingers. He reached up, found another hold, and pulled himself higher, clinging to the wall like a spider, hand and foot, hand after foot.

The wind whipped against him once he cleared the sparse cover they'd had on the hill, and he knew he was exposed if any stray eye turned up from below. He tried not to think of what he'd do if he was spotted and the soldiers came searching through the scrabble at the base of the keep. They were hundreds of paces above the nearest buildings, but still... He climbed, hand and foot, hand after foot.

The wind battered him, like it was trying to rip him off the wall, and by the time he reached the elevation of the windows, his fingers felt like clumsy sticks, banging against the stone sense-lessly. The fingers retained just enough sensation that he could feel the pressure against the stone, and he hoped he could keep trusting the digits with his weight. The windows were darkened, all storerooms or dungeons at that level as he had guessed, just one floor above the living rock of the Spine and the stone foundation the keep was built upon.

Rew kept climbing, nearly blind as the moon hung above the bridge that spanned over his head. Bats flapped by, ignoring the interloper ascending into their domain, caring only for the few insects they could find on the cold, autumn night.

His arms trembling, hand and foot, hand after foot, he kept climbing until he reached the bottom of the first of the two arches that spanned the gap between the keep and the tower. Finally, he risked a look down, but he could see nothing in the darkness below. He glanced back up, and beneath the bridge, he saw a network of ancient wooden spars that were arranged in a matrix, spreading like the fractals of a snowflake, just like he'd seen in his spyglass that morning. The wooden beams had been placed there centuries before, either during construction or during some repair project since, and supported the path of stone above. Rew clambered a little higher and rolled on top of one of the huge wooden support struts.

For a brief moment, his breath caught. The strut was half the width of his back, and as he lay on it, he could feel the cold air kissing his shoulders as they hung over open space. He knew there was nothing but two hundred paces of air beneath him.

Sitting quickly and dangling his legs down on either side of the strut, Rew pulled one of the heavy loops of rope off of his shoulders. He tried to flick one end of it down and around the support beam he was sitting on, but after several failed attempts, he tied a spike to it and tried again. With the extra weight, the end of the rope came swinging up out of the darkness, and he caught it. Blowing on his hands to warm them, he flexed to try and get some feeling back into his cold-numbed fingers. He wiggled the digits and stretched them, sore from the climb and torn from the stone. Then, he tied a knot in the rope. He tugged on it to test how secure it was, and he dropped it so the length slid through his hands and dangled hundreds of paces below him.

With any luck, it would be long enough to reach the ground where the others waited. They'd had to guess the measurement, and it'd taken several shorter lengths tied together to get it as long as they needed. How much length had they lost by tying the strands together? Had he climbed higher than they'd estimated when looking up from below? He wasn't sure, but it was too late to worry about it now.

Hopefully the others would see the rope hanging down, but Rew couldn't wait to be sure. There was much to do before daylight. Rew removed the other rope and stood on the wooden beam. As wide as his shoulders, there was plenty of room for his boots, but when he looked down, all his mind could see was the yawning black that lay on either side of the wooden spar.

He shuddered and reached up to brace himself against a beam that passed overhead. Grunting, he tied the end of his second rope loosely to that beam and adjusted the rope back on his shoulder, feeling the weight tugging him to one side. He glanced down, could not see his boots in the shadow beneath the bridge, and cringed. Walking slowly, his legs trembling, Rew began to move up the slope of the support beam, using spars that passed overhead to steady himself, forcing his eyes ahead and not down. Not that he could see anything below. He was having to feel his way forward, tapping his toe along the support, moving nearly blind.

It was a shade lighter than pitch black beneath the bridge, and as his eyes began to adjust, he could see the shadows of a forest of ancient beams extending ahead of him. The wood was hard, petrified by age, and it held none of the life it once did. When he touched it, he ached to feel the life of living wood, to be within the forest again where trees as massive as these supports grew, but he forced the thought down. He had work to do.

Rew kept walking and unspooled more of the rope from his shoulders, keeping the line going behind him, occasionally feeling the wind tug at it, pulling him toward the open air.

It was cold, nearly freezing, but sweat beaded on his forehead and rolled down his back. To distract himself, he speculated whether the others would be able to ascend the wall even with the help of the knotted rope. Zaine would climb up easily, he thought. The others, probably. For a second, he had a vision of Anne plummeting down the side of the keep and splattering on the rocky soil below. He closed his eyes, and when he reopened them, he decided not to think about that any longer.

It was dry, so he didn't have to worry about slipping down the steep slope of the strut he was climbing, and the bridge was as solid as the bones of the Spine, but the bats were an unforeseen complication. In the darkness beneath the bridge, he could barely see anything, and the small flying rodents came whizzing out of nowhere like bolts from a crossbow. They did not strike him, but they came close before screeching and veering away at the last instant. Several times, his heart lurched, and he nearly jumped at the shrill squeal of the little creatures. If he lost his footing and fell, the King's Ranger killed by a bat... One hand dropped down to his hunting knife, but he wasn't sure what he meant to do with it.

Steadying himself, trying to ignore the squeaking denizens of the underside of the bridge, he continued on, stepping from one strut to another as he crisscrossed the space beneath the bridge. After what seemed most of the night, he reached the peak of the arch, where the struts reached their apex and then started going back down the other way. On his shoulder, he still had several dozen paces of rope. He took it off, found a suitable place near the center, and then tied it tight.

He looked ahead, and as he'd seen from below during the day, the struts culminated at the base of the bridge, and there was a span of about a dozen paces where he'd have no place to put his feet. He'd have to reach up and climb with only his hands across the yawning abyss.

Behind him, a trilling voice asked, "Is this as far as you've gotten?"

He jumped, stumbling.

"Be careful, Ranger. It's quite a drop from here."

Rew peeked back over his shoulder and saw in the gloom that Zaine was standing on one of the struts looking as comfortable as if she was strolling down a city street. She told him, "I thought you'd already be down to the other pillar by now."

"Not yet," he rasped.

"A quarter hour, you think, and I'll tell the others to swing?"

Not trusting his voice, he nodded.

Zaine said, "They're barely making it up that knotted rope. You were right. There's no way the nobles could have traversed the underside without plummeting down below. Did you see those bats? The first squeak and Cinda would have been airborne. I'll send her over first, I think."

Wordlessly, Rew nodded again.

"This might work," said Zaine. "I really didn't think it would." She paused, leaning to the side to look around him. "Is that climb as far as it looks? It looks far. That's a lot of open space, Ranger."

He didn't respond.

"Well, good luck. A quarter hour, and Cinda will come your way, if you've made it." Zaine turned and disappeared back down the strut into the darkness.

Legs quivering like an arrow the moment it struck the target, Rew reached up and grasped a chilly spar of wood with both hands. His breath was fast, panicked even. He practiced lifting himself with his hands, then mumbling a litany of prayers to the Blessed Mother, he reached out with one hand and stepped off the support beam he'd been standing on.

Dangling over the open air, hundreds of paces above a rocky slope, hand over hand, Rew swung out and worked his way across the bottom of the bridge. His heart was hammering, and halfway across, he stopped taking breaths at all. Hand over hand, he climbed, his legs kicking slowly, uselessly beneath him.

Finally, his toe thumped into another beam, and he hauled himself forward to rest his weight on his feet. His arms were quaking uncontrollably, and his vision swam. He looked back into the darkness, only seeing the shadows of what was behind him. Blessed Mother. He started moving again, taking his time now that the slope of the supports had changed and he was moving lower, headed toward the stone pillar that supported the center of the bridge.

When he made it there, evidently in less than a quarter hour, he turned and waited. There was ample room to stand on top of the stone column, so he was comfortable for the first time since he started the climb, but there'd be no warning when someone was coming, so he readied himself and waited nervously.

Suddenly, there was a high-pitched wail, barely audible over the rush of the wind. Out of the darkness, Cinda came swinging at him like a boulder fired from a catapult. Her keening cry seemed to trail her on the air, and for a moment, Rew worried she'd come crashing into him too fast and smash against the hard wood and stone of the underside of the bridge. But as she rose toward him, dangling from the rope, her momentum faded, and Rew reached out, one hand locked around a bolt on the strut, the other grasping for Cinda.

He caught her by the neck of her robe and pulled her tight.

"Blessed Mother!" she choked, her breaths coming in ragged, uneven gasps. Tears were streaming down her face, and as he hugged her tight, he could feel the furious beat of her heart.

He untied her and helped her move to where she could sit.

"Trust me, Ranger," she said, "you're lucky you didn't have to do that."

He thought of climbing hand over hand across the gap and shook his head, not trusting himself to respond. Cinda watched him, and in the dark, he could see the gleam of her white teeth, lips spread in either a rictus of fear or a big grin. Both? Rew snorted and turned back to the open air. He tied the bag of iron spikes to the rope, and he swung it out in front of him, aiming it into the black along the center of the bridge, hoping it'd go directly toward the others.

"That was quite frightening when they pushed me out, but it was easier than I thought it'd be," remarked the young spellcaster from half a dozen paces above Rew's head. "Now that I'm getting my breath, I can admit, not a bad plan, Ranger. Not a bad plan."

Easier? He didn't respond. Instead, he waited for the next member of their party to appear out of the darkness.

"I THINK I BROKE A RIB," GROANED RAIF, HIS VOICE TIGHT, HIS HAND pressed to his side.

Anne reached down and put her hands on his head. After a

moment, she assured him, "A bruise only. I'll do what I can, but this situation is less than optimal for healing."

Rew grinned. They were clinging to the side of the tower after crossing beneath the two arches of the bridge. It was nearly dawn, but they'd made it without being seen, and they'd all survived, which after making the attempt, he decided was a bit surprising.

"At least you weren't stuck out there!" exclaimed Cinda.

"You didn't get stuck," retorted Zaine.

"I almost did," muttered the young spellcaster.

"I caught you."

It was true. The thief had reached out and caught the noble-woman on her second swing when Cinda didn't quite make it all the way to the tower, but Zaine had been in Rew's grip, extending out past his own reach, hanging above the drop below. If she'd missed, Cinda would have been left hanging, tied to the peak of the arch without the momentum to reach either side of it. Rew hadn't considered that issue when he'd originally concocted the plan, and now that he fully appreciated the risks of missing with the swing or getting stuck dangling in the middle, not to mention his own difficulty climbing hand over hand across the gaps like a monkey, he wasn't sure they should return the way they'd come in.

But that was a problem for later. Now, they were all safely beneath the span of the bridge, pressed against the tower and only needing to find a way inside. If they attempted to climb up the side of the tower to where the entrance was, they would have the same problem as if they'd simply walked across. Instead, Rew had thought they could climb to the top from where they were and enter there. No one would expect it. The light was growing, though, and he was getting nervous they'd be seen. On this side of the tower, they'd be exposed to Duke Eeron's soldiers in the keep. He thought he could get around to the backside of the tower and climb up there, but he knew the children wouldn't make it. If they were going to climb to the top, it would be on a rope he dropped down the keep-facing side of the tower. They'd have to scramble up right beside the bridge, right next to the heavily guarded door, and in full view of the soldiers lining the walls of Duke Eeron's keep across the way. So, before he started scaling to the top, Rew had another idea.

"Let me see your greatsword," he said to Raif.

"What?" asked the youth, still pushing gingerly against his bruised side.

"I'll give it back," assured Rew.

Frowning, the youth drew the huge sword and, with the help of his sister, passed it to Rew.

Tucking the sharp blade beneath his arm, Rew awkwardly climbed down the side of the tower a dozen paces. There was a window there, and it was pitch black inside.

"What's in there?" asked the fighter from above.

"The window is covered in iron bars," said Rew. "It's a dungeon, but an empty one."

He tested one of the bars, and then holding onto it, he grasped the hilt of the greatsword with his other hand and slid it inside of the window.

"What are you doing?" worried Raif.

Rew angled the giant blade so that the hilt was inside, positioned between an iron bar and the stone wall, the long length of steel sticking back outside. He gripped the hilt and tugged on it. Nothing happened. He adjusted the hilt, moving it farther inside, improving his leverage.

"Hold on," said Raif from above him. "What are you doing with my family's enchanted greatsword?"

Rew tugged, and again, nothing happened.

Muttering curses, he shifted inside farther, reaching as deep as he could into the room, nearly dropping the greatsword before he caught the hilt, and then straining with everything he had as he hung off the side of the tower, only holding on with one hand around a rusty iron bar. Whispering a prayer to the Blessed Mother, he put his weight on the hilt of the blade, leaning back into the open air.

The iron bar snapped.

Only a strong grip on the remaining bar saved Rew from plunging off the side of the tower. Grinning maniacally, Rew worked the greatsword, pressing the steel against the broken bar, and only thinking later how lucky he was that it was the second bar which had broken, and not the one he was holding onto. Working feverishly, Rew snapped off another hunk of rusty iron, and soon, there was a space large enough that he thought even Raif could squeeze through. It'd be tight, though.

"Zaine, come down here and see if you can get inside," he hissed. "And when you do, keep quiet."

"I am a thief, you know," reminded the girl, scaling easily down the side of the tower. She slipped into the room and made her way across the stone floor. When she returned, she whispered, "It's a cell, but a nicer one than you have back at your ranger station. It has a wooden door but I didn't try it. There's no handle on this side, but there is a light out in the hallway. I couldn't hear anyone."

"Well, cell or not, it's a place we can rest safely," said Rew. He looked up to the others. "Climb down and go inside. Be quiet when you get in. Zaine says there's light in a hallway outside of the room."

"Climb down?" asked Cinda, her voice panicked.

She was looking at Rew and the five-hundred paces of open air beneath him. Rew grimaced. Without his experience climbing or Zaine's natural grace, the others weren't going to make it.

Anne drew her belt knife, reached up, and sawed through the rope they'd swung over on. When she cut it loose, she said, "Let's be honest. Whatever happens, we weren't going to go back that way. Swinging over was a terrible plan, Rew."

"It worked, didn't it?" he asked as she and the others tied off the length of rope.

Cinda began climbing, her hands grasping the rope, her boots slipping down the rough stone of the tower wall.

Rew chose not to hear what the noblewoman was calling him

under her breath. He hung outside of the window and helped her in. Anne came next, and the look she gave him spoke volumes more than Cinda's muttered curses. Raif was silent, barely fitting through the tight gap, the broken iron bar taking a hunk of skin off of him as he wriggled inside.

Clambering in, Rew looked to where Anne was crouched beside the fighter, putting her hands on him to heal the bleeding scrape and his bruised ribs.

"Easier getting in than getting out of these, eh?" Rew asked. The others turned and looked at him blankly. He added, "Remember when you were broken out of my jail cell, Raif? You got shredded down to the bone. I, ah... Never mind."

Zaine put a hand on his arm. "We made it inside, Ranger, but perhaps wait a bit before the jokes?"

❧ 21 ☙

The room was a cell, no doubt about it, but it was a rather nice one. There was a four-poster bed piled with linens and a table with one chair pulled up to it, presumably where the occupant of the cell could enjoy their meals and pen missives to relatives begging they comply with whatever extortion the duke was attempting. There was a ragged, stuffed lounging chair, a tiny bookshelf filled with tattered tomes, a candle, and a thankfully empty chamber pot. The room was made for a high-profile prisoner, and to Rew's eye, it had been freshened recently as if in anticipation of a new arrival. The Investiture swept Vaeldon in waves giant and small.

The party was exhausted from their midnight journey across the bottom of the bridge, but the idea of resting for long in the cell was foolhardy. Rew checked the door, and while it was firmly shut, it was not locked. There was no door handle on the interior, but when he wedged his fingers beneath the gap at the floor, he found with some effort he could tug the heavy slab of wood and iron open.

Zaine, crouched beside him and whispered, "What if there are guards on the other side?"

Rew shrugged but did not respond.

He waved everyone back over to the window, and in low tones, they discussed what to do. The tower appeared to be what Zaine's reconnaissance had uncovered, a luxurious prison. They didn't know what else could be inside the imposing edifice or how many prisoners may be kept there. They didn't know if there were a few guards or several companies. Duke Eeron could have half a dozen spellcasters monitoring the place, for all they knew. Alsayer, Vyar Grund, anyone could be lurking in the hallways. The danger was evident, but it wasn't going to be any less no matter what plan they came up with. The only thing to do was venture out slowly and quietly and try to scout as much of the place as they could without alerting any of the guards. Once they were spotted, it was going to get messy.

"I'll go first, followed by Zaine," said Rew. "I'll try to take down anyone we see. Zaine, only use your arrows if I've missed and you know you've got a shot. The steel tip of an arrow against stone will ring like a bell. Raif, I'm sorry to say it, but stealth is not your style. Wait until we've lost any hope of concealment. Then, you know what to do. Be careful in tight quarters with that greatsword. With little room and in the heat of combat, you could hit us as easily as the enemy. Don't hesitate to use the hilt to batter a man if you don't have room for a swing. Cinda, do not engage unless we're going to die otherwise. I'm certain that somehow, Duke Eeron has protected this tower against high magic. Otherwise, practitioners could be portaling in and out at will and the place would be worthless as a prison. The moment you release your power, we'll have everyone in Duke Eeron's employ on our heels. You should also expect glamours, wards, and other ways to misdirect your casting. We know they've prepared, but we don't know how."

Cinda nodded, her lips pressed tightly together, fire in her eyes. Raif held his greatsword in front of him, prepared for a fight, but he didn't object to Rew's instructions, either. The boy had left his barony to rescue his father, and now that they were on the cusp, he would do anything to accomplish it. Maintaining stealth was common sense, and the youth wasn't going to argue about his own abilities when it came to keeping quiet. Rew glanced at Anne but did not offer her any instruction. She'd stay behind them, and if someone went down, she'd be ready to assist.

With Rew and Zaine beside the door, Raif put his fingers underneath of it and pulled, slowly working it open. The hinges creaked, sounding like the wail of a wraith in the small, stone-walled room, but from outside in the hallway, they heard no shouts of alarm or running feet. As soon as it was open far enough, Rew put his hand on the edge and helped Raif, wincing at the squeal of metal on metal as the rarely used hinges rubbed together.

They stopped when the door was halfway open. Zaine poked her head out and then turned to Rew and shrugged. The ranger padded into the corridor, his soft, leather boots making no sound on the stone.

The hallway was lit at both ends by flickering lanterns. The interior wall was bare stone, the exterior dotted with heavy wooden doors, all of them shut. More prison cells, guessed Rew. As quiet as a falling snow, Rew and Zaine stalked down the corridor while the others clustered in the entrance of the cell.

The ranger and the thief listened at half a dozen doors, hearing nothing from inside of them, before deciding this part of the prison must be empty. It was ready, though, for new occupants. Someone had lit the lanterns, and they must have done so expecting the rooms to be used. Through a few doorways that had been left cracked open, Rew saw that other cells were arranged much like the one they'd entered.

Peering around the corner of the hall, he saw an opening on the interior that he guessed led to a stairwell. It seemed the outside of the tower was rooms—prison cells—and the stairs rose through the core of it. There'd be no avoiding that stairwell.

Rew waved for the others to wait, and then, he and Zaine scouted the rest of the floor they were on. They found nothing, and Rew risked opening a few doors. At the far corner, he found something different and quickly closed the door before Zaine or anyone else saw what was inside.

A wooden table in the center of that room was set on a swivel so it could be stood upright. There were manacles on the top and bottom of the table that could be adjusted for the height of a person. A rack hung on one wall, adorned with iron and steel implements that had only one, grim purpose. Knives and pliers. Scourges and vices. Pincers and tongs. An unlit brazier occupied a corner with a stand of pokers beside it. Rew could smell blood and the sickly sweet stench of burnt flesh in the room. While it seemed none of the prison cells on the floor were currently in use, the torture chamber hadn't been vacant for very long.

Rew and Zaine returned to find the others and led them to the stairs. There was one floor above them that might hold prisoners, and above that was the main level where the bridge connected the tower to the keep. There were certain to be soldiers on that floor.

Rew offered a hope to the Blessed Mother that they would find Baron Fedgley on the next level, and then another hope that once they found him, they could make their way out of the tower unnoticed.

The next floor, though, was unlike the one they'd entered through. As Rew crouched in the stairwell looking over the top step, he saw it was completely open. It was a common room for the soldiers who guarded the place. From the stairwell, they could hear a low murmur of conversation. Two speakers, he thought, and he could see a rack of weapons near the stairs that held halberds and short swords. Beside it was another rack with pieces of armor and miscellaneous equipment for the guards. Most of the hooks on the rack were empty, as if the guards had taken their armaments when they came on duty.

Zaine pointed up and raised an eyebrow.

Rew shook his head. Only two men were speaking. If they balked at confronting two soldiers, they were never going to rescue Baron Fedgley, and while it appeared to be a common room for the guards, there was no telling what was on the other side of the stairwell. They had to clear this floor before proceeding. Rew reached down and drew his two knives from his boots. He flipped them to hold the weapons by the blade.

Zaine slung her bow over her shoulder and drew her daggers as well. She gripped them tightly, her face taut but her hands steady.

Stepping carefully, silently, Rew emerged from the stairs. To either side of him, he saw tables and chairs where men might sit during their break, eating a meal or playing a game of cards. The conversation they overheard was happening on the opposite side of the stairwell. The men were discussing the weather. Rew fought back a snort and skulked through the room. He paused at the corner of the wall, gave Zaine a look, and then darted around it.

Two men were sitting at a table, sipping steaming mugs, the remains of a meal on the table in front of them. Rew flung his dagger at one, switched hands with the second dagger, and met the eyes of a startled soldier.

"Who—"

Rew tossed his second blade and smiled grimly as the sharp steel thunked into the man's throat.

The first man toppled backward, his chair clattering on the stone floor. The second man stared at Rew, his mouth open as if to scream, but only a strangled gurgle emerged, followed by a shower of blood as the man coughed. He slumped forward, his forehead thumping onto the table.

They waited for an alarm or shout, worried someone had heard the falling chair, but there was no reaction from above, and the rest of the room was empty. The party followed Rew and Zaine around the corner and stared, wide-eyed, at the dead soldiers.

Rew collected his knives then turned, peering at the items in the room, hoping for a clue, but there was nothing that pointed to where Baron Fedgley might be held, though it was obvious the tower supported a lot of guards. There were chairs for a dozen of them to sit at once, and presumably if that many were sitting, there were just as many on duty.

Grimacing, Rew went back to the stairwell and started up again. This time, he crouched down on the stairs. Peeking over the top step, he saw a huge door that led from the tower to the bridge and the keep. The double-height door was reinforced and barred with three bolts as thick as his arm. Had they attempted to storm the place, there was no way they would have gotten through that. Worse, there were more than a dozen guards loitering around, some chatting in small groups, others pacing around looking bored.

There was a table to one side of the door with a fat ledger open on top of it. A sealed jar of ink and a quill were beside the ledger, but at the moment, no one was at the table. As Rew watched, one of the guards called out, "They're opening the gate at the keep. Looks like a visitor."

The man was peering through an iron-barred window beside the door. He waved to his companions. Several of the guards started wrestling with the huge bolts, sliding them out of the heavy brackets with difficulty so that they could open the door.

Rew glanced back down the stairwell, wondering if the two men he'd just killed were the ones in charge of the ledger. It could be where they kept a log of their prisoners and their guests. Rew looked at the backs of the dozen guards opening the door and then gestured for Anne and the younglings to go up the stairs.

Whether or not the two men below would be expected to greet a new arrival, they weren't going to have a better chance than now to ascend the stairs with the guards all facing the door. If they could, Rew wanted to find Baron Fedgley before they had to deal with a mass of guards coming after them. If it came to it, they could use the baron's help. Quietly, Rew climbed the stairs, Zaine tight on his heels. Less quietly, Raif started up in a rustle of steel and leather.

Zaine rolled her eyes at Rew, and he held his breath, lurking at the bend in the stairwell, hoping the sound of the scraping metal bolts in the door and the guards' own clattering armor would cover the stomp of Raif's boots and the scrape of his steel.

"It's the girl again," called one of the guards. "Coming to see the baron."

"Pfah," muttered another voice. "She's been coming every day for weeks. The man's not going to crack for her. Give Jonas a bit of time downstairs with the pincers, and he'll pull the baron into line. The duke is wasting his time with this deception, if you ask me."

"The duke needs the baron," argued another soldier. "Jonas could break the man, but that's not what is needed. The duke is smart. Arcanist Salwart is smart. They both know the girl is the way to the baron's heart. She's how they'll get the man working for them, and he'll be glad of it."

Forgoing stealth for speed, the party scrambled up the stairs, knowing that in seconds, the guards would turn and could not possibly miss the five of them standing in the middle of the passageway.

Rew rushed up to the next floor and nearly barreled into a man who was standing in the opening of a room. With no time to think, Rew swung a crisp uppercut and caught the startled soldier on the chin. The man's eyes went dark like a candle that had been snuffed out, and Rew surged forward, catching the body and slowing its descent to the floor.

"Did you just—" began another soldier.

Rew, still crouched over the first man, ripped a knife from his boot and flung it at the second man.

The blade caught the soldier square in the eye. He toppled back, slumping against the wall.

"Nice throw," whispered Zaine.

"I feel strange," said Cinda, staggering into the room.

Rew was staring over the bodies of the two guards to where a trio of doors and a wall blocked half the space on the floor. The rest of the area was covered in thick carpets, comfortable chairs, and a banquet that held fruits, breads, and flagons of wine.

Behind them was a wide glass door that led to a balcony. Through the glass door, Rew saw the bridge between the tower and the keep thrusting across the open air like a spear. Duke Eeron's fortress rose like a monolith beyond. On the bridge, Rew glimpsed half a dozen people walking toward them and disappearing out of sight beneath the balcony. The girl that the guards had mentioned along with an escort, he guessed.

Unlike the prison cells below, the doors on this floor were constructed of solid steel, and one of them was glowing with bright, cerulean patterns traced in silver. Bands of steel, glowing gemstones, and silver ran all along the wall and disappeared, like it was encircling a room.

"King's Sake," muttered Rew, staring in shock at the patterns. "Arcanist Ralcrist's design. They've built these cells specifically for spellcasters. I've never seen anything like it."

Cinda collapsed into a chair, and Anne crouched beside her. The empath muttered, "She's hurting."

"The wards," said Rew.

Only one of the cell doors was locked and glowing. He strode forward and knelt beside the dead guards, pulling a ring of keys off one of the men's belt. There were only three keys. He tried them in the locked door, found the one that worked, and yanked the door open. Immediately, the pulsating glow faded from the cerulean specks embedded in the door and the walls.

"Again?" growled a weary voice from inside.

"We're here to rescue you, Baron Fedgley," said Rew.

"Senior Ranger," said the baron, looking up from where he was sitting hunched over on the foot of an unkempt bed. His arms were bound in glowing shackles, and he appeared to have lost a stone of weight. His face was sallow, his eyes haunted as he peered at Rew, blinking in the sudden light. "Who is we?"

"Your youngest children," said Rew.

Baron Fedgley's eyes fell back to his lap.

"Father!" said Raif, shoving past Rew to get into the cell.

"You shouldn't have come," said Fedgley. "You're only going to get yourself killed, you fool boy."

"We're here to save you, Father," declared Raif.

The baron huffed, not looking up at his son and not rising off the bed.

"Uh, Rew," said Zaine, leaning her head in, "the only thing above us is the roof, and below us are two dozen guards. I think we've got less than a minute before they're coming up here."

Rew stomped over to Baron Fedgley and hauled the man to his feet. The baron's arm felt like nothing more than skin and bone, and his flesh hung loosely off him like a scarecrow's jacket. The ranger dragged the baron out of the cell and into the room outside.

Cinda leapt to her feet. "Father!"

Baron Fedgley's head slumped down at the sound of his daughter's voice. His body was wracked with tremors, as if he was sobbing. Tears of joy? Rew frowned at the broken man, not certain that was why the baron was crying.

"A key, we need a key!" exclaimed Raif, pulling the key ring from the door where Rew had left it. The boy frowned at the keys and then at the manacles on his father's wrists. "I don't think these are going to work…"

Rew shook his head. "It won't be any ordinary key that opens these. The manacles are warded, and I'm certain they will have taken other precautions—like not keeping the key up here, for one. King's Sake. It could be on those men we killed two floors down, or it might not even be in the tower!"

"What do we do, then?" asked Raif, looking from Rew to his father, hoping for answers.

Rew leaned over and studied the manacles on the baron's wrists. The older man didn't object. He didn't do much of anything, except shake his head. He wouldn't look at his two children.

Rew stood up and pointed at Raif's greatsword. "That's your key."

Nodding curtly, Raif pulled his father over to the table the second guard had been seated at and instructed the baron to put his arms on it. He hissed, "Hold them flat."

"Rew!" said Zaine from near the stairwell. She was moving from one foot to the other. "I can hear them downstairs. We're out of time. Do you have a plan?"

Rew glanced back at Raif and Cinda. He said, "Free your father and have him call upon his wraiths. I'll buy us time."

He strode to the top of the stairs beside Zaine and drew his longsword and his hunting knife. He crouched, ready. Behind him, he could hear Raif admonishing his father to hold his hands still, to keep his arms flat. Below, Rew heard the muffled voices of the guards. They were greeting each other, he thought, and then he heard the shuffle of armor as they approached the stairs.

"Should we shut the door?" whispered Zaine, a hand on the sturdy wood barrier that barred the top of the stairwell.

"Not yet," replied Rew.

"What are we waiting on?" questioned Zaine, her words low and harsh. "If we don't shut it now, they're—"

"We're waiting on her," said Rew.

Coming up the stairs were a pair of guards, Kallie Fedgley, and half a dozen soldiers behind her.

"Get the girl, drag her upstairs, and slam that door shut," instructed Rew. "Don't wait on me, Zaine. The baron has the power to protect you, but he'll need time."

The thief nodded.

On the stairs, the first pair of guards paused, confused. One of them barked, "What is this?"

Rew launched himself down the stairs, careening like an avalanche, arresting his momentum when he kicked a boot into the face of the guard who'd spoken.

The man pitched backward, completely unprepared for the attack, though he was more fortunate than his companion. Rew reached across and slid his longsword into that man's throat. The dying guard fell away, and Rew darted around Kallie, who stood rooted in the center of the stairwell, her jaw hanging on her chest.

The guards behind the noblewoman had an extra moment to prepare, but they were packed tightly in the narrow passage and their movements were fouled by the two fallen men who'd collapsed onto them.

Rew put the point of his longsword onto the stone stair and vaulted, lashing out with his feet again, pounding the heel of his boot into another man's chest, forcing the pack of guards farther down the stairs. Surprised at the unexpected attack, the soldiers retreated, dragging their injured companions with them. Rew took advantage of the disarray to spin around and charge back up the stairwell.

Zaine was tugging on Kallie's arms, hauling the girl after her. Rew crashed into the back of them, shoving both girls ahead of him and through the doorway. He spun and slammed the door shut. Zaine was by his side, sliding the bolt home, locking them into the tower room.

"Now what?" the thief asked.

"I'm hoping the baron will do something," muttered Rew, turning to look where Raif was standing next to his father, his greatsword raised above his head.

The big youth brought his sword down, and the enchanted blade crashed against the warded manacles around Baron Fedgley's wrists. The steel shattered beneath the heavy blow in a cloud of acrid smoke and sparks. Rew saw a purple bolt of lightning shiver up the enchanted blade like an uncurling snake, but the charge didn't reach the hilt, and Raif stepped back, looking in surprise at his Father's pale, exposed wrists.

Anne darted forward, clasping the baron's arms. "A slight fracture, no more," she called. "With my healing, it will hold until we get out of here."

"A well-aimed blow," Rew said to Raif. He moved beside the baron and told him, "M'lord, we need you. Call upon your wraiths. We have minutes at the most before Duke Eeron's spellcasters are here, and without your strength, we can't face them all."

The baron, staring morosely at his bare arms and the broken steel around them, whispered, "They have Kallie. They have my daughter, and there was nothing I could do. Now, they'll have the rest of my children. They'll have Cinda. You imbeciles, what have you done?"

Rew blinked and turned to Kallie. "Ah, Kallie is right here, Baron Fedgley."

The man looked up, his eyes hard. "Kallie?"

"Yes, Father," she whispered.

"You escaped," murmured the baron. "I'm surprised. You should have run, though. You should have saved yourself when you could."

"Escaped?" interjected Zaine. "She's been free this entire time."

Kallie scowled at Zaine and muttered, "I recognize you. You're the one who came to my room. I told you to leave this city. Be silent, girl."

Rew shook his head, baffled. Anne glanced at him, but he could only return her confused look.

"That bastard arcanist of Eeron's, Salwart, was holding her, torturing her," said Baron Fedgley, rising slowly to his feet. "They were trying to coerce me into joining them, doing—I couldn't. Not for Kallie. Not for anyone. I am sorry, my girl, but I couldn't do it."

"Torturing her?" spluttered Zaine.

"I said be quiet!" snapped Kallie, glaring at the thief.

"She wasn't a captive, Father," murmured Cinda, staring at her older sister in bewilderment.

"She was," said the baron, drawing himself up hesitantly, feeling the effects of a month of confinement. He raised a hand toward his eldest daughter, but he did not move to embrace her. "They brought her to me every day. I saw the marks on her skin, the horrible evidence of what they'd done to her. I saw it, but I could not break. I would not break! I am sorry, my girl, but you must understand it was for our family. It was the best thing for all of us. I couldn't let them make me—"

"I understand," snapped Kallie, her voice dripping with venom. "All for your family. Those you consider a part of it, that is."

"Kallie," said Cinda, stepping toward her older sister.

Kallie growled at her younger sister. "He thought I was being tortured, but he didn't care. He didn't care, because you were free. You thought I'd run away with you, did you? That you'd forget I was sent away, and that none of you cared? Did you believe I'd really go back with you to Falvar, where I'd be no more than a forgotten woman, dependent on your largess? Why are you here, Cinda? Why did you come?"

"W-We're..." stammered Cinda, "we're here to rescue Father. And you, of course."

"Always Father's little girl, weren't you?" snarled Kallie. "Always his favorite. The reason he and Mother stopped having children. Did you know? You're just like him. A necromancer just like him. You'd do anything for him, wouldn't you?" She glanced at Baron Fedgley and spat, "If you thought Cinda was being held, you would have been soft clay in Arcanist Salwart's hands. What wouldn't you do for her—for the family's magical prodigy? I knew he'd made a mistake thinking you'd join them just to rescue me. I knew you wouldn't do it, but I had to see for myself. I had to—I had to see it."

"Kallie!" cried Baron Fedgley. "Do not speak so disrespectfully. We are the power that is within our blood, and it is Cinda who carries that power for the Fedgleys. She is the future of our line. I hurt for you, my girl, but I had no choice."

Kallie looked away.

Raif shifted uncomfortably, glancing between his older sister and his father. "Father... we have to leave."

The door to the room shattered in a hail of broken wood and twisted metal. Debris peppered Rew's side, and he was thrown off his feet by the concussion of air that screamed through the open doorway. He rolled and then jumped to his feet.

Vyar Grund stood in the doorway. Over the mask that covered the lower-half of his face, his eyes were hard as granite. The ranger commandant raised his arm and pointed at Rew. From around him came two massive simians. They wore heavy, scale armor. Steel spikes poked from bracers on their forearms. Their knuckles were covered in steel-studded gloves. The simians screeched, their mouths opening wide, their yellowed-fangs protruding.

"King's Sake," hissed Rew.

"You should have gone back to the wilderness," boomed Grund. "You should have stayed away."

He snapped his fingers, and his trained simians attacked.

They scampered toward Rew in their odd, halting gait. The steel on their gauntlets scraped against the stone floor as they charged.

"Baron Fedgley, we need your wraiths!" barked Rew.

Before he could turn to see if the baron was listening, the first simian was on him. Rew dodged to the side as the creature grasped for him with its powerful hands. Luckily, if such a thing was possible given how the rest of the day was going, it seemed that while Grund had armed and armored his pets, he hadn't taught them how to effectively make use of their new toys. Instead of trying to grapple with him and slash him with their bracers or smash him with their gauntlets, the simians were reaching for him just like they would with no armor or weapons. Of course, that still meant two beasts, his weight and half again each, were chasing Rew around the open room.

He darted behind the table in the room and kicked it toward the closest simian. He thrust at the second with his longsword, and the tip of the blade bounced off the simian's thick scale armor. Cursing, Rew ducked as the table came flying back at him, narrowly missing his head, and then, he nearly tripped over Zaine, who was crouching behind him.

"Shoot them with your arrows, lass!" he bellowed. "Wait, wait, no. Get everyone to the rooftop, and have the baron summon those damned wraiths before we all join them in death!"

"You want me to—" She cut off in a squawk as one of the simians lumbered toward her.

Rew slashed with his longsword, catching the simian on the upper arm and drawing a deep cut, but he couldn't lean into the blow because the second one was leaping at him. He backed away, slicing his longsword through the air in front of the simians to keep them back, and then was nearly decapitated as Vyar Grund clicked his blades together and scissored them, attempting a dramatic flourish that would have resulted in Rew's body becoming headless.

Rew dropped and spun, kicking out with a leg and catching the ranger commandant on the knee. Grund's feet were swept out from under him, and he crashed down. Rew jumped over the prone body of the ranger commandant and rolled, the simians just behind him, nearly trampling their master as they came after Rew. Spinning again to face his attackers, Rew swung his blade and cleaved through the foot of one of the charging beasts. It went down, skidding and wailing in anger.

The other hurdled its injured companion and reached for Rew, grasping his ankle in a bone-crushing grip. Its other hand swiped at his face. Rew barely turned it aside with his longsword. He jerked his hunting knife free of his belt and slammed it down into the arm that held his ankle. The simian's hand spasmed, and his leg was free. Skipping back to his feet, Rew saw Vyar Grund rise as well. Rew readied himself.

The ranger commandant held his two gleaming falchions wide.

"Who are you working for?" asked Rew. "The king or Valchon?"

The eyes over Grund's mask did not change, and he offered no explanation, just an attack. He came at Rew sweeping both of his falchions in a horizontal slash.

Rew dodged out of the way, knowing how difficult it'd be to block both of the man's weapons at once. Rew struck, swinging a quick counter to Grund's attack, but the commandant caught it with one falchion then thrust with his second blade.

Wincing, Rew backed away again. Grund's style was to wait for an attack and then counter, and it was devastating when one faced him with a single blade and no shield, but Rew sheathed his knife and put both hands on the hilt of his longsword. The smaller blade would be at a horrible disadvantage against Grund's falchions.

The ranger commandant seemed to be waiting for Rew to attack, but when Rew didn't, he came in again, swinging high with one blade and thrusting low with the other.

Rew blocked the high stroke, moved to the side to avoid the thrust, but then paid for it with a long, bloody cut on his hip when Grund turned his falchion and drew it along Rew's side as he stepped back. As Grund pulled his falchion, slicing Rew's skin, Rew swung down with his longsword, taking Grund on the side of the head, shearing away one of the man's ears and sending a spray of crimson blood down Grund's front.

In a blaze of speed, blood flinging from his face, Vyar Grund attacked.

Rew, with no thought of offense, met each blow with his longsword, retreating, trying to buy time for the others, hoping the baron could do something before Grund hacked him in two. Rew had gotten lucky, he knew. The ranger commandant had been overconfident, certain he could easily handle one of his rangers. It had given Rew an opening, but it wouldn't happen again.

Rew retreated. One of the simians skittered close but then backed away as the clanging swords slashed near its face.

Rew and Grund parted as the simian screeched at them. In the momentary break, Grund sheathed one of his falchions and held up his hand. It ignited in a burst of orange and red fire. A shield formed of living flame. Grund advanced.

Rew feinted, drawing Grund's falchion to the side, then swung a quick strike at the man's shield. It wouldn't have reached Grund's body, but Rew needed to know what the barrier was made of. His longsword clinked and bounced off the flaming shield as if he'd struck a steel one, but when Grund advanced, Rew could feel the heat of the fire on his face.

Rew cursed then taunted, "Whichever prince is holding your leash taught you a few tricks?"

Grund's expression didn't change, but Rew saw a flicker of motion in his bright eyes. He ducked.

A huge body slammed into Rew's back, sending him staggering forward onto his knees, a furred arm punching over his head. The simian's steel-covered knuckles missed his spine with a bone-crunching strike only because he'd ducked the second before.

Grund thrust, stabbing down at Rew with his falchion.

Rew twisted, reaching up and grabbing the simian's arm. It was too big for him to throw it off, but he pulled it forward, and the creature's body took the brunt of Grund's attack. The falchion skewered it, and Rew felt the tip of the blade poke out the simian's body, pricking his shoulder.

Kneeling under the weight of the simian on his back, Rew swept a blow beneath Grund's fiery shield and clipped the man across the shin. The strike finally elicited a reaction from the ranger commandant. Grund stumbled back, cursing.

Rew shrugged off the simian and stood. He could see blood showing through the slice in the front of the ranger commandant's boot, but it hadn't shattered Grund's shinbone. Hopefully, it'd slow him a little. The surviving simian was standing again, moving slow as well, the toes of one foot chopped off by Rew.

Rew turned and ran for the stairs, following his companions to the roof. Grund and his remaining simian chased after.

Crashing up the flight of stairs, Rew skidded, slammed against the wall as the stairwell turned, and then shoved off, lurching up toward the open doorway that led to the roof of the tower. He hoped to find Baron Fedgley standing there surrounded by his wraiths. Rew had been counting on the powerful spirits to help them escape, but instead, as he ran into the light of day, Rew saw Alsayer stepping through an open portal.

The spellcaster's thick black eyebrows were raised comically in surprise as he surveyed the scene. Evidently deciding what was going on in the blink of an eye, Alsayer flung a cloud of intense black speckled with brilliant shimmering sparks directly at Rew. From their last encounter, Rew knew the sparks would cut like saw blades. Without thought or grace, Rew dropped to his belly.

A heart-wrenching scream erupted behind him as the simian caught the full force of the spell. Rew didn't need to look to know what had happened to the poor animal, but as he was rising, he was almost engulfed by a giant ball of bubbling, liquid fire coming from behind him.

Alsayer raised his arms, and an invisible wall of solid sound thumped into place, absorbing the glob of fire and splattering heat across the rooftop of the tower. The spellcaster growled, "Grund, what are you doing here?"

Deciding it was best not to lie directly in between the two spellcasters as they dueled, Rew rolled away and, only seconds later, realized his companions were trapped on the other side of the confrontation.

Alsayer's portal blinked out behind him, and the spellcaster stood on the far side of the roof, shaking his head in confusion. "This doesn't involve you, Grund. You shouldn't be here. You're neutral—"

"I don't know what you're up to, you treacherous bastard," snarled Vyar Grund. "but if you think you can slide a blade into Prince Valchon's back and get away with it, you're dead wrong."

The ranger commandant limped out of the stairwell, blood dripping from him like from a sieve. White bone shone on the side of his head where Rew had sliced off his ear and a large flap of skin. The commandant's arm and shoulder were torn with ugly crimson punctures where bits of Alsayer's cloud must have gotten through the simian. Grund limped, each step leaving one bloody footprint, but ignoring the injuries, Grund stepped over the dead body of his simian and strode toward Alsayer.

The spellcaster, a half-smirk twisting his face, said, "Looks like you've had a bit of bad luck, Commandant."

Grund reached up and drew his second falchion. "Enough talk, Spellcaster."

Alsayer shrugged and then unleashed his magic.

22

I t was as if an invisible elephant came running across the rooftop of the tower. A throbbing hum threatened to burst Rew's eardrums, and he couldn't hear the crunch of shattering stone as unseen steps pounded the roof tiles between Alsayer and Vyar Grund.

The ranger commandant's eyes widened and he crossed his falchions in front of himself half a second before Alsayer's spell smashed into him. Grund was thrown back, and Rew lost sight of him in the debris of the shattered structure that had housed the stairwell. The structure, built an age ago, simply flattened like a broken egg. Fragments of stone and wood sprayed from the impact, flying off the edge of the tower in a billowing cloud. It was seconds before the pressure lifted and Rew could hear again.

"Baron Fedgley," declared Alsayer, turning from the destruction he'd caused, "I should be upset you're attempting to escape, but you are a cretin, and I find I can only feel sorry for you. You have no idea the risk your daughter is in, coming here. If you want to preserve your family and their legacy, then the best thing you can do is stay away from them. You should have agreed to assist us, but if you refuse that, you should have remained in the cell behind the wards. I'm constantly surprised men like you even think to involve yourselves in matters like these. This is so far beyond your understanding that I... Ah, why am I bothering? Let's get those chains back on you and send your brood on their way, shall we?"

The baron, shaking off the assistance of Raif, stood straight. His body looked like a man who'd been ravaged by a month of captivity and torture, but his eyes blazed with the same confident fury that Rew had seen in his throne room. The baron raised his arms and, in his deep, arrogant voice, declared, "It is you who've erred, Spellcaster."

Alsayer giggled. "This again?"

From afar, like a scream carried on the wind, they heard the approach of the wraiths. A chill that had nothing to do with the bitter wind swept across the tower, cutting through Rew's cloak and tunic. Despite himself, he shivered.

"Do you never learn? Do you not recall what happened to the last wraiths you summoned?" asked Alsayer, shaking his head in amusement. The spellcaster dropped his hand to his waist and stuck his fingers into a small pouch hanging from his belt. His fingers pushed through the pouch and came out the bottom, which had been slit open. Alsayer froze.

Zaine, standing between Raif and Cinda, held up the small silver box Alsayer had used to capture the wraiths when they were in Falvar. "Looking for this?" She twirled one of her daggers in her other hand and laughed. "And they told me cutting purses would never get me anywhere."

"Blessed Mother!" cried Alsayer. "Lass, you don't know what you're doing!"

The spellcaster raised his arm toward the thief, but before he could cast a spell, Zaine flung the little silver box over the edge of the tower. Alsayer's eyes followed the arc of the throw, his shoulders slumping like the wind leaving a sail. He turned to Baron Fedgley and raised his hands.

"Don't let him kill the baron!" cried Rew, rushing across the broken roof tiles, trying to insert himself between the spellcaster and the baron. He warned the others, "If Fedgley is dead, no one can control the wraiths."

Alsayer, for his part, seemed to agree. The spellcaster stood, his arm held out quivering, but he did not release his magic.

Cackling, the baron curled his fingers and drew the wraiths toward the tower. In the bright light of day, Rew could not see them, but he could feel them. They were ancient, from another time, a race before man. Their age imbued them with immense power. They would feast upon Spinesend if the baron lost control of his charges.

"What do you plan to do, kill me?" asked Alsayer, allowing his hands to fall to his side.

"I'm not going to kill you, Spellcaster," growled Fedgley. "I'm going to bargain with you. Isn't that what men such as you do?"

Alsayer's eyebrows rose, but he did not regain any of his haughty confidence. Rew thought the spellcaster could likely flee before the wraiths struck, but Alsayer hesitated. He was never one to turn from a negotiation.

"You're going to go back to your master, and you're going to tell him that I am finished with groveling for his scraps, being tossed back and forth between him and his brothers like a cat's plaything," instructed Baron Fedgley. "For the last month, I've sat in this tower with nothing to do but think. I'm embarrassed it took so long, but I finally realized why the princes want me and why the king fears me. The House of Fedgley will rise, Spellcaster." The baron gestured to Raif and Cinda. "By my side, my son and daughter will rule. Not the duchy, no. We are beyond that, don't you think? From whichever prince ascends the throne, I demand the entire Eastern Province. We shall rule from Carff, Cinda studying necromancy by my side, Raif ruling our lands and our people with my guidance. Together—"

Baron Fedgley spluttered and looked down at his chest.

Around the tower, the wraiths swirled, their psychic songs penetrating Rew's body. He felt like a filleted fish sitting on a block of ice in the market. He blinked at Fedgley. The man's mouth opened and shut. The baron raised a hand and touched the front of his filthy doublet.

"W-What…" stammered Alsayer. "What have you done?"

Baron Fedgley fell, sprawling face first on the roof of the tower. Behind him, his daughter Kallie was grinning malevolently. A dagger stuck up from Baron Fedgley's back.

"No!" shrieked Alsayer. "No!"

Rew glanced back and forth between the body of the baron and Alsayer. He didn't know what to do.

Kallie spit on her father's corpse before looking at the others. "He believed I was being tortured. He could have saved me with a word, but he didn't. He… You heard him. He had no place for me, his oldest daughter. Family? Family? It was never about that. It was always about him and his foul magic. He's the only one he ever cared about. You're just like him, Cinda, more attuned to the dead than the living, and you, Raif, you must have seen it just like I did, but you've the man bits, eh? You'd take any of father's disrespect if it meant you got to rule the barony. Pfah. You're both as bad as he was."

"K-Kallie…" stammered Cinda.

"I wish you luck, cousin," said Alsayer, raising his voice and looking to Rew. He raised a hand and twisted it. Beside him, a purple and gold vortex formed, and the spellcaster burrowed a tunnel through the ether to a place other than Spinesend. "If you survive the wraiths, we'll meet again. It's all on the lass, now. They'll come for her. They'll keep coming until it's over, Rew. She's the only hope. I don't expect you to believe it yet, but we don't have to be enemies in this. We want the same thing. Think about it."

Without further word and before Rew could respond, Alsayer stepped through his portal. The moment his foot cleared the Spinesend side, it began to close behind him, but before it closed fully, Kallie streaked by Rew and leapt like she was diving into a deep pool. Her hands held out before her, she plunged through the opening, and in a blink, it closed behind her.

"Blessed Mother!" gasped Zaine.

"Father!" cried Raif, falling to his knees beside the body of the baron. He put his hands on his father and looked up at Anne, hope and grief battling on his face. "You can help him. You have to help him!"

"Anne," said Rew, "the wraiths. If you can…"

Nodding, the empath dropped beside the baron and his son. She put her hands on the body of Baron Fedgley. For a brief moment, Rew held his breath, and then Anne looked up and met his eyes. She shook her head.

Rew exhaled, horror replacing the air that left his body. He looked around. He could see nothing in the bright sunlight, but he could feel them. They were close still.

"Do you hear that?" asked Zaine.

She and Rew walked to the side of the tower, and they looked down at the bridge that spanned the gap between the tower and the keep. On the bridge, men were dying. They must have been alerted to the commotion in the tower and had come running from the keep, but now, like a farmer mowing his field with a scythe, the incorporeal forms of the wraiths were sweeping through several companies of Duke Eeron's soldiers. Limbs were severed, blood sprayed, and bodies were mauled as the wraiths tore through the men. The soldiers' armor and weapons were useless against the apparitions, and all the men could do was run or die. Toward the keep, some of them were running, but more soldiers were pouring out onto the bridge. A brief fight erupted between Duke Eeron's own men as some fought to escape and others had no idea what was happening ahead of them.

"Blessed Mother!" Zaine croaked. "How do we stop them?"

Rew shook his head. "We cannot until they are sated. Spirits that old… it's going to be a long time. This is… this is going to be bad."

"We can pray," said Anne. "We can pray to the Blessed Mother."

"That won't work," argued Rew.

"It has to work," declared Anne.

"For the Blessed Mother to intervene," argued Rew, "the old stories say she'd demand a show of faith. Another would be clutched to her bosom—Anne, no!"

Shaking her head, the empath declared, "It is the only way, Rew. How many will those wraiths kill? Thousands?"

"Anne, you don't even know it would work. And how many lives will you save if you live?" demanded Rew. "Maybe the wraiths won't—"

"That's a false choice," she stated, laughing bitterly. She gestured to the bridge. They could see soldiers flinging themselves from the pathway, evidently choosing the quick rush of a fall and deadly impact over the terrible destruction the wraiths were reaping. "When they're done with the soldiers, will the wraiths enter the keep or turn to the tower? We have to act now, while we can."

Rew shook his head angrily. "I've no faith in your Blessed Mother, Anne."

"Rew, I have to do this," replied the empath. "Unless you have a plan, faith is all that we have."

He reached out and gripped both of her arms. "Anne—"

"My father's wraiths," said Cinda, her voice awed. "I-I can feel them."

Anne and Rew held each other's gaze. Then, as one, they turned to Cinda.

"They're killing all of those men," whispered Cinda. "So many deaths. I can feel those as well, those souls being torn away. It's not over when they die, it's... The wraiths are feeding on the departing souls. My father, my family, is this what we are?"

"Cinda—" began Rew, but the girl kept speaking, lost in what she was feeling, seeing.

"My father called these things," said Cinda. "He called them in Falvar. In our home. He called to them knowing what they did! This is the legacy of the Fedgleys! This is what we are."

"Cinda," interrupted Rew, stepping toward her, "your father called to these, but you can send them away."

"W-What?" she stammered.

"He summoned these creatures, and you can banish them," said Anne, taking Cinda's other side.

"How?" asked the girl, quaking, unable to turn from the slaughter on the bridge.

"Send them back to where they came from," replied Anne.

"How?" repeated Cinda.

Anne could only shrug. She looked at Rew hopelessly.

"Try casting them away," suggested Rew. "Try... You can feel them? See if you can shove them away, all of the way back to where they came from. Instead of drawing your magic, push it."

Cinda closed her eyes.

Rew turned and watched as the soldiers fought against something they could not see, could not touch, did not understand, but the wraiths could touch the soldiers, and the bridge was slick with blood and gore. Rew had no idea how many men had perished already, but their remains painted the path from the tower to the keep in bright globs of gleaming crimson and pink.

Suddenly, the killing stopped.

"I think I did something," said Cinda, opening her eyes.

"Are they gone?" wondered Zaine.

Rew shook his head. "No. Can't you still feel them?"

"I feel... Are they coming closer?" asked the thief.

"You got their attention," said Anne to Cinda. "Now, ah, quickly now, banish them back to where they came from."

"I don't know how!" protested Cinda.

The awful presence of the wraiths was climbing the outside of the tower. It felt like ice was freezing the blood in his veins. Rew pushed Cinda back and stood at the battlement, waiting. He didn't know what he would do when those creatures appeared, but he couldn't let them take the girl without a fight.

"Rew, don't be a fool!" snapped Anne.

He had to try.

"Cinda, hurry!" shouted Zaine.

Her voice seemed to echo as the physic energy of the wraiths rolled over them, reverberating strangely, over and over. Rew didn't know if Zaine's shout was being repeated or if time had twisted in the presence of the undead. He stood rooted, his longsword in his hands, but he couldn't see anything. There was nothing for him to strike, nothing for him to do. He felt the wraiths reach the top of the battlement. They hung, insubstantial, appearing to be only the faintest wisps of vapor in the bright sun. They were directly in front of him. Frozen, unable to do anything at all, Rew stood his ground. He waited, and then, the wraiths came for him.

Behind him, Cinda released a primal scream. It sounded as if she was giving birth, as if the wail of her voice could rip open the world. Her scream continued, echoing and growing, and then, it stopped.

Rew blinked.

He was cold, but not from the energy of the wraiths. From the wind, whistling through the crenellations of the battlement, from the chill autumn air. Screams and shouts rose on that wind, but it was silent behind him. He spun. Anne was kneeling, holding Cinda. The girl was pale, but her chest rose and fell with breath.

The empath shook her head. "She'll live, but she's not used to handling such power. It's done damage to her, I think. Rew, she's not going to be moving for hours yet. Maybe days. That took more strength than what she did during the battle. We're going to have to carry her out of here."

Rew grimaced.

Zaine stepped beside him, looking from Cinda's prone form to where Raif still knelt beside his dead father. She turned to Rew. "I don't suppose you—"

She was interrupted by the clatter of stone.

They both looked over and saw Vyar Grund emerging from the edge of the tower where he'd been buried in a pile of rubble. His face was caked with rock dust and blood, and his shoulders were slumped, but he had the strength still to raise his two falchions.

"How is he alive?" Zaine exclaimed.

"He's been magically fortified by the king himself," explained Rew. "The ranger commandant is a hard man to kill."

"I can see that," whispered the thief.

"I'd better get to it, then," said Rew. He raised his longsword and advanced.

Thanks to the king's magic, Vyar Grund, the Ranger Commandant, was a nearly impossible man to kill. Fortunately, they already had a good start.

Dust fell from the commandant, and blood dripped as he stumbled his way through the crumbled remains of the stairwell. He raised his arm, and Rew suspected would have formed a portal, but he couldn't. He'd used too much of his magic surviving Alsayer's attack. Grund stomped his feet and settled himself. Evidently, he had decided there was nothing to do now but fight.

Rew could barely see the commandant's face through the coat of blood and dust on it, but neither of them bothered to speak. Rew didn't need to see his old superior's expression to know there was no mercy there. Grund waited, so Rew attacked.

He thrust straight at Grund's face, expecting the man would easily block it, and when Grund counterattacked, Rew ducked low, spinning on a heel, but instead of sweeping his longsword toward Grund's feet as he had done earlier, he swung up.

Grund jumped, sensing the same attack Rew had used on him successfully in the room below, but he didn't jump high enough to avoid Rew's blade. The longsword sliced across Grund's stomach, almost disemboweling the ranger commandant. Coughing, Grund landed, staggering backward.

Rew twirled his longsword and struck again and again. Grund's counterattacks came slower, and Rew was able to slide a thrust past his guard and pierce the commandant's shoulder. Rew chopped down, drawing a line of sparks and forcing Grund's falchion along the stone roof tiles. Then, Rew whipped his longsword back and severed several of the ranger commandant's toes.

Grund launched a paltry attack, and Rew beat it aside and swung a blow up, catching Grund on the chin, cutting through skin and cracking bone, flinging the man's half-mask away.

Rew's next attack struck the commandant's wrist, though Grund managed to hang onto his falchion. He couldn't do anything with the blade, though, and Rew easily knocked it away and then slammed a thrust into the commandant's chest.

Grund, reeling backward, tried to make room to defend himself, to cast a spell at Rew, to do anything, but Rew kept after him, giving him no space and no time to formulate a plan or to build his magic. There was a strike to Grund's thigh, his hip, and then, Rew chopped hard into the other man's good arm. Grund, fighting silently, elicited a moan at that blow. Any normal man would have been dead three times over, but Grund stumbled away, still on his feet, both of his arms nearly useless. He was walking with the grace of a newborn foal. Rew followed, preparing to take the commandant's head off and end it, but instead of turning to face him, Grund kept shambling away.

"King's Sake," muttered Rew, and he started to chase after his commandant, but he was too late.

Grund stumbled to the battlement, and without pause, he pitched himself over it. There was no scream as the man fell, no shriek of terror, nothing. He was simply gone.

Rew stared at where Grund had jumped off the tower, flummoxed.

"I didn't see that coming," quipped Zaine.

Rew shook his head, walked to the battlement, and looked down. Five hundred paces below them, a tiny speck marked the spot Vyar Grund's body had landed.

Zaine joined Rew. "That ought to do it, huh?"

"Maybe."

"What?" she asked, her head snapping up to look at Rew.

"I told you. Vyar Grund is a hard man to kill," said ranger, studying the fallen body. It wasn't moving, but that didn't mean it wouldn't.

He turned and surveyed the party. Raif's head was bowed against the back of his father's. He knelt beside the dead man, weeping. Anne cradled Cinda, looking up at Rew grim-faced. She'd already thought of what he was now considering. Zaine, showing the most impetus of any of them, was by the stairwell, looking at the mess it used to be. The top of it had been blown back by the force of Alsayer's spell, and much of the rubble had fallen down inside. The roof of the stairs had collapsed.

"We're not getting through here," advised the thief.

Rew walked to the other side of the tower, opposite of where Grund had thrown himself off, and hopped up between two crenellations.

"Rew!" exclaimed Zaine.

"The bridge," he reminded her.

"Oh," she said. She looked over the edge and remarked, "I can make that jump, and you, but the others…"

"We'll catch them," declared Rew. He looked back to Anne. "Are you ready, if we need you?"

She nodded.

"Raif," called Rew, "it's time to go."

The boy did not move. He stayed beside his father, his hands impotently clutching the dead man's clothing. Across the yawning gap between the tower and the keep, Rew could hear alarm bells. He could hear distant orders being shouted, and he knew they wouldn't have much time. The carnage on the bridge would dissuade the regular soldiers, but eventually, Duke Eeron or his spellcasters would force the men out. Soon, they would be coming.

Sighing, Rew hopped down and walked to Raif. He picked up the boy's huge greatsword and declared, "Raif Fedgley, you are now the eldest male of your line. You are Baron Fedgley, lad. You're the head of your house, and we need you."

Raif did not move. He mumbled into his father's body, "The baron of what? Our line is tarnished. Our name means nothing. Our city has been taken, and our liege has betrayed us."

"The name was tarnished, aye," said Rew, "but it doesn't have to end that way, lad. You're alive. Cinda is alive. The line continues."

He thought it best not to mention that as far as they knew, the eldest sister Kallie was alive as well. Another time. It wouldn't matter if they all died in the next few minutes.

Raif stayed with his head bowed over his father.

"Do you want the name Fedgley to stand for a selfish necromancer who called upon wraiths that slaughtered hundreds, or do you want it to mean something else? You have the power, lad, to restore the honor of your name. Only you have that power."

Finally, Raif looked up. His eyes were rimmed in red, and his lips were pressed tightly together. "I know what you're trying to do, Ranger. Don't think to play with me and our honor. It won't work."

Rew snorted. He turned and pointed to Cinda. "I can't get her out of here without you, lad. If you don't help, she's going to die. Forget your name. Forget your honor. I don't care. But will you forget your sister? I thought you were a fighter, Raif. Fight for her."

Scowling at Rew, Raif struggled to his feet. Wordlessly, Rew handed the boy the greatsword. For a moment, he worried Raif was going to use it on him, but instead, Raif asked, "What's your plan?"

❧ 23 ❧

Rew had gone first. He'd been standing between two crenellations on the battlement, looking down at the blood-stained bridge below. It looked like the floor of a charnel house, if the owners hadn't bothered to clean in months. The remains of Duke Eeron's soldiers spread out like carpet, extending from the tower to two-thirds of the way to the keep.

He could see more soldiers clustered in the gate to the keep and along the walls. They were looking at the tower and the people atop it, but none of them were venturing closer. Maybe they knew it was wraiths who'd attacked the previous wave of soldiers, or maybe they didn't. They certainly had no way of knowing that Cinda had banished the wraiths.

Rew frowned. Would knowing Cinda banished the wraiths encourage the soldiers to come closer or keep them away? What was more frightening: wraiths, or a necromancer who could control them?

Until the duke himself forced the men across the bridge, Rew knew his group had a little time. None of those soldiers were going to volunteer to venture across the slaughtered remains of their peers without strong encouragement. Rew certainly wouldn't be walking across that killing ground. Not unless he had to.

"Should I go first?" Zaine asked as she and the ranger stood atop the battlement.

"No, I'll go."

"All right, but you weren't jumping, so I thought..."

"I'll go," the ranger insisted. He fixed his gaze on the bridge, the impossibly narrow looking, gore-slick bridge, and not the five-hundred pace drop on either side of it. The wind whipped his cloak around them, and he felt the wool tugging at his neck, like it was a sail sweeping him out into the open air.

"King's Sake," Rew grumbled. Then, he jumped. For a brief moment, it'd felt like time had stalled, but a breath later he contacted the stone surface of the bridge. He landed heavily and dropped into a roll to disperse his momentum.

Behind him, Zaine dropped before he could even turn, and the light-footed thief landed with no problems. Anne went next, and Rew caught her in his arms. He stumbled and fell on his bottom, but neither of them was hurt worse than an embarrassing bruise. Then, it was the Fedgleys' turn.

"We don't have a lot of time!" warned Zaine, watching the stirring soldiers at the other end of the bridge. "Someone in authority is over there now."

Raif leaned against the battlement, holding his sister by her wrists. He lowered her as far as he could, and then, he dropped her.

Rew caught her easily and lowered her body to lay her down.

"How come you fell when you caught me?" complained Anne, rubbing her elbow which had smacked against the stone of the bridge when they'd collapsed.

"She's as light as a..." began Rew. He swallowed and said, "I was ready for her. You just, ah, I was surprised by how far the drop was. Practice, you know?"

Anne snorted, and Rew turned to look up at Raif.

The big youth was closing his eyes.

"Are you going to catch him too?" wondered Zaine.

"No."

Whether Raif knew that or not was unclear, but after a short hesitation, the fighter dropped off the battlement and landed with the grace of a rock. His leg broke, and his eyes snapped open along with his mouth. He croaked a strangled cry of pain that lasted until Anne was able to draw the agony from him. The empath's mouth tightened, and Rew could see her eyes watering. Drawing the pain from others was what she did, but rarely had she needed to work so quickly in such circumstances.

As soon as Anne nodded that it was safe to do so, Rew grabbed Raif's breastplate and dragged him inside of the tower. Anne followed, walking in a crouch beside the youth with her hands still on him. Zaine struggled with Cinda, pulling the noblewoman's prone body by the arms.

"There in the corner," said Rew, observing the slaughter in the room.

Vyar Grund, on his way up the stairwell, had killed everything in sight. It wasn't quite as messy as the scene out on the bridge, but it was messy enough, and after walking through the wraiths' work, Rew hoped anyone would be shocked into numbness by the glistening, ravaged remains of dead people.

The party arranged themselves in the corner, Anne pouring her empathy into Raif, Cinda breathing evenly but unconscious. Zaine whispered she could watch at the door, but Rew shook his head and told her to stay where she was and to lie still.

With scores of injuries between them, Raif recovering from a broken leg, and Cinda unconscious, it would be suicide to attempt climbing out the way they'd come in. Walking out the bridge, into the bristling legions of Duke Eeron's troops, would be even worse. It was broad daylight, and any way they left the tower, they'd be seen. That meant they had to get creative.

No mundane soldiers would be trusted to investigate what happened. Duke Eeron would send his spellcasters. He would send his best ones, and Rew hoped there wasn't a spellcaster in

Spinesend more powerful than the duke himself. If he was in the city, Duke Eeron would be the one to lead the group to retake his tower. He wouldn't be able to trust anyone else to investigate the attack on his home and what had happened to such a high-profile prisoner. If Duke Eeron did not come himself, he'd look weak and useless in front of his men, not to mention whichever prince he'd have to explain the loss of Baron Fedgley to. No, as much as Vaeldon's nobles preferred to avoid personal risk, Duke Eeron had no choice in these circumstances. It was the Investiture, and any failure could mean death. Duke Eeron would come.

Rew hoped so, at least.

He glanced over the party. They were covered in blood and dust. Perfect. He began to whisper a steady incantation, repeating the same phrases over and over again. He bent down, touching each member of the party, whispering over them, casting a fog of concealment around them. As a group, they lay in the corner, and they blended into the grim tableau of death and destruction.

Low magic, when used in the right circumstances—such as merely confirming what a person expected to see—could be incredibly effective. Even in daylight. Even when used against a high magician of incredible talent. Rew felt confident the party could lie unnoticed for a time. As long as whoever had cast the glamour over Baron Worgon's forces did not turn up, that was. Rew stuttered then took a deep breath before resuming his chant.

Someone had cast a glamour that covered an entire army. They had fooled thousands of people, including Rew. They'd fooled Baron Worgon thoroughly over a period of several days, if not longer. Whoever could cast such a powerful glamour would see through Rew's paltry magic in an instant, but it was all that he had. This was his only idea.

Her calm voice a counterpoint to Rew's chanting, Anne prayed to the Blessed Mother.

Rew was wrong. They did send in the regular soldiers first. The pitiful men were white as fresh milk, and the cursory glance they gave the bodies in the room left Rew wondering whether he'd even needed to cast a fog of concealment over his companions. The soldiers expected to see bodies, and so they did.

Half a dozen of them shuffled up the stairwell, their armor clinking, their breaths bursting from noses like bellows in a forge. Shortly, because the stairwell was completely blocked, Rew heard them come back down the stairs and go to the lower levels. It wasn't long before they returned, and almost jogging, they exited the tower back into the light of day.

His lips curling up as he continued the incantation, Rew resisted turning to his companions. The plan, such as it was, was working. The soldiers had been sent to scout the tower, or more likely, they'd been sent to see whether or not they would return. Duke Eeron wasn't risking his own neck. He'd offered his men as a sacrifice in case anyone was still alive inside. With any luck, the soldiers had at least been thorough enough to see the broken iron bars on the window of the cell below. Rew hoped they would report back to the duke that everyone had fled.

It was several long minutes before they heard footfalls again, and then the duke himself walked in with a coterie of spellcasters and several dozen soldiers. It was too many people for the compact space in the tower, particularly given the ugly mess the dead bodies made scattered across the floor. In the thicket of people, it'd be hard to see anything, and Rew felt a smile truly form on his lips as several of the soldiers were pushed closer to where the party lay hidden. Those men had eyes only for the duke and his spellcasters. They gave the bodies not a second glance.

The duke immediately began issuing orders and directing his people to different parts of the tower. Rew waited patiently. Until they cleared the rubble in the stairwell, the duke's men could not access the roof where Baron Fedgley's body lay, and there was nothing worth seeing below them, but Eeron's men did not know that. Anne and the others remained frozen, and Rew's voice was a whisper on the wind as he continued chanting.

Spellcasters, decked in plush robes, the collars turned up in the chill air, the hems held high as they stepped over pools of blood, stalked about pompously, as if they'd had something to do with stopping the calamity that had occurred in the tower. Soldiers moved slower and more cautiously, perhaps wondering why they were even there. To the soldiers' eyes, no one was left alive in the tower. The arcanists, though, who came in last, actually studied the room. Rew suppressed a quiver of worry. The learned men might see through his illusion or detect that something was amiss, but before they had time to fully observe the room they were in, Duke Eeron growled at them to climb up to where the soldiers were already clearing the rubble. He wanted his arcanists to inspect Baron Fedgley's body, to see if it actually was the baron, and he didn't want a second of delay.

Rew smirked. Duke Eeron was expecting to be fooled by a glamour, but he was looking for the wrong one.

As the arcanists ascended the stairwell and the groups of soldiers formed a line to pass down heavy pieces of shattered stone, the spellcasters went down a level, evidently not wanting to be seen standing around doing nothing. That was the duke's job, which he settled into by stepping aside to give the soldiers room to work. The men passed chunks of mortar down the line and then tossed it off the side of the bridge outside, uncaring about the hovels and shops that surrounded the base of the tower.

Quietly, as if he was stalking through the forest, Rew rose from where he'd been hiding beneath the table the ledger had sat on. Earlier, he'd taken the thick, leather-bound book and stuffed it in his pack then flipped the table over to make his shelter. With the chaotic mess in the room, no one had given the table a second thought. While Eeron's men were still distracted searching the tower and cleaning the rubble, Rew stepped behind the duke and wrapped his arm around the man's neck. With his other hand,

Rew put the tip of his hunting knife against the duke's rib cage and pressed.

"You move, and I push," promised Rew, pressing his knife hard enough that the razor-sharp tip punched through the duke's thickly embroidered doublet and the steel pricked the man's flesh.

Duke Eeron shouted in surprise.

Rew waited, holding the duke tight, keeping his knife firmly against the man's side, where he knew the duke would feel the point dig deeper as he struggled. It wasn't long before Duke Eeron stopped struggling, but he didn't stop screaming.

Soldiers and spellcasters rushed into the room, pushing against each other, the armsmen losing the space they'd need to use their swords, the spellcasters losing the space they'd need to cast a spell without hitting their allies. Rew kept waiting until finally, he pushed harder with his knife and whispered for the duke to shut his mouth.

Blood leaking down his side, the duke complied.

"You and I are going to walk out of here unmolested," said Rew, his voice low so only the duke could hear. "If you object or your men try to stop me, I'll slide this blade right into your heart."

Duke Eeron, regaining his composure, stopped struggling. He waved for his men to pause. Unable to turn and see Rew, he asked, "Who are you?"

"That's not important," said Rew, maneuvering the duke to the doorway where he knew they'd be framed by the bright sunlight outside.

"M'lord, it's the King's Ranger!" exclaimed one of the arcanists from the stairwell.

Rew glared at the man over the duke's shoulder.

"Senior Ranger Rew," murmured Duke Eeron. "I knew I recognized that voice. What are you doing here, Ranger? I thought your kind avoided political entanglements."

Rew whispered, "The king knows about Baron Fedgley. He knows what you and your patron are attempting."

"What are you talking about?" replied the duke, sounding

honestly confused. "What are you saying? The king's never given a fig before about how I manage my duchy. Why would he care that I locked up some country baron? Blessed Mother, I doubt the king even knows who Baron Fedgley is!"

"You don't know," said Rew, actually surprised, thinking quickly what that meant. "That's good. I thought—It was only your arcanist then. It's better this way. It means I don't have to kill you."

"Kill me?" barked Duke Eeron. "What is this madness, Ranger? What do I not know? What do you mean it was my arcanist?"

Duke Eeron, facing his assembled soldiers and spellcasters, was gaining confidence, even though a razor-sharp blade was still stuck in his side.

Rew backed up, stepping onto the bridge.

"Ranger," warned Duke Eeron, his voice loud enough to be heard by everyone in the room, "my men will kill you rather than allowing you to drag me from the keep like this. Tell me why you are doing this."

"I'm an agent of the king, Duke Eeron," replied Rew, his voice still quiet in the duke's ear. "I'm here on his business. Call off your dogs, or I'll have to slide this blade home."

"An agent of the king!" snapped Eeron. "You're a ranger, not a… What are you doing here? The king did not send you! I know that."

"I'm the King's Ranger," said Rew, "but I wasn't always. When the king calls me for darker work, I still answer. Just like you, just like everyone who can feel the swirl of the Investiture, I answered the call. It led me here. King Vaisius Morden wanted Baron Fedgley dead, so he is. I was to kill everyone involved in the plot. The only reason you live, Duke Eeron, is because I don't think you understand why the others wanted the baron."

Duke Eeron was quiet, and Rew wondered what the man did know. They scooted farther back along the bridge, and Rew hoped the other man believed him. It was the truth, sort of. If the king suspected what was afoot, he'd come crashing down on Spine-send with the full weight of the underworld. It wouldn't just be the duke who perished if Vaisius Morden understood what was happening here, but Rew couldn't explain that. He couldn't tell anyone that, or he'd bring it to pass.

Instead, he hoped that the duke was pondering just how crazy Rew might be. Was he crazy enough to invoke the king's name and to lie about it? The duke had to be thinking that no one was that crazy.

The sport of the nobles was betrayal, and they lived their lives for the backstabbing and lies that the Investiture brought, but none of them were bold enough to defy the king. For one, they all knew that Vaisius Morden stayed out of the Investiture. By design, the king had nothing to do with it. The entire point was the competition between the princes, and the king wanted them to prove themselves and their bloodlines.

Dragging the king into the plotting and chicanery simply wasn't done. Plotting against the king at all, in fact, was not done. Vaisius Morden the First's line had been the most powerful users of high magic Vaeldon had seen two hundred years ago, and the Mordens had been breeding and pruning the heirs ever since. The child was always stronger than the parent. There wasn't a high magician in Vaeldon who would even think about challenging the king openly, but working behind his back could be even worse. Each successive king had been born and bred to intrigue, and he'd proven his capability by surviving the Investiture. The king was, by definition, both the most powerful and the most cunning man in Vaeldon.

Claiming you were following the king's orders when you weren't could lead to far worse consequences than an execution. The man was a necromancer, after all. His displeasure could outlast death.

"That's right," hissed Rew, nudging Duke Eeron toward a conclusion. "I killed Baron Fedgley on behalf of the king."

"If you kill me, Prince... The prince will not rest until he has your head."

Rew forced a laugh for the duke's benefit and took another step back onto the bridge.

"Y-You don't know who you're—" spluttered Duke Eeron.

Rew dug the knife deeper. "Yes, I do."

He moved back again, and one of Duke Eeron's spellcasters raised his arm.

"Your men can follow us, but if they attack, you'll die," warned Rew. "Tell them that."

Duke Eeron snorted.

"I'm an agent of the king," whispered Rew, his head next to Eeron's. He kept his voice purposefully harsh and pressed his cheek against the duke's, hoping the spellcaster had little faith in his own aim. "You don't have a caster who can kill me, but I don't want to be dodging those fools until I get out of the keep. Keep them away, and when we reach your gates, I'll let you go. The king hasn't commanded your death, yet."

Duke Eeron waved his hand to warn his men away.

Rew growled, "Don't try it."

He didn't know what Eeron might be thinking of trying. The man was a talented enchanter. His casting would take time and involve certain preparations that he wasn't capable of with a knife in his ribs, but Duke Eeron, like almost all of the nobles with talent for high magic, would have some skill at invoking as well. It was rare there was a noble line in the kingdom that did not have the blood of invokers mixed in. Enchantments took weeks or months, invoking could be done in the blink of an eye. Rew hoped if Duke Eeron was not strong in the art, he would be worried his attack would fail, and the duke knew the consequences of that failure.

"You'll let me go?" asked Duke Eeron as they shuffled onto the bridge, the cool wind whipping Rew's cloak around them. "Why should I trust you? No one is that stupid, Ranger, to leave an enemy like me at your back."

"I'll let you live because you don't know why you were

holding Baron Fedgley," said Rew, "and because you don't want to be my enemy, Duke Eeron. The king watches all of his agents. Besides, Vaisius Morden doesn't want to disrupt the Investiture, and if there is no need to kill you, he'd rather you live in case you still have a role to play in this drama."

Duke Eeron's head shifted slightly, and Rew followed where the man was looking.

He asked Duke Eeron, "Why did Arcanist Salwart tell you he was holding Baron Fedgley in your prison?"

Duke Eeron grunted in response.

"He's the one who arranged it, was he not?" pressed Rew. "He was the one who arranged the cell back in that tower using Arcanist Ralcrist's discovery, didn't he? He met with the thieves' guild and their fixer, Fein. He questioned the baron, and he was the one who suggested you use Kallie Fedgley to crack the baron's will. I know it all, Duke Eeron, except for what they told you— how you allowed a mere arcanist to use you."

"Salwart has been a part of Spinesend since before we were alive, Ranger," hissed Duke Eeron in reply. "He's no mere arcanist."

Rew considered that, but he wasn't sure what the duke meant, and it certainly wasn't time to have a conversation with the man about it, so instead, he asked, "Will you kill him for me, or will I need to come back?"

"I'll handle him," muttered the duke, his eyes fixed ahead, looking at Arcanist Salwart as Rew backed the two of them down the bridge.

Rew guessed that Duke Eeron really meant it, though the arcanist likely had a long, painful journey to his final fate. Duke Eeron, now that he believed his men had roped him into a plot that involved the king, was going to do whatever he had to do to learn the details. Rew worried a bit about what Duke Eeron would find, but for now, he needed Eeron and his forces focused on anything other than wondering where the rest of the party had gone.

Boots slipping on the blood and body parts that littered the bridge, Rew kept backing up, his knife on Duke Eeron, his eyes on the soldiers and the spellcasters that followed them.

"Surely there were easier ways to kill Baron Fedgley," grumbled Duke Eeron as they crossed halfway across the bridge.

Rew chuckled. "I wish there had been, but I'm not a spellcaster."

The duke was silent for a long moment. Then, he asked, "Who was that on the tower, then? We saw the portal. Everyone in the keep could see high magic was being cast up there."

"Who do you think it was?"

"I don't know," barked Duke Eeron, "but I know Baron Fedgley doesn't have the talent to open a portal. I'm certain he was the one who called upon the wraiths, though. It had to be him. I saw what appeared to be his body. Is that really Baron Fedgley, Ranger? If it is, then who banished the wraiths? If you came to kill Fedgley, then who were you fighting, and where did they go? Fedgley called the wraiths, but he couldn't manage half of the rest of what we saw."

"We don't have time for so many questions, but I can tell you the body you saw is Baron Fedgley," assured Rew. "He's dead, as the king wanted. The conspiracy goes deeper than just your arcanist, Duke Eeron. There are other, powerful figures who wanted Fedgley to live. They tried to stop his murder then fled when they couldn't. If you want to know more, you'll have to ask him."

Both Duke Eeron and Rew glanced at Arcanist Salwart, who'd dropped behind the line of spellcasters as everyone slowly shuffled across the bridge. The man looked nervous, but not nervous enough. Rew frowned. Salwart couldn't hear his liege promising his death, but the man had been neck deep in Baron Fedgley's capture and interrogation. Certainly he knew what it meant that the baron had died. To his fellow conspirators, Salwart was now nothing more than a liability.

"He's going to run the moment he gets into the keep,"

warned Rew.

Duke Eeron grunted. Then, he claimed, "You're lying about what occurred on top of that tower. You're lying about coming here on behalf of the king."

"Am I lying?" whispered Rew into the man's ear. "The king knows what Baron Fedgley was supposed to do, even if you do not. He wanted the man dead, and so I killed him. If you doubt me, open a portal to Mordenhold, and let's go ask the king. It will save me the walk, and it will save us all from continuing this farce."

Duke Eeron did not reply. Clearly, he doubted Rew's story, but he faced incredible risk calling Rew's bluff. If Rew was telling the truth, calling attention to the duke's own involvement would be fatal. If Rew was lying, then Duke Eeron had to be wondering whether Vaisius Morden would bother getting to the bottom of what was happening or if he'd simplify matters by killing everyone. The king ruled efficiently, if not kindly.

"If not the king, then maybe one of the princes?" suggested Rew quietly. "Open a portal to your patron, assuming that is, you don't think they'll mind Baron Fedgley dying in your care."

Rew felt Duke Eeron stiffen.

"You see now?" asked Rew after letting the duke remain silent for a moment. "You've no choice but to believe me."

"Let me go," demanded the duke.

"When we reach the gates of the keep, I'll let you go."

"I'll hunt you and I'll kill you," claimed Duke Eeron.

"You can try," responded Rew, "but I'd wager all the coin I have that your patron is going to find you first. Whatever anger you feel toward me, it's in your best interest to run. Take care of Salwart before you do, though, so the king can turn his eyes elsewhere. If Salwart is dead, you need only worry about the princes."

That was the push the duke needed. He'd swam the dangerous currents of the Investiture, and he knew it. He'd gambled on holding Baron Fedgley for whatever benefit his arcanist claimed he'd receive. Duke Eeron had bet everything, and he'd lost. It wasn't unusual, during the Investiture. There was nothing Duke Eeron could say to one of the princes that would cover for his failure to keep Baron Fedgley alive, even if the king had been behind the man's death. And if the king found out, the duke would wish he'd died under the princes' ungentle hands. All Duke Eeron could do now was flee and hope that whenever the Investiture ended, his failure was forgotten.

Duke Eeron was a powerful spellcaster and he had incredible wealth at his disposal. He could portal, and the princes would be busy plotting against each other. It was quite possible Duke Eeron might live to see the crowning of a new king, and then, he might hope that his role would be overlooked. Vengeance could come with the crowning of a new king, but forgiveness as well. With three brothers, most of the nobles didn't start out supporting the victor, after all. Duke Eeron had a chance to survive, but if he was going to do it, he had to start running soon.

"Let's hurry, then," said Duke Eeron with a sigh, evidently coming to the conclusion Rew had hoped he would.

Behind them, all of Duke Eeron's contingent filed out of the tower. Like children on a mother's apron string, they came after the duke, shame-faced but unable to do anything. Rew had his blade in the duke's side, and it'd take a fearless blow to fell the ranger without risking injury to the duke.

As they reached the keep, Rew turned the duke, still keeping their bodies pressed together. The motion twisted the blade in the other man's side and drew a pained curse. Rew didn't need to tell the man. Duke Eeron was already calling out to his soldiers lining the walls, "Clear the way. Clear the way to the gates. Run ahead, you fools! I want the corridors cleared immediately!"

The walk through the keep was tense. Soldiers, servants, and others crowded the cross halls, watching as their liege was dragged through with a knife in his side. Every person in the keep seemed to have come to watch, and Rew grinned at the thought.

Behind them, in the tower, Zaine would be leading the others back to the cell they'd entered through. She'd be climbing out and untying both the ropes they'd left beneath the bridge. They couldn't swing on them, but they could tie the rope to the tower itself and scale down. Zaine could handle the acrobatics beneath the bridge, and they hoped Raif could handle the climb on a healing leg with his sister tied to his back. It'd be dangerous, but it was better than all five of them trying to walk out through the keep. With all eyes on Rew and the duke, the others might be able to climb down unnoticed. Rew's bold play had given them a chance.

Rew adjusted his grip around Duke Eeron's neck, using the man as a human shield. It granted him protection, but it wouldn't have been sufficient for all five of them. The others would have been exposed, and one rash attack from the duke's soldiers or a spellcaster could have gotten them all killed.

As Rew and the duke entered the grand foyer that led from the throne room to the main entrance of the keep, Duke Eeron whispered, "I could have killed you, you know? I'm not the strongest invoker, but I'm strong enough."

"Maybe," acknowledged Rew.

"If you really are working for the king, remember that," said Duke Eeron. "I played it straight."

"Once a knife was in your ribs," retorted Rew.

Duke Eeron laughed then coughed, evidently regretting the motion while Rew's knife was still pricking his side. "Betrayal is the cup we all sip from, Ranger. Turning us against each other, letting us tear each other apart, that's what has kept Mordens on the throne all of these centuries. You know that better than anyone. They sit the throne, and we die. Remember, I could have fought you, but I didn't."

"And I could have killed you for taking Baron Fedgley," said Rew, "but I didn't."

"You may as well have," responded the duke darkly. "The prince will be on my heels by sundown."

"Which prince?" asked Rew.

The duke snorted. "So you did lie."

"I didn't lie about all of it," insisted Rew. "You're better off not knowing why the prince and your arcanist were holding Baron Fedgley. That's the truth. Kill Salwart and flee, and then you might live long enough to bow to the new king. Pray to the Blessed Mother it's not the prince you've been involved with. You've got two out of three odds, Duke Eeron. That's not bad, if you manage to escape today."

"If you aren't working for the king, Ranger, I'll enjoy hearing about your long, pathetic demise," said the duke.

"We'll see," replied Rew.

He backed his way out the open gates of the keep. A dozen guards flanked them on the steps leading into the city and beyond. The citizens of Spinesend carried about their day, still unaware of the chaos that had occurred on the bridge and in the tower. Few of them noticed what was happening in the gate to the keep, and those who did notice only hurried away. Commoners, one and all, knew it was best to stay out of the matters of nobility.

Rew removed the knife from the duke's side, spun the duke around, and punched the man square in the face. "Good luck, Eeron. Believe it or not, I wish you no ill will."

The duke stumbled and fell onto his bottom, sitting on the stone stairs to his keep.

"I don't wish you the same luck," Duke Eeron muttered after leaning over and spitting a thick globule of blood. Soldiers shifted, moving around the duke in the open gate, but Eeron waved them back. He looked past Rew and snickered. "He'll be dead soon enough, and his blood won't be on our hands."

Rew, his skin crawling, turned his back on the man and walked into the courtyard and the crowd. Within moments, he was lost in the flow of the citizens of Spinesend, but he couldn't help noticing one woman who had been standing still, watching. A heavy woolen cloak hid her body, but the tall shock of blonde hair atop her head and the crawling blue tattoos over her ears were impossible to miss.

❧ 24 ❧

Mistress Clae.

Rew cursed. If Zaine was correct, and he had no reason to think she wasn't, then the woman was an assassin for the Spinesend thieves' guild. She'd attacked them in the woods outside of Umdrac and must have guessed they'd eventually turn up in the city. The crowd surrounded him, but the woman had been looking right at him as he'd left Duke Eeron. There was no way she missed him.

Rew was exceptionally skilled at moving through the forest stealthily, but in broad daylight in the middle of the city, there was nothing he could do to slip away. They were on her ground, not his. He strode quickly but not yet running. He took a convoluted path down the twisting stairs and sloped streets, dodging through narrow alleys, careening around sharp turns, and trying to use the maze of Spinesend's buildings to lose the woman.

She matched his pace, staying close but not close enough that she could launch an attack. Whether by sound or some city-born sense Rew did not understand, she followed him around each corner and through each passageway. She was doing nothing to hide per pursuit. Her wild hair and the tattoos would stand out in any crowd, and by the way he was moving, she must have known she'd been seen.

He frowned.

She'd stand out in any crowd except for those in the foreign quarter of Jabaan, the capital of the western province. There was a contingent of refugees there from somewhere across the southern sea. They'd come generations ago and had been captured and stranded. A century later, little was known about where they'd come from, even by them, but the Morden kings had not stamped them out, and their cultural identity was strong enough that they did not assimilate into the hodgepodge of Vaeldon's peoples. What was the woman doing in Spinesend working with the thieves' guild? More importantly, why was she following him?

As he walked, he decided the second of those answers was easy. The woman had no interest in the King's Ranger; she wanted the children.

Moving around a slow-moving cart laden with giant melons that was being painfully tugged uphill by a pair of sweating, swearing porters, Rew ducked into a narrow alley, sped up, and then took another turn.

He wasn't sprinting, but he wasn't short of a run, either. The woman was easy enough to spot, but he hadn't identified any companions. If she'd survived the confrontation in the woods against Duke Eeron's men, then surely some of her minions had as well. And if they had, and they were with her, he needed to know. He figured by pushing his pace, he would force them to hurry into the open if they wanted to keep up with him.

His mind churning, Rew realized that while she'd tangled with Duke Eeron's men in the forest, the duke had recognized her outside of the gate of his keep. The duke knew her, but she wasn't working for him. He'd claimed his hands would be clean.

Rew trotted down a narrow staircase, listening for footsteps above him. Near the bottom, he placed a hand on the railing and vaulted over, dropping a dozen steps down to the other side. He kept going, weaving through the tangled streets and paths of Spinesend.

Fedgley and Worgon thought they were working with Prince Valchon, which meant the woman behind him probably was not. If she'd been in Prince Valchon's employ, simply speaking honestly to the children in the forest would have gotten them into her clutches. If she was allied with the Fedgleys, there'd been no reason for the threat of violence.

Prince Calb ruled Jabaan. Could she be working for him, a spy of sorts in the eastern province of Calb's older brother, Valchon? But if she was a spy, she was a rather obvious one. Her hair and tattoos marked her clearly as coming from that far, western city.

Scowling, Rew saw the woman's head poke around a corner fifty paces behind him, and he hurried, taking the narrow, little used back streets and alleys that trickled down the slopes of Spinesend like vines hanging from a tree. The woman had shown herself, which meant she intended him to know she was there, but she hadn't attacked. She wanted to talk.

Rew punched a wall beside him as he hurried by.

She wanted to talk, and he needed to talk as well. The alliances, the secrets, it was too complicated for him to untangle without more information, but there wasn't anyone who was going to volunteer that information unless he offered something in return.

He kept going, moving down through the city, until he found a stairwell with a hairpin turn that was wedged between two tall, windowless buildings. There was a small platform between the flights of the stairs where residents of the buildings had left ladders that climbed up to a web of laundry lines. Fresh air whistled between the buildings, stirring the clothing and linens overhead. The tenements rose sharply on either side like walls of a cliff. From that spot on the stairwell, Rew had a view both up and down the narrow street. He glanced over the edge of the platform and saw a roof one hundred paces below. No one was coming up from that direction.

He turned, waiting for the assassin to catch up to him. She didn't take long, and she showed no surprise when she saw him standing there. She stopped on the stairs, still covered from the neck down in her heavy cloak. Rew eyed her, waiting for the strange woman to speak, but she did not. He shifted his feet, his eyes roaming around, looking for her minions. Finally, he decided no one else was coming, and he was tired of waiting. He asked, "Why are you following me?"

"You know why I'm following you, Ranger," she drawled. "I want the children."

"You think I'll take you to them?"

"I decided that you were going to see me following you, whether I hid or did not hide, and that once you saw me, you were too smart to lead me right back to them," she explained. "That meant I had to speak with you and work this out."

Rew reached up and scratched his beard.

She asked calmly, "Where are they?"

"Why would I tell you that?"

"Because if you tell me where I can find them, I won't kill you."

Rew laughed.

It was the woman's turn to frown. "Ranger, you were saved before by Duke Eeron's men stumbling across us, but we both know that will not happen again. If the duke meant to interfere, he would have when he saw me. I suspect the duke believes I will kill you, and after whatever trouble you were causing in his keep, he is content with that knowledge. Duke Eeron knows me, Ranger, and he knows that I am thorough."

Rew leaned back against the railing for a moment before recalling just how far the drop on the other side was. He stepped forward two paces but did not climb the stairs toward her.

"What were you doing in the keep?" asked Mistress Clae.

Rew shook his head. "You think a threat to kill me is going to make me talk?"

The woman pushed back her cloak, revealing her leather

bracers tipped with the gleaming steel claws he'd seen in the forest. "It's enough for most people." She held up a hand. "This steel cuts like a razor, but those who know me do not fear that. I slather a toxic preparation along my blades. It won't kill you, but it will feel like your flesh is aflame. That's what the arcanists' books say, at least. It's much worse, Ranger. I've seen people attempt to flay themselves to stop the terrible agony. If I've disarmed them, they'll use their own teeth between breaths begging me to kill them. Imagine that, gnawing away at your own skin because it hurts so terribly. I tell you this because it is not the threat of death that should worry you, Ranger. It is the pain I will cause you before you die. We do not have to be rude, though, do we? Talk to me, and I will let you go. My employer cares nothing for you, just the children."

"Who is your employer?" asked Rew.

The woman smirked at him and did not reply.

"It seems we're at a bit of an impasse," remarked Rew.

The woman shook her wrists, and the claws slid out, extending a hand past the end of her fingers.

"If we kill each other," mentioned Rew, "then neither of us gets what we want."

"I won't kill you right away," said the woman. "I will cut you, and then you will beg for me to kill you. Before the pain overtakes you, Ranger, understand that all I want is the location of the children. Tell me where they are, and I will do you the kindness of finishing you."

"Prince Calb, is it?" asked Rew, guessing randomly.

The woman looked back at him impassively.

"I had a fifty-fifty chance," muttered Rew. "Prince Heindaw, then. You've been working for him some time, I'm guessing, acting as a spy and assassin deep in Valchon's territory? If you were ever discovered, Valchon might assume you were in Calb's employ. You are from Jabaan, are you not? Does Heindaw know it is me you are chasing?"

"I'm chasing the children," responded the woman. "Neither of us care a fig for you."

"He doesn't know," surmised Rew. "If Heindaw knew you were standing here, threatening me with death to solicit information from me, he'd tell you not to bother."

The woman's face remained impassive. She raised her hand, the gleaming claw flashing in the mid-day sun. She paused, looking along the blade, as if studying the steel for whatever mixture she'd applied to it. "Humor me, Ranger. Why would the prince tell me not to bother?"

"Because Prince Heindaw knows me," growled Rew, "and he knows to stay away."

Mistress Clae smirked. "Ranger, there's not a man in this kingdom that Prince Heindaw is afraid of, and there's not many I'm afraid of, either. You've started to bore me. Tell me where the children are, and I'll spare your life. Or don't tell me, and your life will end in excruciating pain right after you blather what I want to know."

"That's where you're wrong," said Rew, drawing himself up, flexing his hands and rolling his shoulders. "You ever wonder why neither Prince Heindaw nor even Prince Valchon visit the Eastern Territory? It's because I'm here. I told them I wanted nothing to do with the family, and I told them what would happen if they ever disturbed me. You were wrong, Clae. There are men in this kingdom that Heindaw is afraid of, and I'm one of them."

Mistress Clae laughed.

"You're an assassin, right?" questioned Rew, putting a boot on the step above him.

Mistress Clae gave him a sly wink and spread her arms wide, the steel blades protruding from her gauntlets flashing in the narrow bands of sunlight that trickled between the flapping laundry above them. She stepped down the stairs toward him. "You have no idea who I am, Ranger."

"I don't care who you are," growled Rew, "but I'll feel a lot better about this knowing you're a killer."

He charged up the stairwell.

Mistress Clae launched herself like a raven streaking toward its prey, but Rew had expected that. The woman was a killer, a talented one probably, but she had no idea who she was facing. It meant she'd be overconfident, expecting to carve him like a roasted chicken with those claws of hers. She swung, and he ducked.

Rew felt a brush of air as Mistress Clae's swing whipped over-head. He didn't bother to draw his own weapons. Instead, he surged upward, rising behind her swing, grabbing her other wrist, and punching into her midriff. He flung her over his head.

Mistress Clae, kicking and flipping in the air like a cat falling from a roof, twisted around to look at him, her mouth open, her eyes wide as she soared over the balustrade and out into the open air. Drying laundry flapped several paces above her, out of her reach. She had nothing to grab onto. There was nothing she could do to stop herself from falling. For a brief second, Rew saw her stunned realization that she was going to die, and then, she plummeted out of view.

He scowled. The woman was a murderer. By all rights, she deserved what she'd gotten, but he hated that he was the one to give it to her. He hated that Prince Heindaw had set the woman on the trail of the children, bringing the situation about. He hated what all of the princes were doing to the kingdom in an effort to kill each other. He hated that the king was the one orchestrating the entire bloody show from behind his curtain. Rew hated it so much that ten years ago, he'd run, and he'd never looked back.

He walked to the railing and glanced down. Far below, on top of a weather-beaten shingle roof, was Mistress Clae's body. Blood leaked from her, staining the shingles and then dripping off the edge of the roof. Cold wind blew through the gap in the two buildings where Rew stood, and his cloak whipped around behind him.

Ten years ago, killing the woman would have sent him into a furious frenzy. He would have raged at what he'd been forced to do, and then, he would have vanished into the wilderness for weeks or even months, walking until there wasn't another soul within days of him. He wouldn't have called it hiding, but it was. He'd always known it was. Heindaw and the rest of them had understood, and they would have let him run off, afraid of what would happen if they kicked the hornet's nest one too many times. Just weeks ago, he wouldn't have felt the same rage, but Rew would have still walked away from it all. He would have returned to Eastwatch, hoping to be left alone there.

But not anymore.

Much had changed in the last weeks. He had changed. Looking down at Mistress Clae's body, he thought sourly of his conversation with Raif, the one about life, the one when Rew had realized he was helping the children as more than a favor to Anne. He was doing it because it was the right thing to do, and because if he didn't do it, there was no one else who could. Rew thought about Raif, and his sister Cinda. He thought about how ten years ago, he'd realized what it would take to stop all of this madness, and that he didn't have the skill to do it. He'd run away then, like he always had, knowing that despite what he was capable of, he couldn't do what was necessary.

But she could.

She could, and she would, if he asked it of her. Cinda and her brother were part of the terrible system that had ruled Vaeldon for two hundred years, but not because they chose it. They were part of it because of their birth, just as he had been, until he'd chosen to run. Running hadn't changed anything for anyone, not even for him. He was still a part of that system, and always would be, as long as it still existed. He snorted. It'd taken two noble children— ignorant of the world—to show him the truth, but they had. And now, he was done running. Now, he knew what must happen. Rew checked his weapons, cracked his neck, and started down the stairs. He had work to do.

His body aching, Rew clambered up the rough, rock-strewn slope of the hill. The sun was setting, and he figured he had half an hour before darkness. Half an hour before he'd told Anne and the others to leave with or without him. The wounds Vyar Grund had given him stung every time he stepped or reached up with a hand to climb. There were bruises on him he didn't recall receiving, and his head was throbbing with each beat of his heart.

For the last two hours, Rew had been skirting through Spinesend, making sure he lost any tails that had followed him from the keep or from his encounter with Mistress Clae. Duke Eeron had told his men to let Rew go, but that didn't mean the duke had not changed his mind once the ranger's knife left his side. It didn't mean that no one had disobeyed the duke and set out on their own. Mistress Clae's men, if any had survived the forest, would certainly be wondering where she was. King's Sake, there were probably dozens of spies in the city working for both the duke's enemies and his allies, and Rew had given them every reason to be interested in him.

He'd involved himself publicly now, and he was at risk like anyone who was caught in the swirl of the Investiture. There were no rules, no formal guide to how the nobles should conduct themselves in the generational bloodbath, except that if someone was not with you, they were against you. Winning was always easier if you removed a few pieces from the board, and killing someone was easier than converting them as an ally. Not that Rew had any allies of his own or want of them. From all quarters now, Rew had enemies.

But Duke Eeron had been exposed as well, and he was experienced enough to know what it meant. Rew hoped that would give him enough time to find the others and escape. Even now, the duke would be gathering his things and preparing to flee. Maybe he'd already left, or maybe one of the princes had learned of the duke's failure and had come for him.

Rew wondered if they would. Duke Eeron had to be allied with Prince Calb, since Mistress Clae had been in league with Heindaw, and both Fedgley and Worgon thought they'd been in concert with Valchon. Would Calb come to punish the duke for allowing Fedgley to die, or would Valchon or Heindaw move against Eeron now that his allegiance was in the open? King's Sake. He wondered if Calb had even known the duke was holding Worgon. Heindaw would have, and he wouldn't be happy the baron had been killed. He'd be even less happy that his plotting may have been exposed. Duke Eeron was right to worry that they would come. Any of the three princes had reason to take the man's head.

As he considered it, Rew suspected the princes would not come. Not yet, at least. Rew didn't think they'd risk Spinesend while he was there unless they thought it meant their own lives. They wouldn't want to force a confrontation and then leave themselves weakened for the others. The princes wouldn't want to face Rew until they'd killed a brother or two first.

He scowled. They'd wait, but he wouldn't. He was done running, done hiding, and done ignoring the world and the dark shadow looming over the kingdom. He was finished pretending he had no part in that darkness and that, by ignoring it, he was any better than those at the heart of the Investiture. He'd been born a part of it like so many others, but now he was ready to fight and to tear it all down. The princes didn't need to come to Spinesend. He'd go to them.

Rew looked up the slope at the tower rising above him and sighed. After more years than he cared to think of, his head felt clear. He finally knew what needed to be done, but he had the children to watch out for now. They—very obviously—were not ready for what was to come. He could leave them, but he wouldn't. He had work to do, and they were a part of it, and he was a part of them. Rew sighed. With any luck, all eyes would be on Duke Eeron. Whether the man had already fled or would attempt to stay and fight, Rew hoped Eeron would draw everyone's attention. For any arrivals portaling into the city to see what had happened, they'd all be starting at the keep, and there was plenty there to keep them busy.

The party didn't have a lot of time, but they might have enough.

Rew stopped walking. Zaine was sitting on a boulder looking down at him. Beneath her, purple in the fading light, was a giant pool of tacky blood. Rew put his hands on his hips.

"He's hard to kill, huh?" she asked. "When we finally managed to climb down from the tower, he was already gone. I found bloody footprints, but they disappear two dozen paces through those bushes. There are marks where it looks to me he might have opened a portal and fled."

Rew didn't bother to check the thief's claims. He found he trusted her instincts. Blessed Mother, he trusted her. He replied, "I told you, the commandant has the king's own magic fortifying him. It'll take more than a fall to do him in."

"The box, the one Alsayer used to capture the wraiths, is gone as well," said Zaine, gesturing around them. "At least, I couldn't find it. Would he have taken it?"

Rew grimaced and nodded. "He'd take it if he found it. The others?"

"Anne is tired from healing, but she's all right," replied Zaine. "Raif's leg is tender, and it will pain him to walk, but he's confident he can make it to where we can hide in the city. Cinda is unconscious still, but her breathing and heartbeat are steady. Anne says it's a deeper exhaustion than physical. She says Cinda needs sleep and some broth if we can find it for her."

Rew shook his head.

"What?" asked Zaine. "You think someone is on your tail?"

"I hope not. Doesn't much matter, though. We've got to leave."

"Leave?" asked the thief. "Didn't you hear what I just—"

"Zaine," he interrupted, "we've a momentary interruption where all eyes will be on the keep, but it won't be for long. Lingering allies of Duke Eeron, minions of the princes, the princes themselves! King's Sake, the king—Pfah. What if Vyar Grund is actually still working for the king and that's where he fled?"

Zaine raised an eyebrow. "You don't think Grund is still working for the king?"

Rew shook his head. "Later."

Zaine frowned.

"We have to find my sister," declared Raif, stepping out of the gloom behind the thief. "She killed our father. We have to—we have to find her."

"Revenge won't make you feel any better about what happened, lad," warned Rew.

His head dropping, the big fighter admitted, "I know. It's not revenge I seek. It's answers. Why did she do it? How did she grow to hate us so?"

"Didn't she just tell you?" asked Rew.

"She's all that's left of our family, and family stays together," responded Raif, looking back up to meet the ranger's gaze. The three of them stood silently for a long moment. Then, Raif added, "Where else do we have to go? We can't go back to Falvar, can we? You can't go to Eastwatch."

Rew crossed his arms over his chest. The boy had a point, but even if he didn't, Rew wasn't interested in going back to those places. The time for crouching in the Eastern Territory, pretending he couldn't feel what was happening in the kingdom, was over. The time for action was now.

"Where would we even start?" wondered Zaine, fiddling with the hilt of one of her daggers. "Alsayer, I guess. Where we find that treacherous bastard, we'll find Kallie."

"Maybe, maybe not," said Rew.

Anne joined Raif on the hillside. "I heard the lad, Rew. He's right. Where else would we go? Tracking Alsayer will be dangerous but not much more so than running. Years ago, you told me that sometimes when you're stuck in the brambles, the only way out is forward."

"I was talking about actual brambles," said Rew with a laugh.

Anne tilted her head, waiting on him.

Rew grunted and then told the group, "They went to Carff."

"What?" exclaimed Zaine.

"How do you know?" demanded Raif.

"I smelled the air from Alsayer's portal," explained Rew. "There's only one place that smells like that. I don't know if they'll still be there when we arrive, but I've got to... We've got to start somewhere. We may as well start with Carff."

He left unsaid that Carff was the seat of Prince Valchon. Was it possible Alsayer was actually working for the eldest of the princes? Rew doubted it, but he was certain that was where his cousin had fled with Kallie Fedgley jumping after him. Looking for the eldest of the Fedgley children and perhaps stopping to visit the oldest of the Mordens while they were there... Why not?

"Should we find somewhere to rest tonight and leave at dawn?" wondered Raif, stretching his injured leg out in front of him and tentatively putting a little weight on it.

Rew shook his head. "I know it will pain you, lad, but we have to get out of Spinesend. We have to put leagues between here and ourselves. We're no longer at the fringes of the Investiture—we're at the heart of it. So wherever there are powerful people, we'll be in serious danger. Right now, they know where we are, and I'd rather they didn't. Besides, if you want to walk to Carff, it's a long journey, and we won't get there unless we get started."

Raif looked as if he meant to object, but then, he acknowledged, "I suppose you're right."

Rew nodded. "I'll gather your sister. With your leg healing, you're in no shape to carry her."

He moved up the hill to the base of the tower where the others had left the girl. He put his arms under her, and as he was lifting her, he heard soft footsteps behind him.

"How did you know your plan would work?" asked Anne. "Duke Eeron has some skill at invoking, does he not? He's not strong, but strong enough to call your bluff if he'd wanted. If he'd opened a portal to Mordenhold, what would you have done?"

Rew smirked. "He never would have."

"Bringing the king into this was dangerous, Rew," said Anne. "I'm not certain the duke was even involved. It worked to get us out of that tower, but the king—"

"King Vaisius Morden is the last person in the kingdom that Duke Eeron wants to face," retorted Rew. "You're right, by the way, Duke Eeron wasn't involved. It was the Arcanist Salwart who kidnapped Baron Fedgley, and he didn't tell Eeron the whole truth. Salwart didn't tell Duke Eeron they were holding Fedgley on behalf of Prince Calb. Duke Eeron has no idea what all of this is about. It's almost enough to make you feel sorry for the man."

"You're sure?" questioned Anne.

"Duke Eeron either missed his calling of the stage, or he was telling the truth," replied Rew. "Though, it doesn't matter if he was behind it or not. No one would risk going to see the king."

Anne looked worried. "If he talks…"

"Trust me. Duke Eeron won't say a word of what happened to the king," said Rew. "The princes won't either, and I'd bet gold Vyar Grund is in the thrall of Prince Valchon. None of them—even Alsayer, whatever he is up to—can afford the attention of the king. Vaisius Morden does not look kindly on this sort of thing."

"How can you be sure no one will talk?" pressed Anne. "Rew, there's so much we don't—"

"They took Baron Fedgley because they're plotting against the king," interjected Rew. "That's why none of them will talk. Even if they're not behind the plot, none of the princes will risk their father's wrath."

"I don't understand," said Anne. "Why would the princes plot against the king? What would they gain from that?"

Rew started down the hill, Cinda in his arms, but Anne caught the sleeve of his tunic.

He turned. In a low voice, he told her, "If Vaisius Morden knew what Prince Calb had planned with Arcanist Salwart and Baron Fedgley, the king would have come here himself. He would have leveled Spinesend to stop it. And then, he'd start to wonder what the other princes knew. Alsayer has worked for all three, and others will have done the same. The Investiture is built on tangled webs of alliances and betrayals. Not even Vaisius Morden could sort it all out and be certain of which prince knows what. So instead, he'd stamp the betrayal out. All of it."

Anne still looked worried.

"The Investiture doesn't have to end with one of the princes taking the throne, Anne," Rew told her. "The king does not have to relinquish his seat. If he finds one of his sons plotting against him, he'll kill all the conspirators he can find, but would he allow the other two to continue the Investiture? Will he start all over again? The three princes are not the king's only children. They're just the oldest of his brood that can command high magic. There are other sons in Mordenhold who could replace the three, if the king desired. The princes know that, but they don't know how their father will react to treachery in the family, so no matter what, they won't risk him finding out about this."

"If the king would have reacted like that... If he would come personally to kill Fedgley..." started Anne. She frowned and glanced at Cinda. "Rew..."

"I know," said the ranger, shifting the unconscious spellcaster's form. "That's why we have to get away tonight."

"What are they planning to do with her?" questioned Anne.

"It's best you don't know," said Rew. "I wish that I did not. If I told you, you'd be in as much danger as the lass. While the Mordens rule, she'll never be clear of it. It's too late for her. But as long as you don't know, Anne, then maybe one day you can be free."

"You have to tell me something," insisted Anne.

"Let's take the children to Carff," said Rew. "Alsayer and Kallie went there, though I've no idea if they'll stay. Wherever he goes, I need to find that bastard spellcaster and talk to him. He's known this entire time... I need to find out what else he's hiding."

"You want us to follow you while you keep deadly secrets from the group?" questioned Anne.

"Have faith in this," said Rew. "It's a long journey to Carff, and we'll never make it if we don't leave now. We can't let the princes find Cinda, Anne. The princes, the king, none of them can find her."

Without further word, they left, and they walked through a city buzzing with word of the turmoil and rumors about what had happened at the keep. They walked through the gates of the city moments before they were closed, and then, they walked long into the night.

THANKS FOR READING!

My biggest thanks to the readers! If it wasn't for you, I wouldn't be doing this. Those of you who enjoyed the book, I can always use a good review—or even better—tell a friend.

My eternal gratitude to: Felix Ortiz for the breath-taking cover and social media illustrations. Shawn T King for his incredible graphic design. Kellerica for inking this world into reality. Nicole Zoltack coming back yet again as my long-suffering proofreader, joined this round by Anthony Holabird for the final polish. And of course, I'm honored to continue working with living legend Simon Vance on the audio. When you read my words, I hope it's in his voice.

Terrible 10... you know.

Thanks again, and hope to hear from you!

AC

WANT MORE? REMOVE THE SHROUD: THE KING'S RANGER BOOK 3 is scheduled for an April 1st, 2021 release!

To check out my other books (I have a lot), find larger versions of the maps, series artwork, my newsletter, and other goodies go to accobble.com.

CPSIA information can be obtained
at www.ICGtesting.com
Printed in the USA
FSHW010653200221
78782FS

9 781947 683266